Henry James

Son of the metaphysician and lecturer, Henry James, Sr., and brother of the philosopher, William—Henry James was born on April 15, 1843. His early life was spent in New York City and then, on and off, during the impressionable years from twelve to seventeen, in Europe. In 1866, after an interlude in Newport, the James family settled in Cambridge, where they renewed acquaintance with the literary men of New England, including the editors of the *North American Review* and *The Atlantic Monthly*, to which James made his first acknowledged contributions of criticism (1864) and fiction (1865). Here he formed his lifelong friendship with William Dean Howells and Henry Adams. Between 1869 and 1875, James made three trips to Europe, where he met Turgenev, Flaubert, and Zola. Renewing his acquaintance with New York in 1874-75, he there wrote his first important novel, *Roderick Hudson*. In the following year, he chose England for permanent residence. Among his distinguished novels and stories, the best known are *The American* (1877), *Daisy Miller* (1878), *The Portrait of a Lady* (1877), *The Turn of the Screw* (1898), and *The Ambassadors* (1903). With the onset of the First World War Henry James devoted much of his time to visiting the wounded and the refugees, also giving freely of writing and his money to war charities. In July, he became a British subject, and shortly before death on February 28, 1916, the British Government conferred on him the Order of Merit.

The Madonna of the Future
and Other Early Stories

by HENRY JAMES

With a Foreword by WILLARD THORP

 A SIGNET CLASSIC

Published by THE NEW AMERICAN LIBRARY

First Printing, March, 1962

SIGNET CLASSICS are published by
The New American Library of World Literature, Inc.
501 Madison Avenue, New York 22, New York

PRINTED IN THE UNITED STATES OF AMERICA

Contents

Foreword

ONCE Henry James found his metier, at the age of twenty-one—as a critic, with a review of Nassau W. Senior's *Essays on Fiction,* and as a teller of tales, with "A Tragedy of Error"—there was no letup in a writing life which lasted fifty-two years, from 1864 to 1916. In the years represented by the eight stories collected here, 1865–1877, he published nearly two hundred reviews, taking on everything the editors sent along—fiction, poetry, historical works, travel writing. He also wrote a large number of sketches of travel, which he soon collected in *Transatlantic Sketches* (1875) and *Portraits of Places* (1883). In the same stretch he published his first three novels, *Watch and Ward* (serial publication, 1871), *Roderick Hudson* (serial publication, 1875), and *The American* (1877).

The short stories of this period number twenty-nine. This prodigal outpouring was not a warming-up stage. James had no public period of maturing as a writer of short fiction. Some of these early stories are masterly; all of them are interesting. Yet, they have been strangely neglected.

Henry James, Jr., as he signed himself until the death of his father in 1882, was the second of five children. His elder brother William was destined for fame as a psychologist and philosopher. The two younger brothers, Wilkinson and Robertson, were officers at an early age in the Civil War, and never recovered fully from their experiences in combat. There was a younger sister, Alice, an invalid most of her life. It was a close-knit family with affection flowing both ways between parents and children.

The senior Henry James inherited a fortune sufficient to permit him to be a man of leisure. He held unusual ideas about the education of children and had the time and money to carry them out. The James boys should have the finest education which private schools, private tutors, and foreign travel could provide. The father moved the children about restlessly, seeking in each move the kind of environment and instruction which was suited to what he thought they needed. From 1855 to 1858 the family was in Geneva, London, and Paris. Then followed a year in Newport, not yet the gaudy resort of its zenith. Then another year at Geneva where, at the Institution Rochette, young Henry patiently endured the curriculum designed for architects and engineers. In 1860 the three older boys were sent to Bonn for still further educational polishing.

Their father had no intention of dictating what professions the boys should enter. His sole wish was to procure for them the best instruction in languages, letters, and science. Still, he was amazed when William announced during the Bonn sojourn that he had decided to be a painter. True to his principles, the father brought the family back to Newport so that William might study under William Morris Hunt. Henry junior had his corner in the studio, where he copied from plaster casts without much show of talent.

Henry was the quietest of this high-spirited family, and he was in those early years under the shadow of the brilliant William, only one year his senior. He was a great reader, a lover of the theater and of painting and architecture. Most important for his future career, he was an observer, and he remembered all that he observed— faces, gestures, scenes, places, types of individuals, traits of personality. Later, when he needed to recall the look of the road of the Furca ("At Isella," 1871) or the port city of Le Havre ("Four Meetings," 1877) he had only to search his memory and the scene came to hand. He was speaking for himself when he makes a character remark, in "The Ghostly Rental" (1876):

"Observe closely enough," she once said, "and it doesn't matter where you are. You may be in a pitch-dark closet. All you want is something to start with; one thing leads to another, and all things are mixed up. Shut me up in a dark closet and I will observe after a while, that some places in it are darker than others. After that (give me time), and I will tell you what the President of the United States is going to have for dinner."

We know that young Henry was beginning to take himself seriously as a writer at least as early as May, 1860. Wilkie James let the secret out in a letter to Thomas Sergeant Perry. Wilkie had peeked into Henry's room and "saw some poetical manuscripts lying on the table, and himself looking in a most authorlike way." "The only difference there is between Willy and Harry's labours," Wilkie continues, "is that the former always shows his production while the modest little Henry wouldn't let a soul or even a spirit see his."

While William was working in Hunt's studio, Henry was given a nudge in the direction he should go by John La Farge, another of Hunt's pupils. LaFarge, seven years older than Henry, was to him a romantic figure who talked as well as he painted. When he told Henry he must read Balzac and Mérimée and learn from them, Henry obeyed. He was soon writing stories in which, according to "Sarge" Perry, the heroines seemed "to have read all Balzac in the cradle and to be positively dripping with lurid crimes." Henry was now seventeen, the age at which his brother Wilkie would soon march to war.

The line was crossed into a profession four years later. The two older James boys had not joined the Union ranks. William was studying science at Harvard instead, and Henry followed him there in 1862. He was enrolled in the law school, though he showed no more aptitude for the law than he had for painting. That he was going on with his writing during this waiting period we know from his own testimony. He brought away from law school "certain rolls of manuscript" which were not summaries of cases or lectures. They were "small sickly seed, no doubt, but to be sown and to sprout up into such flowers as they might, in a much less trimmed and ordered garden than that of the law."

We are still not certain that Henry James's first published story has been found. It was long supposed that "The Story of a Year," published in the *Atlantic Monthly* in March, 1865, was his first. In 1953 James's biographer,

Leon Edel, discovered an unsigned story, "A Tragedy of Error," printed in the *Continental Monthly* for February, 1864. There may be other "firsts."

Whatever the year of his beginning as a story-writer, the speed with which he turned out his pieces and the maturity of his writing are remarkable. He was accepted at once by the best magazines of the day and was in his early twenties sought after by such excellent editors as James T. Fields of the *Atlantic Monthly,* Charles Eliot Norton of the *North American Review,* and E. L. Godkin of the *Nation.* When James had published only six signed stories, the *Nation* averred that "within the somewhat narrow limits to which he confines himself Mr. James is . . . the best writer of short stories in America. . . . He is never commonplace, never writes without knowing what he wants to do, and never has an incident or character that is not in some way necessary to the production of such effects as he aims at."

Because James had not fought in the Civil War, he deliberately stayed away from stories about combat, but the effects of the War on those who had fought he dealt with twice, in "The Story of a Year" (1865*), and in "A Most Extraordinary Case" (1868). His interest in the problems of the painter shows up early—in "The Story of a Masterpiece" (1868) and "The Madonna of the Future" (1873). All his life James would be fascinated by supernatural phenomena and their fictional possibilities. Some of his most famous stories, for example "The Turn of the Screw" (1898), deal with the subject, and he left unpublished at his death a ghost novel, *The Sense of the Past.* We should expect to find some ghostly tales among these first twenty-nine stories, and there are three: "The Romance of Certain Old Clothes" (1868), a Hawthorne-like account of a ghost's revenge on her sister; "The Last of the Valerii" (1874), in which a modern Roman reverts to the pagan religion of his ancestors, moves back in time, and joins them briefly; and "The Ghostly Rental" (1876), a "straight" ghost story, equipped with a haunted

* The date of each story mentioned in the Foreword is the year of its magazine publication.

house and a pale-faced ghost who manifests herself every
quarter to pay the rent.

In the best sense of the word Henry James was a
moralist, and his later stories and novels usually turn on
a moral decision which must be faced. His finest characters are men and women who do the thing which decency and humanity require. Their antagonists are weak,
or vengeful, or, most often, corrupt. Surprisingly, only
two of these early tales are stories which have a moral
dilemma at the center. "Guest's Confession" (1872) is
one of James's earliest commemorations of the virtue of
renunciation. "A Light Man" (1869) is his first study of a
corrupt human being.

Though by the time he began publishing James had
spent five of his twenty-one years in Europe and had
stored up memories of which he made abundant use later
on, the twelve stories from "The Story of a Year" (1865)
through "A Light Man" (1869) are set in America (Europe enters in a few flashbacks), and the characters are
all American, including an Indian squaw, in "A Problem"!
The influence of Hawthorne may have been decisive in
this deliberate choosing of American subjects. Years later,
in *Notes of a Son and Brother* (1914), James recalled
how deeply Hawthorne's death in 1864 affected him. In
commenting on the "full and rare tone of prose" which
Hawthorne could command, he notes how Hawthorne's
achievement had influenced his own work: "And the
tone had been, in its beauty—for me at least—ever so
appreciably American; which proved to what a use
American matter could be put by an American hand."

That the young James wanted to be "American enough"
so that he could write with vigor about the American
scene we know from a letter to T. S. Perry, to whom he
wrote more fully about his ambitions than to any member
of his family. To be an American "is an excellent preparation for culture." We have exquisite qualities as a race
and are ahead of the European races in that we can
"pick and choose and assimilate and in short (aestheti-
cally &c) claim our property wherever we find it."

"We must of course have something of our own—something distinctive & homogeneous—& I take it that we
shall find it in our moral consciousness, our unprece-

dented spiritual lightness and vigour. In this sense at least
we shall have a national *cachet*."

James's turn to European settings resulted from his
travels abroad in 1869–1870. He was free of his family
and on his own. Homesick at first and suffering from
his persistent "backache," he was soon well enough to
wander about London and to meet some of England's
literary notables, including John Ruskin, George Eliot,
and Dante Gabriel Rossetti. But Italy made the greatest
impression. For some reason Henry James, Sr., had never
taken his family there, and Italy's beauty and antiquity
came as a revelation. The rapture he felt is conveyed in
the words of the narrator in "Travelling Companions"
(1870), his first story in which a modern European setting becomes part of the action.

In these dead cities of Verona, Mantua, Padua, how life
had revelled and postured in its strength! How sentiment
and passion had blossomed and flowered! How much of history had been performed! What a wealth of mortality had
ripened and decayed! I have never elsewhere got so deep an
impression of the social secrets of mankind.

Of the remaining sixteen stories (of the twenty-nine)
nine are set in Europe. Themes on which James would
compose variations in later stories and novels begin to
emerge. In "At Isella" (1871), he presents for the first
time an innocent and romantic American confronting a
hardheaded and scheming European, in this instance an
Italian woman fleeing from her husband to her lover.
"The Secret of M. Briseux" (1873) adumbrates "The
Aspern Papers" of 1888. "Madame de Mauves" (1874) is
James's first study of a rigidly moral American woman
who makes a romantic marriage with a European. When
he turns out to be as cynically immoral as such gentle-
men in the early James fiction usually are, Madame de
Mauves sticks by her bargain and also refuses to let the
Baron escape. There are thematic hints here of *The
Portrait of a Lady* (1881) and *The Golden Bowl* (1904).
In the last of these early stories, "Four Meetings" (1877),
James works out his America vs. Europe theme on
both sides of the Atlantic. Pathetic little Miss Spencer's

dream trip in Europe lasts only thirteen hours. What she gets instead of Paris and Byron's Castle of Chillon is a lifetime of waiting on her vulgar European sister-in-law. This device of bringing Europe to America James would use again, a year later, in *The Europeans*.

These early stories have many virtues besides their variety of theme and setting. William James singled out one excellence in a letter written after he received "The Story of a Masterpiece" and "The Romance of Certain Old Clothes." William takes his brother to task for exhibiting in the first of these stories (as too often in his "male *vs.* female subjects") "a want of heartiness or unction." But he goes on to analyze correctly the reason for this fault. "I fancy that this rather dainty and disdainful treatment of yours comes from a wholesome dread of being gushing and over-abounding in power of expression, like most of your rivals in the *Atlantic*. . . . and that is excellent, in fact it is the instinct of truth against humbug and twaddle, and when it governs the treatment of a rich material it produces first class works." There is no humbug, very little twaddle, and no gushing in these stories.

William might have noted another virtue. If some of these stories are thin, many of them are strong enough to satisfy the most avid lover of melodrama. Henry had seen scores of blood and thunder plays in the New York and Paris theaters and, during the family's stay in London in 1855–1856, he had read his way through many three-decker melodramatic novels. In studies of James's fiction not enough stress has been put on the sudden and sometimes shocking turn of events in many of his later works: the destruction by fire of the great house with all its treasures in *The Spoils of Poynton* (1897); the agonized death of little Miles in "The Turn of the Screw" (1898). What Henry was already attempting to do in some of these early stories was to convert "strong" situations, which could have been handled as mere melodrama, into believable plots. His first story, "A Tragedy of Error" (1864), is a somewhat crude attempt to convert melodrama into realism. The story reprinted here which represents this genre of transmuted melodrama is his fifth, "My Friend Bingham" (1867). The central episode is the accidental killing of a little boy by a wealthy young man

(Bingham) while he is casually shooting at gulls by the seashore. Fifteen pages later Bingham marries the widowed and aggrieved mother. It is fascinating to watch James working to make this melodramatic ending plausible. He accomplishes his purpose in the simplest and best way, by showing us how their inevitable love for each other overcomes the tragedy.

As we look back on these early stories what seems most remarkable about them—aside from the variety of themes—is the excellence of the plotting. This master of the art of fiction, who would in time do more for the craft than any other novelist, had his eye on method from the beginning. In the stories printed here there are a few instances of awkward handling of material—but only a few. In "The Story of a Masterpiece," for example, James did not know how to manage the necessary flashback which tells us of Marian's dubious flirtations in Europe. He is forced to write lamely: "I may as well take advantage of the moment rapidly to make plain to the reader the events to which the above conversation refers."

James experimented with almost every conceivable way of presenting action. In his early reviews of novels he speculated about narrative method and often took the novelists to task for the sloppiness of their work. The results of these speculations are apparent in his own practice. One device he particularly disliked—the use of the "omniscient author," who is at liberty to intrude where he pleases and shift the point of view at will. James did not use this slovenly method in any of these stories. Twice he presents us with a diary, which is used effectively in "A Light Man" to reveal ironically the despicable character of the man who has written it. A few times he employs the device of the "framed" story, in which the situation at the opening presents the narrator with the occasion to tell his tale. Though James later developed an aversion to the first-person narrative—all the author has to do, he once observed, is to throw the reins on his hero's neck and let them flap there "as free as in 'Gil Blas' or in 'David Copperfield' "—he used this method in "My Friend Bingham" (1867), "Travelling Companions" (1870), "Guest's Confession" (1872), and "The Ghostly Rental" (1876).

A cardinal point of James's developed theory of fiction is that the reader must be brought close to the action by means of a "fine central intelligence" on whom the action is making an impression. As R. P. Blackmur states this theory: "James never put his reader in direct contact with his subjects; he believed it was impossible to do so, because his subject really was not what happened but what someone felt about what happened, and this could be directly known only through an intermediate intelligence."

James's search for the right kind of "intermediate intelligence" is the most engrossing thing to watch in these stories, so far as method is concerned. By the end of the 1870's he was making frequent use of "the impersonal author's concrete deputy or delegate," who is close to the center of action but not so emotionally involved in what is happening as to be incapable of having "impressions." Two of the tales which employ this method are "The Madonna of the Future" and "Four Meetings." The youthful amateur of painting in the first of these and the experienced young traveler of the second are in exactly the right relation to the action to see, feel, and comprehend, and so to engage the reader.

Thus James did not for some time come to the realization of how effective this method could be in short fiction. (He used much more elaborate devices of indirect presentation in his later novels.) Most of the earliest stories are close to the "omniscient author" technique. There are, for instance, authorial side remarks in his second tale, "The Story of a Year," but they could easily be lifted out, and if they were, we should have the omniscient author as the teller. In all the stories of the 1860's which make use of the "author's deputy" the narrator is anonymous and is not even slightly characterized. Suddenly, with "The Madonna of the Future," the narrator-deputy who is also a "fine central intelligence" makes his appearance.

In 1873, then, James found what he had been seeking— the best way to present his subject. Years later, in writing the Preface to *The Golden Bowl* volume in the New York Edition, he commented on this best of methods.

My instinct appears repeatedly to have been that to arrive at the facts retailed and the figures introduced by the given help of some other conscious and confessed agent is essentially to find the whole business—that is, as I say, its effective interest-enriched *by the way*. I have in other words constantly inclined to the idea of the particular attaching case *plus* some near individual view of it; that nearness quite having thus to become an imagined observer's, a projected, charmed painter's or poet's—however avowed the "minor" quality in the latter—close and sensitive contact with it. Anything, in short, I now reflect, must always have seemed to me better—better for the process and the effect of representation, my irrepressible ideal—than the mere miffled majesty of irresponsible "authorship".

This method had not, as he remembered, "always" seemed to him better. It had taken him nine years to work his way to it.

WILLARD THORP
Princeton University

The Madonna of the Future
and Other Early Stories

The Story of a Year

1

MY story begins as a great many stories have begun within the last three years—and, indeed, as a great many have ended, for when the hero is dispatched, does not the romance come to a stop?

In early May, two years ago, a young couple I wot of strolled homeward from an evening walk, a long ramble among the peaceful hills which enclosed their rustic home. Into these peaceful hills the young man had brought, not the rumor (which was an old inhabitant), but some of the reality of war—a little whiff of gunpowder, the clanking of a sword—for, although Mr. John Ford had his campaign still before him, he wore a certain comely air of camp life which stamped him a very Hector to the steady-going villagers, and a very pretty fellow to Miss Elizabeth Crowe, his companion in this sentimental stroll. And was he not attired in the great brightness of blue and gold which befits a freshly made lieutenant? This was a strange sight for these happy northern glades; for, although the first Revolution had boomed awhile in their midst, the honest yeomen who defended them were clad in sober homespun, and it is well known that His Majesty's troops wore red.

These young people, I say, had been roaming. It was plain that they had wandered into spots where the brambles were thick and the dews heavy—nay, into swamps and puddles where the April rains were still undried. Ford's boots and trousers had imbibed a deep foretaste of the Virginia mud; his companion's skirts were fearfully bedraggled. What great enthusiasm had made our friends so unmindful of their steps? What blinding ardor had kindled these strange phenomena: a young lieutenant

19

scornful of his first uniform, a well-bred young lady reckless of her stockings?

Good reader, this narrative is averse to retrospect.

Elizabeth (as I shall not scruple to call her outright)
was leaning upon her companion's arm, half-moving in
concert with him, and half-allowing herself to be led, with
that instinctive acknowledgment of dependence natural
to a young girl who has just received the assurance of
lifelong protection. Ford was lounging along with that
calm, swinging stride which often bespeaks, when you can
read it aright, the answering consciousness of a sudden
rush of manhood. A spectator might have thought him at
this moment profoundly conceited. The young girl's blue
veil was dangling from his pocket; he had shouldered her
sun umbrella after the fashion of a musket on a march
—he might carry these trifles. Was there not a vague
longing expressed in the strong expansion of his stalwart
shoulders, in the fond accommodation of his pace to hers
—her pace so submissive and slow that, when he tried to
match it, they almost came to a delightful standstill, a
silent desire for the whole fair burden?

They made their way up a long, swelling mound whose
top commanded the sunset. The dim landscape, which had
been brightening all day to the green of spring, was now
darkening to the gray of evening. The lesser hills, the
farms, the brooks, the fields, orchards, and woods made
a dusky gulf before the great splendor of the west. As
Ford looked at the clouds, it seemed to him that their
imagery was all of war, their great uneven masses were
marshaled into the semblance of a battle. There were
columns charging and columns flying and standards floating—tatters of the reflected purple; and great captains on
colossal horses; and a rolling canopy of cannon smoke
and fire and blood. The background of the clouds, indeed, was like a land on fire, or a battleground illumined
by another sunset, a country of blackened villages and
crimsoned pastures. The tumult of the clouds increased;
it was hard to believe them inanimate. You might have
fancied them an army of gigantic souls playing at football
with the sun. They seemed to sway in confused splendor;
the opposing squadrons bore each other down; and then
suddenly they scattered, bowling with equal velocity to-

ward north and south and gradually fading into the pale
evening sky. The purple pennons sailed away and sank
out of sight, caught, doubtless, upon the brambles of the
intervening plain. Day contracted itself into a fiery ball
and vanished.

Ford and Elizabeth had quietly watched this great mystery of the heavens.

"That is an allegory," said the young man, as the sun
went under, looking into his companion's face, where a
pink flush seemed still to linger. "It means the end of the
war. The forces on both sides are withdrawn. The blood
that has been shed gathers itself into a vast globule and
drops into the ocean."

"I'm afraid it means a shabby compromise," said
Elizabeth. "Light disappears, too, and the land is in darkness."

"Only for a season," answered the other. "We mourn
our dead. Then light comes again, stronger and brighter
than ever. Perhaps you'll be crying for me, Lizzie, at that
distant day."

"Oh, Jack, didn't you promise not to talk about that?"
says Lizzie, threatening to anticipate the performance in
question.

Jack took this rebuke in silence, gazing soberly at the
empty sky. Soon the young girl's eyes stole up to his face.
If he had been looking at anything in particular, I think
she would have followed the direction of his glance, but
as it seemed to be a very vacant one, she let her eyes
rest.

"Jack," said she after a pause, "I wonder how you'll
look when you get back."

Ford's soberness gave way to a laugh.

"Uglier than ever. I shall be all encrusted with mud
and gore. And then I shall be magnificently sun-burned,
and I shall have a beard."

"Oh, you dreadful!" and Lizzie gave a little shout.
"Really, Jack, if you have a beard, you'll not look like a
gentleman."

"Shall I look like a lady, pray?" says Jack.

"Are you serious?" asked Lizzie.

"To be sure. I mean to alter my face as you do your
misfitting garments,—take in on one side and let out on

the other. Isn't that the process? I shall crop my head and cultivate my chin."

"You've a very nice chin, my dear, and I think it's a shame to hide it."

"Yes, I know my chin's handsome—but wait till you see my beard."

"Oh, the vanity!" cried Lizzie, "the vanity of men in their faces! Talk of women!" and the silly creature looked up at her lover with most inconsistent satisfaction.

"Oh, the pride of women in their husbands!" said Jack, who of course knew what she was about.

"You're not my husband, sir. There's many a slip—" But the young girl stopped short.

"—'Twixt the cup and the lip," said Jack. "Go on. I can match your proverb with another. 'There's many a true word,' and so forth. No, my darling, I'm not your husband. Perhaps I never shall be. But if anything happens to me, you'll take comfort, won't you?"

"Never!" said Lizzie tremulously.

"Oh, but you must; otherwise, Lizzie, I should think our engagement inexcusable. Stuff! Who am I that you should cry for me?"

"You are the best and wisest of men. I don't care; you *are.*"

"Thank you for your great love, my dear. That's a delightful illusion. But I hope time will kill it, in his own good way, before it hurts anyone. I know so many men who are worth infinitely more than I—men wise, generous, and brave—that I shall not feel as if I were leaving you in an empty world."

"Oh, my dear friend!" said Lizzie after a pause, "I wish you could advise me all my life."

"Take care, take care," laughed Jack; "you don't know what you are bargaining for. But will you let me say a word now? If by chance I'm taken out of the world, I want you to beware of that tawdry sentiment which enjoins you to be 'constant to my memory.' My memory be hanged! Remember me at my best—that is, fullest of the desire of humility. Don't inflict me on people. There are some widows and bereaved sweethearts who remind me of the peddler in that horrible murder story who carried a corpse in his pack. Really, it's their stock in trade. The only justification of a man's personality is his rights. What rights has a dead man?—Let's go down."

They turned southward and went jolting down the hill.

"Do you mind this talk, Lizzie?" asked Ford.

"No," said Lizzie, swallowing a sob, unnoticed by her companion in the sublime egotism of protection; "I like it."

"Very well," said the young man, "I want my memory to help you. When I am down in Virginia, I expect to get a vast deal of good from thinking of you,—to do my work better, and to keep straighter altogether. Like all lovers, I'm horribly selfish. I expect to see a vast deal of shabbiness and baseness and turmoil, and in the midst of it all I'm sure the inspiration of patriotism will sometimes fail. Then I'll think of you. I love you a thousand times better than my country, Liz. Wicked? So much the worse. It's the truth. But if I find your memory makes a milksop of me, I shall thrust you out of the way without ceremony; I shall clap you into my box, or between the leaves of my Bible, and only look at you on Sunday."

"I shall be very glad, sir, if that makes you open your Bible frequently," says Elizabeth rather demurely.

"I shall put one of your photographs against every page," cried Ford; "and then I think I shall not lack a text for my meditations. Don't you know how Catholics keep little pictures of their adored Lady in their prayer-books?"

"Yes, indeed," said Lizzie; "I should think it would be a very soul-stirring picture, when you are marching to the front, the night before a battle—a poor, stupid girl, knitting stupid socks, in a stupid Yankee village."

Oh, the craft of artless tongues! Jack strode along in silence a few moments, splashing straight through a puddle; then, ere he was quite clear of it, he stretched out his arm and gave his companion a long embrace.

"And pray what am I to do," resumed Lizzie, wondering, rather proudly perhaps, at Jack's averted face, "while you are marching and countermarching in Virginia?"

"Your duty, of course," said Jack, in a steady voice, which belied a certain little conjecture of Lizzie's. "I think you will find the sun will rise in the east, my dear, just as it did before you were engaged."

"I'm sure I didn't suppose it wouldn't," says Lizzie.

"By duty I don't mean anything disagreeable, Liz," pursued the young man. "I hope you'll take your pleasure, too. I wish you might go to Boston, or even to Leatherborough, for a month or two."

"What for, pray?"

"What for? Why, for the fun of it: to 'go out,' as they say."

"Jack, do you think me capable of going to parties while you are in danger?"

"Why not? Why should I have all the fun?"

"Fun? I'm sure you're welcome to it all. As for me, I mean to make a new beginning."

"Of what?"

"Oh, of everything. In the first place, I shall begin to improve my mind. But don't you think it's horrid for women to be reasonable?"

"Hard, say you?"

"Horrid—yes, and hard too. But I mean to become so. Oh, girls are such fools, Jack! I mean to learn to like boiled mutton and history and plain sewing, and all that. Yet, when a girl's engaged, she's not expected to do anything in particular."

Jack laughed and said nothing, and Lizzie went on.

"I wonder what your mother will say to the news. I think I know."

"What?"

"She'll say you've been very unwise. No, she won't: she never speaks so to you. She'll say I've been very dishonest or indelicate, or something of that kind. No, she won't either: she doesn't say such things, though I'm sure she thinks them. I don't know what she'll say."

"No, I think not, Lizzie, if you indulge in such conjectures. My mother never speaks without thinking. Let us hope that she may think favorably of our plan. Even if she doesn't—"

Jack did not finish his sentence, nor did Lizzie urge him. She had a great respect for his hesitations. But in a moment, he began again.

"I was going to say this, Lizzie: I think for the present our engagement had better be kept quiet."

Lizzie's heart sank with a sudden disappointment. Imagine the feelings of the damsel in the fairytale, whom the disguised enchantress had just empowered to utter diamonds and pearls, should the old beldame have straightway added that for the present mademoiselle had better hold her tongue. Yet the disappointment was brief. I think this enviable young lady would have tripped home talking very hard to herself, and have been not ill pleased to find her little mouth turning into a tightly clasped jewel casket. Nay, would she not on this occasion have been thankful for a large mouth—a mouth huge and unnatural—stretching from ear to ear? Who wish to cast their pearls before swine? The young lady of the pearls was, after all, but a barnyard miss. Lizzie was too proud of Jack to be vain. It's well enough to wear our own hearts upon our sleeves, but for those of others, when entrusted to our keeping, I think we had better find a more secluded lodging.

"You see, I think secrecy would leave us much freer," said Jack; "leave *you* much freer."

"Oh, Jack, how can you?" cried Lizzie. "Yes, of course; I shall be falling in love with someone else. Freer! Thank you, sir!"

"Nay, Lizzie, what I'm saying is really kinder than it sounds. Perhaps you *will* thank me one of these days."

"Doubtless! I've already taken a great fancy to George Mackenzie."

"Will you let me enlarge on my suggestion?"

"Oh, certainly! You seem to have your mind quite made up."

"I confess I like to take account of possibilities. Don't you know mathematics are my hobby? Did you ever study algebra? I always have an eye on the unknown quantity."

"No, I never studied algebra. I agree with you that we had better not speak of our engagement."

"That's right, my dear. You're always right. But mind, I don't want to bind you to secrecy. Hang it, do as you please! Do what comes easiest to you, and you'll do the best thing. What made me speak is my dread of the horrible publicity which clings to all this business. Nowadays, when a girl's engaged, it's no longer, 'Ask Mama,' simply; but, 'Ask Mrs. Brown, and Mrs. Jones, and my large circle of acquaintance—Mrs. Grundy, in short.' I say nowadays, but I suppose it's always been so."

"Very well, we'll keep it all nice and quiet," said Lizzie, who would have been ready to celebrate her nuptials according to the rites of the Esquimaux, had Jack seen fit to suggest it.

"I know it doesn't look well for a lover to be so cautious," pursued Jack; "but you understand me, Lizzie, don't you?"

"I don't entirely understand you, but I quite trust you."

"God bless you! My prudence, you see, is my best strength. Now, if ever, I need my strength. When a man's awooing, Lizzie, he is all feeling—or he ought to be. When he's accepted, then he begins to think."

"And to repent, I suppose you mean."

"Nay, to devise means to keep his sweetheart from repenting. Let me be frank. Is it the greatest fools only that are the best lovers? There's no telling what may happen, Lizzie. I want you to marry me with your eyes open. I don't want you to feel tied down or taken in. You're very young, you know. You're responsible to yourself of a year hence. You're at an age when no girl can count safely from year's end to year's end."

"And you, sir!" cries Lizzie; "one would think you were a grandfather."

"Well, I'm on the way to it. I'm a pretty old boy. I mean what I say. I may not be entirely frank, but I think I'm sincere. It seems to me as if I'd been fibbing all my life before I told you that your affection was necessary to my happiness. I mean it out and out. I never loved anyone before, and I never will again. If you had refused me half an hour ago, I should have died a bachelor. I have no fear for myself. But I have for you. You said a few minutes ago that you wanted me to be your adviser. Now you know the function of an adviser is to perfect his victim in the art of walking with his eyes shut. I shan't be so cruel."

Lizzie saw fit to view these remarks in a humorous light. "How disinterested!" quoth she: "how very self-sacrificing! Bachelor indeed! For my part, I think I shall become a Mormon!" I verily believe the poor misinformed creature fancied that in Utah it is the ladies who are guilty of polygamy.

Before many minutes they drew near home. There stood Mrs. Ford at the garden gate, looking up and down the road, with a letter in her hand.

"Something for you, John," said his mother as they approached. "It looks as if it came from camp. Why, Elizabeth, look at your skirts!"

"I know it," says Lizzie, giving the articles in question a shake. "What is it, Jack?"

"Marching orders!" cried the young man. "The regiment leaves day after tomorrow. I must leave by the early train in the morning. Hurray!" And he diverted a sudden, gleeful kiss into a filial salute.

They went in. The two women were silent, after the manner of women who suffer. But Jack did little else than laugh and talk and circumnavigate the parlor, sitting first here and then there,—close beside Lizzie and on the opposite side of the room. After a while Miss Crowe joined in his laughter, but I think her mirth might have been resolved into articulate heartbeats. After tea she went to bed, to give Jack opportunity for his last filial *épanchements*. How generous a man's intervention makes women! But Lizzie promised to see her lover off in the morning.

"Nonsense!" said Mrs. Ford. "You'll not be up. John will want to breakfast quietly."

"I shall see you off, Jack," repeated the young lady from the threshold.

Elizabeth went upstairs buoyant with her young love. It had dawned upon her like a new life—a life positively worth the living. Hereby she would subsist and cost nobody anything. In it, she was boundlessly rich. She would make it the hidden spring of a hundred praiseworthy deeds. She would begin the career of duty; she would enjoy boundless equanimity; she would raise her whole being to the level of her sublime passion. She would practice charity, humility, piety—in fine, all the virtues, together with certain *morceaux* of Beethoven and Chopin. She would walk the earth like one glorified. She would do homage to the best of men by inviolate secrecy. Here, by I know not what gentle transition, as she lay in the quiet darkness, Elizabeth covered her pillow with a flood of tears.

Meanwhile Ford, downstairs, began in this fashion. He was lounging at his manly length on the sofa, in his slippers.

"May I light a pipe, Mother?"

"Yes, my love. But please be careful of your ashes. There's a newspaper."

"Pipes don't make ashes. Mother, what do you think?" he continued, between the puffs of his smoking. "I've got a piece of news."

"Ah?" said Mrs. Ford, fumbling for her scissors; "I hope it's good news."

"I hope you'll think it so. I've been engaging myself"— puff—puff—"to Lizzie Crowe." A cloud of puffs between his mother's face and his own. When they cleared away, Jack felt his mother's eyes. Her work was in her lap. "To be married, you know," he added.

In Mrs. Ford's view, like the king in that of the British Constitution, her only son could do no wrong. Prejudice is a stout bulwark against surprise. Moreover, Mrs. Ford's motherly instinct had not been entirely at fault. Still, it had by no means kept pace with fact. She had been silent, partly from doubt, partly out of respect for her son. As long as John did not doubt of himself, he was right. Should he come to do so, she was sure he would speak. And now, when he told her the matter was settled, she persuaded herself that he was asking her advice.

"I've been expecting it," she said at last.

"You have? why didn't you speak?"

"Well, John, I can't say I've been hoping it."

"Why not?"

"I am not sure of Lizzie's heart," said Mrs. Ford, who, it may be well to add, was very sure of her own.

Jack began to laugh. "What's the matter with her heart?"

"I think Lizzie's shallow," said Mrs. Ford, and there was that in her tone which betokened some satisfaction with this adjective.

"Hang it! She is shallow," said Jack. "But when a thing's shallow, you can see to the bottom. Lizzie doesn't pretend to be deep. I want a wife, Mother, that I can understand. That's the only wife I can love. Lizzie's the only girl I ever understood, and the first I ever loved. I love her very much—more than I can explain to you."

"Yes, I confess it's inexplicable. It seems to me," she added, with a bad smile, "like infatuation."

Jack did not like the smile; he liked it even less than the remark. He smoked steadily for a few moments, and then he said:

"Well, Mother, love is notoriously obstinate, you know. We shall not be able to take the same view of this subject. Suppose we drop it."

"Remember that this is your last evening at home, my son," said Mrs. Ford.

"I do remember. Therefore I wish to avoid disagreement."

There was a pause. The young man smoked, and his mother sewed, in silence.

"I think my position, as Lizzie's guardian," resumed Mrs. Ford, "entitles me to an interest in the matter."

"Certainly, I acknowledged your interest by telling you of our engagement."

Further pause.

"Will you allow me to say," said Mrs. Ford after a while, "that I think this a little selfish?"

"Allow you? Certainly, if you particularly desire it. Though I confess it isn't very pleasant for a man to sit and hear his future wife pitched into,—by his own mother, too."

"John, I am surprised at your language."

"I beg your pardon," and John spoke more gently. "You mustn't be surprised at anything from an accepted lover. I'm sure you misconceive her. In fact, Mother, I don't believe you know her."

Mrs. Ford nodded with an infinite depth of meaning, and from the grimness with which she bit off the end of her thread, it might have seemed that she fancied herself to be executing a human vengeance.

"Ah, I know her only too well!"

"And you don't like her?"

Mrs. Ford performed another decapitation of her thread.

"Well, I'm glad Lizzie has one friend in the world," said Jack.

"Her best friend," said Mrs. Ford, "is the one who flatters her least. I see it all, John. Her pretty face has done the business."

The young man flushed impatiently.

"Mother," said he, "you are very much mistaken. I'm not a boy nor a fool. You trust me in a great many things; why not trust me in this?"

"My dear son, you are throwing yourself away. You deserve for your companion in life a higher character than that girl."

I think Mrs. Ford, who had been an excellent mother, would have liked to give her son a wife fashioned on her own model.

"Oh, come, Mother," said he, "that's twaddle. I should be thankful if I were half as good as Lizzie."

"It's the truth, John, and your conduct—not only the step you've taken, but your talk about it—is a great disappointment to me. If I have cherished any wish of late, it is that my darling boy should get a wife worthy of him. The household governed by Elizabeth Crowe is not the home I should desire for any one I love."

"It's one to which you should always be welcome, ma'am," said Jack.

"It's not a place I should feel at home in," replied his mother.

"I'm sorry," said Jack. And he got up and began to walk about the room. "Well, well, Mother," he said at last, stopping in front of Mrs. Ford, "we don't understand each other. One of these days we shall. For the present let us have done with discussion. I'm half-sorry I told you."

"I'm glad of such a proof of your confidence. But if you hadn't, of course Elizabeth would have done so."

"No, ma'am, I think not."

"Then she is even more reckless of her obligations than I thought her."

"I advised her to say nothing about it."

Mrs. Ford made no answer. She began slowly to fold up her work.

"I think we had better let the matter stand," continued

her son. "I'm not afraid of time. But I wish to make a request of you: you won't mention this conversation to Lizzie, will you, nor allow her to suppose that you know of our engagement? I have a particular reason."

Mrs. Ford went on smoothing out her work. Then she suddenly looked up.

"No, my dear, I'll keep your secret. Give me a kiss."

2

I HAVE no intention of following Lieutenant Ford to the scat of war. The exploits of his campaign are recorded in the public journals of the day, where the curious may still peruse them. My own taste has always been for unwritten history, and my present business is with the reverse of the picture.

After Jack went off, the two ladies resumed their old homely life. But the homeliest life had now ceased to be repulsive to Elizabeth. Her common duties were no longer wearisome: for the first time, she experienced the delicious companionship of thought. Her chief task was still to sit by the window knitting soldiers' socks; but even Mrs. Ford could not help owning that she worked with a much greater diligence; yawned, rubbed her eyes, gazed up and down the road less; and, indeed, produced a much more comely article. Ah, me! If half the lovesome fancies that flitted through Lizzie's spirit in those busy hours could have found their way into the texture of the dingy yarn, as it was slowly wrought into shape, the eventual wearer of the socks would have been as lightfooted as Mercury. I am afraid I should make the reader sneer were I to rehearse some of this little fool's diversions. She passed several hours daily in Jack's old chamber: it was in this sanctuary, indeed, at the sunny south window, overlooking the long road, the wood-crowned heights, the gleaming river, that she worked with most pleasure and profit. Here she was removed from the untiring glance of the elder lady, from her jarring questions and commonplaces; here she was alone with her love— that greatest commonplace in life. Lizzie felt in Jack's

room a certain impress of his personality. The idle fancies
of her mood were bodied forth in a dozen sacred relics.
Some of these articles Elizabeth carefully cherished. It
was rather late in the day for her to assert a literary
taste—her reading having begun and ended (naturally
enough) with the ancient fiction of the "Scottish Chiefs."
So she could hardly help smiling, herself, sometimes, at
her interest in Jack's old college tomes. She carried several of them to her own apartment and placed them at
the foot of her little bed on a bookshelf adorned, besides,
with a pot of spring violets, a portrait of General McClel-
lan, and a likeness of Lieutenant Ford. She had a vague
belief that a loving study of their well-thumbed verses
would remedy, in some degree, her sad intellectual defi-
ciencies. She was sorry she knew so little—as sorry, that
is, as she might be, for we know that she was shallow.
Jack's omniscience was one of his most awful attributes.
And yet she comforted herself with the thought that, as
he had forgiven her ignorance, she herself might surely
forget it. Happy Lizzie, I envy you this easy path to
knowledge! The volume she most frequently consulted
was an old German *Faust,* over which she used to fum-
ble with a battered lexicon. The secret of this preference
was in certain marginal notes in pencil, signed "J." I hope
they were really of Jack's making.

Lizzie was always a small walker. Until she knew Jack,
this had been quite an unsuspected pleasure. She was
afraid, too, of the cows, geese, and sheep—all the ag-
ricultural *spectra* of the feminine imagination. But now
her terrors were over. Might she not play the soldier,
too, in her own humble way? Often with a beating heart,
I fear, but still with resolute, elastic steps, she revisited
Jack's old haunts; she tried to love Nature as he had
seemed to love it; she gazed at his old sunsets; she
fathomed his old pools with bright plummet glances, as
if seeking some lingering trace of his features in their
brown depths, stamped there as on a fond human heart;
she sought out his dear name, scratched on the rocks
and trees—and when night came on, she studied, in her
simple way, the great starlit canopy under which, perhaps,
her warrior lay sleeping; she wandered through the green
glades, singing snatches of his old ballads in a clear voice

made tuneful with love, and as she sang, there mingled with the everlasting murmur of the trees the faint sound of a muffled bass, borne upon the south wind like a distant drumbeat, responsive to a bugle. So she led for some months a very pleasant, idyllic life, face to face with a strong, vivid memory which gave everything and asked nothing. These were doubtless to be (and she half-knew it) the happiest days of her life. Has life any bliss so great as this pensive ecstasy? To know that the golden sands are dropping one by one makes servitude freedom and poverty riches.

In spite of a certain sense of loss, Lizzie passed a very blissful summer. She enjoyed the deep repose which, it is to be hoped, sanctifies all honest betrothals. Possible calamity weighed lightly upon her. We know that when the columns of battle smoke leave the field, they journey through the heavy air to a thousand quiet homes and play about the crackling glaze of as many firesides. But Lizzie's vision was never clouded. Mrs. Ford might gaze into the thickening summer dusk and wipe her spectacles, but her companion hummed her old ballad ends with an unbroken voice. She no more ceased to smile under evil tidings than the brooklet ceases to ripple beneath the projected shadow of the roadside willow. The self-given promises of that tearful night of parting were forgotten. Vigilance had no place in Lizzie's scheme of heavenly idleness. The idea of moralizing in Elysium!

It must not be supposed that Mrs. Ford was indifferent to Lizzie's mood. She studied it watchfully and kept note of all its variations. And among the things she learned was that her companion knew of her scrutiny and was, on the whole, indifferent to it. Of the full extent of Mrs. Ford's observation, however, I think Lizzie was hardly aware. She was like a reveler in a brilliantly lighted room, with a curtainless window, conscious, and yet heedless, of passers-by. And Mrs. Ford may not inaptly be compared to the chilly spectator on the dark side of the pane. Very few words passed on the topic of their common thoughts. From the first, as we have seen, Lizzie guessed at her guardian's probable view of her engagement—an abasement incurred by John. Lizzie lacked what is called a sense of duty, and unlike the majority of such tempera-

ments, which contrive to be buoyant on the glistening
bubble of dignity, she had likewise a modest estimate of
her dues. Alack, my poor heroine had no pride! Mrs.
Ford's silent censure awakened no resentment. It sounded
in her ears like a dull, soporific hum. Lizzie was deeply
enamored of what a French book terms her *aises intellec-
tuelles*. Her mental comfort lay in the ignoring of
problems. She possessed a certain native insight which
revealed many of the horrent inequalities of her path-
way, but she found it so cruel and disenchanting a faculty
that blindness was infinitely preferable. She preferred repose to order and mercy to justice. She was speculative,
without being critical. She was continually wondering, but
she never inquired. This world was the riddle; the next
alone would be the answer.

So she never felt any desire to have an "understanding"
with Mrs. Ford. Did the old lady misconceive her? it was
her own business. Mrs. Ford apparently felt no desire to
set herself right. You see, Lizzie was ignorant of her
friend's promise. There were moments when Mrs. Ford's
tongue itched to speak. There were others, it is true,
when she dreaded any explanation which would compel
her to forfeit her displeasure. Lizzie's happy self-suffi-
ciency was most irritating. She grudged the young girl
the dignity of her secret; her own actual knowledge of it
rather increased her jealousy, by showing her the importance of the scheme from which she was excluded.
Lizzie, being in perfect good humor with the world and
with herself, abated no jot of her personal deference to
Mrs. Ford. Of Jack, as a good friend and her guardian's
son, she spoke very freely. But Mrs. Ford was mistrust-
ful of this semiconfidence. She would not, she often said
to herself, be wheedled against her principles. Her principles! Oh, for some shining blade of purpose to hew
down such stubborn stakes! Lizzie had no thought of
flattering her companion. She never deceived anyone but
herself. She could not bring herself to value Mrs. Ford's
good will. She knew that Jack often suffered from his
mother's obstinacy. So her unbroken humility shielded no
unavowed purpose. She was patient, and kindly from nature, from habit. Yet I think that, if Mrs. Ford could have
measured her benignity, she would have preferred, on the

whole, the most open defiance. "Of all things," she would
sometimes mutter, "to be patronized by that little piece!"
It was very disagreeable, for instance, to have to listen to
portions of her own son's letters.

These letters came week by week, flying out of the
South like white-winged carrier doves. Many and many a
time, for very pride, Lizzie would have liked a larger
audience. Portions of them certainly deserved publicity.
They were far too good for her. Were they not better
than that stupid war correspondence in the *Times,* which
she so often tried in vain to read? They contained long
details of movements, plans of campaigns, military opinions and conjectures, expressed with the emphasis habitual to young sublieutenants. I doubt whether General
Halleck's dispatches laid down the law more absolutely
than Lieutenant Ford's. Lizzie answered in her own fashion. It must be owned that hers was a dull pen. She told
her dearest, dearest Jack how much she loved and honored him, and how much she missed him, and how delightful his last letter was (with those beautifully drawn
diagrams), and the village gossip, and how stout and
strong his mother continued to be—and again, how she
loved, etc., etc., and that she remained his loving L. Jack
read these effusions as became one so beloved. I should
not wonder if he thought them very brilliant.

The summer waned to its close, and through myriad
silent stages began to darken into autumn. Who can tell
the story of those red months? I have to chronicle another
silent transition. But as I can find no words delicate and
fine enough to describe the multifold changes of Nature,
so, too, I must be content to give you the spiritual facts
in gross.

John Ford became a veteran down by the Potomac.
And, to tell the truth, Lizzie became a veteran at home.
That is, her love and hope grew to be an old story. She
gave way, as the strongest must, as the wisest will, to
time. The passion which, in her simple, shallow way, she
had confided to the woods and waters reflected their out-
ward variations; she thought of her lover less, and with
less positive pleasure. The golden sands had run out. Perfect rest was over. Mrs. Ford's tacit protest began to be
annoying. In a rather resentful spirit, Lizzie forebore to

read any more letters aloud. These were as regular as
ever. One of them contained a rough camp photograph
of Jack's newly bearded visage. Lizzie declared it was "too
ugly for anything," and thrust it out of sight. She found
herself skipping his military dissertations, which were still
as long and written in as handsome a hand as ever. The
"too good," which used to be uttered rather proudly, was
now rather a wearisome truth. When Lizzie in certain
critical moods tried to qualify Jack's temperament, she
said to herself that he was too literal. Once he gave her a
little scolding for not writing oftener. "Jack can make no
allowances," murmured Lizzie. "He can understand no
feelings but his own. I remember he used to say that
moods were diseases. His mind is too healthy for such
things; his heart is too stout for ache or pain. The
night before he went off he told me that reason, as he
calls it, was the rule of life. I suppose he thinks it the rule
of love, too. But his heart is younger than mine—younger
and better. He has lived through awful scenes of danger
and bloodshed and cruelty, yet his heart is purer." Lizzie
had a horrible feeling of being blasé of this one affection.
"Oh, God bless him!" she cried. She felt much better for
the tears in which this soliloquy ended. I fear she had
begun to doubt her ability to cry about Jack.

3

CHRISTMAS came. The Army of the Potomac had
stacked its muskets and gone into winter quarters. Miss
Crowe received an invitation to pass the second fortnight
in February at the great manufacturing town of Leatherborough. Leatherborough is on the railroad, two hours
south of Glenham, at the mouth of the great river Tan,
where this noble stream expands into its broadest smile,
or gapes in too huge a fashion to be disguised by a
bridge.

"Mrs. Littlefield kindly invites you for the last of the
month," said Mrs. Ford, reading a letter behind the tea
urn.

It suited Mrs. Ford's purpose—a purpose which I have

not space to elaborate—that her young charge should now go forth into society and pick up acquaintants.

Two sparks of pleasure gleamed in Elizabeth's eyes. But, as she had taught herself to do of late with her protectress, she mused before answering.

"It is my desire that you should go," said Mrs. Ford, taking silence for dissent.

The sparks went out.

"I intend to go," said Lizzie rather grimly. "I am much obliged to Mrs. Littlefield."

Her companion looked up.

"I intend you shall. You will please to write this morning."

For the rest of the week the two stitched together over muslins and silks, and were very good friends. Lizzie could scarcely help wondering at Mrs. Ford's zeal on her behalf. Might she not have referred it to her guardian's principles? Her wardrobe, hitherto fashioned on the Glenham notion of elegance, was gradually raised to the Leatherborough standard of fitness. As she took up her bedroom candle the night before she left home, she said:

"I thank you very much, Mrs. Ford, for having worked so hard for me, for having taken so much interest in my outfit. If they ask me at Leatherborough who made my things, I shall certainly say it was you."

Mrs. Littlefield treated her young friend with great kindness. She was a good-natured, childless matron. She found Lizzie very ignorant and very pretty. She was glad to have so great a beauty and so many lions to show.

One evening Lizzie went to her room with one of the maids, carrying half a dozen candles between them. Heaven forbid that I should cross that virgin threshold—for the present! But we will wait. We will allow them two hours. At the end of that time, having gently knocked, we will enter the sanctuary. Glory of glories! The faithful attendant has done her work. Our lady is robed, crowned, ready for worshipers.

I trust I shall not be held to a minute description of our dear Lizzie's person and costume. Who is so great a recluse as never to have beheld young ladyhood in full dress? Many of us have sisters and daughters. Not a few of us, I hope, have female connections of another degree, yet no less dear. Others have looking glasses. I give you my word for it that Elizabeth made as pretty a show as it is possible to see. She was, of course, well-dressed. Her skirt was of voluminous white, puffed and trimmed in wondrous sort. Her hair was profusely ornamented with curls and braids of its own rich substance. From her waist depended a ribbon, broad and blue. White with coral ornaments, as she wrote to Jack in the course of the week. Coral ornaments, forsooth! And pray, miss, what of the other jewels with which your person was decorated —the rubies, pearls, and sapphires? One by one Lizzie assumes her modest gimcracks: her bracelet, her gloves, her handkerchief, her fan, and then—her smile. Ah, that strange crowning smile!

An hour later, in Mrs. Littlefield's pretty drawing room, amid music, lights, and talk, Miss Crowe was sweeping a grand curtsy before a tall, sallow man whose name she caught from her hostess's redundant murmur as Bruce. Five minutes later, when the honest matron gave a glance at her newly started enterprise from the other side of the room, she said to herself that really, for a plain country girl, Miss Crowe did this kind of thing very well. Her next glimpse of the couple showed them whirling round the room to the crashing thrum of the piano. At eleven o'clock she beheld them linked by their fingertips in the dazzling mazes of the reel. At half-past eleven she discerned them charging shoulder to shoulder in the serried columns of the Lancers. At midnight she tapped her young friend gently with her fan.

"Your sash is unpinned, my dear. I think you have danced often enough with Mr. Bruce. If he asks you again, you had better refuse. It's not quite the thing. Yes, my dear, I know. Mr. Simpson, will you be so good as to take Miss Crowe down to supper?"

I'm afraid young Simpson had rather a snappish partner.

After the proper interval, Mr. Bruce called to pay his respects to Mrs. Littlefield. He found Miss Crowe also in the drawing room. Lizzie and he met like old friends. Mrs. Littlefield was a willing listener, but it seemed to her that she had come in at the second act of the play. Bruce went off with Miss Crowe's promise to drive with

him in the afternoon. In the afternoon he swept up to
the door in a prancing, tinkling sleigh. After some minutes
of hoarse jesting and silvery laughter in the keen wintry
air, he swept away again with Lizzie curled up in the
buffalo robe beside him, like a kitten in a rug. It was
dark when they returned. When Lizzie came in to the
sitting-room fire, she was congratulated by her hostess
upon having made a "conquest."

"I think he's a most gentlemanly man," says Lizzie.

"So he is, my dear," said Mrs. Littlefield; "Mr. Bruce
is a perfect gentleman. He's one of the finest young men
I know. He's not so young either. He's a little too yellow
for my taste, but he's beautifully educated. I wish you
could hear his French accent. He has been abroad I
don't know how many years. The firm of Bruce and
Robertson does an immense business."

"And I'm so glad," cries Lizzie, "he's coming to Glenham in March! He's going to take his sister to the water
cure."

"Really? Poor thing! She has very good manners."

"What do you think of his looks?" asked Lizzie,
smoothing her feather.

"I was speaking of Jane Bruce. I think Mr. Bruce has
fine eyes."

"I must say I like tall men," says Miss Crowe.

"Then Robert Bruce is your man," laughs Mrs. Littlefield.
"He's as tall as a bell tower. And he's got a bell clapper
in his head, too."

"I believe I will go and take off my things," remarks
Miss Crowe, flinging up her curls.

Of course, it behooved Mr. Bruce to call the next day
and see how Miss Crowe had stood her drive. He set a
veto upon her intended departure and presented an invitation from his sister for the following week. At Mrs.
Littlefield's instance, Lizzie accepted the invitation, dispatched a laconic note to Mrs. Ford, and stayed over for
Miss Bruce's party. It was a grand affair. Miss Bruce was
a very great lady: she treated Miss Crowe with every
attention. Lizzie was thought by some persons to look
prettier than ever. The vaporous gauze, the sunny hair,
the coral, the sapphires, the smile, were displayed with
renewed success. The master of the house was unable to

dance; he was summoned to sterner duties. Nor could Miss Crowe be induced to perform, having hurt her foot on the ice. This was, of course, a disappointment; let us hope that her entertainers made it up to her.

On the second day after the party, Lizzie returned to Glenham. Good Mr. Littlefield took her to the station, stealing a moment from his precious business hours.

"There are your checks," said he; "be sure you don't lose them. Put them in your glove."

Lizzie gave a little scream of merriment.

"Mr. Littlefield, how can you? I've a reticule, sir. But I really don't want you to stay."

"Well, I confess," said her companion—"Hullo! There's your Scottish chief! I'll get him to stay with you till the train leaves. He may be going. Bruce!"

"Oh, Mr. Littlefield, don't!" cries Lizzie. "Perhaps Mr. Bruce is engaged."

Bruce's tall figure came striding toward them. He was astounded to find that Miss Crowe was going by this train. Delightful! He had come to meet a friend who had not arrived.

"Littlefield," said he, "you can't be spared from your business. I will see Miss Crowe off."

When the elder gentleman had departed, Mr. Bruce conducted his companion into the car and found her a comfortable seat, equidistant from the torrid stove and the frigid door. Then he stowed away her shawls, umbrella, and reticule. She would keep her muff? She did well. What a pretty fur!

"It's just like your collar," said Lizzie. "I wish I had a muff for my feet," she pursued, tapping on the floor.

"Why not use some of those shawls?" said Bruce; "let's see what we can make of them."

And he stooped down and arranged them as a rug, very neatly and kindly. And then he called himself a fool for not having used the next seat, which was empty; and the wrapping was done over again.

"I'm so afraid you'll be carried off!" said Lizzie. "What would you do?"

"I think I should make the best of it. And you?"

"I would tell you to sit down *there*"; and she indicated

the seat facing her. He took it. "Now you'll be sure to," said Elizabeth.

"I'm afraid I shall, unless I put the newspaper between us." And he took it out of his pocket. "Have you seen the news?"

"No," says Lizzie, elongating her bonnet ribbons. "What is it? Just look at that party."

"There's not much news. There's been a scrimmage on the Rappahannock. Two of our regiments engaged,— the Fifteenth and the Twenty-Eighth. Didn't you tell me you had a cousin or something in the Fifteenth?"

"Not a cousin, no relation, but an intimate friend—my guardian's son. What does the paper say, please?" inquires Lizzie, very pale.

Bruce cast his eye over the report. "It doesn't seem to have amounted to much; we drove back the enemy and recrossed the river at our ease. Our loss only fifty. There are no names," he added, catching a glimpse of Lizzie's pallor; "none in this paper at least."

In a few moments appeared a newsboy crying the New York journals.

"Do you think the New York papers would have any names?" asked Lizzie.

"We can try," said Bruce. And he bought a *Herald*, and unfolded it. "Yes, there *is* a list," he continued, some time after he had opened out the sheet. "What's your friend's name?" he asked from behind the paper.

"Ford, John Ford, second lieutenant," said Lizzie.

There was a long pause.

At last Bruce lowered the sheet, and showed a face in which Lizzie's pallor seemed faintly reflected.

"There *is* such a name among the wounded," he said, and folding the paper down, he held it out and gently crossed to the seat beside her.

Lizzie took the paper and held it close to her eyes. But Bruce could not help seeing that her temples had turned from white to crimson.

"Do you see it?" he asked; "I sincerely hope it's nothing very bad."

"*Severely*," whispered Lizzie.

"Yes, but that proves nothing. Those things are most unreliable. *Do* hope for the best."

Lizzie made no answer. Meanwhile passengers had been brushing in, and the car was full. The engine began to puff, and the conductor to shout. The train gave a jog.

"You'd better go, sir, or you'll be carried off," said Lizzie, holding out her hand, with her face still hidden.

"May I go on to the next station with you?" said Bruce.

Lizzie gave him a rapid look, with a deepened flush. He had fancied that she was shedding tears. But those eyes were dry; they held fire rather than water.

"No, no, sir; you must not. I insist. Good-by."

Bruce's offer had cost him a blush, too. He had been prepared to back it with the assurance that he had business ahead, and, indeed, to make a little business in order to satisfy his conscience. But Lizzie's answer was final.

"Very well," said he, "*good*-by. You have my real sympathy, Miss Crowe. Don't despair. We shall meet again."

The train rattled away. Lizzie caught a glimpse of a tall figure with lifted hat on the platform. But she sat motionless, with her head against the window frame, her veil down and her hands idle.

She had enough to do to think, or rather to feel. It is fortunate that the utmost shock of evil tidings often comes first. After that everything is for the better. Jack's name stood printed in that fatal column like a stern signal for despair. Lizzie felt conscious of a crisis which almost arrested her breath. Night had fallen at midday: what was the hour? A tragedy had stepped into her life: was she spectator or actor? She found herself face to face with death: was it not her own soul masquerading in a shroud? She sat in a half-stupor. She had been aroused from a dream into a waking nightmare. It was like hearing a murder shriek while you turn the page of your novel. But I cannot describe these things. In time, the crushing sense of calamity loosened its grasp. Feeling lashed her pinions. Thought struggled to rise. Passion was still, stunned, floored. She had recoiled like a receding wave for a stronger onset. A hundred ghastly fears and fancies strutted a moment, pecking at the young girl's naked heart, like sandpipers on the weltering beach. Then, as with a great murmurous rush, came the meaning of her grief. The floodgates of emotion were opened.

At last, passion exhausted itself, and Lizzie thought. Bruce's parting words rang in her ears. She did her best to hope. She reflected that wounds, even severe wounds, did not necessarily mean death. Death might easily be warded off. She would go to Jack; she would nurse him; she would watch by him; she would cure him. Even if death had already beckoned, she would strike down his hand: if life had already obeyed, she would issue the stronger mandate of love. She would stanch his wounds; she would unseal his eyes with her kisses; she would call till he answered her.

Lizzie reached home and walked up the garden path. Mrs. Ford stood in the parlor as she entered, upright, pale, and rigid. Each read the other's countenance. Lizzie went toward her slowly and giddily. She must of course kiss her patroness. She took her listless hand and bent toward her stern lips. Habitually Mrs. Ford was the most undemonstrative of women. But as Lizzie looked closer into her face, she read the signs of a grief infinitely more potent than her own. The formal kiss gave way: the young girl leaned her head on the old woman's shoulder and burst into sobs. Mrs. Ford acknowledged those tears with a slow inclination of the head, full of a certain grim pathos. She put out her arms and pressed them closer to her heart.

At last, Lizzie disengaged herself and sat down.

"I am going to him," said Mrs. Ford.

Lizzie's dizziness returned. Mrs. Ford was going—and she, she?

"I am going to nurse him, and with God's help to save him."

"How did you hear?"

"I have a telegram from the surgeon of the regiment." And Mrs. Ford held out a paper.

Lizzie took it and read: "Lieutenant Ford dangerously wounded in the action of yesterday. You had better come on."

"I should like to go myself," said Lizzie: "I think Jack would like to have me."

"Nonsense! A pretty place for a young girl! I am not going for sentiment: I am going for use."

Lizzie leaned her head back in her chair and closed her eyes. From the moment they had fallen upon Mrs.

Ford, she had felt a certain quiescence. And now it was a relief to have responsibility denied her. Like most weak persons, she was glad to step out of the current of life, now that it had begun to quicken into action. In emergencies, such persons are tacitly counted out, and they as tacitly consent to the arrangement. Even to the sensitive spirit there is a certain meditative rapture in standing on the quiet shore (beside the ruminating cattle) and watching the hurrying, eddying flood, which makes up for the loss of dignity. Lizzie's heart resumed its peaceful throbs. She sat, almost dreamily, with her eyes shut.

"I leave in an hour," said Mrs. Ford. "I am going to get ready. Do you hear?"

The young girl's silence was a deeper consent than her companion supposed.

4

IT was a week before Lizzie heard from Mrs. Ford. The letter, when it came, was very brief. Jack still lived. The wounds were three in number, and very serious; he was unconscious; he had not recognized her; but still the chances either way were thought equal. They would be much greater for his recovery nearer home, but it was impossible to move him. "I write from the midst of horrible scenes," said the poor lady. Subjoined was a list of necessary medicines, comforts, and delicacies to be boxed up and sent.

For a while Lizzie found occupation in writing a letter to Jack, to be read in his first lucid moment, as she told Mrs. Ford. This lady's man of business came up from the village to superintend the packing of the boxes. Her directions were strictly followed, and in no point were they found wanting. Mr. Mackenzie bespoke Lizzie's admiration for their friend's wonderful clearness of memory and judgment. "I wish we had that woman at the head of affairs," said he. " 'Gad, I'd apply for a brigadier-generalship."—"I'd apply to be sent South," thought Lizzie.

When the boxes and letter were dispatched, she sat down to await more news. Sat down, say I? Sat down, and rose, and wondered, and sat down again. These were lonely, weary days. Very different are the idleness of love and the idleness of grief. Very different is it to be alone with your hope and alone with your despair. Lizzie failed to rally her musings. I do not mean to say that her sorrow was very poignant, although she fancied it was. Habit was a great force in her simple nature, and her chief trouble now was that habit refused to work. Lizzie had to grapple with the stern tribulation of a decision to make, a problem to solve. She felt that there was some spiritual barrier between herself and repose. So she began in her usual fashion to build up a false repose on the hither side of belief. She might as well have tried to float on the Dead Sea. Peace eluding her, she tried to resign herself to tumult. She drank deep at the well of self-pity, but found its waters brackish. People are apt to think that they may temper the penalties of misconduct by self-commiseration, just as they season the long aftertaste of beneficence by a little spice of self-applause. But the power of good is a more grateful master than the Devil. What bliss to gaze into the smooth gurgling wake of a good deed, while the comely bark sails on with floating pennon! What horror to look into the muddy sediment which floats round the piratic keel! Go, sinner, and dissolve it with your tears! And you, scoffing friend, there is the way out! Or would you prefer the window? I'm an honest man forever-more.

One night Lizzie had a dream— a rather disagreeable one—which haunted her during many waking hours. It seemed to her that she was walking in a lonely place with a tall, dark-eyed man who called her Wife. Suddenly, in the shadow of a tree, they came upon an unburied corpse. Lizzie proposed to dig him a grave. They dug a great hole and took hold of the corpse to lift him in, when suddenly he opened his eyes. Then they saw that he was covered with wounds. He looked at them intently for some time, turning his eyes from one to the other. At last he solemnly said, "Amen!" and closed his eyes. Then she and her companion placed him in the grave, and shoveled the earth over him, and stamped it down with their feet.

He of the dark eyes and he of the wounds were the

two constantly recurring figures of Lizzie's reveries. She
could never think of John without thinking of the courteous Leatherborough gentleman, too. These were the
data of her problem. These two figures stood like opposing knights (the black and the white), foremost on
the great chessboard of fate. Lizzie was the wearied,
puzzled player. She would idly finger the other pieces and
shift them carelessly hither and thither, but it was of no
avail—the game lay between the two knights. She would
shut her eyes and long for some kind hand to come and
tamper with the board; she would open them and see
the two knights standing immovable, face to face. It was
nothing new. A fancy had come in and offered defiance to
a fact; they must fight it out. Lizzie generously inclined
to the fancy, the unknown champion, with a reputation
to make. Call her blasé, if you like, this little girl, whose
record told of a couple of dances and a single lover,
heartless, old before her time. Perhaps she deserves your
scorn. I confess she thought herself ill used. By whom?
By what? Wherein? These were questions Miss Crowe was
not prepared to answer. Her intellect was unequal to
the stern logic of human events. She expected two and two
to make five: as why should they not for the nonce? She
was like an actor who finds himself on the stage with a
half-learned part and without sufficient wit to extempo-
rize. Pray, where is the prompter? Alas, Elizabeth, that
you had no mother! Young girls are prone to fancy that
when once they have a lover, they have everything they
need, a conclusion inconsistent with the belief entertained by many persons that life begins with love. Lizzie's fortunes became old stories to her before she had
half-read them through. Jack's wounds and danger were
an old story. Do not suppose that she had exhausted the
lessons, the suggestions of these awful events, their in-
spirations, exhortations—that she had wept as became
the horror of the tragedy. No: the curtain had not yet
fallen, yet our young lady had begun to yawn. To yawn?
Ay, and to long for the afterpiece. Since the tragedy
dragged, might she not divert herself with that well-
bred man beside her?

Elizabeth was far from owning to herself that she had
fallen away from her love. For my own part, I need no

better proof of the fact than the dull persistency with which she denied it. What accusing voice broke out of the stillness? Jack's nobleness and magnanimity were the hourly theme of her clogged fancy. Again and again she declared to herself that she was unworthy of them, but that, if he would only recover and come home, she would be his eternal bond-slave. So she passed a very miserable month. Let us hope that her childish spirit was being tempered to some useful purpose. Let us hope so.

She roamed about the empty house with her footsteps tracked by an unlaid ghost. She cried aloud and said that she was very unhappy; she groaned and called herself wicked. Then, sometimes, appalled at her moral perplexities, she declared that she was neither wicked nor unhappy; she was contented, patient, and wise. Other girls had lost their lovers: it was the present way of life. Was she weaker than most women? Nay, but Jack was the best of men. If he would only come back directly, without delay, as he was, senseless, dying even, that she might look at him, touch him, speak to him! Then she would say that she could no longer answer for herself, and wonder (or pretend to wonder) whether she were not going mad. Suppose Mrs. Ford should come back and find her in an unswept room, pallid and insane? Or suppose she should die of her troubles? What if she should kill herself—dismiss the servants, and close the house, and lock herself up with a knife? Then she would cut her arm to escape from dismay at what she had already done; and then her courage would ebb away with her blood, and having so far pledged herself to despair, her life would ebb away with her courage; and then, alone, in darkness, with none to help her, she would vainly scream, and thrust the knife into her temple, and swoon to death. And Jack would come back, and burst into the house, and wander through the empty rooms, calling her name, and for all answer get a death scent! These imaginings were the more creditable or discreditable to Lizzie, that she had never read *Romeo and Juliet*. At any rate, they served to dissipate time—heavy, weary time—the more heavy and weary as it bore dark foreshadowings of some momentous event. If that event would only come, whatever it was, and sever this Gordian knot of doubt!

The days passed slowly: the leaden sands dropped one by one. The roads were too bad for walking, so Lizzie was obliged to confine her restlessness to the narrow bounds of the empty house, or to an occasional journey to the village, where people sickened her by their dull indifference to her spiritual agony. Still they could not fail to remark how poorly Miss Crowe was looking. This was true, and Lizzie knew it. I think she even took a certain comfort in her pallor and in her failing interest in her dress. There was some satisfaction in displaying her white roses amid the apple-cheeked prosperity of Main Street. At last Miss Cooper, the doctor's sister, spoke to her:

"How is it, Elizabeth, you look so pale, and thin, and worn out? What you been doing with yourself? Falling in love, eh? It isn't right to be so much alone. Come down and stay with us awhile—till Mrs. Ford and John come back," added Miss Cooper, who wished to put a cheerful face on the matter.

For Miss Cooper, indeed, any other face would have been difficult. Lizzie agreed to come. Her hostess was a busy, unbeautiful old maid, sister and housekeeper of the village physician. Her occupation here below was to perform the forgotten tasks of her fellow men—to pick up their dropped stitches, as she herself declared. She was never idle, for her general cleverness was commensurate with mortal needs. Her own story was that she kept moving so that folks couldn't see how ugly she was. And, in fact, her existence was manifest through her long train of good deeds—just as the presence of a comet is shown by its tail. It was doubtless on the above principle that her visage was agitated by a perpetual laugh.

Meanwhile more news had been coming from Virginia. "What an absurdly long letter you sent John," wrote Mrs. Ford, in acknowledging the receipt of the boxes. "His first lucid moment would be very short, if he were to take upon himself to read your effusions. Pray keep your long stories till he gets well." For a fortnight the young soldier remained the same—feverish, conscious only at intervals. Then came a change for the worse, which, for many weary days, however, resulted in nothing decisive. "If he could only be moved to Glenham, home, and old sights," said his mother, "I should have hope. But think of the journey!" By this time Lizzie had stayed out ten days of her visit.

One day Miss Cooper came in from a walk, radiant with tidings. Her face, as I have observed, wore a continual smile— being dimpled and punctured all over with merriment—so that, when an unusual cheerfulness was superdiffused, it resembled a tempestuous little pool into which a great stone has been cast.

"Guess who's come," said she, going up to the piano, which Lizzie was carelessly fingering, and putting her hands on the young girl's shoulders. "Just guess!"

Lizzie looked up.

"Jack," she half-gasped.

"Oh, dear, no, not that! How stupid of me! I mean Mr. Bruce, your Leatherborough admirer."

"Mr. Bruce! Mr. Bruce!" said Lizzie. "Really?"

"True as I live. He's come to bring his sister to the water cure. I met them at the post office."

Lizzie felt a strange sensation of good news. Her fingertips were on fire. She was deaf to her companion's rattling chronicle. She broke into the midst of it with a fragment of some triumphant, jubilant melody. The keys rang beneath her flashing hands. And then she suddenly stopped, and Miss Cooper, who was taking off her bonnet at the mirror, saw that her face was covered with a burning flush.

That evening, Mr. Bruce presented himself at Doctor Cooper's with whom he had a slight acquaintance. To Lizzie he was infinitely courteous and tender. He assured her, in very pretty terms, of his profound sympathy with her in her cousin's danger—her cousin he still called him—and it seemed to Lizzie that until that moment no one had begun to be kind. And then he began to rebuke her, playfully and in excellent taste, for her pale cheeks.

"Isn't it dreadful?" said Miss Cooper. "She looks like a ghost. I guess she's in love."

"He must be a good-for-nothing lover to make his mistress look so sad. If I were you, I'd give him up, Miss Crowe."

"I didn't know I looked sad," said Lizzie.

"You don't now," said Miss Cooper. "You're smiling and blushing. An't she blushing, Mr. Bruce?"

"I think Miss Crowe has no more than her natural color," said Bruce, dropping his eyeglass. "What have you been doing all this while since we parted?"

"All this while? It's only six weeks. I don't know. Nothing. What have you?"

"I've been doing nothing, too. It's hard work."

"Have you been to any more parties?"

"Not one."

"Any more sleigh rides?"

"Yes. I took one more dreary drive all alone—over that same road, you know. And I stopped at the farmhouse again and saw the old woman we had the talk with. She remembered us and asked me what had become of the young lady who was with me before. I told her you were gone home, but that I hoped soon to go and see you. So she sent you her love."

"Oh, how nice!" exclaimed Lizzie.

"Wasn't it? And then she made a certain little speech; I won't repeat it, or we shall have Miss Cooper talking about your blushes again."

"I know," cried the lady in question; "she said she was very——"

"Very what?" said Lizzie.

"Very h-a-n-d—what everyone says."

"Very handy?" asked Lizzie. "I'm sure no one ever said that."

"Of course," said Bruce; "and I answered what everyone answers."

"Have you seen Mrs. Littlefield lately?"

"Several times. I called on her the day before I left town, to see if she had any messages for you."

"Oh, thank you! I hope she's well."

"Oh, she's as jolly as ever. She sent you her love and hoped you would come back to Leatherborough very soon again. I told her that, however it might be with the first message, the second should be a joint one from both of us."

"You're very kind. I should like very much to go again. Do you like Mrs. Littlefield?"

"Like her? Yes. Don't you? She's thought a very pleasing woman."

"Oh, she's very nice. I don't think she has much conversation."

"Ah, I'm afraid you mean she doesn't backbite. We've always found plenty to talk about."

"That's a very significant tone. What, for instance?"

"Well, we *have* talked about Miss Crowe."

"Oh, you have? Do you call that having plenty to talk about?"

"We *have* talked about Mr. Bruce,—haven't we, Elizabeth?" said Miss Cooper, who had her own notion of being agreeable.

It was not an altogether bad notion, perhaps, but Bruce found her interruptions rather annoying and insensibly allowed them to shorten his visit. Yet, as it was, he sat till eleven o'clock—a stay quite unprecedented at Glenham.

When he left the house, he went splashing down the road with a very elastic tread, springing over the starlit puddles and trolling out some sentimental ditty. He reached the inn and went up to his sister's sitting room.

"Why, Robert, where have you been all this while?" said Miss Bruce.

"At Dr. Cooper's."

"Dr. Cooper's? I should think you had! Who's Dr. Cooper?"

"Where Miss Crowe's staying."

"Miss Crowe? Ah, Mrs. Littlefield's friend! Is she as pretty as ever?"

"Prettier—prettier—prettier. *Tara-ta! tara-la!*"

"Oh, Robert, do stop that singing! You'll rouse the whole house."

5

LATE one afternoon, at dusk, about three weeks after Mr. Bruce's arrival, Lizzie was sitting alone by the fire, in Miss Cooper's parlor, musing, as became the place and hour. The doctor and his sister came in, dressed for a lecture.

"I'm sorry you won't go, my dear," said Miss Cooper.

"It's a most interesting subject: 'A Year of the War.' All the battles and things described, you know."

"I'm tired of war," said Lizzie.

"Well, well, if you're tired of the war, we'll leave you in peace. Kiss me good-by. What's the matter? You look sick. You are homesick, an't you?"

"No, no; I'm very well."

"Would you like me to stay at home with you?"

"Oh, no! Pray, don't!"

"Well, we'll tell you all about it. Will they have programs, James? I'll bring her a program. But you really feel as if you were going to be ill. Feel her skin, James."

"No, you needn't, sir," said Lizzie. "How queer of you, Miss Cooper! I'm perfectly well."

And at last her friends departed. Before long the servant came with the lamp, ushering Mr. Mackenzie.

"Good evening, miss," said he. "Bad news from Mrs. Ford."

"Bad news?"

"Yes, miss. I've just got a letter stating that Mr. John is growing worse and worse, and that they look for his death from hour to hour. It's very sad," he added as Elizabeth was silent.

"Yes, it's very sad," said Lizzie.

"I thought you'd like to hear it."

"Thank you."

"He was a very noble young fellow," pursued Mr. Mackenzie.

Lizzie made no response.

"There's the letter," said Mr. Mackenzie, handing it over to her.

Lizzie opened it.

"How long she is reading it!" thought her visitor. "You can't see so far from the light, can you, miss?"

"Yes," said Lizzie. "His poor mother! Poor woman!"

"Aye, indeed, miss—she's the one to be pitied."

"Yes, she's the one to be pitied," said Lizzie. "Well!" and she gave him back the letter.

"I thought you'd like to see it," said Mackenzie, drawing on his gloves; and then, after a pause, "I'll call again, miss, if I hear anything more. Good night!"

Lizzie got up and lowered the light, and then went back to her sofa by the fire.

Half an hour passed; it went slowly; but it passed. Still lying there in the dark room on the sofa, Lizzie heard a ring at the doorbell, a man's voice and a man's tread in the hall. She rose and went to the lamp. As she turned it up, the parlor door opened. Bruce came in.

"I was sitting in the dark," said Lizzie, "but when I heard you coming, I raised the light."

"Are you afraid of me?" said Bruce.

"Oh, no! I'll put it down again. Sit down."

"I saw your friends going out," pursued Bruce, "so I knew I should find you alone. What are you doing here in the dark?"

"I've just received very bad news from Mrs. Ford about her son. He's much worse, and will probably not live."

"Is it possible?"

"I was thinking about that."

"Dear me! Well, that's a sad subject. I'm told he was a very fine young man."

"He was, very," said Lizzie.

Bruce was silent awhile. He was a stranger to the young officer, and felt that he had nothing to offer beyond the commonplace expressions of sympathy and surprise. Nor had he exactly the measure of his companion's interest in him.

"If he dies," said Lizzie, "it will be under great injustice."

"Ah! What do you mean?"

"There wasn't a braver man in the Army."

"I suppose not."

"And, oh, Mr. Bruce," continued Lizzie, "he was so clever and good and generous! I wish you had known him."

"I wish I had. But what do you mean by injustice? Were these qualities denied him?"

"No, indeed! Everyone that looked at him could see that he was perfect."

"Where's the injustice, then? It ought to be enough for him that you should think so highly of him."

"Oh, he knew that," said Lizzie.

Bruce was a little puzzled by his companion's manner. He watched her as she sat with her cheek on her hand, looking at the fire. There was a long pause. Either they were too friendly or too thoughtful for the silence to be embarrassing. Bruce broke it at last.

"Miss Crowe," said he, "on a certain occasion, some time ago, when you first heard of Mr. Ford's wounds, I offered you my company, with the wish to console you as far as I might for what seemed a considerable shock. It was, perhaps, a bold offer for so new a friend, but, nevertheless, in it even then my heart spoke. You turned me off. Will you let me repeat it? Now, with a better right, will you let me speak out all my heart?"

Lizzie heard this speech, which was delivered in a slow and hesitating tone, without looking up or moving her head, except, perhaps, at the words "turned me off." After Bruce had ceased, she still kept her position.

"You'll not turn me off now?" added her companion.

She dropped her hand, raised her head, and looked at him a moment. He thought he saw the glow of tears in her eyes. Then she sank back upon the sofa with her face in the shadow of the mantelpiece.

"I don't understand you, Mr. Bruce," said she.

"Ah, Elizabeth! Am I such a poor speaker? How shall I make it plain? When I saw your friends leave home half an hour ago, and reflected that you would probably be alone, I determined to go right in and have a talk with you that I've long been wanting to have. But first I walked half a mile up the road, thinking hard—thinking how I should say what I had to say. I made up my mind to nothing, but that somehow or other I should say it. I would trust—I *do* trust to your frankness, kindness, and sympathy, to a feeling corresponding to my own. Do you understand that feeling? Do you know that I love you? I do, I do, I do! You *must* know it. If you don't, I solemnly swear it. I solemnly ask you, Elizabeth, to take me for your husband."

While Bruce said these words, he rose, with their rising passion, and came and stood before Lizzie. Again she was motionless.

"Does it take you so long to think?" said he, trying to

read her indistinct features; and he sat down on the sofa beside her and took her hand.

At last Lizzie spoke.

"Are you sure," said she, "that you love me?"

"As sure as that I breathe. Now, Elizabeth, make me as sure that I am loved in return."

"It seems very strange, Mr. Bruce," said Lizzie.

"What seems strange? Why should it? For a month I've been trying, in a hundred dumb ways, to make it plain; and now, when I swear it, it only seems strange!"

"What do you love me for?"

"For? For yourself, Elizabeth."

"Myself? I am nothing."

"I love you for what your are—for your deep, kind heart—for being so perfectly a woman."

Lizzie drew away her hand, and her lover rose and stood before her again. But now she looked up into his face, questioning when she should have answered, drinking strength from his entreaties for her replies. There he stood before her, in the glow of the firelight, in all his gentlemanhood, for her to accept or reject. She slowly rose and gave him the hand she had withdrawn.

"Mr. Bruce, I shall be very proud to love you," she said.

And then, as if this effort was beyond her strength, she half-staggered back to the sofa again. And still holding her hand, he sat down beside her. And there they were still sitting when they heard the doctor and his sister come in.

For three days Elizabeth saw nothing of Mr. Mackenzie. At last, on the fourth day, passing his office in the village, she went in and asked for him. He came out of his little back parlor with his mouth full and a beaming face.

"Good day, Miss Crowe, and good news!"

"*Good* news?" cried Lizzie.

"Capital!" said he, looking hard at her, while he put on his spectacles. "She writes that Mr. John—won't you take a seat?—has taken a sudden and unexpected turn for the better. Now's the moment to save him; it's an equal risk. They were to start for the North the second day after date. The surgeon comes with them. So they'll be home —of course they'll travel slowly—in four or five days.

Yes, miss, it's a remarkable Providence. And that noble young man will be spared to the country, and to those who love him, as I do."

"I had better go back to the house and have it got ready," said Lizzie for an answer.

"Yes, miss, I think you had. In fact, Mrs. Ford made that request."

The request was obeyed. That same day Lizzie went home. For two days she found it her interest to over-look, assiduously, a general sweeping, scrubbing, and provisioning. She allowed herself no idle moment until bedtime. Then—but I would rather not be the chamber-lain of her agony. It was the easier to work, as Mr. Bruce had gone to Leatherborough on business.

On the fourth evening, at twilight, John Ford was borne up to the door on his stretcher, with his mother stalking beside him in rigid grief, and kind, silent friends pressing about with helping hands.

> Home they brought her warrior dead,
> She nor swooned nor uttered cry.

It was, indeed, almost a question whether Jack was not dead. Death is not thinner, paler, stiller. Lizzie moved about like one in a dream. Of course, when there are so many sympathetic friends, a man's family has nothing to do—except exercise a little self-control. The women huddled Mrs. Ford to bed; rest was imperative; she was killing herself. And it was significant of her weakness that she did not resent this advice. In greeting her, Lizzie felt as if she were embracing the stone image on the top of a sepulchre. She, too, had her cares anticipated. Good Doctor Cooper and his sister stationed themselves at the young man's couch.

The doctor prophesied wondrous things of the change of climate; he was certain of a recovery. Lizzie found herself very shortly dealt with as an obstacle to this consummation. Access to John was prohibited. "Perfect stillness, you know, my dear," whispered Miss Cooper, opening his chamber door on a crack, in a pair of very creaking shoes. So for the first evening that her old friend was at home Lizzie caught but a glimpse of his pale, senseless face as she hovered outside the long train of his attendants. If we may suppose any of these kind people to have had eyes for aught but the sufferer, we may be sure that they saw another visage, equally sad and white. The sufferer? It was hardly Jack, after all.

When Lizzie was turned from Jack's door, she took a covering from a heap of draperies that had been hurriedly tossed down in the hall—it was an old army blanket. She wrapped it round her and went out on the veranda. It was nine o'clock, but the darkness was filled with light. A great wanton wind—the ghost of the raw blast which travels by day—had arisen, bearing long, soft gusts of inland spring. Scattered clouds were hurrying across the white sky. The bright moon, careering in their midst, seemed to have wandered forth in frantic quest of the hidden stars.

Lizzie nestled her head in the blanket and sat down on the steps. A strange, earthy smell lingered in that faded old rug, and with it a faint perfume of tobacco. Instantly the young girl's senses were transported as they had never been before to those faroff southern battlefields. She saw men lying in swamps, puffing their kindly pipes, drawing their blankets closer, canopied with the same luminous dusk that shone down upon her comfortable weakness. Her mind wandered amid these scenes till recalled to the present by the swinging of the garden gate. She heard a firm, well-known tread crunching the gravel. Mr. Bruce came up the path. As he drew near the steps, Lizzie arose. The blanket fell back from her head and Bruce started at recognizing her.

"Hullo! You, Elizabeth? What's the matter?"

Lizzie made no answer.

"Are you one of Mr. Ford's watchers?" he continued, coming up the steps; "how is he?"

Still she was silent. Bruce put out his hands to take hers and bent forward as if to kiss her. She half-shook him off and retreated toward the door.

"Good heavens!" cried Bruce. "What's the matter? Are you moonstruck? Can't you speak?"

"No—no—not tonight," said Lizzie in a choking voice. "Go away—go away!"

She stood, holding the door handle and motioning him

off. He hesitated a moment and then advanced. She opened the door rapidly and went in. He heard her lock it. He stood looking at it stupidly for some time and then slowly turned round and walked down the steps.

The next morning Lizzie arose with the early dawn and came downstairs. She went into the room where Jack lay and gently opened the door. Miss Cooper was dozing in her chair. Lizzie crossed the threshold and stole up to the bed. Poor Ford lay peacefully sleeping. There was his old face, after all—his strong, honest features refined, but not weakened, by pain. Lizzie softly drew up a low chair and sat down beside him. She gazed into his face—the dear and honored face into which she had so often gazed in health. It was strangely handsomer—body stood for less. It seemed to Lizzie that, as the fabric of her lover's soul was more clearly revealed—the veil of the temple rent well nigh in twain—she could read the justification of all her old worship. One of Jack's hands lay outside the sheet—those strong, supple fingers, once so cunning in workmanship, so frank in friendship, now thinner and whiter than her own. After looking at it for some time, Lizzie gently grasped it. Jack slowly opened his eyes. Lizzie's heart began to throb—it was as if the stillness of the sanctuary had given a sign. At first there was no recognition in the young man's gaze. Then the dull pupils began visibly to brighten. There came to his lips the commencement of that strange moribund smile which seems so ineffably satirical of the things of this world. O imposing spectacle of death! O blessed soul, marked for promotion! What earthly favor is like thine? Lizzie sank down on her knees, and still clasping John's hand, bent closer over him.

"Jack—dear, dear Jack," she whispered, "do you know me?"

The smile grew more intense. The poor fellow drew out his other hand and slowly, feebly placed it on Lizzie's head, stroking down her hair with his fingers.

"Yes, yes," she murmured; "you know me, don't you? I am Lizzie, Jack. Don't you remember Lizzie?"

Ford moved his lips inaudibly and went on patting her head.

"This is home, you know," said Lizzie; "this is Glenham. You haven't forgotten Glenham? You are with your mother and me and your friends. Dear, darling Jack!"

Still he went on stroking her head, and his feeble lips tried to emit some sound. Lizzie laid her head down on the pillow beside his own, and still his hand lingered caressingly on her hair.

"Yes, you know me," she pursued; "you are with your friends now forever—with those who will love and take care of you—oh, forever!"

"I'm very badly wounded," murmured Jack, close to her ear.

"Yes, yes, my dear boy, but your wounds are healing. I will love you and nurse you forever."

"Yes, Lizzie, our old promise," said Jack; and his hand fell upon her neck, and with its feeble pressure he drew her closer, and she wet his face with her tears.

Then Miss Cooper, awakening, rose and drew Lizzie away.

"I am sure you excite him, my dear. It is best he should have none of his family near him—persons with whom he has associations, you know."

Here the doctor was heard gently tapping on the window, and Lizzie went round to the door to admit him.

She did not see Jack again all day. Two or three times she ventured into the room, but she was banished by a frown, or a finger raised to the lips. She waylaid the doctor frequently. He was blithe and cheerful, certain of Jack's recovery. This good man used to exhibit as much moral elation at the prospect of a cure as an orthodox believer at that of a new convert: it was one more body gained from the Devil. He assured Lizzie that the change of scene and climate had already begun to tell: the fever was lessening, the worst symptoms disappearing. He answered Lizzie's reiterated desire to do something by directions to keep the house quiet and the sickroom empty.

Soon after breakfast, Miss Dawes, a neighbor, came in to relieve Miss Cooper, and this indefatigable lady transferred her attention to Mrs. Ford. Action was forbidden her. Miss Cooper was delighted for once to be able to lay down the law to her vigorous neighbor, of whose fine judgment she had always stood in awe. Having bullied Mrs. Ford into taking her breakfast in the little sitting

room, she closed the doors and prepared for "a good long
talk." Lizzie was careful not to break in upon this interview. She had bidden her patroness good morning, asked
after her health, and received one of her temperate oscu-
lations. As she passed the invalid's door, Doctor Cooper
out and asked her to go and look for a certain roll of
bandages, in Mr. John's trunk, which had been carried
into another room. Lizzie hastened to perform this task.
In fumbling through the contents of the trunk, she came
across a packet of letters in a well-known feminine hand-
writing. She pocketed it, and after disposing of the bandages, went to her own room, locked the door, and sat
down to examine the letters. Between reading and thinking and sighing and (in spite of herself) smiling, this
process took the whole morning. As she came down to
dinner, she encountered Mrs. Ford and Miss Cooper,
emerging from the sitting room, the good long talk being
only just concluded.

"How do you feel, ma'am?" she asked of the elder lady.
"Rested?"

For all answer Mrs. Ford gave a look—I had almost
said a scowl—so hard, so cold, so reproachful that Lizzie
was transfixed. But suddenly its sickening meaning was
revealed to her. She turned to Miss Cooper, who stood
pale and fluttering beside the mistress, her everlasting
smile glazed over with a piteous, deprecating glance; and
I fear her eyes flashed out the same message of angry
scorn they had just received. These telegraphic operations are very rapid. The ladies hardly halted: the next
moment found them seated at the dinner table, with Miss
Cooper scrutinizing her napkin mark and Mrs. Ford
saying grace.

Dinner was eaten in silence. When it was over, Lizzie
returned to her own room. Miss Cooper went home, and
Mrs. Ford went to her son. Lizzie heard the firm, low
click of the lock as she closed the door. Why did she lock
it? There was something fatal in the silence that followed. The plot of her little tragedy thickened. Be it so
—she would act her part with the rest. For the second
time in her experience, her mind was lightened by the
intervention of Mrs. Ford. Before the scorn of her own
conscience (which never came), before Jack's deepest

reproach, she was ready to bow down—but not before
that long-faced nemesis in black silk. The leaven of resentment began to work. She leaned back in her chair and
folded her arms, brave to await results. But before long
she fell asleep. She was aroused by a knock at her chamber door. The afternoon was far gone. Miss Dawes stood
without.

"Elizabeth, Mr. John wants very much to see you, with
his love. Come down very gently—his mother is lying
down. Will you sit with him while I take my dinner? Better? Yes, ever so much."

Lizzie betook herself with trembling haste to Jack's bedside.

He was propped up with pillows. His pale cheeks were
slightly flushed. His eyes were bright. He raised himself
and, for such feeble arms, gave Lizzie a long, strong
embrace.

"I've not seen you all day, Lizzie," said he. "Where
have you been?"

"Dear Jack, they wouldn't let me come near you. I
begged and prayed. And I wanted so to go to you in
the Army; but I couldn't. I wish, I wish I had!"

"You wouldn't have liked it, Lizzie. I'm glad you didn't.
It's a bad, bad place."

He lay quietly, holding her hands and gazing at her.

"Can I do anything for you, dear?" asked the young
girl. "I would work my life out. I'm so glad you're better!"

It was some time before Jack answered:

"Lizzie," said he, at last, "I sent for you to look at
you. You are more wondrously beautiful than ever. Your
hair is brown—like—like nothing; your eyes are blue;
your neck is white. Well, well!"

He lay perfectly motionless, but for his eyes. They
wandered over her with a kind of peaceful glee, like
sunbeams playing on a statue. Poor Ford lay, indeed,
not unlike an old wounded Greek who, at falling dusk,
has crawled into a temple to die, steeping the last dull
interval in idle admiration of sculptured Artemis.

"Ah, Lizzie, this is already heaven!" he murmured.

"It will be heaven when you get well," whispered Lizzie.

He smiled into her eyes:

"You say more than you mean. There should be perfect truth between us. Dear Lizzie, I am not going to get well. They are all very much mistaken. I am going to die. I've done my work. Death makes up for everything. My great pain is in leaving you. But you, too, will die one of these days; remember that. In all pain and sorrow, remember that."

Lizzie was able to reply only by the tightening grasp of her hands.

"But there is something more," pursued Jack. "Life *is* as good as death. Your heart has found its true keeper; so we shall all three be happy. Tell him I bless him and honor him. Tell him God, too, blesses him. Shake hands with him for me," said Jack, feebly moving his pale fingers. "My mother," he went on, "be very kind to her. She will have great grief, but she will not die of it. She'll live to great age. Now, Lizzie, I can't talk any more; I wanted to say farewell. You'll keep me farewell—you'll stay with me awhile—won't you? I'll look at you till the last. For a little while you'll be mine, holding my hands— so—until death parts us."

Jack kept his promise. His eyes were fixed in a firm gaze long after the sense had left them.

In the early dawn of the next day, Elizabeth left her sleepless bed, opened the window, and looked out on the wide prospect, still cool and dim with departing night. It offered freshness and peace to her hot head and restless heart. She dressed herself hastily, crept down stairs, passed the death chamber, and stole out of the quiet house. She turned away from the still sleeping village and walked toward the open country. She went a long way without knowing it. The sun had risen high when she bethought herself to turn. As she came back along the brightening highway and drew near home, she saw a tall figure standing beneath the budding trees of the garden, hesitating, apparently, whether to open the gate. Lizzie came upon him almost before he had seen her. Bruce's first movement was to put out his hands, as any lover might, but as Lizzie raised her veil, he dropped them.

"Yes, Mr. Bruce," said Lizzie, "I'll give you my hand once more—in farewell."

"Elizabeth!" cried Bruce, half-stupefied, "in God's name, what do you mean by these crazy speeches?"

"I mean well. I mean kindly and humanely to you. And I mean justice to my old—old love."

She went to him, took his listless hand, without looking into his wild, smitten face, shook it passionately, and then, wrenching her own from his grasp, opened the gate and let it swing behind her.

"No! no! no!" she almost shrieked, turning about in the path. "I forbid you to follow me!"

But for all that, he went in.

My Friend Bingham

CONSCIOUS as I am of a deep aversion to stories of a painful nature, I have often asked myself whether, in the events here set forth, the element of pain is stronger than that of joy. An affirmative answer to this question would have stood as a veto upon the publication of my story, for it is my opinion that the literature of horrors needs no extension. Such an answer, however, I am unwilling to pronounce; while, on the other hand, I hesitate to assume the responsibility of a decided negative. I have therefore determined to leave the solution to the reader. I may add that I am very sensible of the superficial manner in which I have handled my facts. I bore no other part in the accomplishment of these facts than that of a cordial observer, and it was impossible that, even with the best will in the world, I should fathom the emotions of the actors. Yet, as the very faintest reflection of human passions, under the pressure of fate, possesses an immortal interest, I am content to appeal to the reader's sympathy and to assure him of my own fidelity.

Toward the close of summer, in my twenty-eighth year, I went down to the seaside to rest from a long term of work and to enjoy, after several years of separation, a tête-à-tête with an intimate friend. My friend had just arrived from Europe, and we had agreed to spend my vacation together by the side of the sounding sea and within easy reach of the city. On taking possession of our lodgings, we found that we should have no fellow idlers, and we hailed joyously the prospect of the great marine solitudes which each of us declared that he found so abundantly peopled by the other. I hasten to impart to the reader the following facts in regard to the man whom I found so good a companion.

George Bingham had been born and bred among people for whom, as he grew to manhood, he learned to entertain a most generous contempt—people in whom the hereditary possession of a large property—for he assured me that the facts stood in the relation of cause and effect—had extinguished all intelligent purpose and principle. I trust that I do not speak rhetorically when I describe in these terms the combined ignorance and vanity of my friend's progenitors. It was their fortune to make a splendid figure while they lived, and I feel little compunction in hinting at their poverty in certain human essentials. Bingham was no declaimer, and indeed no great talker, and it was only now and then, in an allusion to the past as the field of a wasted youth, that he expressed his profound resentment. I read this for the most part in the severe humility with which he regarded the future, and under cover of which he seemed to salute it as void at least (whatever other ills it might contain) of those domestic embarrassments which had been the bane of his first manhood. I have no doubt that much may be said, within limits, for the graces of that society against which my friend embodied so violent a reaction, and especially for its good humor—that home-keeping benevolence which accompanies a sense of material repletion. It is equally probable that to persons of a simple constitution these graces may wear a look of delightful and enduring mystery, but poor Bingham was no simpleton. He was a man of opinions numerous, delicate, and profound. When, with the lapse of his youth, he awoke to a presentiment of these opinions and cast his first interrogative glance upon the world, he found that in his own little section of it he and his opinions were a piece of melancholy impertinence. Left, at twenty-three years of age, by his father's death, in possession of a handsome property and absolute master of his actions, he had thrown himself blindly into the world. But, as he afterwards assured me, so superficial was his knowledge of the real world—the world of labor and inquiry—that he had found himself quite incapable of intelligent action. In this manner he had wasted a great deal of time. He had traveled much, however, and being a keen observer of men and women, he had acquired a certain practical knowledge of human nature. Nevertheless, it was not till he was nearly thirty years old that he had begun to live for himself. "By myself," he explained, "I mean something else than this monstrous hereditary faculty for doing nothing and thinking of nothing." And he led me to believe, or I should rather say he allowed me to believe, that at this moment he had made a serious attempt to study. But upon this point he was not very explicit, for if he blushed for the manner in which he had slighted his opportunities, he blushed equally for the manner in which he had used them. It is my belief that he had but a limited capacity for study, and I am certain that to the end of his days there subsisted in his mind a very friendly relation between fancies and facts.

Bingham was par excellence a moralist, a man of sentiment. I know—he knew himself—that, in this busy western world, this character represents no recognized avocation; but in the absence of such avocation, its exercise was nevertheless very dear to him. I protest that it was very dear to me, and that, at the end of a long morning devoted to my office desk, I have often felt as if I had contributed less to the common cause than I have felt after moralizing—or, if you please, sentimentalizing—half an hour with my friend. He was an idler, assuredly, but his candor, his sagacity, his good taste, and, above all, a certain diffident enthusiasm which followed its objects with the exquisite trepidation of an unconfessed and despairing lover—these things, and a hundred more, redeemed him from vulgarity. For three years before we came together, as I have intimated, my impressions of my friend had rested on his letters; and yet, from the first hour which we spent together, I felt that they had done him no wrong. We were genuine friends. I don't know that I can offer better proof of this than by saying that, as our old personal relations resumed their force and the time-shrunken outlines of character filled themselves out, I greeted the reappearance of each familiar foible on Bingham's part quite as warmly as I did that of the less punctual virtue. Compared, indeed, with the comrade of earlier years, my actual companion was a

well-seasoned man of the world; but with all his acquired
humility and his disciplined bonhomie, he had failed to
divest himself of a certain fastidiousness of mind, a certain formalism of manner, which are the token and the
prerogative of one who has not been obliged to address
himself to practical questions. The charm bestowed by
these facts upon Bingham's conversation—a charm often
vainly invoked in their absence—is explained by his honest indifference to their action, and his indisposition to
turn them to account in the interest of the picturesque—
an advantage but too easy of conquest for a young man
rich, accomplished, and endowed with good looks and a
good name. I may say, perhaps, that to a critical mind
my friend's prime distinction would have been his very
positive refusal to drape himself, after the current taste,
with those brilliant stuffs which fortune had strewn at
his feet.

Of course, a great deal of our talk bore upon Bingham's recent travels, adventures, and sensations. One of
these last he handled very frankly, and treated me to a
bit of genuine romance. He had been in love, and had been
cruelly jilted, but had now grown able to view the matter
with much of the impartial spirit of those French critics
whose works were his favorite reading. His account of
the young lady's character and motives would, indeed,
have done credit to many a clever *feuilleton*. I was the
less surprised, however, at his severely dispassionate tone
when, in retracing the process of his opinions, I discerned
the traces—the ravages, I may almost say—of a solemn
act of renunciation. Bingham had forsworn marriage. I
made haste to assure him that I considered him quite too
young for so austere a resolve.

"I can't help it," said he; "I feel a foreboding that I
shall live and die alone."

"A foreboding?" said I. "What's a foreboding worth?"

"Well, then, rationally considered, my marriage is
improbable."

"But it's not to be rationally considered," I objected.
"It belongs to the province of sentiment."

"But you deny me sentiment. I fall back upon my foreboding."

"That's not sentiment—it's superstition," I answered.

"Your marrying will depend upon your falling in love, and your falling in love will certainly not depend upon yourself."

"Upon whom, then?"

"Upon some unknown fair one—Miss A, B, or C."

"Well," said Bingham submissively, "I wish she would make haste and reveal herself."

These remarks had been exchanged in the hollow of a cliff which sloped seaward, and where we had lazily stretched ourselves at length on the grass. The grass had grown very long and brown, and as we lay with our heads quite on a level with it, the view of the immediate beach and the gentle breakers was so completely obstructed by the rank, coarse herbage that our prospect was reduced to a long, narrow band of deep blue ocean traversing its black fibers, and to the great vault of the sky. We had strolled out a couple of hours before, bearing each a borrowed shotgun and accompanied by a friendly water dog, somewhat languidly disposed towards the slaughter of wild ducks. We were neither of us genuine sportsmen, and it is certain that, on the whole, we meant very kindly to the ducks. It was at all events fated that on that day they should suffer but lightly at our hands. For the half-hour previous to the exchange of the remarks just cited, we had quite forgotten our real business, and with our pieces lost in the grass beside us, and our dog, weary of inaction, wandering far beyond call, we looked like any straw-picking truants. At last Bingham rose to his feet, with the asseveration that it would never do for us to return empty-handed. "But, behold," he exclaimed as he looked down across the breadth of the beach, "there is our friend of the cottage, with the sick little boy."

I brought myself into a sitting posture and glanced over the cliff. Down near the edge of the water sat a young woman, tossing stones into it for the amusement of a child, who stood lustily crowing and clapping his hands. Her title to be called our friend lay in the fact that, on our way to the beach, we had observed her issuing from a cottage hard by the hotel, leading by the hand a pale-faced little boy muffled like an invalid. The hotel, as I have said, was all but deserted, and this young woman had been the first person to engage our idle observation.

We had seen that, although plainly dressed, she was young, pretty, and modest, and, in the absence of heavier cares, these facts had sufficed to make her interesting. The question had arisen between us whether she was a native of the shore, or a visitor like ourselves. Bingham inclined to the former view of the case, and I to the latter. There was, indeed, a certain lowliness in her aspect, but I had contended that it was by no means a rustic lowliness. Her dress was simple, but it was well-made and well-worn, and I noticed that as she strolled along, leading her little boy, she cast upon sky and sea the lingering glance of one to whom, in their integrity, these were unfamiliar objects. She was the wife of some small tradesman, I argued, who had brought her child to the seaside by the physician's decree. But Bingham declared that it was utterly illogical to suppose her to be a mother of five years' motherhood, and that, for his part, he saw nothing in her appearance inconsistent with rural influences. The child was her nephew, the son of a married sister, and she a sentimental maiden aunt. Obviously the volume she had in her hand was Tennyson. In the absence on both sides of authentic data, of course, the debate was not prolonged, and the subject of it had passed from our memories some time before we again met her on the beach. She soon became aware of our presence, however, and with a natural sense of intrusion, we immediately resumed our walk. The last that I saw of her, as we rounded a turn in the cliff which concealed the backward prospect, was a sudden grasp of the child's arm, as if to withdraw him from the reach of a hastily advancing wave.

Half an hour's farther walk led us to a point which we were not tempted to exceed. We shot between us some half a dozen birds, but as our dog—whose talents had been sadly misrepresented—proved very shy of the deep water and succeeded in bringing no more than a couple of our victims to shore, we resolved to abstain from further destruction and to return home quietly along the beach, upon which we had now descended.

"If we meet our young lady," said Bingham, "we can gallantly offer her our booty."

Some five minutes after he had uttered these words, a

couple of great seagulls came flying landward over our heads and, after a long gyration in mid-air, boldly settled themselves on the slope of the cliff at some three hundred yards in front of us, a point at which it projected almost into the waves. After a momentary halt, one of them rose again on his long pinions and soared away seaward; the other remained. He sat perched on a jutting boulder some fifteen feet high, sunning his fishy breast.

"I wonder if I could put a shot into him," said Bingham.

"Try," I answered, and, as he rapidly charged and leveled his piece, I remember idly repeating, while I looked at the great bird,

> God save thee, ancient mariner,
> From the fiends that plague thee thus!
> Why look'st thou so? "With my cross-bow
> I shot the albatross."

"He's going to rise," I added.

But Bingham had fired. The creature rose, indeed, half-sluggishly, and yet with too hideous celerity. His movement drew from us a cry which was almost simultaneous with the report of Bingham's gun. I cannot express our relation to what followed it better than by saying that it exposed to our sight, beyond the space suddenly left vacant, the happy figure of the child from whom we had parted but an hour before. He stood with his little hands extended and his face raised toward the retreating bird. Of the sickening sensation which assailed our common vision as we saw him throw back his hands to his head and reel downward out of sight, I can give no verbal account, nor of the rapidity with which we crossed the smooth interval of sand, and rounded the bluff.

The child's companion had scrambled up the rocky bank toward the low ledge from which he had fallen, and to which access was of course all too easy. She had sunk down upon the stones, and was wildly clasping the boy's body. I turned from this spectacle to my friend, as to an image of equal woe. Bingham, pale as death, bounded over the stones and fell on his knees. The woman let him take the child out of her arms, and bent over, with her fore-

head on a rock, moaning. I have never seen helplessness
so vividly embodied as in this momentary group.

"Did it strike his head?" cried Bingham. "What the
devil was he doing up there?"

"I told him he'd get hurt," said the young woman with
harrowing simplicity. "To shoot straight at him! He's
killed!"

"Great heavens! Do you mean to say that I saw him!"
roared Bingham. "How did I know he was there? Did
you see us?"

The young woman shook her head. "Of course I didn't
see you. I saw you with your guns before. Oh, he's killed!"

"He's not killed. It was mere duck shot. Don't talk
such stuff. My own poor little man!" cried George.
"Charles, where *were* our eyes?"

"He wanted to catch the bird," moaned our companion. "Baby, my boy! Open your eyes. Speak to your
mother. For God's sake, get some help!"

She had put out her hands to take the child from Bingham, who had half-angrily lifted him out of her reach.
The senseless movement with which, as she disengaged
him from Bingham's grasp, he sank into her arms, was
clearly the senselessness of death. She burst into sobs. I
went and examined the child.

"He *may* not be killed," I said, turning to Bingham;
"keep your senses. It's not your fault. We *couldn't* see
each other."

Bingham rose stupidly to his feet.

"She must be got home," I said.

"We must get a carriage. Will you go or stay?"

I saw that he had seen the truth. He looked about him
with an expression of miserable impotence. "Poor little
devil!" he said hoarsely.

"Will you go for a carriage?" I repeated, taking his
hand, "or will you stay?"

Our companion's sobs redoubled their violence.

"I'll stay," said he. "Bring some woman."

I started at a hard run. I left the beach behind me,
passed the white cottage at whose garden gate two women
were gossiping, and reached the hotel stable, where I had
the good fortune to find a vehicle at my disposal. I
drove straight back to the white cottage. One of the

women had disappeared, and the other was lingering among her flowers—a middle-aged, keen-eyed person. As I descended and hastily addressed her, I read in her rapid glance an anticipation of evil tidings.

"The young woman who stays with you—" I began.

"Yes," she said, "my second cousin. Well?"

"She's in trouble. She wants you to come to her. Her little boy has hurt himself." I had time to see that I need fear no hysterics.

"Where did you leave her?" asked my companion.

"On the beach."

"What's the matter with the child?"

"He fell from a rock. There's no time to be lost." There was a certain antique rigidity about the woman which was at once irritating and reassuring. I was impelled both to quicken her apprehensions and to confide in her self-control. "For all I know, ma'am," said I, "the child is killed."

She gave me an angry stare. "For all you know!" she exclaimed. "Where were your wits? Were you afraid to look at him?"

"Yes, half-afraid."

She glanced over the paling at my vehicle. "Am I to get into that?" she asked.

"If you will be so good."

She turned short about and re-entered the house, where, as I stood out among the dahlias and the pinks, I heard a rapid opening and shutting of drawers. She shortly reappeared, equipped for driving, and having locked the house door and pocketed the key, came and faced me, where I stood ready to help her into the wagon.

"We'll stop for the doctor," she began.

"The doctor," said I, "is of no use."

A few moments of hard driving brought us to my starting point. The tide had fallen perceptibly in my absence, and I remember receiving a strange impression of the irretrievable nature of the recent event from the sight of poor Bingham, standing down at the low-water mark and looking seaward with his hands in his pockets. The mother of his little victim still sat on the heap of stones where she had fallen, pressing her child to her breast. I helped my companion to descend, which she did with

great deliberation. It is my belief that, as we drove along
the beach, she derived from the expression of Bingham's
figure, and from the patient aversion of his face, a suspicion of his relation to the opposite group. It was not
till the elder woman had come within a few steps of her
that the younger became aware of her approach. I merely
had time to catch the agonized appeal of her upward
glance, and the broad compassion of the other's stooping
movement, before I turned my back upon their encounter and walked down toward my friend. The monotonous murmur of the waves had covered the sound of
our wagon wheels, and Bingham stood all unconscious
of the coming of relief—distilling I know not what divine
relief from the simple beauty of sea and sky. I had laid
my hand on his shoulder before he turned about. He
looked toward the base of the cliff. I knew that a great
effusion of feeling would occur in its natural order, but
how should I help him across the interval?

"That's her cousin," I said at random. "She seems a
very capable woman."

"The child is quite dead," said Bingham, for all answer. I was struck by the plainness of his statement. In
the comparative freedom of my own thoughts I had
failed to make allowance for the embarrassed movement
of my friend's. It was not, therefore, until afterward
that I acknowledged he had thought to better purpose
than I, inasmuch as the very simplicity of his tone im-
plied a positive acceptance (for the moment) of the
dreadful fact which he uttered.

"The sooner they get home, the better," I said. It was
evident that the elder of our companions had already embraced this conviction. She had lifted the child and
placed him in the carriage, and she was now turning toward his mother and inviting her to ascend. Even at the
distance at which I stood, the mingled firmness and tenderness of her gestures were clearly apparent. They
seemed, moreover, to express a certain indifference to
our movements, an independence of our further interference, which—fanciful as the assertion may look—was
not untinged with irony. It was plain that, by whatever
rapid process she had obtained it, she was already in possession of our story. "Thank God for strong-minded wom-

en!" I exclaimed, and yet I could not repress a feeling
that it behooved me, on behalf of my friend, to treat as
an equal with the vulgar movement of antipathy which
he was destined to encounter, and of which, in the irresistible sequence of events, the attitude of this good
woman was an index.

We walked toward the carriage together. "I shall not
come home directly," said Bingham, "but don't be alarmed
about me."

I looked at my watch. "I give you two hours," I said
with all the authority of my affection.

The newcomer had placed herself on the back seat of
the vehicle beside the sufferer, who on entering had again
possessed herself of her child. As I went about to mount
in front, Bingham came and stood by the wheel. I read
his purpose in his face—the desire to obtain from the
woman he had wronged some recognition of his *human*
character, some confession that she dimly distinguished
him from a wild beast or a thunderbolt. One of her hands
lay exposed, pressing together on her knee the lifeless
little hands of her boy. Bingham removed his hat and
placed his right hand on that of the young woman. I saw
that she started at his touch, and that he vehemently
tightened his grasp.

"It's too soon to talk of forgiveness," said he, "for it's
too soon for me to think intelligently of the wrong I have
done you. God has brought us together in a very strange
fashion."

The young woman raised her bowed head and gave my
friend, if not just the look he coveted, at least the most
liberal glance at her command—a look which, I fancy,
helped him to face the immediate future. But these are
matters too delicate to be put into words.

I spent the hours that elapsed before Bingham's return
to the inn in gathering information about the occupants
of the cottage. Impelled by that lively intuition of calamity
which is natural to women, the housekeeper of the hotel,
a person of evident kindliness and discretion, lost no
time in winning my confidence. I was not unwilling that
the tragic incident which had thus arrested our idleness
should derive its earliest publicity from my own lips; and
I was forcibly struck with the exquisite impartiality with

which this homely creature bestowed her pity. Miss Horner, I learned, the mistress of the cottage, was the last representative of a most respectable family, native to the neighboring town. It had been for some years her practice to let lodgings during the summer. At the close of the present season, she had invited her kinswoman, Mrs. Hicks, to spend the autumn with her. That this lady was the widow of a Baptist minister; that her husband had died some three years before; that she was very poor; that her child had been sickly, and that the care of his health had so impeded her exertions for a livelihood that she had been intending to leave him with Miss Horner for the winter and obtain a "situation" in town—these facts were the salient points of the housekeeper's somewhat prolix recital.

The early autumn dusk had fallen when Bingham returned. He looked very tired. He had been walking for several hours, and, as I fancied, had grown in some degree familiar with his new responsibilities. He was very hungry, and made a vigorous attack upon his supper. I had been indisposed to eat, but the sight of his healthy appetite restored my own. I had grown weary of my thoughts, and I found something salutary in the apparent simplicity and rectitude of Bingham's state of mind.

"I find myself taking it very quietly," he said in the course of his repast. "There is something so absolute in the nature of the calamity that one is compelled to accept it. I don't see how I could endure to have mutilated the poor little mortal. To kill a human being is, after all, the least injury you can do him." He spoke these words deliberately, with his eyes on mine, and with an expression of perfect candor. But as he paused, and in spite of my perfect assent to their meaning, I could not help mentally reverting to the really tragic phase of the affair, and I suppose my features revealed to Bingham's scrutiny the process of my thoughts. His pale face flushed a burning crimson, his lips trembled. "Yes, my boy!" he cried, "that's where it's damnable." He buried his head in his hands, and burst into tears.

We had a long talk. At the end of it, we lit our cigars and came out upon the deserted piazza. There was a lovely starlight, and after a few turns in silence, Bingham left my side and strolled off toward a bend in the road, in the direction of the sea. I saw him stand motionless for a long time, and then I heard him call me. When I reached his side, I saw that he had been watching a light in the window of the white cottage. We heard the village bell in the distance striking nine.

"Charles," said Bingham, "suppose you go down there and make some offer of your services. God knows whom the poor creatures have to look to. She has had a couple of men thrust into her life. She must take the good with the bad."

I lingered a moment. "It's a difficult task," I said. "What shall I say?"

Bingham silently puffed his cigar. He stood with his arms folded and his head thrown back, slowly measuring the starry sky. "I wish she could come out here and look at that sky," he said at last. "It's a sight for bereaved mothers. Somehow, my dear boy," he pursued, "I never felt less depressed in my life. It's none of my doing."

"It would hardly do for me to tell her that," said I.

"I don't know," said Bingham. "This isn't an occasion for the exchange of compliments. I'll tell you what you may tell her. I suppose they will have some funeral services within a day or two. Tell her that I should like very much to be present."

I set off for the cottage. Its mistress in person introduced me into the little parlor.

"Well, sir?" she said in hard, dry accents.

"I've come," I answered, "to ask whether I can be of any assistance to Mrs. Hicks."

Miss Horner shook her head in a manner which deprived her negation of half its dignity. "What assistance is possible?" she asked.

"A man," said I, "may relieve a woman of certain cares——"

"Oh, men are a blessed set! You had better leave Mrs. Hicks to me."

"But will you at least tell me how she is—if she has in any degree recovered herself?"

At this moment the door of the adjoining room was opened, and Mrs. Hicks stood on the threshold, bearing a lamp—a graceful and pathetic figure. I now had occasion to observe that she was a woman of decided beauty. Her fair hair was drawn back into a single knot behind her head, and the lamplight deepened the pallor of her face and the darkness of her eyes. She wore a calico dressing gown and a shawl.

"What do you wish?" she asked in a voice clarified, if I may so express it, by long weeping.

"He wants to know whether he can be of any assistance," said the elder lady.

Mrs. Hicks glanced over her shoulder into the room she had left. "Would you like to look at the child?" she asked in a whisper.

"Lucy!" cried Miss Horner.

I walked straight over to Mrs. Hicks, who turned and led the way to a little bed. My conductress raised her lamp aloft and let the light fall gently on the little white-draped figure. Even the bandage about the child's head had not dispelled his short-lived prettiness. Heaven knows that to remain silent was easy enough; but Heaven knows, too, that to break the silence—and to break it as I broke it—was equally easy. "He must have been a very pretty child," I said.

"Yes, he was very pretty. He had black eyes. I don't know whether you noticed."

"No, I didn't notice," said I. "When is he to be buried?"

"The day after tomorrow. I am told that I shall be able to avoid an inquest."

"Mr. Bingham has attended to that," I said. And then I paused, revolving his petition.

But Mrs. Hicks anticipated it. "If you would like to be present at the funeral," she said, "you are welcome to come. And so is your friend."

"Mr. Bingham bade me ask leave. There is a great deal that I should like to say to you for him," I added, "but I won't spoil it by trying. It's his own business."

The young woman looked at me with her deep, dark eyes. "I pity him from my heart," she said, pressing her hands to her breast. "I had rather have my sorrow than his."

"They are pretty much one sorrow," I answered. "I don't see that you can divide it. You are two to bear it.

Bingham is a wise, good fellow," I went on. "I have shared a great many joys with him. In Heaven's name," I cried, "don't bear hard on him!"

"How can I bear hard?" she asked, opening her arms and letting them drop. The movement was so deeply expressive of weakness and loneliness that, feeling all power to reply stifled in a rush of compassion, I silently made my exit.

On the following day, Bingham and I went up to town, and on the third day returned in time for the funeral. Besides the two ladies, there was no one present but ourselves and the village minister, who of course spoke as briefly as decency allowed. He had accompanied the ladies in a carriage to the graveyard, while Bingham and I had come on foot. As we turned away from the grave, I saw my friend approach Mrs. Hicks. They stood talking beside the freshly turned earth, while the minister and I attended Miss Horner to the carriage. After she had seated herself, I lingered at the door, exchanging sober commonplaces with the reverend gentleman. At last Mrs. Hicks followed us, leaning on Bingham's arm.

"Margaret," she said, "Mr. Bingham and I are going to stay here awhile. Mr. Bingham will walk home with me. I'm *very* much obliged to you, Mr. Bland," she added, turning to the minister and extending her hand.

I bestowed upon my friend a glance which I felt to be half-interrogative and half-sympathetic. He gave me his hand, and answered the benediction by its pressure, while he answered the inquiry by his words. "If you are still disposed to go back to town this afternoon," he said, "you had better not wait for me. I may not have time to catch the boat."

I, of course, made no scruple of returning immediately to the city. Some ten days elapsed before I again saw Bingham; but I found my attention so deeply engrossed with work that I scarcely measured the interval. At last, one morning, he came into my office.

"I take for granted," I said, "that you have not been all this time at B——."

"No, I've been on my travels. I came to town the day after you came. I found at my rooms a letter from a lawyer in Baltimore, proposing the sale of some of my

property there, and I seized upon it as an excuse for
making a journey to that city. I felt the need of movement, of action of some kind. But when I reached Baltimore, I didn't even go to see my correspondent. I pushed
on to Washington, walked about for thirty-six hours, and
came home."

He had placed his arm on my desk, and stood, sup-
porting his head on his hand, with a look of great physical exhaustion.

"You look very tired," said I.

"I haven't slept," said he. "I had such a talk with that
woman!"

"I'm sorry that you should have felt the worse for it."

"I feel both the worse and the better. She talked about
the child."

"It's well for her," said I, "that she was able to do it."

"She wasn't able, strictly speaking. She began calmly
enough, but she very soon broke down."

"Did you see her again?"

"I called upon her the next day, to tell her that I was
going to town, and to ask if I could be useful to her. But
she seems to stand in perfect isolation. She assured me
that she was in want of nothing."

"What sort of a woman does she seem to be, taking her
in herself?"

"Bless your soul! I can't take her in herself!" cried
Bingham with some vehemence. "And yet, stay," he added;
"she's a very pleasing woman."

"She's very pretty."

"Yes, she's very pretty. In years, she's little more than
a young girl. In her ideas, she's one of 'the people.'"

"It seems to me," said I, "that the frankness of her
conduct toward you is very much to her credit."

"It doesn't offend you, then?"

"Offend me? It gratifies me beyond measure."

"I think that, if you had seen her as I have seen her, it
would interest you deeply. I'm at a loss to determine
whether it's the result of great simplicity or great sagacity.
Of course, it's absurd to suppose that, ten days ago, it
could have been the result of anything but a beautiful
impulse. I think that tomorrow I shall again go down to
B——."

I allowed Bingham time to have made his visit and to have brought me an account of his further impressions; but as three days went by without his reappearance, I called at his lodgings. He was still out of town. The fifth day, however, brought him again to my office.

"I've been at B—— constantly," he said, "and I've had several interviews with our friend."

"Well, how fares it?"

"It fares well. I'm forcibly struck with her good sense. In matters of mind—in matters of soul, I may say—she has the touch of an angel, or rather the touch of a woman. That's quite sufficient."

"Does she keep her composure?"

"Perfectly. You can imagine nothing simpler and less sentimental than her manner. She makes me forget myself most divinely. The child's death colors our talk, but it doesn't confine or obstruct it. You see she has her religion: she can afford to be natural."

Weary as my friend looked, and shaken by his sudden subjection to care, it yet seemed to me, as he pronounced these words, that his eye had borrowed a purer light and his voice a fresher tone. In short, where I discerned it, how I detected it, I know not, but I felt that he carried a secret. He sat, poking with his walking stick at a nail in the carpet, with his eyes dropped. I saw about his mouth the faint promise of a distant smile—a smile which six months would bring to maturity.

"George," said I, "I have a fancy."

He looked up. "What is it?"

"You've lost your heart."

He stared a moment, with a sudden frown. "To whom?" he asked.

"To Mrs. Hicks."

With a frown, I say, but a frown that was as a smile to the effect of my rejoinder. He rose to his feet; all his color deserted his face and rushed to his eyes.

"I beg your pardon if I'm wrong," I said.

Bingham had turned again from pale to crimson. "Don't beg *my* pardon," he cried. "You may say what you please. Beg *hers!*" he added bitterly.

I resented the charge of injustice. "I've done *her* no wrong!" I answered. "I haven't said"—I went on with a certain gleeful sense that I was dealing with massive truths—"I haven't said that she had lost her heart to you!"

"Good God, Charles!" cried Bingham, "what a horrid imagination you have!"

"I am not responsible for my imagination."

"Upon my soul, I hope *I*'m not!" cried Bingham passionately. "I have enough without that."

"George," I said after a moment's reflection, "if I thought I had insulted you, I would make amends. But I have said nothing to be ashamed of. I believe that I have hit the truth. Your emotion proves it. I spoke hastily, but you must admit that, having caught a glimpse of the truth, I couldn't stand indifferent to it."

"The truth! The truth! What truth?"

"Aren't you in love with Mrs. Hicks? Admit it like a man."

"Like a man! Like a brute. Haven't I done the woman wrong enough?"

"Quite enough, I hope."

"Haven't I turned her simple joys to bitterness?"

"I grant it."

"And now you want me to insult her by telling her that I love her?"

"I want you to tell her nothing. What you tell her is your own affair. Remember that, George. It's as little mine as it is the rest of the world's."

Bingham stood listening, with a contracted brow and his hand grasping his stick. He walked to the dusty office window and halted a moment, watching the great human throng in the street. Then he turned and came toward me. Suddenly he stopped short. "God forgive me!" he cried; "I believe I do love her."

The fountains of my soul were stirred. "Combining my own hasty impressions of Mrs. Hicks with yours, George," I said, "the consummation seems to me exquisitely natural."

It was in these simple words that we celebrated the sacred fact. It seemed as if, by tacit agreement, the evolution of this fact was result enough for a single interview.

A few days after this interview, in the evening, I called

at Bingham's lodgings. His servant informed me that my friend was out of town, although he was unable to indicate his whereabouts. But as I turned away from the door, a hack drew up, and the object of my quest descended, equipped with a traveling bag. I went down and greeted him under the gaslamp.

"Shall I go in with you?" I asked, "or shall I go my way?"

"You had better come in," said Bingham. "I have something to say. I have been down to B——," he resumed, when the servant had left us alone in his sitting room. His tone bore the least possible tinge of a confession, but of course it was not as a confessor that I listened.

"Well," said I, "how is our friend?"

"Our friend—" answered Bingham. "Will you have a cigar?"

"No, I thank you."

"Our friend. . . . Ah, Charles, it's a long story."

"I sha'n't mind that, if it's an interesting one."

"To a certain extent it's a painful one. It's painful to come into collision with incurable vulgarity of feeling."

I was puzzled. "Has that been your fortune?" I asked.

"It has been my fortune to bring Mrs. Hicks into a great deal of trouble. The case, in three words, is this. Miss Horner has seen fit to resent, in no moderate terms, what she calls the 'extraordinary intimacy' existing between Mrs. Hicks and myself. Mrs. Hicks, as was perfectly natural, has resented her cousin's pretension to regulate her conduct. Her expression of this feeling has led to her expulsion from Miss Horner's house."

"Has she any other friend to turn to?"

"No one, except some relatives of her husband, who are very poor people, and of whom she wishes to ask no favors."

"Where has she placed herself?"

"She is in town. We came up together this afternoon. I went with her to some lodgings which she had formerly occupied, and which were fortunately vacant."

"I suppose it's not to be regretted that she has left B——. She breaks with sad associations."

"Yes, but she renews them, too, on coming to town."

"How so?"

"Why, damn it," said Bingham with a tremor in his voice, "the woman is utterly poor."

"Has she no resources whatever?"

"A hundred dollars a year, I believe—worse than nothing."

"Has she any marketable talents or accomplishments?"

"I believe she is up to some pitiful needlework or other. Such a woman! O horrible world!"

"Does *she* say so?" I asked.

"She? No indeed. She thinks it's all for the best. I suppose it is. But it seems but a bad best."

"I wonder," said I after a pause, "whether I might see Mrs. Hicks. Do you think she would receive me?"

Bingham looked at me an instant keenly. "I suppose so," said he. "You can try."

"I shall go, not out of curiosity," I resumed, "but out of——"

"Out of what?"

"Well, in fine, I should like to see her again."

Bingham gave me Mrs. Hicks's address, and in the course of a few evenings I called upon her. I had abstained from bestowing a fine name upon the impulse which dictated this act, but I am nevertheless free to declare that kindliness and courtesy had a large part in it. Mrs. Hicks had taken up her residence in a plain, small house, in a decent bystreet, where, upon presenting myself, I was ushered into a homely sitting room (apparently her own) and left to await her coming. Her greeting was simple and cordial and not untinged with a certain implication of gratitude. She had taken for granted, on my part, all possible sympathy and good will, but as she had regarded me besides as a man of many cares, she had thought it improbable that we should meet again. It was no long time before I became conscious of that generous charm which Bingham had rigorously denominated her good sense. Good sense assuredly was there, but good sense mated and prolific. Never had I seen, it seemed to me as the moments elapsed, so exquisitely modest a use of such charming faculties—an intelligence so sensible of its obligations and so indifferent to its privileges. It was obvious that she had been a woman of plain associations—her allusions were to homely facts, and her manner direct and unstudied—and yet, in spite of these limitations, it was equally obvious that she was a person to be neither patronized, dazzled, nor deluded. Oh, the satisfaction which, in the course of that quiet dialogue, I took in this sweet infallibility! How it effaced her loneliness and poverty and added dignity to her youth and beauty! It made her, potentially at least, a woman of the world. It was an anticipation of the self-possession, the wisdom, and perhaps even in some degree of the wit which comes through the experience of society—the result, on Mrs. Hicks's part, of I know not what hours of suffering, despondency, and self-dependence. With whatever intentions, therefore, I might have come before her, I should have found it impossible to address her as any other than an equal, and to regard her affliction as anything less than an absolute mystery. In fact, we hardly touched upon it, and it was only covertly that we alluded to Bingham's melancholy position. I will not deny that in a certain sense I regretted Mrs. Hicks's reserve. It is true that I had a very informal claim upon her confidence, but I had gone to her with a half-defined hope that this claim would be liberally interpreted. It was not even recognized; my vague intentions of counsel and assistance had lain undivined, and I departed with the impression that my social horizon had been considerably enlarged, but that my charity had by no means secured a pensioner.

Mrs. Hicks had given me permission to repeat my visit, and after the lapse of a fortnight I determined to do so. I had seen Bingham several times in the interval. He was, of course, much interested in my impressions of our friend, and I fancied that my admiration gave him even more pleasure than he allowed himself to express. On entering Mrs. Hicks's parlor a second time, I found him in person, standing before the fireplace and talking apparently with some vehemence to Mrs. Hicks, who sat listening on the sofa. Bingham turned impatiently to the door as I crossed the threshold, and Mrs. Hicks rose to welcome me with all due composure. I was nevertheless sensible that my entrance was ill-timed; yet a retreat was impossible. Bingham kept his place on the hearth rug, and mechanically gave me his hand,—standing irresolute, as I

thought, between annoyance and elation. The fact that I
had interrupted a somewhat passionate interview was
somehow so obvious that, at the prompting of a very delicate feeling, Mrs. Hicks hastened to anticipate my apologies.

"Mr. Bingham was giving me a lecture," she said; and
there was perhaps in her accent a faint suspicion of bitterness. "He will doubtless be glad of another auditor."

"No," said Bingham, "Charles is a better talker than
listener. You shall have two lectures instead of one." He
uttered this sally without even an attempt to smile.

"What is your subject?" said I. "Until I know that, I
shall promise neither to talk nor to listen."

Bingham laid his hand on my arm. "He represents
the world," he said, addressing our hostess. "You're afraid
of the world. There, make your appeal."

Mrs. Hicks stood silent a moment, with a contracted
brow and a look of pain on her face. Then she turned
to me with a half-smile. "I don't believe you represent the
world," she said; "you are too good."

"She flatters you," said Bingham. "You wish to corrupt
him, Mrs. Hicks."

Mrs. Hicks glanced for an instant from my friend to
myself. There burned in her eyes a far-searching light,
which consecrated the faint irony of the smile which
played about her lips. "Oh you men!" she said, "you are so
wise, so deep!" It was on Bingham that her eyes rested
last; but after a pause, extending her hand, she transferred them to me. "Mr. Bingham," she pursued, "seems
to wish you to be admitted to our counsels. There is
every reason why his friends should be my friends. You
will be interested to know that he has asked me to be
his wife."

"Have you given him an answer?" I asked.

"He was pressing me for an answer when you came
in. He conceives me to have a great fear of the judg-
ments of men, and he was saying very hard things about
them. But they have very little, after all, to do with the
matter. The world may heed it, that Mr. Bingham should
marry Mrs. Hicks, but it will care very little whether or
no Mrs. Hicks marries Mr. Bingham. You are the world,
for me," she cried with beautiful inconsequence, turning

to her suitor; "I know no other." She put out her hands, and he took them.

I am at a loss to express the condensed force of these rapid words—the amount of passion, of reflection, of experience, which they seemed to embody. They were the simple utterance of a solemn and intelligent choice, and as such, the whole phalanx of the *Best Society* assembled in judgment could not have done less than salute them. What honest George Bingham said, what I said, is of little account. The proper conclusion of my story lies in the highly dramatic fact that out of the depths of her bereavement—out of her loneliness and her pity—this richly gifted woman had emerged, responsive to the passion of him who had wronged her all but as deeply as he loved her. The reader will decide, I think, that this catastrophe offers as little occasion for smiles as for tears. My narrative is a piece of genuine prose.

It was not until six months had elapsed that Bingham's marriage took place. It has been a truly happy one. Mrs. Bingham is now, in the fullness of her bloom, with a single exception, the most charming woman I know. I have often assured her—once too often, possibly—that, thanks to that invaluable good sense of hers, she is also the happiest. She has made a devoted wife, but—and in occasional moments of insight it has seemed to me that this portion of her fate is a delicate tribute to a fantastic principle of equity—she has never again become a mother. In saying that she has made a devoted wife, it may seem that I have written Bingham's own later history. Yet as the friend of his younger days, the comrade of his *belle jeunesse*, the partaker of his dreams, I would fain give him a sentence apart. What shall it be? He is a truly incorruptible soul; he is a confirmed philosopher; he has grown quite stout.

The Story of a Masterpiece

NO longer ago than last summer, during a six weeks'
stay at Newport, John Lennox became engaged to
Miss Marian Everett of New York. Mr. Lennox was a
widower, of large estate, and without children. He was
thirty-five years old, of a sufficiently distinguished appearance, of excellent manners, of an unusual share of sound
information, of irreproachable habits, and of a temper
which was understood to have suffered a trying and
salutary probation during the short term of his wedded
life. Miss Everett was, therefore, all things considered,
believed to be making a very good match and to be
having by no means the worst of the bargain.

And yet Miss Everett, too, was a very marriageable
young lady—the pretty Miss Everett, as she was called,
to distinguish her from certain plain cousins with whom,
owing to her having no mother and no sisters, she was
constrained, for decency's sake, to spend a great deal of
her time—rather to her own satisfaction, it may be conjectured, than to that of these excellent young women.

Marian Everett was penniless, indeed, but she was richly
endowed with all the gifts which make a woman charming.
She was, without dispute, the most charming girl in the
circle in which she lived and moved. Even certain of
her elders, women of a larger experience, of a heavier
caliber, as it were, and—thanks to their being married
ladies—of greater freedom of action, were practically not
so charming as she. And yet, in her emulation of the
social graces of these, her more fully licensed sisters, Miss
Everett was quite guiltless of any aberration from the
strict line of maidenly dignity. She professed an almost
religious devotion to good taste, and she looked with
horror upon the boisterous graces of many of her com-

panions. Beside being the most entertaining girl in New York, she was, therefore, also the most irreproachable. Her beauty was, perhaps, contestable, but it was certainly uncontested. She was the least bit below the middle height, and her person was marked by a great fullness and roundness of outline; and yet, in spite of this comely ponderosity, her movements were perfectly light and elastic. In complexion she was a genuine blonde—a warm blonde—with a midsummer bloom upon her cheek and the light of a midsummer sun wrought into her auburn hair. Her features were not cast upon a classical model, but their expression was in the highest degree pleasing. Her forehead was low and broad, her nose small, and her mouth—well, by the envious her mouth was called *enormous*. It is certain that it had an immense capacity for smiles, and that when she opened it to sing (which she did with infinite sweetness), it emitted a copious flood of sound. Her face was, perhaps, a trifle too circular, and her shoulders a trifle too high, but as I say, the general effect left nothing to be desired. I might point out a dozen discords in the character of her face and figure, and yet utterly fail to invalidate the impression they produced. There is something essentially uncivil and, indeed, unphilosophical, in the attempt to verify or to disprove a woman's beauty in detail, and a man gets no more than he deserves when he finds that, in strictness, the aggregation of the different features fails to make up the total. Stand off, gentlemen, and let *her* make the addition. Beside her beauty, Miss Everett shone by her good nature and her lively perceptions. She neither made harsh speeches nor resented them; and, on the other hand, she keenly enjoyed intellectual cleverness, and even cultivated it. Her great merit was that she made no claims or pretensions. Just as there was nothing artificial in her beauty, so there was nothing pedantic in her acuteness and nothing sentimental in her amiability. The one was all freshness, and the others all bonhomie.

John Lennox saw her, then loved her and offered her his hand. In accepting it Miss Everett acquired, in the world's eye, the one advantage which she lacked—a complete stability and regularity of position. Her friends took no small satisfaction in contrasting her brilliant and comfortable future with her somewhat precarious past. Lennox, nevertheless, was congratulated on the right hand and on the left, but none too often for his faith. That of Miss Everett was not put to so severe a test, although she was frequently reminded by acquaintances of a moralizing turn that she had reason to be very thankful for Mr. Lennox's choice. To these assurances Marian listened with a look of patient humility, which was extremely becoming. It was as if for *his* sake she could consent even to be bored.

Within a fortnight after their engagement had been made known, both parties returned to New York. Lennox lived in a house of his own, which he now busied himself with repairing and refurnishing, for the wedding had been fixed for the end of October. Miss Everett lived in lodgings with her father, a decayed old gentleman who rubbed his idle hands from morning till night over the prospect of his daughter's marriage.

John Lennox, habitually a man of numerous resources, fond of reading, fond of music, fond of society and not averse to politics, passed the first weeks of the autumn in a restless, fidgety manner. When a man approaches middle age, he finds it difficult to wear gracefully the distinction of being engaged. He finds it difficult to discharge with becoming alacrity the various *petits soins* incidental to the position. There was a certain pathetic gravity, to those who knew him well, in Lennox's attentions. One-third of his time he spent in foraging in Broadway, whence he returned half a dozen times a week, laden with trinkets and gimcracks, which he always finished by thinking it puerile and brutal to offer his mistress. Another third he passed in Mr. Everett's drawing room, during which period Marian was denied to visitors. The rest of the time he spent, as he told a friend, God knows how. This was stronger language than his friend expected to hear, for Lennox was neither a man of precipitate utterance, nor, in his friend's belief, of a strongly passionate nature. But it was evident that he was very much in love, or at least very much off his balance.

"When I'm with her, it's all very well," he pursued, "but when I'm away from her, I feel as if I were thrust out of the ranks of the living."

"Well, you must be patient," said his friend; "you're destined to live hard, yet."

Lennox was silent, and his face remained rather more somber than the other liked to see it.

"I hope there's no particular difficulty," the latter resumed; hoping to induce him to relieve himself of whatever weighed upon his consciousness.

"I'm afraid sometimes I—afraid sometimes she doesn't really love me."

"Well, a little doubt does no harm. It's better than to be too sure of it, and to sink into fatuity. Only be sure you love her."

"Yes," said Lennox, solemnly, "that's the great point."

One morning, unable to fix his attention on books and papers, he bethought himself of an expedient for passing an hour.

He had made, at Newport, the acquaintance of a young artist named Gilbert, for whose talent and conversation he had conceived a strong relish. The painter, on leaving Newport, was to go to the Adirondacks and to be back in New York on the first of October, after which time he begged his friend to come and see him.

It occurred to Lennox on the morning I speak of that Gilbert must already have returned to town, and would be looking for his visit. So he forthwith repaired to his studio.

Gilbert's card was on the door, but, on entering the room, Lennox found it occupied by a stranger—a young man in painter's garb at work before a large panel. He learned from this gentleman that he was a temporary sharer of Mr. Gilbert's studio, and that the latter had stepped out for a few moments. Lennox accordingly prepared to await his return. He entered into conversation with the young man, and finding him very intelligent as well as, apparently, a great friend of Gilbert, he looked at him with some interest. He was of something less than thirty, tall and robust, with a strong, joyous, sensitive face and a thick, auburn beard. Lennox was struck with his face, which seemed both to express a great deal of human sagacity and to indicate the essential temperament of a painter.

"A man with that face," he said to himself, "does work at least worth looking at."

He accordingly asked his companion if he might come and look at his picture. The latter readily assented, and Lennox placed himself before the canvas.

It bore a representation of a half-length female figure, in a costume and with an expression so ambiguous that Lennox remained uncertain whether it was a portrait or a work of fancy: a fair-haired young woman, clad in a rich medieval dress, and looking like a countess of the Renaissance. Her figure was relieved against a somber tapestry, her arms loosely folded, her head erect and her eyes on the spectator, toward whom she seemed to move—*"Dans un flot de velours trainant ses petits pieds."*

As Lennox inspected her face, it seemed to reveal a hidden likeness to a face he well knew—the face of Marian Everett. He was, of course, anxious to know whether the likeness was accidental or designed.

"I take this to be a portrait," he said to the artist, "a portrait 'in character.' "

"No," said the latter, "it's a mere composition: a little from here and a little from there. The picture has been hanging about me for the last two or three years, as a sort of receptacle of waste ideas. It has been the victim of innumerable theories and experiments. But it seems to have survived them all. I suppose it possesses a certain amount of vitality."

"Do you call it anything?"

"I called it originally after something I'd read— Browning's poem, 'My Last Duchess.' Do you know it?"

"Perfectly."

"I am ignorant of whether it's an attempt to embody the poet's impression of a portrait actually existing. But why should I care? This is simply an attempt to embody my own private impression of the poem, which has always had a strong hold on my fancy. I don't know whether it agrees with your own impression and that of most readers. But I don't insist upon the name. The possessor of the picture is free to baptize it afresh."

The longer Lennox looked at the picture, the more he liked it, and the deeper seemed to be the correspondence between the lady's expression and that with which he had

invested the heroine of Browning's lines. The less accidental, too, seemed that element which Marian's face
and the face on the canvas possessed in common. He
thought of the great poet's noble lyric and of its exquisite significance, and of the physiognomy of the woman
he loved having been chosen as the fittest exponent of
that significance.

He turned away his head; his eyes filled with tears. "If
I were possessor of the picture," he said, finally, answering the artist's last words, "I should feel tempted to call it
by the name of a person of whom it very much reminds
me."

"Ah?" said Baxter; and then, after a pause, "a person
in New York?"

It had happened a week before that, at her lover's request, Miss Everett had gone in his company to a photog-
rapher's and had been photographed in a dozen different
attitudes. The proofs of these photographs had been sent
home for Marian to choose from. She had made a choice
of half a dozen—or rather Lennox had made it—and the
latter had put them in his pocket with the intention of
stopping at the establishment and giving his orders. He
now took out his pocketbook and showed the painter
one of the cards.

"I find a great resemblance," said he, "between your
duchess and that young lady."

The artist looked at the photograph. "If I am not mistaken," he said, after a pause, "the young lady is Miss
Everett."

Lennox nodded assent.

His companion remained silent a few moments, exam-
ining the photograph with considerable interest; but, as
Lennox observed, without comparing it with his picture.

"My duchess very probably bears a certain resemblance
to Miss Everett, but a not exactly intentional one," he
said at last. "The picture was begun before I ever saw
Miss Everett. Miss Everett, as you see—or as you know
—has a very charming face, and during the few weeks in
which I saw her, I continued to work upon it. You know
how a painter works—how artists of all kinds work—
they claim their property wherever they find it. What I
found to my purpose in Miss Everett's appearance I didn't

hesitate to adopt, especially as I had been feeling about in the dark for a type of countenance which her face effectually realized. The duchess was an Italian, I take it, and I had made up my mind that she was to be a blonde. Now, there is a decidedly southern depth and warmth of tone in Miss Everett's complexion, as well as that breadth and thickness of feature which is common in Italian women. You see, the resemblance is much more a matter of type than of expression. Nevertheless, I'm sorry if the copy betrays the original."

"I doubt," said Lennox, "whether it would betray it to any other perception than mine. I have the honor," he added after a pause, "to be engaged to Miss Everett. You will, therefore, excuse me if I ask whether you mean to sell your picture?"

"It's already sold—to a lady," rejoined the artist, with a smile; "a maiden lady, who is a great admirer of Browning."

At this moment, Gilbert returned. The two friends exchanged greetings, and their companion withdrew to a neighboring studio. After they had talked a while of what had happened to each since they parted, Lennox spoke of the painter of the duchess and of his remarkable talent, expressing surprise that he shouldn't have heard of him before and that Gilbert should never have spoken of him.

"His name is Baxter—Stephen Baxter," said Gilbert, "and until his return from Europe, a fortnight ago, I knew little more about him than you. He's a case of improvement. I met him in Paris in '62; at the time he was doing absolutely nothing. He has learned what you see in the interval. On arriving in New York, he found it impossible to get a studio big enough to hold him. As, with my little sketches, I need only occupy one corner of mine, I offered him the use of the other three, until he should be able to bsetow himself to his satisfaction. When he began to unpack his canvases I found I had been entertaining an angel unawares."

Gilbert then proceeded to uncover, for Lennox's inspection, several of Baxter's portraits, both of men and women. Each of these works confirmed Lennox's impression of the painter's power. He returned to the pic-

ture on the easel. Marian Everett reappeared at his silent
call and looked out of the eyes with a most penetrating
tenderness and melancholy.

"He may say what he pleases," thought Lennox, "the
resemblance *is*, in some degree, also a matter of expression. Gilbert," he added, wishing to measure the force of
the likeness, "whom does it remind you of?"

"I know," said Gilbert, "of whom it reminds *you*."

"And do you see it yourself?"

"They are both handsome, and both have auburn hair.
That's all I can see."

Lennox was somewhat relieved. It was not without a
feeling of discomfort—a feeling by no means inconsistent
with his first moment of pride and satisfaction—that he
thought of Marian's peculiar and individual charms having been subjected to the keen appreciation of another
than himself. He was glad to be able to conclude that
the painter had merely been struck with what was most
superficial in her appearance, and that his own imagination supplied the rest. It occurred to him, as he walked
home, that it would be a not unbecoming tribute to the
young girl's loveliness on his own part to cause her portrait to be painted by this clever young man. Their engagement had as yet been an affair of pure sentiment,
and he had taken an almost fastidious care not to give
himself the vulgar appearance of a mere purveyor of
luxuries and pleasures. Practically, he had been as yet
for his future wife a poor man—or rather a man, pure
and simple, and not a millionaire. He had ridden with her,
he had sent her flowers, and he had gone with her to the
opera. But he had neither sent her sugar plums, nor made
bets with her, nor made her presents of jewelry. Miss
Everett's female friends had remarked that he hadn't as
yet given her the least little betrothal ring, either of
pearls or of diamonds. Marian, however, was quite content.
She was, by nature, a great artist in the *mise en scène* of
emotions, and she felt instinctively that this classical
moderation was but the converse presentment of an immense matrimonial abundance. In his attempt to make it
impossible that his relations with Miss Everett should be
tinged in any degree with the accidental condition of the
fortunes of either party, Lennox had thoroughly under-

stood his own instinct. He knew that he should some day feel a strong and irresistible impulse to offer his mistress some visible and artistic token of his affection, and that his gift would convey a greater satisfaction from being sole of its kind. It seemed to him now that his chance had come. What gift could be more delicate than the gift of an opportunity to contribute by her patience and good will to her husband's possession of a perfect likeness of her face?

On that same evening, Lennox dined with his future father-in-law, as it was his habit to do once a week.

"Marian," he said, in the course of the dinner, "I saw, this morning, an old friend of yours."

"Ah," said Marian, "who was that?"

"Mr. Baxter, the painter."

Marian changed color—ever so little; no more, indeed, than was natural to an honest surprise.

Her surprise, however, could not have been great, inasmuch as she now said that she had seen his return to America mentioned in a newspaper, and as she knew that Lennox frequented the society of artists. "He was well, I hope," she added, "and prosperous."

"Where did you know this gentleman, my dear?" asked Mr. Everett.

"I knew him in Europe two years ago—first in the summer in Switzerland, and afterward in Paris. He is a sort of cousin of Mrs. Denbigh." Mrs. Denbigh was a lady in whose company Marian had recently spent a year in Europe—a widow, rich, childless, an invalid, and an old friend of her mother. "Is he always painting?"

"Apparently, and extremely well. He has two or three as good portraits there as one may reasonably expect to see. And he has, moreover, a certain picture which reminded me of you."

"His 'Last Duchess?'" asked Marian, with some curiosity. "I should like to see it. If you think it's like me, John, you ought to buy it up."

"I wanted to buy it, but it's sold. You know it then?"

"Yes, through Mr. Baxter himself. I saw it in its rudimentary state, when it looked like nothing that I should care to look like. I shocked Mrs. Denbigh very much by telling him I was glad it was his 'last.' The picture, indeed, led to our acquaintance."

"And not vice versa," said Mr. Everett facetiously.

"How vice versa?" asked Marian innocently. "I met Mr. Baxter for the first time at a party in Rome."

"I thought you said you met him in Switzerland," said Lennox.

"No, in Rome. It was only two days before we left. He was introduced to me without knowing I was with Mrs. Denbigh, and indeed without knowing that she had been in the city. He was very shy of Americans. The first thing he said to me was that I looked very much like a picture he had been painting."

"That you realized his ideal, etc."

"Exactly, but not at all in that sentimental tone. I took him to Mrs. Denbigh; they found they were sixth cousins by marriage; he came to see us the next day and insisted upon our going to his studio. It was a miserable place. I believe he was very poor; at least, Mrs. Denbigh offered him some money, and he frankly accepted it. She attempted to spare his sensibilities by telling him that if he liked, he could paint her a picture in return. He said he would, if he had time. Later, he came up into Switzerland, and the following winter we met him in Paris."

If Lennox had had any mistrust of Miss Everett's relations with the painter, the manner in which she told her little story would have effectually blighted it. He forthwith proposed that in consideration not only of the young man's great talent, but of his actual knowledge of her face, he should be invited to paint her portrait.

Marian assented without reluctance and without alacrity, and Lennox laid his proposition before the artist. The latter requested a day or two to consider, and then replied (by note) that he would be happy to undertake the task.

Miss Everett expected that in view of the projected renewal of their old acquaintance, Stephen Baxter would call upon her under the auspices of her lover. He called in effect, alone, but Marian was not at home, and he failed to repeat the visit. The day for the first sitting was therefore appointed through Lennox. The artist had not as yet obtained a studio of his own, and the latter cordially offered him the momentary use of a spacious and well-lighted apartment in his house, which had been intended as a billiard room but was not yet fitted up. Lennox expressed no wishes with regard to the portrait, being content to leave the choice of position and costume to the parties immediately interested. He found the painter perfectly well acquainted with Marian's "points," and he had an implicit confidence in her own good taste.

Miss Everett arrived on the morning appointed, under her father's escort, Mr. Everett, who prided himself largely upon doing things in proper form, having caused himself to be introduced beforehand to the painter. Between the latter and Marian there was a brief exchange of civilities, after which they addressed themselves to business. Miss Everett professed the most cheerful deference to Baxter's wishes and fancies, at the same time that she made no secret of possessing a number of strong convictions as to what should be attempted and what should be avoided.

It was no surprise to the young man to find her convictions sound and her wishes thoroughly sympathetic. He found himself called upon to make no compromise with stubborn and unnatural prejudices, nor to sacrifice his best intentions to a shortsighted vanity.

Whether Miss Everett was vain or not need not here be declared. She had at least the wit to perceive that the interests of an enlightened sagacity would best be served by a painting which should be good from the painter's point of view, inasmuch as these are the painting's chief end. I may add, moreover, to her very great credit, that she thoroughly understood how great an artistic merit should properly attach to a picture executed at the behest of a passion, in order that it should be anything more than a mockery—a parody—of the duration of that passion; and that she knew instinctively that there is nothing so chilling to an artist's heat as the interference of illogical self-interest, either on his own behalf or that of another.

Baxter worked firmly and rapidly, and at the end of a couple of hours he felt that he had begun his picture. Mr. Everett, as he sat by, threatened to be a bore, laboring apparently under the impression that it was his duty to beguile the session with cheap aesthetic small talk. But Marian good-humoredly took the painter's share of the dialogue, and he was not diverted from his work.

The next sitting was fixed for the morrow. Marian wore the dress which she had agreed upon with the painter, and in which, as in her position, the "picturesque" element had been religiously suppressed. She read in Baxter's eyes that she looked supremely beautiful, and she saw that his fingers tingled to attack his subject. But she caused Lennox to be sent for, under the pretense of obtaining his adhesion to her dress. It was black, and he might object to black. He came, and she read in his kindly eyes an augmented edition of the assurance conveyed in Baxter's. He was enthusiastic for the black dress, which, in truth, seemed only to confirm and enrich, like a grave maternal protest, the young girl's look of undiminished youth.

"I expect you," he said to Baxter, "to make a masterpiece."

"Never fear," said the painter, tapping his forehead. "It's made."

On this second occasion, Mr. Everett, exhausted by the intellectual strain of the preceding day and encouraged by his luxurious chair, sank into a tranquil sleep. His companions remained for some time, listening to his regular breathing, Marian with her eyes patiently fixed on the opposite wall, and the young man with his glance mechanically traveling between his figure and the canvas. At last he fell back several paces to survey his work. Marian moved her eyes, and they met his own.

"Well, Miss Everett," said the painter, in accents which might have been tremulous if he had not exerted a strong effort to make them firm.

"Well, Mr. Baxter," said the young girl.

And the two exchanged a long, firm glance, which at last ended in a smile—a smile which belonged decidedly to the family of the famous laugh of the two angels behind the altar in the temple.

"Well, Miss Everett," said Baxter, going back to his work; "such is life!"

"So it appears," rejoined Marian. And then, after a

pause of some moments: "Why didn't you come and see me?" she added.

"I came and you weren't at home."

"Why didn't you come again?"

"What was the use, Miss Everett?"

"It would simply have been more decent. We might have become reconciled."

"We seem to have done that as it is."

"I mean 'in form.' "

"That would have been absurd. Don't you see how true an instinct I had? What could have been easier than our meeting? I assure you that I should have found any talk about the past and mutual assurances or apologies extremely disagreeable."

Miss Everett raised her eyes from the floor and fixed them on her companion with a deep, half-reproachful glance, "Is the past, then," she asked, "so utterly disagreeable?"

Baxter stared, half-amazed. "Good heavens!" he cried, "of course it is."

Miss Everett dropped her eyes and remained silent.

I may as well take advantage of the moment rapidly to make plain to the reader the events to which the above conversation refers.

Miss Everett had found it expedient, all things considered, not to tell her intended husband the whole story of her acquaintance with Stephen Baxter; and when I have repaired her omissions, the reader will probably justify her discretion.

She had, as she said, met this young man for the first time at Rome, and there in the course of two interviews had made a deep impression upon his heart. He had felt that he would give a great deal to meet Miss Everett again. Their reunion in Switzerland was therefore not entirely fortuitous, and it had been the more easy for Baxter to make it possible for the reason that he was able to claim a kind of roundabout relationship with Mrs. Denbigh, Marian's companion. With this lady's permission he had attached himself to their party. He had made their route of travel his own; he had stopped when they stopped and been prodigal of attentions and civilities. Before a week was over, Mrs. Denbigh, who was the soul of con-

fiding good nature, exulted in the discovery of an invaluable kinsman. Thanks not only to her naturally un-
exacting disposition, but to the apathetic and inactive
habits induced by constant physical suffering, she proved
a very insignificant third in her companions' spending
of the hours. How delightfully these hours were spent it
requires no great effort to imagine. A suit conducted in
the midst of the most romantic scenery in Europe is
already half-won. Marian's social graces were largely enhanced by the satisfaction which her innate intelligence
of natural beauty enabled her to take in the magnificent
scenery of the Alps. She had never appeared to such
advantage; she had never known such perfect freedom and
frankness and gaiety. For the first time in her life she
had made a captive without suspecting it. She had sur-
rendered her heart to the mountains and the lakes, the
eternal snows and the pastoral valleys, and Baxter, standing by, had intercepted it. He felt his long-projected
Swiss tour vastly magnified and beautified by Miss Everett's part in it—by the constant feminine sympathy which
gushed within earshot, with the coolness and clearness of
a mountain spring. Oh, if only it too had not been fed by
the eternal snows! And then her beauty—her indefatigable
beauty—was a continual enchantment. Miss Everett looked
so thoroughly in her place in a drawing room that it
was almost logical to suppose that she looked well no-
where else. But in fact, as Baxter learned, she looked
quite well enough in the character of what ladies call a
"fright"—that is, sunburned, travel-stained, overheated,
exhilarated, and hungry—to elude all invidious comparisons.

At the end of three weeks, one morning as they stood
together on the edge of a falling torrent, high above the
green concavities of the hills, Baxter felt himself irresistibly urged to make a declaration. The thunderous
noise of the cataract covered all vocal utterance, so, taking
out his sketch-book, he wrote three short words on a
blank leaf. He handed her the book. She read his message
with a beautiful change of color and a single rapid glance
at his face. She then tore out the leaf.

"Don't tear it up!" cried the young man.

She understood him by the movement of his lips and

shook her head with a smile. But she stooped, picked up a little stone, and wrapping it in the bit of paper, prepared to toss it into the torrent.

Baxter, uncertain, put out his hand to take it from her. She passed it into the other hand and gave him the one he had attempted to take.

She threw away the paper, but she let him keep her hand.

Baxter had still a week at his dispoal, and Marian made it a very happy one. Mrs. Denbigh was tired; they had come to a halt, and there was no interruption to their being together. They talked a great deal of the long future, which, on getting beyond the sound of the cataract, they had expeditiously agreed to pursue in common.

It was their misfortune both to be poor. They determined, in view of this circumstance, to say nothing of their engagement until Baxter, by dint of hard work, should have at least quadrupled his income. This was cruel, but it was imperative, and Marian made no complaint. Her residence in Europe had enlarged her conception of the material needs of a pretty woman, and it was quite natural that she should not, close upon the heels of this experience, desire to rush into marriage with a poor artist. At the end of some days, Baxter started for Germany and Holland, portions of which he wished to visit for purposes of study. Mrs. Denbigh and her young friend repaired to Paris for the winter. Here, in the middle of February, they were rejoined by Baxter, who had achieved his German tour. He had received, while absent, five little letters from Marian, full of affection. The number was small, but the young man detected in the very temperance of his mistress a certain delicious flavor of implicit constancy. She received him with all the frankness and sweetness that he had a right to expect, and listened with great interest to his account of the improvement in his prospects. He had sold three of his Italian pictures and had made an invaluable collection of sketches. He was on the high road to wealth and fame, and there was no reason their engagement should not be announced. But to this latter proposition Marian demurred—demurred so strongly, and yet on grounds so arbitrary, that a somewhat painful scene ensued. Stephen left her, irritated and perplexed. The next day, when he called, she was unwell and unable to see him; and the next; and the next. On the evening of the day that he had made his third fruitless call at Mrs. Denbigh's, he overheard Marian's name mentioned at a large party. The interlocutors were two elderly women. On giving his attention to their talk, which they were taking no pains to keep private, he found that his mistress was under accusal of having trifled with the affections of an unhappy young man, the only son of one of the ladies. There was apparently no lack of evidence or of facts which might be construed as evidence. Baxter went home, *la mort dans l'âme*, and on the following day called again on Mrs. Denbigh. Marian was still in her room, but the former lady received him. Stephen was in great trouble, but his mind was lucid, and he addressed himself to the task of interrogating his hostess, Mrs. Denbigh, with her habitual indolence, had remained unsuspicious of the terms on which the young people stood.

"I'm sorry to say," Baxter began, "that I heard Miss Everett accused last evening of very sad conduct."

"Ah, for heaven's sake, Stephen," returned his kinswoman, "don't go back to that. I've done nothing all winter but defend and palliate her conduct. It's hard work. Don't make me do it for you. You know her as well as I do. She was indiscreet, but I know she is penitent, and for that matter she's well out of it. He was by no means a desirable young man."

"The lady whom I heard talking about the matter," said Stephen, "spoke of him in the highest terms. To be sure, as it turned out, she was his mother."

"His mother? You're mistaken. His mother died ten years ago."

Baxter folded his arms with a feeling that he needed to sit firm. *"Allons,"* said he, "of whom do you speak?"

"Of young Mr. King."

"Good heavens," cried Stephen. "So there are two of them?"

"Pray, of whom do *you* speak?"

"Of a certain Mr. Young. The mother is a handsome old woman with white curls."

"You don't mean to say there has been anything between Marian and Frederic Young?"

"Voilà! I only repeat what I hear. It seems to me, my dear Mrs. Denbigh, that you ought to know."

Mrs. Denbigh shook her head with a melancholy movement. "I'm sure I don't," she said. "I give it up. I don't pretend to judge. The manners of young people to each other are very different from what they were in my day. One doesn't know whether they mean nothing or everything."

"You know, at least, whether Mr. Young has been in your drawing room?"

"Oh, yes, frequently. I'm very sorry that Marian is talked about. It's very unpleasant for me. But what can a sick woman do?"

"Well," said Stephen, "so much for Mr. Young. And now for Mr. King."

"Mr. King is gone home. It's a pity he ever came away."

"In what sense?"

"Oh, he's a silly fellow. He doesn't understand young girls."

"Upon my word," said Stephen, *with expression,* as the music sheets say, "he might be very wise and not do that."

"Not but that Marian was injudicious. She meant only to be amiable, but she went too far. She became adorable. The first thing she knew he was holding her to an account."

"Is he good looking?"

"Well enough."

"And rich?"

"Very rich, I believe."

"And the other?"

"What other—Marian?"

"No, no; your friend Young."

"Yes, he's quite handsome."

"And rich, too?"

"Yes, I believe he's also rich."

Baxter was silent a moment. "And there's no doubt," he resumed, "that they were both far gone?"

"I can only answer for Mr. King."

"Well, I'll answer for Mr. Young. His mother wouldn't have talked as she did unless she'd seen her son suffer. After all, then, it's perhaps not so much to Marian's discredit. Here are two handsome young millionaires, madly smitten. She refuses them both. She doesn't care for good looks and money."

"I don't say that," said Mrs. Denbigh sagaciously. "She doesn't care for those things alone. She wants talent and all the rest of it. Now, if you were only rich, Stephen—" added the good lady innocently.

Baxter took up his hat. "When you wish to marry Miss Everett," he said, "you must take good care not to say too much about Mr. King and Mr. Young."

Two days after this interview, he had a conversation with the young girl in person. The reader may like him the less for his easily shaken confidence, but it is a fact that he had been unable to make light of these lightly made revelations. For him, his love had been a passion; for *her,* he was compelled to believe, it had been a vulgar pastime. He was a man of a violent temper; he went straight to the point.

"Marian," he said, "you've been deceiving me."

Marian knew very well what he meant; she knew very well that she had grown weary of her engagement and that, however little of a fault her conduct had been to Messrs. Young and King, it had been an act of grave disloyalty to Baxter. She felt that the blow was struck and that their engagement was clean broken. She knew that Stephen would be satisfied with no half-excuses or half-denials, and she had none others to give. A hundred such would not make a perfect confession. Making no attempt, therefore, to save her "prospects," for which she had ceased to care, she merely attempted to save her dignity. Her dignity for the moment was well enough secured by her natural, half-cynical coolness of temper. But this same vulgar placidity left in Stephen's memory an impression of heartlessness and shallowness, which in that particular quarter, at least, was destined to be forever fatal to her claims to real weight and worth. She denied the young man's right to call her to account and to interfere with her conduct, and she almost anticipated his proposal that they should consider their

engagement at an end. She even declined the use of the
simple logic of tears. Under these circumstances, of
course, the interview was not of long duration.

"I regard you," said Baxter as he stood on the threshold, "as the most superficial, most heartless of women."

He immediately left Paris and went down into Spain,
where he remained till the opening of the summer. In
the month of May, Mrs. Denbigh and her protégée
went to England, where the former, through her husband, possessed a number of connections, and where Marian's thoroughly un-English beauty was vastly admired.
In September, they sailed for America. About a year
and a half, therefore, had elapsed between Baxter's
separation from Miss Everett and their meeting in New
York.

During this interval, the young man's wounds had had
time to heal. His sorrow, although violent, had been short-
lived, and when he finally recovered his habitual equanimity, he was very glad to have purchased exemption
at the price of a simple heart-ache. Reviewing his im
pressions of Miss Everett in a calmer mood, he made up
his mind that she was very far from being the woman
of his desire, and that she had not really been the woman
of his choice. "Thank God," he said to himself, "it's
over. She's irreclaimably light. She's hollow, trivial, vulgar." There had been in his addresses something hasty
and feverish, something factitious and unreal in his fancied passion. Half of it had been the work of the scenery,
of the weather, of mere juxtaposition, and, above all,
of the young girl's picturesque beauty—to say nothing
of the almost suggestive tolerance and indolence of poor
Mrs. Denbigh. And finding himself very much interested
in Velasquez, at Madrid, he dismissed Miss Everett from
his thoughts. I do not mean to offer his judgment of
Miss Everett as final, but it was at least conscientious.
The ample justice, moreover, which, under the illusion
of sentiment, he had rendered to her charms and graces,
gave him a right, when free from that illusion, to register
his estimate of the arid spaces of her nature. Miss Everett
might easily have accused him of injustice and brutality,
but this fact would still stand to plead in his favor, that
he cared with all his strength for truth. Marian, on the

contrary, was quite indifferent to it. Stephen's angry sentence on her conduct had awakened no echo in her contracted soul.

The reader has now an adequate conception of the feelings with which these two old friends found themselves face to face. It is needful to add, however, that the lapse of time had very much diminished the force of those feelings. A woman, it seems to me, ought to desire no easier company, none less embarrassed or embarrassing, than a disenchanted lover; premising, of course, that the process of disenchantment is thoroughly complete, and that some time has elapsed since its completion.

Marian herself was perfectly at her ease. She had not retained her equanimity—her philosophy, one might almost call it—during that painful last interview to go and lose it now. She had no ill feeling toward her old lover. His last words had been—like all words in Marian's estimation—a mere *façon de parler*. Miss Everett was in so perfect a good humor during these last days of her maidenhood that there was nothing in the past that she could not have forgiven.

She blushed a little at the emphasis of her companion's remark, but she was not discountenanced. She summoned up her good humor. "The truth is, Mr. Baxter," she said, "I feel at the present moment on perfect good terms with the world. I see everything *en rose,* the past as well as the future."

"I, too, am on very good terms with the world," said Baxter, "and my heart is quite reconciled to what you call the past. But, nevertheless, it's very disagreeable to me to think about it."

"Ah then," said Miss Everett with great sweetness, "I'm afraid you're not reconciled."

Baxter laughed—so loud that Miss Everett looked about at her father. But Mr. Everett still slept the sleep of gentility. "I've no doubt," said the painter, "that I'm far from being so good a Christian as you. But I assure you I'm very glad to see you again."

"You've but to say the word and we're friends," said Marian.

"We were very foolish to have attempted to be anything else."

" 'Foolish,' yes. But it was a pretty folly."

"Ah no, Miss Everett. I'm an artist, and I claim a right of property in the word 'pretty.' You mustn't stick it in there. Nothing could be pretty which had such an ugly termination. It was all false."

"Well—as you will. What have you been doing since we parted?"

"Traveling and working. I've made great progress in my trade. Shortly before I came home, I became engaged."

"Engaged?—*à la bonne heure*. Is she good?—is she pretty?"

"She's not nearly so pretty as you."

"In other words, she's infinitely more good. I'm sure I hope she is. But why did you leave her behind you?"

"She's with a sister, a sad invalid who is drinking mineral waters on the Rhine. They wished to remain there to the cold weather. They're to be home in a couple of weeks, and we are straightway to be married."

"I congratulate you, with all my heart," said Marian.

"Allow me to do as much, sir," said Mr. Everett, waking up, which he did by instinct whenever the conversation took a ceremonious turn.

Miss Everett gave her companion but three more sittings, a large part of his work being executed with the assistance of photographs. At these interviews also, Mr. Everett was present, and still delicately sensitive to the soporific influences of his position. But both parties had the good taste to abstain from further reference to their old relation and to confine their talk to less personal themes.

One afternoon, when the picture was nearly finished, John Lennox went into the empty painting room to ascertain the degree of its progress. Both Baxter and Marian had expressed a wish that he should not see it in its early stages, and this, accordingly, was his first view. Half an hour after he had entered the room, Baxter came in, unannounced, and found him sitting before the canvas, deep in thought. Baxter had been furnished with a house key, so that he might have immediate and easy access to his work whenever the humor came upon him.

"I was passing," he said, "and I couldn't resist the impulse to come in and correct an error which I made this morning, now that a sense of its enormity is fresh in my mind." He sat down to work, and the other stood watching him.

"Well," said the painter finally, "how does it satisfy you?"

"Not altogether."

"Pray develop your objections. It's in your power materially to assist me."

"I hardly know how to formulate my objections. Let me, at all events, in the first place, say that I admire your work immensely. I'm sure it's the best picture you've painted."

"I honestly believe it is. Some parts of it," said Baxter frankly, "are excellent."

"It's obvious. But either those very parts or others are singularly disagreeable. That word isn't criticism, I know, but I pay you for the right to be arbitrary. They are too hard, too strong, of too frank a reality. In a word, your picture frightens me, and if I were Marian, I should feel as if you'd done me a certain violence."

"I'm sorry for what's disagreeable; but I meant it all to be real. I go in for reality; you must have seen that."

"I approve you; I can't too much admire the broad and firm methods you've taken for reaching this same reality. But you can be real without being brutal—without attempting, as one may say, to be *actual*."

"I deny that I'm brutal. I'm afraid, Mr. Lennox, I haven't taken quite the right road to please you. I've taken the picture too much *au sérieux*. I've striven too much for completeness. But if it doesn't please you, it will please others."

"I've no doubt of it. But that isn't the question. The picture is good enough to be a thousand times better."

"That the picture leaves room for infinite improvement, I, of course, don't deny; and, in several particulars, I see my way to make it better. But, substantially, the portrait is there. I'll tell you what you miss. My work isn't 'classical'; in fine, I'm not a man of genius."

"No; I rather suspect you are. But, as you say, your work isn't classical. I adhere to my term *brutal*. Shall

I tell you? It's too much of a study. You've given poor
Miss Everett the look of a professional model."

"If that's the case, I've done very wrong. There never
was an easier, a less conscious sitter. It's delightful to look
at her."

"Confound it, you've given all her ease, too. Well, I
don't know what's the matter. I give up."

"I think," said Baxter, "you had better hold your verdict in abeyance until the picture is finished. The classical element is there, I'm sure, but I've not brought
it out. Wait a few days, and it will rise to the surface."

Lennox left the artist alone, and the latter took up
his brushes and painted hard till nightfall. He laid them
down only when it was too dark to see. As he was going
out, Lennox met him in the hall.

"Exegi monumentum," said Baxter; "it's finished. Go
and look at your ease. I'll come tomorrow and hear
your impressions."

The master of the house, when the other had gone, lit
half a dozen lights and returned to the study of the picture. It had grown prodigiously under the painter's recent handling, and whether it was that, as Baxter had
said, the classical element had disengaged itself, or that
Lennox was in a more sympathetic mood, it now impressed him as an original and powerful work, a genuine
portrait, the deliberate image of a human face and figure.
It was Marian, in very truth, and Marian most patiently
measured and observed. Her beauty was there, her sweetness, and her young loveliness and her aerial grace, imprisoned forever, made inviolable and perpetual. Nothing
could be more simple than the conception and composition of the picture. The figure sat peacefully, looking
slightly to the right, with the head erect and the hands
—the virginal hands, without rings or bracelets—lying
idle on its knees. The blonde hair was gathered into a
little knot of braids on the top of the head (in the
fashion of the moment), and left free the almost childish
contour of the ears and cheeks. The eyes were full of
color, contentment, and light; the lips were faintly parted.
Of color in the picture, there was, in strictness, very little;
but the dark draperies told of reflected sunshine, and
the flesh-spaces of human blushes and pallors, of throb-

bing life and health. The work was strong and simple; the figure was thoroughly void of affection and stiffness, and yet supremely elegant.

"That's what it is to be an artist," thought Lennox. "All this has been done in the past two hours."

It was his Marian, assuredly, with all that had charmed him—with all that still charmed him when he saw her: her appealing confidence, her exquisite lightness, her feminine enchantments. And yet, as he looked, an expression of pain came into his eyes, and lingered there, and grew into a mortal heaviness.

Lennox had been as truly a lover as a man may be, but he loved with the discretion of fifteen years' experience of human affairs. He had a penetrating glance, and he liked to use it. Many a time when Marian, with eloquent lips and eyes, had poured out the treasures of her nature into his bosom, and he had taken them in his hands and covered them with kisses and passionate vows, he had dropped them all with a sudden shudder and cried out in silence, "But ah! Where is the heart?" One day he had said to her (irrelevantly enough, doubtless), "Marian, where *is* your heart?"

"*Where*—what do you mean?" Miss Everett had said.

"I think of you from morning till night. I put you together and take you apart, as people do in that game where they make words out of a parcel of given letters. But there's always one letter wanting. I can't put my hand on your heart."

"My heart, John," said Marian ingeniously, "is the whole word. My heart's everywhere."

This may have been true enough. Miss Everett had distributed her heart impartially throughout her whole organism, so that, as a natural consequence, its native seat was somewhat scantily occupied. As Lennox sat and looked at Baxter's consummate handiwork, the same question rose again to his lips; and if Marian's portrait suggested it, Marian's portrait failed to answer it. It took Marian to do that. It seemed to Lennox that some strangely potent agency had won from his mistress the confession of her inmost soul and had written it there upon the canvas in firm yet passionate lines. Marian's person was lightness—her charm was lightness; could it be that her soul was levity too? Was she a creature without faith and without conscience? What else was the meaning of that horrible blankness and deadness that quenched the light in her eyes and stole away the smile from her lips? These things were the less to be eluded because in so many respects the painter had been profoundly just. He had been as loyal and sympathetic as he had been intelligent. Not a point in the young girl's appearance had been slighted; not a feature but had been forcibly and delicately rendered. Had Baxter been a man of marvelous insight—an unparalleled observer—or had he been a mere patient and unflinching painter, building infinitely better than he knew? Would not a mere painter have been content to paint Miss Everett in the strong, rich, objective manner of which the work was so good an example, and to do nothing more? For it was evident that Baxter had done more. He had painted with something more than knowledge—with imagination, with feeling. He had almost *composed,* and his composition had embraced the truth. Lennox was unable to satisfy his doubts. He would have been glad to believe that there was no imagination in the picture but what his own mind supplied, and that the unsubstantial sweetness on the eyes and lips of the image was but the smile of youth and innocence. He was in a muddle—he was absurdly suspicious and capricious; he put out the lights and left the portrait in kindly darkness. Then, half as a reparation to his mistress, and half as a satisfaction to himself, he went up to spend an hour with Marian. She, at least, as he found, had no scruples. She thought the portrait altogether a success, and she was very willing to be handed down in that form to posterity. Nevertheless, when Lennox came in, he went back into the painting room to take another glance. This time he lit but a single light. Faugh! It was worse than with a dozen. He hastily turned out the gas.

Baxter came the next day, as he had promised. Meanwhile, poor Lennox had had twelve hours of uninterrupted reflection, and the expression of distress in his eyes had acquired an intensity which, the painter saw, proved it to be of far other import than a mere tribute to his power.

"Can the man be jealous?" thought Baxter. Stephen had been so innocent of any other design than that of painting a good portrait that his conscience failed to reveal to him the source of his companion's trouble. Nevertheless, he began to pity him. He had felt tempted, indeed, to pity him from the first. He had liked him and esteemed him; he had taken him for a man of sense and of feeling, and he had thought it a matter of regret that such a man—a creature of strong spiritual needs—should link his destiny with that of Marian Everett. But he had very soon made up his mind that Lennox knew very well what he was about, and that he needed no enlightenment. He was marrying with his eyes open, and had weighed the risks against the profits. Everyone had his particular taste, and at thirty-five years of age John Lennox had no need to be told that Miss Everett was not quite all that she might be. Baxter had thus taken for granted that his friend had designedly selected as his second wife a mere pretty woman—a woman with a genius for receiving company, and who would make a picturesque use of his money. He knew nothing of the serious character of the poor man's passion, nor of the extent to which his happiness was bound up in what the painter would have called his delusion. His only concern had been to do his work well, and he had done it the better because of his old interest in Marian's bewitching face. It is very certain that he had actually infused into his picture that force of characterization and that depth of reality which had arrested his friend's attention, but he had done so wholly without effort and without malice. The artistic half of Baxter's nature exerted a lusty dominion over the human half—fed upon its disappointments and grew fat upon its joys and tribulations. This, indeed, is simply saying that the young man was a true artist. Deep, then, in the unfathomed recesses of his strong and sensitive nature, his genius had held communion with his heart and had transferred to canvas the burden of its disenchantment and its resignation. Since his little affair with Marian, Baxter had made the acquaintance of a young girl whom he felt that he could love and trust forever; and, sobered and strengthened by this new emotion, he had been able to resume with more distinctness the shortcomings of his earlier love. He had, therefore, painted with feeling. Miss Everett could not have expected him to do otherwise. He had done his honest best, and conviction had come in unbidden and made it better.

Lennox had begun to feel very curious about the history of his companion's acquaintance with his destined bride; but he was far from feeling jealous. Somehow he felt that he could never again be jealous. But in ascertaining the terms of their former intercourse, it was of importance that he should not allow the young man to suspect that he discovered in the portrait any radical defect.

"Your old acquaintance with Miss Everett," he said frankly, "has evidently been of great use to you."

"I suppose it has," said Baxter "Indeed, as soon as I began to paint, I found her face coming back to me like a half-remembered tune. She was wonderfully pretty at that time."

"She was two years younger."

"Yes, and I was two years younger. Decidedly, you are right. I *have* made use of my old impressions."

Baxter was willing to confess to so much, but he was resolved not to betray anything that Marian had herself kept secret. He was not surprised that she had not told her lover of her former engagement; he expected as much. But he would have held it inexcusable to attempt to repair her omission.

Lennox's faculties were acutely sharpened by pain and suspicion, and he could not help detecting in his companion's eyes an intention of reticence. He resolved to baffle it.

"I am curious to know," he said, "whether you were ever in love with Miss Everett?"

"I have no hesitation in saying yes," rejoined Baxter, fancying that a general confession would help him more than a particular denial. "I'm one of a thousand, I fancy. Or one, perhaps, of only a hundred. For you see I've got over it. I'm engaged to be married."

Lennox's countenance brightened. "That's it," said he. "Now I know what I didn't like in your picture—the point of view. I'm not jealous," he added. "I should like the picture better if I were. You evidently care nothing for the poor girl. You have got over your love rather too well. You loved her, she was indifferent to you, and now you take your revenge." Distracted with grief, Lennox was taking refuge in irrational anger.

Baxter was puzzled. "You'll admit," said he with a smile, "that it's a very handsome revenge." And all his professional self-esteem rose to his assistance. "I've painted for Miss Everett the best portrait that has yet been painted in America. She herself is quite satisfied."

"Ah!" said Lennox with magnificent dissimulation; "Marian is generous."

"Come, then," said Baxter; "what do you complain of? You accuse me of scandalous conduct, and I'm bound to hold you to an account." Baxter's own temper was rising, and with it his sense of his picture's merits. "How have I perverted Miss Everett's expression? How have I mis-represented her? What does the portrait lack? Is it ill-drawn? Is it vulgar? Is it ambiguous? Is it immodest?" Baxter's patience gave out as he recited these various charges. "Fiddlesticks!" he cried; "you know as well as I do that the picture is excellent."

"I don't pretend to deny it—only, I wonder that Marian was willing to come to you."

It is very much to Baxter's credit that he still adhered to his resolution not to betray the young girl, and that rather than do so he was willing to let Lennox suppose that he had been a rejected adorer.

"Ah, as you say," he exclaimed, "Miss Everett is so generous!"

Lennox was foolish enough to take this as an admission. "When I say, Mr. Baxter," he said, "that you have taken your revenge, I don't mean that you've done so wantonly or consciously. My dear fellow, how could you help it? The disappointment was proportionate to the loss and the reaction to the disappointment."

"Yes, that's all very well; but, meanwhile, I wait in vain to learn wherein I've done wrong."

Lennox looked from Baxter to the picture, and from the picture back to Baxter.

"I defy you to tell me," said Baxter. "I've simply kept Miss Everett as charming as she is in life."

"Oh, damn her charms!" cried Lennox.

"If you were not the gentleman, Mr. Lennox," continued the young man, "which, in spite of your high temper, I believe you to be, I should believe you——"

"Well, you should believe me?"

"I should believe you simply bent on cheapening the portrait."

Lennox made a gesture of vehement impatience. The other burst out laughing, and the discussion closed. Baxter instinctively took up his brushes and approached his canvas with a vague desire to detect latent errors, while Lennox prepared to take his departure.

"Stay!" said the painter, as he was leaving the room; "if the picture really offends you, I'll rub it out. Say the word," and he took up a heavy brush, covered with black paint.

But Lennox shook his head with decision and went out. The next moment, however, he reappeared. "You *may* rub it out," he said. "The picture is, of course, already mine."

But now Baxter shook his head. "Ah! now it's too late," he answered. "Your chance is gone."

Lennox repaired directly to Mr. Everett's apartments. Marian was in the drawing room with some morning callers, and her lover sat by until she had got rid of them. When they were alone together, Marian began to laugh at her visitors and to parody certain of their affectations, which she did with infinite grace and spirit. But Lennox cut her short and returned to the portrait. He had thought better of his objections of the preceding evening; he liked it.

"But I wonder, Marian," he said, "that you were willing to go to Mr. Baxter."

"Why so?" asked Marian, on her guard. She saw that her lover knew something, and she intended not to commit herself until she knew how much he knew.

"An old lover is always dangerous."

"An old lover?" and Marian blushed a good honest blush. But she rapidly recovered herself. "Pray where did you get that charming news?"

"Oh, it slipped out," said Lennox.

Marian hesitated a moment. Then with a smile: "Well, I was brave," she said. "I went."

"How came it," pursued Lennox, "that you didn't tell me?"

"Tell you what, my dear John?"

"Why, about Baxter's little passion. Come, don't be modest."

Modest! Marian breathed freely. "What do you mean, my dear, by telling your wife not to be modest? Pray don't ask me about Mr. Baxter's passions. What do I know about them?"

"Did you know nothing of this one?"

"Ah, my dear, I know a great deal too much for my comfort. But he's got bravely over it. He's engaged."

"Engaged, but not quite disengaged. He's an honest fellow, but he remembers his penchant. It was as much as he could do to keep his picture from turning to the sentimental. He saw you as he fancied you—as he wished you—and he has given you a little look of what he imagines moral loveliness, which comes within an ace of spoiling the picture. Baxter's imagination isn't very strong, and this same look expresses, in point of fact, nothing but inanity. Fortunately he's a man of extraordinary talent, and a real painter, and he has made a good portrait in spite of himself."

To such arguments as these was John Lennox reduced, to stifle the evidence of his senses. But when once a lover begins to doubt, he cannot cease at will. In spite of his earnest efforts to believe in Marian as before, to accept her without scruple and without second thought, he was quite unable to repress an impulse of constant mistrust and aversion. The charm was broken, and there is no mending a charm. Lennox stood half-aloof, watching the poor girl's countenance, weighing her words, analyzing her thoughts, guessing at her motives.

Marian's conduct under this trying ordeal was truly heroic. She felt that some subtle change had taken place in her future husband's feelings, a change which, although she was powerless to discover its cause, yet obviously imperiled her prospects. Something had snapped between them; she had lost half of her power. She was horribly distressed, and the more so because that superior

depth of character which she had all along gladly con-
ceded to Lennox might now, as she conjectured, cover
some bold and portentous design. Could he meditate a
direct rupture? Could it be his intention to dash from her
lips the sweet, the spiced and odorous cup of being the
wife of a good-natured millionaire? Marian turned a
tremulous glance upon her past and wondered if he had
discovered any dark spot. Indeed, for that matter, might
she not defy him to do so? She had done nothing really
amiss. There was no visible blot in her history. It was
faintly discolored, indeed, by a certain vague moral
dinginess, but it compared well enough with that of other
girls. She had cared for nothing but pleasure, but to what
else were girls brought up? On the whole, might she not
feel at ease? She assured herself that she might, but
she nevertheless felt that if John wished to break off
his engagement, he would do it on high abstract grounds,
and not because she had committed a naughtiness the
more or the less. It would be simply because he had
ceased to love her. It would avail her but little to assure
him that she would kindly overlook this circumstance
and remit the obligations of the heart. But, in spite of
her hideous apprehensions, she continued to smile and
smile.

The days passed by, and John consented to be still
engaged. Their marriage was only a week off—six days,
five days, four. Miss Everett's smile became less mechanical. John had apparently been passing through a
crisis—a moral and intellectual crisis, inevitable in a man
of his constitution, and with which she had nothing to
do. On the eve of marriage he had questioned his heart;
he had found that it was no longer young and capable of
the vagaries of passion, and he had made up his mind
to call things by their proper names, and to admit to
himself that he was marrying not for love, but for friendship, and a little, perhaps, for prudence. It was only out
of regard for what he supposed Marian's own more exalted theory of the matter that he abstained from revealing to her this common-sense view of it. Such was
Marian's hypothesis.

Lennox had fixed his wedding day for the last Thursday
in October. On the preceding Friday, as he was passing

up Broadway, he stopped at Goupil's to see if his order for the framing of the portrait had been fulfilled. The picture had been transferred to the shop, and, when duly framed, had been, at Baxter's request and with Lennox's consent, placed for a few days in the exhibition room. Lennox went up to look at it.

The portrait stood on an easel at the end of the hall, with three spectators before it—a gentleman and two ladies. The room was otherwise empty. As Lennox went toward the picture, the gentleman turned out to be Baxter. He proceeded to introduce his friend to his two companions, the younger of whom Lennox recognized as the artist's betrothed. The other, her sister, was a plain, pale woman, with the look of ill health, who had been provided with a seat and made no attempt to talk. Baxter explained that these ladies had arrived from Europe but the day before, and that his first care had been to show them his masterpiece.

"Sarah," said he, "has been praising the model very much to the prejudice of the copy."

Sarah was a tall, black-haired girl of twenty, with irregular features, a pair of luminous dark eyes, and a smile radiant of white teeth—evidently an excellent person. She turned to Lennox with a look of frank sympathy and said in a deep, rich voice:

"She must be very beautiful."

"Yes, she's very beautiful," said Lennox with his eyes lingering on her own pleasant face. "You must know her —she must know you."

"I'm sure I should like very much to see her," said Sarah.

"This is very nearly as good," said Lennox. "Mr. Baxter is a great genius."

"I know Mr. Baxter is a genius. But what is a picture, at the best? I've seen nothing but pictures for the last two years, and I haven't seen a single pretty girl."

The young girl stood looking at the portrait in very evident admiration, and while Baxter talked to the elder lady, Lennox bestowed a long, covert glance upon his fiancée. She had brought her head into almost immediate juxtaposition with that of Marian's image, and, for a moment, the freshness and the strong animation which bloomed upon her features seemed to obliterate the lines and colors on the canvas. But the next moment, as Lennox looked, the roseate circle of Marian's face blazed into remorseless distinctness, and her careless blue eyes looked with cynical familiarity into his own.

He bade an abrupt good morning to his companions and went toward the door. But beside it he stopped. Suspended on the wall was Baxter's picture, "My Last Duchess." He stood amazed. Was *this* the face and figure that, a month ago, had reminded him of his mistress? Where was the likeness now? It was as utterly absent as if it had never existed. The picture, moreover, was a very inferior work to the new portrait. He looked back at Baxter, half-tempted to demand an explanation, or at least to express his perplexity. But Baxter and his sweetheart had stooped down to examine a minute sketch near the floor, with their heads in delicious contiguity.

How the week elapsed it was hard to say. There were moments when Lennox felt as if death were preferable to the heartless union which now stared him in the face, and as if the only possible course was to transfer his property to Marian and to put an end to his existence. There were others, again, when he was fairly reconciled to his fate. He had but to gather his old dreams and fancies into a fagot and break them across his knee, and the thing were done. Could he not collect in their stead a comely cluster of moderate and rational expectations and bind them about with a wedding favor? His love was dead, his youth was dead—that was all. There was no need of making a tragedy of it. His love's vitality had been but small, and since it was to be short-lived it was better that it should expire before marriage than after. As for marriage, that should stand, for that was not of necessity a matter of love. He lacked the brutal consistency necessary for taking away Marian's future. If he had mistaken her and overrated her, the fault was his own, and it was a hard thing that she should pay the penalty. Whatever were her failings, they were profoundly involuntary, and it was plain that with regard to himself her intentions were good. She would be no companion, but she would be at least a faithful wife.

With the help of this grim logic, Lennox reached the

eve of his wedding day. His manner toward Miss Everett during the preceding week had been inveterately tender and kind. He felt that in losing his love she had lost a heavy treasure, and he offered her instead the most unfailing devotion. Marian had questioned him about his lassitude and his preoccupied air, and he had replied that he was not very well. On the Wednesday afternoon, he mounted his horse and took a long ride. He came home toward sunset, and was met in the hall by his old housekeeper.

"Miss Everett's portrait, sir," she said, "has just been sent home, in the most beautiful frame. You gave no directions, and I took the liberty of having it carried into the library. I thought," and the old woman smiled deferentially, "you'd like best to have it in your own room."

Lennox went into the library. The picture was standing on the floor, back to back with a high armchair, and catching through the window the last horizontal rays of the sun. He stood before it a moment, gazing at it with a haggard face.

"Come!" said he, at last, "Marian may be what God has made her, but *this* detestable creature I can neither love nor respect!"

He looked about him with an angry despair, and his eye fell on a long, keen poinard, given him by a friend who had bought it in the East, and which lay as an ornament on his mantelshelf. He seized it and thrust it, with barbarous glee, straight into the lovely face of the image. He dragged it downward and made a long fissure in the living canvas. Then, with half a dozen strokes, he wantonly hacked it across. The act afforded him an immense relief.

I need hardly add that on the following day Lennox was married. He had locked the library door on coming out the evening before, and he had the key in his waistcoat pocket as he stood at the altar. As he left town, therefore, immediately after the ceremony, it was not until his return, a fortnight later, that the fate of the picture became known. It is not necessary to relate how he explained his exploit to Marian and how he disclosed it to Baxter. He at least put on a brave face. There is a rumor current of his having paid the painter an enormous sum of money. The amount is probably exaggerated, but there can be no doubt that the sum was very large. How he has fared—how he is destined to fare—in matrimony it is rather too early to determine. He has been married scarcely three months.

A Light Man

And I—what I seem to my friend, you see—
　What I soon shall seem to his love, you guess.
What I seem to myself, do you ask of me?
　No hero, I confess.
　　　　A LIGHT WOMAN. BROWNING'S MEN AND WOMEN.

APRIL 4, 1857. I have changed my sky without changing my mind. I resume these old notes in a new world. I hardly know of what use they are, but it's easier to preserve the habit than to break it. I have been at home now a week—at home, forsooth! And yet, after all, it is home. I'm dejected, I'm bored, I'm blue. How can a man be more at home than that? Nevertheless, I'm the citizen of a great country, and for that matter, of a great city. I walked today some ten miles or so along Broadway, and on the whole I don't blush for my native land. We're a capable race and a good-looking withal, and I don't see why we shouldn't prosper as well as another. This, by the way, ought to be a very encouraging reflection. A capable fellow and a good-looking withal; I don't see why he shouldn't die a millionaire. At all events, he must set bravely to work. When a man has, at thirty-two, a net income of considerably less than nothing, he can scarcely hope to overtake a fortune before he himself is overtaken by age and philosophy—two deplorable obstructions. I'm afraid that one of them has already planted itself in my path. What am I? What do I wish? Whither do I tend? What do I believe? I am constantly beset by these impertinent whisperings. Formerly, it was enough that I was Maximus Austin; that I was endowed with a cheerful mind and a good digestion; that one day or another, when I had come to the end, I should return to America and begin at the beginning; that, meanwhile, existence was sweet in—in the Rue Tranchet. But now! Has the sweetness really passed out of life? Have I eaten the plums and left nothing but the bread and milk and cornstarch, or whatever the horrible concoction is (we had it to-day for dinner)? Pleasure, at least, I imagine—pleasure pure and simple, pleasure crude, brutal, and vulgar—this poor, flimsy delusion has lost all its prettiness. I shall never again care for certain things—and, indeed, for certain persons. Of such things, of such persons, I firmly maintain, however, that I was never an enthusiastic votary. It would be more to my credit, I suppose, if I had been. More would be forgiven me if I had loved a little more, if into all my folly and egotism I had put a little more naïveté and sincerity. Well, I did the best I could, I was at once too bad and too good for it all. At present, it's far enough off; I've put the sea between us. I'm stranded. I sit high and dry, scanning the horizon for a friendly sail, or waiting for a high tide to set me afloat. The wave of pleasure has planted me here in the sand. Shall I owe my rescue to the wave of pain? At moments my heart throbs with a sort of ecstatic longing to expiate my stupid peccadilloes. I see, as through a glass, darkly, the beauty of labor and love. Decidedly, I'm willing to work. It's written.

7th. My sail is in sight; it's at hand; I've all but boarded the vessel. I received this morning a letter from the best man in the world. Here it is:

DEAR MAX: I see this very moment, in the old newspaper which had already passed through my hands without yielding up its most precious item, the announcement of your arrival in New York. To think of your having perhaps missed the grasp of my hand. Here it is, dear Max—to rap on the knuckles, if you like. When I say I have just read of your arrival, I mean that twenty minutes have elapsed by the clock. These have been spent in conversation with my excellent friend Mr. Frederick Sloane—your excellent self being the subject. I haven't time to say more about Mr. Sloane than that he is very anxious to make your acquaintance, and that, if your time is not otherwise predestined, he would esteem it a particular favor to have you pass a month under his roof—the ample roof which covers my own devoted head.

It appears that he knew your mother very intimately, and he has a taste for visiting the amenities of the parents upon the children; the original ground of my own connection with him was that he had been a particular friend of my father. You may have heard your mother speak of him—a perfect eccentric, but a charming one. He will make you most welcome. But whether or no you come for his sake, come for mine. I have a hundred questions on the end of my pen, but I can't drop them, lest I should lose the mail. You'll not refuse me without an excellent reason, and I shan't excuse you, even then. So the sooner the better. Yours more than ever,

THEODORE LISLE

Theodore's letter is, of course, very kind, but it's perfectly obscure. My mother may have had the highest regards for Mr. Sloane, but she never mentioned his name in my hearing. Who is he, what is he, and what is the nature of his relations with Theodore? I shall learn betimes. I have written to Theodore that I gladly accept (I believe I suppressed the "gladly" though) his friend's invitation, and that I shall immediately present myself. What better can I do? I shall, at the narrowest calculation, obtain food and lodging while I invoke the fates. I shall have a basis of operations. D., it appears, is a long day's journey, but delicious when you reach it. I'm curious to see a delicious American town. And a month's stay! Mr. Frederick Sloane, whoever you are, *vous faites bien les choses,* and the little that I know of you is very much to your credit. You enjoyed the friendship of my dear mother, you possess the esteem of my incomparable Theodore, you commend yourself to my own affection. At this rate, I shan't grudge it.

D——, 14th. I have been here since Thursday evening —three days. As we rattled up to the tavern in the village, I perceived from the top of the coach, in the twilight, Theodore beneath the porch, scanning the vehicle, with all his affectionate soul in his eyes. I made hardly more than two downward strides into his arms—or, at all events, into his hands. He has grown older, of course, in these five years, but less so than I had expected. His is one of those smooth, unwrinkled souls that infuse a perennial fairness and freshness into the body. As tall as ever, moreover, and as lean and clean. How short and fat and dark and debauched he makes one feel! By nothing he says or means, of course, but merely by his old unconscious purity and simplicity—that slender aspiring rectitude which makes him remind you of the tower of an English abbey. He greeted me with smiles, and stares, and formidable blushes. He assures me that he never would have known me, and that five years have quite transformed my physiognomy. I asked him if it was for the better. He looked at me hard for a moment with his eyes of blue, and then, for all answer, he blushed again.

On my arrival, we agreed to walk over from the village. He dismissed his wagon with my trunk, and we went arm-in-arm through the dusk. The town is seated at the foot of certain mountains, whose names I have yet to learn, and at the head of a vast sheet of water which, as yet, too, I know only as "The Lake." The road hitherward soon leaves the village and wanders in rural loveliness by the lakeside. Sometimes the water is hidden by clumps of trees, behind which we heard it lapping and gurgling in the darkness; sometimes it stretches out from your feet in unspotted beauty, offering its broad, white bosom to the embrace of the dark, fraternal hills. The walk from the tavern takes some half an hour, in which space Theodore had explained his position to my comparative satisfaction. Mr. Sloane is old, widowed, and rich; his age is seventy-two, and as his health is thoroughly broken, is practically even greater; and his fortune —Theodore, characteristically, doesn't know its numerical formula. It's probably a round million. He has lived much abroad and in the thick of things; he has had adventures and passions and all that sort of thing; and now, in the evening of his days, like an old French diplomat, he takes it into his head to write his memoirs. To this end, he has taken poor Theodore to his generous side to serve as his guide, philosopher, and friend. He has been a great scribbler, says Theodore, all his days, and he proposes to incorporate a large amount of promiscuous literary matter into this singular record of his existence. Theodore's principal function seems to be to get him to leave things out. In fact, the poor boy seems troubled in conscience. His patron's lucubrations have taken the turn of all memoirs and become *tout bonnement* immoral. On the whole, he declares they are a very odd mixture— a jumble of pretentious trash and of excellent good sense. I can readily understand it. The old man bores me, puzzles me, and amuses me.

He was in waiting to receive me. We found him in his library—which, by the way, is simply the most delightful apartment that I ever smoked a cigar in—a room for a lifetime. At one end stands a great fireplace, with a florid, fantastic mantelpiece in carved white marble—an importation, of course, and as one may say, an interpolation, the groundwork of the house, the "fixtures," being throughout plain, solid, and domestic. Over the mantelshelf is a large landscape painting, a *soi-disant* Gainsborough, full of the mellow glory of an English summer. Beneath it stands a fantastic litter of French bronzes and outlandish *chinoiseries*. Facing the door, as you enter, is a vast window set in a recess, with cushioned seats and large, clear panes, stationed as it were at the very apex of the lake (which forms an almost perfect oval) and commanding a view of its whole extent. At the other end, opposite the fireplace, the wall is studded, from floor to ceiling, with choice foreign paintings, placed in relief against the orthodox crimson screen. Elsewhere, the walls are covered with books, arranged neither in formal regularity nor quite helter-skelter, but in a sort of genial mutual incongruity, which tells that sooner or later each volume feels sure of leaving the ranks and returning into different company. Mr. Sloane uses his books. His two passions, according to Theodore, are reading and talking, but to talk, he must have a book in his hand. The charm of the room lies in the absence of the portentous soberness—the browns, and blacks, and grays—which distinguish most rooms of its class. It's a sort of female study. There are half a dozen light colors scattered about— pink in the carpet, tender blue in the curtains, yellow in the chairs. The result is a general look of brightness, and lightness, and unpedantic elegance. You perceive the place to be the home, not of a man of learning, but of a man of fancy.

He rose from his chair, the man of fancy, to greet me, the man of fact. As I looked upon him, in the lamplight, it seemed to me, for the first five minutes, that I had seldom seen a worse-favored human creature. It took me then five minutes to get the point of view; then I began to admire. He is undersized, or, at best, of my own moderate stature bent and contracted with years; thin, however, where I am stout, and light where I am heavy. In color, we're about equally dark. Mr. Sloane, however, is curiously pale, with a dead, opaque, yellow pallor. Literally, it's a magnificent yellow. His skin is of just the hue and apparent texture of some old crumpled Oriental scroll. I know a dozen painters who would give more than they have to arrive at the exact "tone" of his thick-veined, saffron-colored hands—his polished ivory knuckles. His eyes are circled with red, but within their unhealthy orbits they scintillate like black diamonds. His nose, owing to the falling away of other portions of his face, has assumed a grotesque, unnatural prominence; it describes an immense arch, gleaming like parchment stretched on ivory. He has kept his teeth, but replaced his hair by a dead black wig; of course, he's clean-shaven. In his dress he has a muffled, wadded look, and an apparent aversion to linen, inasmuch as none is visible on his person. He seems neat enough, but not fastidious. At first, as I say, I fancied him monstrously ugly, but on further acquaintance I perceived that what I had taken for ugliness is nothing but the incomplete remains of remarkable good looks. The lines of his features are delicate; his nose, *ceteris paribus,* would be extremely handsome; his eyes are the eyes of a mind, not of a body. There is intelligence on his brow and sweetness on his lips.

He offered his two hands, as Theodore introduced me; I gave him my own, and he stood smiling upon me like some quaint old image in ivory and ebony, scanning my face with the somber sparkle of his gaze. "Good heaven!" he said at last, "how much you look like your father." I sat down, and for half an hour we talked of many things—of my journey, of my impressions of home, of my reminiscences of Europe, and, by implication, of my prospects. His voice is aged and cracked, but he uses it with immense energy. Mr. Sloane is not yet in his dotage, by a long shot. He nevertheless makes himself out a woefully old man. In reply to an inquiry I made about his health, he favored me with a long list of his infirmities (some of which are very trying, certainly) and assured me that he had but a mere pinch of vitality left.

"I live," he said, "out of mere curiosity."

"I have heard of people dying," I answered, "from the same motive."

He looked at me a moment, as if to ascertain whether I was making light of his statement. And then, after a pause, "Perhaps you don't know," said he with a certain vague pomposity, "that I disbelieve in a future life."

Poor Theodore! At these words he got up and walked to the fire.

"Well, we shan't quarrel about that," said I. Theodore turned around, staring.

"Do you mean that you agree with me?" the old man asked.

"I certainly haven't come here to talk theology. Dear me, Mr. Sloane," I said, "don't ask me to disbelieve, and I'll never ask you to believe."

"Come," cried Mr. Sloane, rubbing his hands, "you'll not persuade me you're a Christian—like your friend Theodore there."

"Like Theodore—assuredly not." And then, somehow, I don't know why, at the thought of Theodore's Christianism, I burst into a laugh. "Excuse me, my dear fellow," I said, "you know, for the last ten years I have lived in Catholic countries."

"Good, good, good!" cried Mr. Sloane, rubbing his hands and clapping them together, and laughing with high relish.

"Dear me," said Theodore, smiling, but vaguely apprehensive, too—and a little touched, perhaps, by my involuntary reflection upon the quality of his faith, "I hope you're not a Roman Catholic."

I saw the old man, with his hands locked, eying me shrewdly and waiting for my answer. I pondered a moment in mock gravity. "I shall make my confession," I said. "I've been in the East, you know. I'm a Mohammedan!"

Hereupon Mr. Sloane broke out into a wheezy ecstasy

of glee. Verily, I thought, if he lives for curiosity, he's easily satisfied.

We went into dinner, in the constitution of which I should have been at loss to suggest the shadow of an improvement. I observed, by the way, that for a victim of paralysis, neuralgia, dyspepsia, and a thousand other ills, Mr. Sloane plies a most inconsequential knife and fork. Sweets, and spices, and condiments seem to be the chief of his diet. After dinner he dismissed us, in consideration of my natural desire to see my friend in private. Theodore has capital quarters—a chamber and sitting room as luxurious as a man (or as a woman, for that matter) could possibly wish. We talked till near midnight—of ourselves and of our lemon-colored host below. That is, I spoke of myself and Theodore listened; and then Theodore told of Mr. Sloane and I listened. His commerce with the old man has sharpened his wits. Sloane has taught him to observe and judge, and Theodore turns around, observes, judges—him! He has become quite the critic and analyst. There is something very pleasant in the sagacity of virtue, in discernment without bitterness, penetration without spite. Theodore has all these unalloyed graces, to say nothing of an angelic charity. At midnight, we repaired to the library to take leave of our host till the morrow—an attention which, under all circumstances, he formally exacts. As I gave him my hand, he held it again and looked at me as he had done on my arrival. "Good heaven," he said at last, "how much you look like your mother!"

Tonight, at the end of my third day, I begin to feel decidedly at home. The fact is, I'm supremely comfortable. The house is pervaded by an indefinable, irresistible air of luxury and privacy. Mr. Frederick Sloane must be a horribly corrupt old mortal. Already in his hateful, delightful presence I have become heartily reconciled to doing nothing. But with Theodore on one side, I honestly believe I can defy Mr. Sloane on the other. The former asked me this morning, with real solicitude, in allusion to the bit of dialogue I have quoted above on matters of faith, if I had actually ceased to care for divine things. I assured him that I would rather utterly lose my sense of the picturesque than do anything to detract from the splendor of religious worship. Some of the happiest hours of my life, I told him, have been spent in cathedrals. He looked at me awhile, in friendly sadness. "I hardly know," he said, "whether you are worse than Mr. Sloane, or better."

But Theodore is, after all, in duty bound to give a man a long rope in these matters. His own rope is one of the longest. He reads Voltaire with Mr. Sloane, and Emerson in his own room. He's the stronger man of the two; he has the bigger stomach. Mr. Sloane delights, of course, in Voltaire, but he can't read a line of Emerson. Theodore delights in Emerson, and has excellent taste in the matter of Voltaire. It appears that since we parted in Paris, five years ago, his conscience has dwelt in many lands. C'est toute une histoire—which he tells very nicely. He left college determined to enter the ministry and came abroad to lay the basis of his theological greatness in some German repository of science. He appears to have studied, not wisely, but too well. Instead of faith full-armed and serene, there sprang from the labor of his brain a myriad abortive doubts, piping for sustenance. He went for a winter to Italy, where, I take it, he was not quite so much afflicted as he ought to have been at the sight of the beautiful spiritual repose which he had missed. It was after this that we spent those three months together in Britanny—the best-spent three months of my whole ten years abroad. Theodore inoculated me, I think, with a little of his sacred fermentation, and I infused into his conscience something of my vulgar indifference; and we agreed together that there were a few good things left—health, friendship, a summer sky, and the lovely byways of an old French province. He came home, returned to theology, accepted a "call," and made an attempt to respond to it. But the inner voice failed him. His outlook was cheerless enough. During his absence, his married sister—the elder one—had taken the other to live with her, relieving Theodore of the charge of contribution to her support. But suddenly, behold the husband, the brother-in-law, dies, leaving a mere fragment of property, and the two ladies, with their two little girls, are afloat in the wide world. Theodore finds himself at twenty-six without an income, without a profession, and with a family of four females to support. Well, in his quiet way, he draws on his courage. The history of the two years which preceded his initiation here is a simple record of practical manly devotion. He rescued his sisters and nieces from the deep waters, placed them high and dry, established them somewhere in decent gentility—and then found at last that his strength had left him—had dropped dead like an overridden horse. In short, he had worked himself ill. It was now his sisters' turn. They nursed him with all the added tenderness of gratitude for the past and terror of the future and brought him safely through a grievous malady. Meanwhile, Mr. Sloane, having decided to treat himself to a private secretary and suffered dreadful mischance in three successive experiments, had heard of Theodore's situation and his merits; had furthermore recognized in him the son of an early and intimate friend, and had finally offered him the very comfortable position which he now occupies. There is a decided incongruity between Theodore as a man—as Theodore, in fine—and the dear fellow as the intellectual agent, confidant, complaisant, purveyor, pander—what you will—of a battered old cynic and worldly dilettante. There seems at first sight a perfect want of agreement between his character and his function. One is gold and the other brass, or something very like it. But, on reflection, I perfectly conceive that he should, under the circumstances, have accepted Mr. Sloane's offer and been content to do his duties. Just heaven! Theodore's contentment in such a case is a theme for the moralist—a better moralist than I. The best and purest mortals are an odd mixture, and in none of us does honesty exist *totus, teres, atque rotundus*. Ideally, Theodore hasn't the smallest business *dans cette galère*. It offends my sense of propriety to find him here. I feel like admonishing him as a friend that he has knocked at the wrong door, and that he had better retreat before he is brought to the blush. Really, as I say, I suppose he might as well be here as reading Emerson "evenings," in the back parlor, to those two very plain sisters— judging from their photographs. Practically it hurts no one to compromise with his tendencies. Poor Theodore was weak, depressed, out of work. Mr. Sloane offers him a lodging and a salary in return for—after all, merely a little forebearance. All he has to do is to read to the old man, lay down the book awhile, with his finger in the place, and let him talk; take it up again, read another dozen pages and submit to another commentary. Then to write a dozen pages under his dictation —to suggest a word, polish off a period, or help him out with a reluctant idea or a half-remembered fact. This is all, I say, and yet this is much. Theodore's apparent success proves it to be much, as well as the old man's satisfaction. It's a part; he plays it. He uses tact; he has taken a reef in his pride; he has clipped the sting of his conscience, he listens, he talks, conciliates, accommodates, flatters—does it as well as many a worse man— does it far better than I. I might dominate Mr. Sloane, but I doubt that I could serve him. But, after all, it's not a matter of better and worse. In every son of woman, there are two men—the practical man and the dreamer. We live for our dreams—but meanwhile, we live by our wits. When the dreamer is a poet, his brother is an artist. Theodore is essentially a man of taste. If he were not destined to become a high priest among moralists, he might be a prince among connoisseurs. He plays his part, then, artistically, with taste, with relish—with all the finesse of his delicate fancy. How can Mr. Sloane fail to believe that he possesses a paragon? He is no such fool as to misconceive a *belle âme* when a *belle âme* comes in his way. He confidentially assured me this morning that Theodore has the most beautiful mind in the world, but that it's a pity he's so simple as not to suspect it. If he only doesn't ruin him with his flattery!

19th. I'm certainly fortunate among men. This morning when, tentatively, I spoke of understaying my month, Mr. Sloane rose from his seat in horror and declared that for the present I must regard his house as my home. "Come, come," he said, "when you leave this place, where do you intend to go?" Where, indeed? I graciously allowed Mr. Sloane to have the best of the argument. Theodore assures me that he appreciates these and other affabilities, and that I have made what he calls a "conquest" of his venerable heart. Poor, battered, bamboozled old organ! He would have one believe that it has a most tragical record of capture and recapture. At all events, it appears that I'm master of the citadel. For the present, I have no wish to evacuate. I feel, nevertheless, in some faroff corner of my soul, that I ought to shoulder my victorious banner and advance to more fruitful triumphs.

I blush for my slothful inaction. It isn't that I'm willing to stay here a month, but that I'm willing to stay here six. Such is the charming, disgusting truth. Have I actually outlived the age of energy? Have I survived my ambition, my integrity, my self-respect? Verily, I ought to have survived the habit of asking myself silly questions. I made up my mind long ago that I care deeply for nothing save my own personal comfort, and I don't care for that sufficiently to secure it at the cost of acute temporary suffering. I have a passion for nothing—not even for life. I know very well the appearance I make in the world. I pass for intelligent, well-informed, accomplished, amiable, strong. I'm supposed to have a keen relish for letters, for music, for science, for art. There was a time when I fancied I cared for scientific research, but I know now that I care for it as little as I really do for Shakespeare, for Rubens, for Rossini. When I was younger, I used to find a certain entertainment in the contemplation of men and women. I liked to see them hurrying on each other's heels across the stage. But I'm sick and tired of them now; not that I'm a misanthrope, God forbid. They're not worth hating. I never knew but one creature who was, and her I went and loved. To be consistent, I ought to have hated my mother—and now I ought to hate Theodore. But I don't—truly, on the whole, I don't—any more than I love him. I firmly believe that a large portion of his happiness rests upon his devout conviction that I really care for him. He believes in that, as he believes in all the rest of it—in my knowledge, my music, my underlying "earnestness," my sense of beauty and love of truth. Oh, for a *man* among them all—a fellow with eyes in his head—eyes that would look me through and through and flash out in scorn of my nothingness. Then, perhaps, I might answer him with rage; *then*, perhaps, I might feel a simple, healthy emotion.

In the name of bare nutrition—in the fear of starvation—what am I to do? (I was obliged this morning to

borrow ten dollars from Theodore, who remembered gleefully that he has been owing me no less than twenty-five
dollars for the past four years, and in fact has preserved
a note to this effect.) Within the last week, I have
hatched a desperate scheme. I have deliberately conceived the idea of marrying money. Why not accept and
utilize the goods of the gods? It is not my fault, after all,
if I pass for a superior fellow. Why not admit that practically, mechanically—as I may say—maritally, I *may*
be a superior fellow? I warrant myself, at least, thoroughly
gentle. I should never beat my wife; I doubt that I
should ever snub her. Assume that her fortune has the
proper number of zeros and that she herself is one of
them, and I can actually imagine her adoring me. It's not
impossible that I've hit the nail and solved my riddle.
Curiously, as I look back upon my brief career, it all
seems to tend in a certain way to this consummation.
It has its graceful curves and crooks, indeed, and here
and there a passionate tangent, but on the whole, if I
were to unfold it here *à la* Hogarth, what better legend
could I scrawl beneath the series of pictures than So-and-
So's Progress to a Mercenary Marriage?

Coming events do what we all know with their shadows. My glorious destiny is, perhaps, not far off. I already feel throughout my person a magnificent lan-
guor—as from the possession of past opulence. Or is it
simply my sense of perfect well-being in this perfectly
appointed home? Is it simply the absolutely comfortable
life I lead in this delicious old house? At all events, the
house *is* delicious, and my only complaint of Mr. Sloane
is that instead of an old widower, he's not an old widow
(or I a young maid) so that I might marry him, survive
him, and dwell forever in this rich and mellow home. As
I write here, at my bedroom table, I have only to stretch
out an arm and raise the window curtain to see the
thick-planted garden budding and breathing and growing
in the moonshine. Far above, in the liquid darkness, sails
the glory-freighted orb of the moon; beneath, in its light,
lies the lake, in murmuring, troubled sleep; around stand
the gentle mountains, wearing the gold reflection on
their shoulders, or hiding it away in their glens. So much
for midnight. Tomorrow the sun will be lovely with the

beauty of day. Under one aspect or another, I have it always before me. At the end of the garden is moored a boat, in which Theodore and I have repeatedly explored the surface of the lake and visited the mild wilderness of its shores. What lovely landward caves and bays—what alder-smothered creeks—what lily-sheeted pools—what sheer, steep hillsides, darkening the water with the downward image of their earthy greenness. I confess that in these excursions, Theodore does the rowing and I the contemplation. Mr. Sloane avoids the water—on account of the dampness, he says; but because he's afraid of drowning, I suspect.

22d. Theodore is right. The *bonhomme* has taken me into his favor. I protest I don't see how he was to escape it. I doubt that there has ever been a better flattered man. I don't blush for it. In one coin or another I must repay his hospitality—which is certainly very liberal. Theodore advises him, helps him, comforts him; I amuse him, surprise him, deprave him. This is speaking vastly well for my power. He pretends to be surprised at nothing and to possess in perfection—poor, pitiable old fop—the art *nil admirari;* but repeatedly, I know, I have clear outskipped his fancy. As for his depravity, it's a very pretty piece of wickedness, but it strikes me as a purely intellectual matter. I imagine him never to have had any downright senses. He may have been unclean; morally, he's not oversavory now; but he never can have been what the French call a *viveur.* He's too delicate, he's of a feminine turn—and what woman was ever a *viveur?* He likes to sit in his chair and read scandal, talk scandal, make scandal so far as he may without catching a cold or incurring a headache. I already feel as if I had known him a lifetime. I read him as clearly, I think, as if I had. I know the type to which he belongs; I have encountered, first and last, a round dozen of specimens. He's neither more nor less than a gossip—a gossip flanked by a coxcomb and an egotist. He's shallow, vain, cold, superstitious, timid, pretentious, capiricious—a pretty jumble of virtues! And yet, for all this, he has his good points. His caprices are sometimes generous, I imagine, and his aversion to the harsh, cruel, and hideous frequently takes the form of positive kindness and charity. His memory (for trifles) is remarkable, and (where his own performances are not involved) his taste is excellent. He has no will for evil more than for good. He is the victim, however, of more illusions with regard to himself than I ever knew a human heart to find lodging for. At the age of twenty, poor, ignorant and remarkably handsome, he married a woman of immense wealth many years his senior. At the end of three years, she very considerately went out of the world and left him to the enjoyment of his freedom and riches. If he had remained poor, he might from time to time have rubbed at random against the truth, and would still be wearing a few of its sacred smutches on his sleeve. But he wraps himself in his money, as in a wadded dressing gown, and goes trundling through life on his little gold wheels, as warm and close as an unweaned baby. The greater part of his career, from his marriage to within fifteen years ago, was spent in Europe, which, superficially, he knows very well. He has lived in fifty places, known hundreds of people, and spent thousands of dollars. At one time, I believe, he spent a few thousands too many, trembled for an instant on the verge of a pecuniary crash; but recovered himself, and found himself more frightened than hurt, but loudly admonished to lower his pitch. He passed five years in a species of penitent seclusion on the lake of—I forget what (his genius seems to be partial to lakes)—and formed the rudiments of his present magnificent taste for literature; I can't call it anything but magnificent, so long as it must needs have Theodore Lisle as a ministrant. At the close of this period, by economy, he had become a rich man again. The control and discipline exercised during these years upon his desires and his natural love of luxury must have been the sole act of real resolution in the history of Mr. Sloane's life. It was rendered possible by his morbid, his actually pusillanimous dread of poverty; he doesn't feel safe without half a million between him and starvation. Meanwhile, he had turned from a young man into an old man; his health was broken, his spirit was jaded, and I imagine, to do him justice, that he began to feel certain natural, filial longings for this dear American mother of us all. They say the most hopeless truants and triflers have come to it. He came to it, at all events; he packed up his books and pictures and gimcracks and bade farewell to Europe. This house which he now occupies belonged to his wife's estate. She had, for sentimental reasons of her own, commended it to his particular regard. On his return, he came to see it, fancied it, turned a parcel of carpenters and upholsterers into it, and by inhabiting it for twelve years, transformed it into the perfect dwelling which I find it. Here he has spent all his time, with the exception of a regular winter's visit to New York—a practice recently discontinued owing to the aggravation of his physical condition and the projection of these famous memoirs. His life has finally come to be passed in comparative solitude. He tells of various distant relatives, as well as intimate friends of both sexes, who used formerly to be largely entertained at his cost, but with each of them, in the course of time, he seems to have clipped the thread of intercourse. Throughout life, evidently, he has shown great delicacy of tact in keeping himself clean of parasites. Rich, lonely, and vain, he must have been fair game for the race of social sycophants and cormorants, and it's richly to the credit of his shrewdness and good sense that he has suffered so little havoc in substance and happiness. Apparently they've been a sad lot of bunglers. I maintain that he's to be—how shall I say it?—possessed. But you must work in obedience to certain definite laws. Doctor Jones, his physician, tells me that in point of fact he has had for the past ten years an unbroken series of favorites, *protégés,* and heirs presumptive, but that each, in turn, by some fatally false movement has fairly unjointed his nose. The doctor declares, moreover, that they were, at best, a woefully common set of people. Gradually, the old man seems to have developed a preference for two or three strictly exquisite intimates, over a throng of your vulgar charmers. His tardy literary schemes, too—fruit of his all but sapless senility—have absorbed more and more of his time and attention. The end of it all is, therefore, that Theodore and I have him quite to ourselves, and that it behooves us to keep our noses on our faces and our heads on our shoulders.

Poor, pretentious old simpleton! It's not his fault, after all, that he fancies himself a great little man. How are you to judge of the stature of mankind when men have forever addressed you on their knees? Peace and joy to his innocent fatuity! He believes himself the most rational of men; in fact, he's the most vapidly sentimental. He fancies himself a philosopher, a thinker, a student. His philosophy and his erudition are quite of a piece; they would lie at ease in the palm of Theodore's hand. He prides himself on his good manners, his urbanity, his unvarying observance of the becoming. My private impression is that his cramped old bosom contains unsuspected treasures of cunning impertinence. He takes his stand on his speculative audacity—his direct, undaunted gaze at the universe; in truth, his mind is haunted by a hundred, dingy, old-world specters and theological phantasms. He fancies himself one of the weightiest of men; he is essentially one of the lightest. He deems himself ardent, impulsive, passionate, magnanimous—capable of boundless enthusiasm for an idea or a sentiment. It is clear to me that on no occasion of pure, disinterested action can he ever have taken a timely, positive second step. He fancies, finally, that he has drained the cup of life to the dregs; that he has known, in its bitterest intensity, every emotion of which the human spirit is capable; that he has loved, struggled, and suffered. Stuff and nonsense, all of it. He has never loved anyone but himself; he has never suffered from anything but an undigested supper or an exploded pretension; he has never touched with the end of his lips the vulgar bowl from which the mass of mankind quaffs its great floods of joy and sorrow. Well, the long and short of it all is that I honestly pity him. He may have given sly knocks in his life, but he can't hurt *me*. I pity his ignorance, his weakness, his timidity. He has tasted the real sweetness of life no more than its bitterness; he has never dreamed, or wandered, or dared; he has never known any but mercenary affection; neither men nor women have risked aught for *him*—for his good spirits, his good looks, and his poverty. How I should like to give him, for once, a real sensation!

26th. I took a row this morning with Theodore a couple of miles along the lake, to a point where we went ashore and lounged away an hour in the sunshine, which is still very comfortable. Poor Theodore seems troubled about many things. For one, he is troubled about me; he is actually more anxious about my future than I myself; he thinks better of me than I do of myself; he is so deucedly conscientious, so scrupulous, so averse to giving offense or to *brusquer* any situation before it has played itself out that he shrinks from betraying his apprehensions or asking any direct questions. But I know that he is dying to extort from me some positive profession of practical interest and faith. I catch myself in the act of taking—Heaven forgive me!—a half-malicious joy in confounding his expectations—leading his generous sympathies off the scent by various extravagant protestations of mock cynicism and malignity. But in Theodore I have so firm a friend that I shall have a long row to hoe if I ever find it needful to make him forswear his devotion—abjure his admiration. He admires me—that's absolute; he takes my moral infirmities for the eccentricities of genius, and they only impart an extra flavor—a *haut goût*—to the richness of my charms. Nevertheless, I can see that he is disappointed. I have even less to show, after this lapse of years, than he had hoped. Heaven help us! Little enough it must strike him as being. What an essential absurdity there is in our being friends at all. I honestly believe we shall end with hating each other. They are all very well now—our diversity, our oppugnancy, our cross-purposes; now that we are at play together, they serve as a theme for jollity. But when we settle down to work—ah me, for the tug of war. I wonder, as it is, that Theodore keeps his patience with me. His education since we parted should tend logically to make him despise me. He has studied, thought, suffered, loved—loved those very plain sisters and nieces. Poor me! How should I be virtuous? I have no sisters, plain or pretty! Nothing to love, work for, live for. Friend Theodore, if you are going one of these days to despise me and drop me, in the sacred name of comfort, come to the point at once and make an end of our common agony!

He is troubled, too, about Mr. Sloane. His attitude toward the *bonhomme* quite passes my comprehension. It's the queerest jumble of contraries. He penetrates him, contemns him—yet respects and admires him. It all comes of the poor boy's shrinking New England conscience. He's afraid to give his perceptions a fair chance, lest, forsooth, they should look over his neighbor's wall. He'll not understand that he may as well sacrifice the old man for a lamb as for a sheep. His view of the gentleman, therefore, is a perfect tissue of cobwebs—a jumble of half-way sorrows, and wide-drawn charities, and hairbreadth 'scapes from utter damnation, and sudden platitudes of generosity—fit, all of it, to make an angel curse!

"The man's a perfect egotist and fool," say I, "but I like him." Now Theodore likes him—or rather wants to like him, but he can't reconcile it to his self-respect—fastidious deity!—to like a fool. Why the deuce can't he leave it alone altogether? It's a purely practical matter. He ought to do the duties of his place all the better for having his head clear of officious sentiment. I don't believe in disinterested service, and Theodore is too desperately bent on preserving his disinterestedness. With me, it's different. I'm perfectly free to love the *bonhomme*—for a fool. I'm neither a scribe nor a Pharisee, I'm—ah me, *what* am I?

And then, Theodore is troubled about his sisters. He's afraid he's not doing his duty by them. He thinks he ought to be with them—to be getting a larger salary—to be teaching his nieces. I'm not versed in such questions. Perhaps he ought.

MAY 3d. This morning Theodore sent me word that he was ill and unable to get up, upon which I immediately repaired to his bedside. He had caught cold, was sick and a little feverish. I urged him to make no attempt to leave his room and assured him that I would do what I could to reconcile Mr. Sloane to his nonattendance. This I found an easy matter. I read to him for a couple of hours, wrote four letters—one in French—and then talked a good two hours more. I have done more talking, by the way, in the last fortnight than in any previous twelve months—much of it, too, none of the wisest, nor, I may add, of the most fastidiously veracious. In a little discussion two or three days ago with Theodore, I came to the point and roundly proclaimed that in gossiping with Mr. Sloane I made no scruple, for our common satisfaction, of discreetly using the embellishments of fiction.

My confession gave him "that turn," as Mrs. Gamp would say, that his present illness may be the result of it. Nevertheless, poor, dear fellow, I trust he'll be on his legs tomorrow. This afternoon, somehow, I found myself really in the humor of talking. There was something propitious in the circumstances; a hard, cold rain without, a wood fire in the library, the *bonhomme* puffing cigarettes in his armchair, beside him a portfolio of newly imported prints and photographs, and—Theodore tucked safely away in bed. Finally, when I brought our tête-à-tête to a close (taking good care to understay my welcome), Mr. Sloane seized me by both hands and honored me with one of his venerable grins. "Max," he said, "—you must let me call you Max—you're the most delightful man I ever knew."

Verily, there's some virtue left in me yet. I believe I fairly blushed.

"Why didn't I know you ten years ago?" the old man went on. "Here are ten years lost."

"Ten years ago, my dear Mr. Sloane," quoth Max, "I was hardly worth your knowing."

"But I did know you!" cried the *bonhomme*. "I knew you in knowing your mother."

Ah! My mother again. When the old man begins that chapter, I feel like telling him to blow out his candle and go to bed.

"At all events," he continued, "we must make the most of the years that remain. I'm a poor, sick, old fellow, but I've no notion of dying. You'll not get tired of me and want to go away?"

"I'm devoted to you, sir," I said. "But I must be looking up some work, you know."

"Work! Bah! I'll give you work. I'll give you wages."

"I'm afraid," I said with a smile, "that you'll want to give me the wages without the work." And then I declared that I must go up and look at poor Theodore.

The *bonhomme* still kept my hands. "I wish very much," he said, "that I could get you to love me as well as you do poor Theodore."

"Ah, don't talk about love, Mr. Sloane. I'm no lover."

"Don't you love your friend?"

"Not as he deserves."

"Nor as he loves you, perhaps?"

"He loves me, I'm afraid, far more than I deserve."

"Well, Max," my host pursued, "we can be good friends all the same. We don't need a hocus-pocus of false sentiment. We are *men*, aren't we—men of sublime good sense?" And just here, as the old man looked at me, the pressure of his hands deepened to a convulsive grasp and the bloodless mask of his countenance was suddenly distorted with a nameless fear. "Ah, my dear young man!" he cried, "come and be a son to me—the son of my age and desolation! For God's sake, don't leave me to pine and die alone!"

I was amazed—and I may say I was moved. Is it true, then, that this poor old heart contains such measureless depths of horror and longing? I take it that he's mortally afraid of death. I assured him on my honor that he may henceforth call upon me for any service.

8th. Theodore's indisposition turned out more serious than I expected. He has been confined to his room till today. This evening he came down to the library in his dressing gown. Decidedly, Mr. Sloane is an eccentric, but hardly, as Theodore thinks, a "charming" one. There is something extremely curious in the exhibition of his caprices—the incongruous fits and starts, as it were, of his taste. For some reason best known to himself, he took it into his head to deem it a want of delicacy, of respect, of *savoir-vivre*—of heaven knows what—that poor Theodore, who is still weak and languid, should enter the sacred precinct of his study in the vulgar drapery of a dressing gown. The sovereign trouble with the *bonhomme* is an absolute lack of the instinct of justice. He's of the real feminine turn—I believe I have written it before—without a ray of woman's virtues. I honestly believe that I might come into his study in my nightshirt and he would smile upon it as a picturesque *dishabillé*. But for poor Theodore tonight, there was nothing but scowls and frowns and barely a civil inquiry about his health. But poor Theodore is not such a fool, either; he'll not die of a snubbing; I never said he was a weakling. Once he fairly saw from what quarter the wind blew, he bore the master's brutality with the utmost coolness and gallantry. Can it be that Mr. Sloane really wishes to drop him? The delicious old brute! He understands favor and friendship only as a selfish rapture—a reaction, an infatuation, an act of aggressive, exclusive patronage. It's not a bestowal with him, but a transfer, and half his pleasure in causing his sun to shine is that—being woefully near its setting—it will produce a number of delectable shadows. He wants to cast my shadow, I suppose, on Theodore; fortunately, I'm not altogether an opaque body. Since Theodore was taken ill, he has been into his room but once and has sent him none but the scantiest messages. I, too, have been much less attentive than I should have wished to be, but my time has not been my own. It has been—every moment of it— at Mr. Sloane's disposal. He actually runs after me; he devours me; he makes a fool of himself, and is trying hard to make one of me. I find that he will stand—that, in fact, he actually enjoys—a certain kind of humorous snubbing. He likes anything that will tickle his fancy, impart a flavor to our relations, remind him of his old odds and ends of novels and memoirs. I have fairly stepped into Theodore's shoes and done—with what I feel in my bones to be vastly inferior skill and taste—all the reading, writing, condensing, expounding, transcribing, and advising that he has been accustomed to do. I have driven with the *bonhomme;* played chess and cribbage with him; and beaten him, bullied him, contradicted him; and forced him into going out on the water under my charge. Who shall say, after this, that I haven't done my best to discourage his advances, confound his benevolence? As yet, my efforts are vain; in fact, they quite turn to my own confusion. Mr. Sloane is so vastly thankful at having escaped from the lake with his life that he seems actually to look upon me as a kind of romantic preserver and protector. Faugh! What tiresome nonsense it all is! But one thing is certain, it can't last forever. Admit that he *has* cast Theodore out and taken me in. He will speedily discover that he has made a pretty mess of it, and that he had much better have left well enough alone. He likes my reading and writing now, but in a month he'll begin to hate them. He'll miss Theodore's healthy, unerring, impersonal judgment. What an advantage that pure and luminous nature has over mine, after all. I'm for days, he's for years; he for the long run, I for the short. I, perhaps, am intended for success, but he alone for happiness. He holds in his heart a tiny, sacred particle which leavens his whole being and keeps it pure and sound—a faculty of admiration and respect. For him human nature is still a wonder and a mystery; it bears a divine stamp—Mr. Sloane's tawdry organism as well as the best.

13th. I have refused, of course, to supplant Theodore further, in the exercise of his functions, and he has resumed his morning labors with Mr. Sloane. I, on my side, have spent these morning hours in scouring the country on that capital black mare, the use of which is one of the perquisites of Theodore's place. The days have been magnificent—the heat of the sun tempered by a murmuring, wandering wind, the whole north a mighty ecstasy of sound and verdure, the sky a faraway vault of bended blue. Not far from the mill at M., the other end of the lake, I met, for the third time, that very pretty young girl who reminds me so forcibly of A. L. She makes so very frank and fearless a use of her eyes that I ventured to stop and bid her good morning. She seems nothing loath to an acquaintance. She's an out-and-out barbarian in speech, but her eyes look as if they had drained the noonday heavens of their luster. These rides do me good; I had got into a sadly worrying, brooding habit of thought.

What has got into Theodore I know not; his illness seems to have left him strangely affected. He has fits of somber reserve, alternating with spasms of extravagant gaiety. He avoids me at times for hours together, and then he comes and looks at me with an inscrutable smile, as if he were on the verge of a burst of confidence—which again is swallowed up in the darkness of his silence. Is he hatching some astounding benefit to his species? Is he working to bring about my removal to a higher sphere of action? *Nous verrons bien.*

18th. Theodore threatens departure. He received this morning a letter from one of his sisters—the young widow—announcing her engagement to a minister whose acquaintance she has recently made and intimating her expectation of an immediate union with the gentleman—a ceremony which would require Theodore's attendance.

Theodore, in high good humor, read the letter aloud
at breakfast—and to tell the truth a charming letter it
was. He then spoke of his having to go on to the
wedding, a proposition to which Mr. Sloane graciously
assented—but with truly startling amplitude. "I shall
be sorry to lose you after so happy a connection," said
the old man. Theodore turned pale, stared a moment,
and then, recovering his color and his composure, declared that he should have no objection in life to coming
back.

"Bless your soul!" cried the *bonhomme,* "you don't
mean to say you'll leave your little sister all alone?"

To which Theodore replied that he would arrange for
her to live with his brother-in-law. "It's the only proper
thing," he declared in a tone which was not to be gain-
said. It has come to this, then, that Mr. Sloane actually wants to turn him out of the house. Oh, the
precious old fool! He keeps smiling an uncanny smile,
which means, as I read it, that if the poor boy once
departs, he shall never return on the old footing—for
all his impudence!

20th. This morning, at breakfast, we had a terrific
scene. A letter arrives for Theodore; he opens it, turns
white and red, frowns, falters, and then informs us that
the clever widow has broken off her engagement. No
wedding, therefore, and no departure for Theodore. The
bonhomme was furious. In his fury he took the liberty
of calling poor Mrs. Parker (the sister) a very impolite
name. Theodore rebuked him, with perfect good taste,
and kept his temper.

"If my opinions don't suit you, Mr. Lisle," the old
man broke out, "and my mode of expressing them dis-
pleases you, you know you can easily remove yourself
from within my jurisdiction."

"My dear Mr. Sloane," said Theodore, "your opinions,
as a general rule, interest me deeply, and have never
ceased to act most beneficially upon the formation of
my own. Your mode of expressing them is charming,
and I wouldn't for the world, after all our pleasant intercourse, separate from you in bitterness. Only, I repeat,
your qualification of my sister's conduct was perfectly

uncalled for. If you knew her, you would be the first to admit it."

There was something in Theodore's aspect and manner, as he said these words, which puzzled me all the morning. After dinner, finding myself alone with him, I told him I was glad he was not obliged to go away. He looked at me with the mysterious smile I have mentioned—a smile which actually makes him handsome—thanked me, and fell into meditation. As this bescribbled chronicle is the record of my follies as well as of my *haut faits,* I needn't hesitate to say that, for a moment, I was keenly exasperated. What business has poor, transparent Theodore to put on the stony mask of the sphinx and play the inscrutable? What right has he to do so with me especially, in whom he has always professed an absolute confidence? Just as I was about to cry out, "Come, my dear boy, this affectation of mystery has lasted quite long enough—favor me at last with the result of your cogitation!"—as I was on the point of thus expressing my impatience of his continued solemnity of demeanor, the oracle at last addressed itself to utterance.

"You see, my dear Max," he said, "I can't, in justice to myself, go away in obedience to any such intimation as that vouchsafed to me this morning. What do you think of my actual footing here?"

Theodore's actual footing here seemed to me essentially uncomfortable—of course, I said so.

"Nay, I assure you it's not," he answered. "I should feel, on the contrary, very uncomfortable to think that I'd come away, except by my own choice. You see a man can't afford to cheapen himself. What are you laughing at?"

"I'm laughing, in the first place, my dear fellow, to hear on your lips the language of cold calculation; and in the second place, at your odd notion of the process by which a man keeps himself up in the market."

"I assure you that it's the correct notion. I came here as a favor to Mr. Sloane; it was expressly understood so. The occupation was distasteful to me. I had from top to bottom to accommodate myself to my duties. I had to compromise with a dozen convictions, preferences, prejudices. I don't take such things easily; I take them hard;

and when once the labor is achieved, I can't consent to have it thrown away. If Mr. Sloane needed me then, he needs me still. I am ignorant of any change having taken place in his intentions, or in his means of satisfying them. I came not to amuse him, but to do a certain work; I hope to remain until the work is completed. To go away sooner is to make a confession of incapacity which, I protest, costs too great a sacrifice to my vanity."

Theodore spoke these words with a face which I have never seen him wear; a fixed, mechanical smile; a hard, dry glitter in his eyes; a harsh, strident tone in his voice—in his whole physiognomy a gleam, as it were, a note of defiance. Now, I confess that for defiance I have never been conscious of an especial relish. When I'm defied, I'm ugly. "My dear man," I replied, "your sentiments do you prodigious credit. Your very ingenious theory of your present situation, as well as your extremely pronounced sense of your personal value, are calculated to insure you a degree of practical success which can very well dispense with the furtherance of my poor good wishes." Oh, the grimness of his listening smile — and I suppose, I may add, of my own physiognomy! But I have ceased to be puzzled. Theodore's conduct for the past ten days is suddenly illumined with a backward, lurid ray. Here are a few plain truths, which it behooves me to take to heart—commit to memory. Theodore is jealous of me. Theodore hates me. Theodore has been seeking for the past three months to see his name written, last but not least, in a certain testamentary document: "Finally, I bequeath to my dear young friend, Theodore Lisle, in return for invaluable services and unfailing devotion, the bulk of my property, real and personal, consisting of—" (hereupon follows an exhaustive enumeration of houses, lands, public securities, books, pictures, horses, and dogs). It is for this that he has toiled, and watched, and prayed; submitted to intellectual weariness and spiritual torture; made his terms with levity, blasphemy, and insult. For this he sets his teeth and tightens his grasp; for this he'll fight. Merciful powers! it's an immense weight off one's mind. There are nothing, then, but vulgar, common laws; no sublime exceptions, no transcendent anomalies. Theodore's a knave, a hypo—nay, nay; stay, irreverent hand!—Theodore's a *man!* Well, that's all I want. *He* wants fight—he shall have it. Have I got, at last, my simple, natural emotion?

21st. I have lost no time. This evening late, after I had heard Theodore go to his room (I had left the library early, on the pretext of having letters to write), I repaired to Mr. Sloane, who had not yet gone to bed, and informed him that it is necessary I shall at once leave him and seek some occupation in New York. He felt the blow; it brought him straight down on his marrow bones. He went through the whole gamut of his arts and graces; he blustered, whimpered, entreated, flattered. He tried to drag in Theodore's name; but this I, of course, prevented. But, finally, why, *why,* WHY, after all my promises of fidelity, must I thus cruelly desert him? Then came my supreme avowal: I have spent my last penny; while I stay, I'm a beggar. The remainder of this extraordinary scene I have no power to describe: how the *bonhomme,* touched, inflamed, inspired by the thought of my destitution, and at the same time annoyed, perplexed, bewildered at having to commit himself to any practical alleviation of it, worked himself into a nervous frenzy which deprived him of a clear sense of the value of his words and his actions; how I, prompted by the irresistible spirit of my desire to leap astride of his weakness and ride it hard into the goal of my dreams, cunningly contrived to keep his spirit at the fever point so that strength, and reason and resistance should burn themselves out. I shall probably never again have such a sensation as I enjoyed tonight—actually feel a heated human heart throbbing, and turning, and struggling in my grasp; know its pants, its spasms, its convulsions, and its final senseless quiescence. At half-past one o'clock, Mr. Sloane got out of his chair, went to his secretary, opened a private drawer, and took out a folded paper. "This is my will," he said, "made some seven weeks ago. If you'll stay with me, I'll destroy it."

"Really, Mr. Sloane," I said, "if you think my purpose is to exert any pressure upon your testamentary inclinations——"

"I'll tear it in pieces," he cried; "I'll burn it up. I

shall be as sick as a dog tomorrow; but I'll do it. A-a-h!"

He clapped his hand to his side, as if in sudden, over-whelming pain, and sank back fainting into his chair. A single glance assured me that he was unconscious. I possessed myself of the paper, opened it, and perceived that the will is almost exclusively in Theodore's favor. For an instant, a savage, pucrile feeling of hate sprang erect in my bosom, and I came within an ace of obeying my foremost impulse—that of casting the document into the fire. Fortunately, my reason overtook my passion, though for a moment 'twas an even race. I replaced the paper in the secretary, closed it, and rang the bell for Robert (the old man's servant). Before he came I stood watching the poor, pale remnant of mortality be-fore me and wondering whether those feeble life gasps were numbered. He was as white as a sheet, grimacing with pain—horribly ugly. Suddenly, he opened his eyes; they met my own; I fell on my knees and took his hands. They closed on mine with a grasp strangely akin to the rigidity of death. Nevertheless, since then he has revived and has relapsed again into a comparatively healthy sleep. Robert seems to know how to deal with him.

22d. Mr. Sloane is seriously ill—out of his mind and unconscious of people's identity. The doctor has been here, off and on, all day, but this evening reports improvement. I have kept out of the old man's room and confined myself to my own, reflecting largely upon the odd contingency of his immediate death. Does Theodore know of the will? Would it occur to him to divide the property? Would it occur to me, in his place? We met at dinner and talked in a grave, desultory, friendly fashion. After all, he's an excellent fellow. I don't hate him. I don't even dislike him. He jars on me, *il m'agace,* but that's no reason why I should do him an evil turn. Nor shall I. The property is a fixed idea, that's all. I shall get it if I can. We're fairly matched. Before heaven, no, we're not fairly matched! Theodore has a conscience.

23d. I'm restless and nervous—and for good reasons. Scribbling here keeps me quiet. This morning Mr. Sloane is better; feeble and uncertain in mind, but unmistakably on the mend. I may confess now that I feel relieved of a weighty burden. Last night, I hardly slept a wink. I lay awake listening to the pendulum of my clock. It seemed to say "He lives—he dies." I fully expected to have it stop suddenly at *dies*. But it kept going all the morning, and to a decidedly more lively tune. In the afternoon, the old man sent for me. I found him in his great muffled bed, with his face the color of damp chalk, and his eyes glowing faintly, like torches half-stamped out. I was forcibly struck with the utter loneliness of his lot. For all human attendance, my villainous self grinning at his bedside, and old Robert without, listening, doubtless at the keyhole. The *bonhomme* stared at me stupidly, then seemed to know me and greeted me with a sickly smile. It was some moments before he was able to speak. At last he faintly bade me to descend into the library, open the secret drawer of the secretary (which he contrived to direct me how to do), possess myself of his will, and burn it up. He appears to have forgotten his having removed it, night before last. I told him that I had an insurmountable aversion to any personal dealings with the document. He smiled, patted the back of my hand, and requested me, in that case, to get it, at least, and bring it to him. I couldn't deny him that favor? No, I couldn't, indeed. I went down to the library, therefore, and on entering the room found Theodore standing by the fireplace with a bundle of papers. The secretary was open. I stood still, looking from the ruptured cabinet to the documents in his hand. Among them I recognized, by its shape and size, the paper of which I had intended to possess myself. Without delay I walked straight up to him. He looked surprised, but not confused. "I'm afraid I shall have to trouble you," I said, "to surrender one of those papers."

"Surrender, Max? To anything of your own you are perfectly welcome. I didn't know, however, that you made use of Mr. Sloane's secretary. I was looking up some notes of my own making, in which I conceive I have a property."

"This is what I want, Theodore," I said, and I drew the will, unfolded, from between his hands. As I did so his eyes fell upon the superscription, "Last Will and Testament. March. F. S." He flushed a splendid, furious crimson. Our eyes met. Somehow—I don't know how or why, or for that matter why not—I burst into a violent peal of laughter. Theodore stood staring, with two hot, bitter tears in his eyes.

"Of course you think," he said, "that I came to ferret out that thing."

I shrugged my shoulders—those of my body only. I confess, morally, I was on my knees with contrition, but there was a fascination in it—a fatality. I remembered that in the hurry of my movements the other evening, I had replaced the will simply in one of the outer drawers of the cabinet, among Theodore's own papers; doubtless where he had taken it up. "Mr. Sloane sent me for it," I said.

"Very good, I'm glad to hear he's well enough to think of such things."

"He means to destroy it."

"I hope, then, he has another made."

"Mentally, I suppose he has."

"Unfortunately, his weakness isn't mental—or exclusively so."

"Oh, he'll live to make a dozen more," I said. "Do you know the purport of this one?"

Theodore's color, by this time, had died away into a somber paleness. He shook his head. The doggedness of the movement provoked me. I wished to arouse his curiosity. "I have his commission," I rejoined, "to destroy it."

Theodore smiled superbly. "It's not a task I envy you," he said.

"I should think not—especially if you knew the import of the will." He stood with folded arms, regarding me with the remote contempt of his rich blue eyes. I couldn't stand it. "Come, it's your property," I cried. "You're sole legatee. I give it up to you." And I thrust the paper into his hand.

He received it mechanically, but after a pause, bethinking himself, he unfolded it and cast his eyes over the contents. Then he slowly refolded it and held it a moment with a tremulous hand. "You say that Mr. Slone directed you to destroy it?" he finally asked.

"I say so."

"And that you know the contents?"

"Exactly."

"And that you were about to comply?"

"On the contrary, I declined."

Theodore fixed his eyes, for a moment, on the superscription and then raised them again to my face. "Thank you, Max," he said. "You've left me a real satisfaction." He tore the sheet across and threw the bits into the fire. We stood watching them burn. "Now he can make another," said Theodore.

"Twenty others," I replied.

"No," said Theodore, "you'll take care of that."

"Upon my soul," I cried, "you're bitter!"

"No, not now. I worked off all my bitterness in these few words."

"Well, in consideration of that, I excuse them."

"Just as you please."

"Ah," said I, "there's a little bitterness left!"

"No, nothing but indifference. Farewell." And he put out his hand.

"Are you going away?"

"Of course I am. Farewell."

"Farewell, then. But isn't your departure rather sudden?"

"I ought to have gone three weeks ago—three weeks ago." I had taken his hand, he pulled it away, covered his face, and suddenly burst into tears.

"Is *that* indifference?" I asked.

"It's something you'll never know," he cried. "It's shame! I'm not sorry you should see it. It will suggest to you, perhaps, that my heart has never been in this filthy contest. Let me assure you, at any rate, that it hasn't; that it has had nothing but scorn for the base perversion of my pride and my ambition. These tears are tears of joy at their return—the return of the prodigals! Tears of sorrow—sorrow——"

He was unable to go on. He sank into a chair, burying his face in his handkerchief.

"For God's sake, Theodore," I said, "stick to the joy."

He rose to his feet again. "Well," he said, "it was for your sake that I parted with my self-respect; with your assistance I recover it."

"How for my sake?"

"For whom but you would I have gone as far as I did? For what other purpose than that of keeping our friendship whole would I have borne you company into this narrow pass? A man whom I loved less I would long since have parted with. You were needed—you and your incomparable gifts—to bring me to this. You ennobled, exalted, enchanted the struggle. I *did* value my prospects of coming into Mr. Sloane's property. I valued them for my poor sister's sake, as well as for my own, so long as they were the natural reward of conscientious service and not the prize of hypocrisy and cunning. With another man than you I never would have contested such a prize. But I loved you, even as my rival. You played with me, deceived me, betrayed me. I held my ground, hoping and longing to purge you of your error by the touch of your old pledges of affection. I carried them in my heart. For Mr. Sloane, from the moment that, under your magical influence, he revealed his extraordinary foibles, I had nothing but contempt."

"And for me now?"

"Don't ask me. I don't trust myself."

"Hate, I suppose."

"Is that the best you can imagine? Farewell."

"Is it a serious farewell—farewell forever?"

"How can there be any other?"

"I'm sorry that such should be your point of view. It's characteristic. All the more reason then that I should say a word in self-defense. You accuse me of having 'played with you, deceived you, betrayed you.' It seems to me that you're quite off the track. You say you loved me. If so, you ought to love me still. It wasn't for my virtue, for I never had any, or pretended to any. In anything I have done recently, therefore, there has been no inconsistency. I never pretended to love you. I don't understand the word, in the sense you attach to it. I don't understand the feeling, between men. To me, love means quite another thing. You give it a meaning of your own; you enjoy the profit of your invention; it's no more than just that you should pay the penalty. Only, it seems to me rather hard that *I* should pay it." Theodore remained silent, but his brow slowly contracted into an inexorable frown. "Is it still a 'serious farewell'?" I went on. "It seems a pity. After this clearing up, it actually seems to me that I shall be on better terms with you. No man can have a deeper appreciation of your excellent faculties, a keener enjoyment of your society, your talk. I should very much regret the loss of them."

"Have we, then, all this while," said Theodore, "understood each other so little?"

"Don't say 'we' and 'each other.' I think I have understood you."

"Very likely. It's not for want of my having confessed myself."

"Well, Theodore, I do you justice. To me you've always been overgenerous. Try now, and be just."

Still he stood silent, with his cold, hard frown. It was plain that if he was to come back to me, it would be from a vast distance. What he was going to answer I know not. The door opened, and Robert appeared, pale, trembling, his eyes starting in his head.

"I verily believe, gentlemen," he cried, "that poor Mr. Sloane is dead in his bed."

There was a moment's perfect silence. "Amen," said I. "Yes, Theodore, try and be just." Mr. Sloane had quietly died in my absence.

24th. Theodore went up to town this morning, having shaken hands with me in silence before he started. Doctor Jones and Brookes the attorney have been very officious, and, by their advice, I have telegraphed to a certain Miss Meredith, a maiden lady, by their account the nearest of kin—or, in other words, simply a discarded half-niece of the defunct. She telegraphs back that she will arrive in person for the funeral. I shall remain till she comes. I have lost a fortune, but have I irretrievably lost a friend? I'm sure I can't say.

❧

At Isella

MY story begins properly, I suppose, with my journey, and my journey began properly at Lucerne. It had been on the point of beginning a number of times before. About the middle of August I actually started. I had been putting it off from day to day in deference to the opinion of several discreet friends, who solemnly assured me that a man of my make would never outweather the rage of an Italian August. But ever since deciding to winter in Italy, instead of subsiding unimaginatively upon Paris, I had had a standing quarrel with Switzerland. What was Switzerland after all? Little else but brute Nature surely, of which at home we have enough and to spare. What we seek in Europe is Nature refined and transmuted to art. In Switzerland, what a pale historic coloring, what a penury of relics and monuments! I pined for a cathedral or a gallery. Instead of dutifully conning my Swiss Baedeker, I had fretfully deflavored my Murray's *North Italy*. Lucerne, indeed, is a charming little city, and I had learned to know it well. I had watched the tumbling Reuss, blue from the melting pinnacles which know the blue of heaven, come rushing and swirling beneath those quaintly timbered bridges, vaulted with mystical paintings in the manner of Holbein, and through the severed mass of the white, compact town. I had frequented the great, bald, half-handsome, half-hideous church of the Jesuits, and listened in the twilight to the seraphic choir which breathes through its mighty organ tubes. I had taken the most reckless pleasure in the fact that this was Catholic Switzerland. I had strolled and restrolled across the narrow marketplace at Altorf, and kept my countenance in the presence of that ludicrous plaster cast of the *genius loci* and his crossbow. I had peregrinated further to the little hamlet of Bürglen, and peeped into the frescoed chapel which commemorates the hero's natal scene. I had also investigated that sordid lakeside sanctuary, with its threshold lapped by the waves and its walls defiled by cockneys, which consecrates the spot at which the great mountaineer, leaping from among his custodians in Gesler's boat, spurned the stout skiff with his invincible heel. I had contemplated from the deck of the steamer the images of the immortal trio, authors of the oath of liberation, which adorn the pier at Brunnen. I had sojourned at that compact little State of Gersau, sandwiched between the lake and the great wall of the Righi, and securely niched somewhere in history as the smallest and most perpetual of republics. The traveler's impatience hereabouts is quickened by his nearness to one of the greatest of the Alpine highways. Here he may catch a balmy side wind, stirred from the ranks of southward-trooping pilgrims. The Saint Gothard route begins at Lucerne, where you take your place in the diligence and register your luggage. I used to fancy that a great wave of southern life rolled down this mighty channel to expire visibly in the blue lake and ripple to its green shores. I used to imagine great gusts of warm wind hovering about the coach office at Fluelen, scented with oleander and myrtle. I used to buy at Fluelen, to the great peril of my digestion, certain villainous peaches and plums offered by little girls at the steamboat landing, and of which it was currently whispered that they had ripened on those further Italian slopes.

One fine morning I marked my luggage *Milan!* with a great imaginative flourish—which may have had something to do with my subsequent difficulty in recovering it in the Lombard capital—banished it for a fortnight from sight and mind, and embarked on the steamboat at Lucerne with the interval's equipment in a knapsack. It is noteworthy how readily, on leaving Switzerland, I made my peace with it. What a pleasure-giving land it is, in truth! Besides the massive glory of its mountains, how it heaps up the measure of delight with the unbargained grace of town and tower, of remembered name and deed! As we passed away from Lucerne, my eyes lingered with a fresher fondness than before upon an admirable bit of the civic picturesque—a great line of mellow-stuccoed dwellings, with verdurous water steps and grated basements, rising squarely from the rushing cobalt of the Reuss. It was a palpable foretaste of Venice. I am not ashamed to say how soon I began to look out for premonitions of Italy. It was better to begin too soon than too late, so, to miss nothing, I began to note "sensations" at Altorf, the historic heart of Helvetia. I remember here certain formal burgher mansions, standing back from the dusty high road beyond spacious, well-swept courts, into which the wayfarer glances through immense gates of antique wrought iron. I had a notion that deserted Italian palazzos took the lingering sunbeams at somewhat such an angle, with just that coarse glare. I wondered, of course, who lived in them, and how they lived, and what was society in Altorf; longing plaintively, in the manner of roaming Americans, for a few stray crumbs from the native social board; with my fancy vainly beating its wings against the great blank wall, behind which, in travel-haunted Europe, all gentle private interests nestle away from intrusion. Here, as everywhere, I was struck with the mere surface relation of the Western tourist to the soil he treads. He filters and trickles through the dense social body in every possible direction, and issues forth at last the same virginal water drop. "Go your way," these antique houses seemed to say, from their quiet courts and gardens; "the road is yours and welcome, but the land is ours. You may pass and stare and wonder, but you may never know us." The Western tourist consoles himself, of course, by the reflection that the gentry of Altorf and other ancient burghs gain more from the imagination possibly than they might bestow upon it.

I confess that so long as I remained in the land, as I did for the rest of the afternoon—a pure afternoon of late summer, charged with mellow shadows from the teeming verdure of the narrow lowland, beyond which tomorrow and Italy seemed merged in a vague bright identity—I felt that I was not fairly under way. The land terminates at Amstaeg, where I lay that night. Early the next morning, I attacked the mighty slopes. Just beyond Amstaeg, if I am not mistaken, a narrow granite bridge spans the last mountain plunge of the Reuss; and just

here the great white road begins the long toil of its ascent.
To my sense, these mighty Alpine highways have a grand
poetry of their own. I lack, doubtless, that stout stomach
for pure loneliness which leads your genuine mountaineer
to pronounce them a desecration of the mountain stillness. As if the mountain stillness were not inviolable!
Gleaming here and there against the dark sides of the
gorges, unrolling their measured bands further and higher,
doubling and stretching and spanning, but always climbing, they break it only to the anxious eye. The Saint
Gothard road is immensely long drawn, and, if the truth
be told, somewhat monotonous. As you follow it to its
uppermost reaches, the landscape takes on a darker local
color. Far below the wayside, the yellow Reuss tumbles
and leaps and foams over a perfect torture bed of broken
rock. The higher slopes lie naked and raw, or coated
with slabs of gray. The valley lifts and narrows and darkens
into the scenic mountain pass of the fancy. I was haunted
as I walked by an old steel plate in a French book that I
used to look at as a child, lying on my stomach on the
parlor floor. Under it was written "Saint Gothard." I
remembered distinctly the cold, gray mood which this
picture used to generate; the same tone of feeling is produced by the actual scene. Coming at last to the Devil's
Bridge, I recognized the source of the steel plate of my
infancy. You have no impulse here to linger fondly. You
hurry away after a moment's halt, with an impression
fierce and chaotic as the place itself. A great torrent of
wind, sweeping from a sudden outlet and snatching uproar
and spray from the mad torrent of water leaping in
liquid thunderbolts beneath; a giddy, deafened, deluged
stare, with my two hands to my hat; and a rapid shudder-
ing retreat—these are my chief impressions of the Devil's
Bridge. If, on leaving Amstaeg in the morning, I had been
asked whither I was bending my steps, "To Italy!" I
would have answered, with a grand absence of detail. The
radiance of this broad fact had quenched the possible side-
lights of reflection. As I approached the summit of the
pass, it became a profoundly solemn thought that I might,
by pushing on with energy, lay my weary limbs on an
Italian bed. There was something so delightful in the mere
protracted, suspended sense of approach that it seemed a

pity to bring it to so abrupt a close. And then suppose, metaphysical soul of mine, that Italy should not, in vulgar parlance, altogether come up to time? Why not prolong awhile the possible bliss of ignorance—of illusion? Something short of the summit of the Saint Gothard pass, the great road of the Furca diverges to the right, passes the Rhône Glacier enters the Rhône Valley, and conducts you to Brieg and the foot of the Simplon. Reaching in due course this divergence of the Furca road, I tarried awhile beneath the mountain sky, debating whether or not delay would add to pleasure. I opened my Baedeker and read that within a couple of hours' walk from my halting place was the *Albergo di San Gothardo, vaste et sombre auberge Italienne.* To think of being at that distance from a vast, somber Italian inn! On the other hand, there were some very pretty things said of the Simplon. I tossed up a napoleon; the head fell uppermost. I trudged away to the right. The road to the Furca lies across one of those high desolate plateaus which represent the hard prose of mountain scenery. Naked and stern it lay before me, rock and grass, without a shrub, without a tree, without a grace—like the dry bed of some gigantic river of prehistoric times.

The stunted hamlet of Realp, beside the road dwarfed by the huge scale of things, seemed little more than a cluster of naked, sun-blackened boulders. It contained an inn, however, and the inn contained the usual Alpine larder of cold veal and cheese, and, as I remember, a very affable maidservant, who spoke excellent lowland French and confessed in the course of an after-dinner conversation that the winters in Realp were *un peu tristes*. This conversation took place as I sat resting outside the door in the late afternoon, watching the bright, hard light of the scene grow gray and cold beneath a clear sky and wondering to find humanity lodged in such an exaltation of desolation.

The road of the Furca, as I discovered the next morning, is a road and little else. Its massive bareness, however, gives it an incontestable grandeur. The broad, serpentine terrace uncoils its slanting *cordons* with a multiplicity of curves and angles and patient reaches of circumvention, which give it the air of some wanton revelry of engineering genius. Finally, after a brief level of repose, it plunges down to the Rhône Glacier. I had the good fortune to see this great spectacle on the finest day of the year. Its perfect beauty is best revealed beneath the scorching glare of an untempered sun. The sky was without a cloud—the air incredibly lucid. The glacier dropped its billowy sheet —a soundless tumult of whiteness, a torrent of rolling marble—straight from the blue of heaven to the glassy margin of the road. It seems to gather into its bosom the whole diffused light of the world, so that around about it all objects lose their color. The rocks and hills stand sullen and neutral; the luster of the sky is turned to blackness. At the little hotel near the glacier I waited for the coach to Brieg, and started thitherward in the early afternoon, sole occupant of the coupé.

Let me not, however, forget to commorate the French priest whom we took in at one of the squalid villages of the dreary Haut-Valais, through which on that bright afternoon we rattled so superbly. It was a Sunday, and throughout this long, dark chain of wayside hamlets the peasants were straddling stolidly about the little central *place* in the hideous festal accouterments of the rustic Swiss. He came forth from the tavern, gently cleaving the staring crowd, accompanied by two brother ecclesiastics. These were portly, elderly men; he was young and pale and priestly in the last degree. They had a little scene of adieus at the coach door. They whispered gently, gently holding each other's hands and looking lovingly into each other's eyes, and then the two elders saluted their comrade on each cheek, and, as we departed, blew after him just the least little sacramental kiss. It was all, dramatically speaking, delightfully low in tone. Before we reached Brieg the young priest had gained a friend to console him for those he had lost. He proved to be a most amiable person, full of homely frankness and appealing innocence of mundane things, and invested withal with a most pathetic air of sitting there as a mere passive object of transmission—a simple priestly particle in the great ecclesiastical body, transposed by the logic of an inscrutable *thither!* and *thus!* On learning that I was an American, he treated me so implicitly as a traveled man of the world that he almost persuaded me for the time I was one. He was on pins and needles with his sense of the possible hazards of travel. He asked questions the most innocently *saugrenues*. He was convinced on general grounds that our driver was drunk, and that he would surely overturn us into the Rhône. He seemed possessed at the same time with a sort of schoolboy relish for the profane humor of things. Whenever the coach made a lurch toward the riverbank or swung too broadly round a turn, he would grasp my arm and whisper that our hour had come; and then, before our pace was quite readjusted, he would fall to nursing his elbows and snickering gently to himself. It seemed altogether a larger possibility than any he had been prepared for that on his complaining of the cold I should offer him the use of my overcoat. Of this and of other personal belongings he ventured to inquire the price, and indeed seemed oppressed with the sudden expensiveness of the world. But now that he was fairly launched he was moving in earnest. He was to reach Brieg, if possible, in time for the night diligence over the Simplon, which was to deposit him at the hospice on the summit.

By a very early hour the next morning I had climbed apace with the sun. Brieg was far below me in the valley. I had measured an endless number of the giant elbows of the road, and from the bosky flank of the mountain I looked down at nestling gulfs of greenness, cool with shade; at surging billows of forest crested with the early brightness; at slopes in light and cliffs in shadow; at all the heaving mountain zone which belongs to the verdant nearness of earth; and then straight across to the sacred pinnacles which take their tone from heaven.

If weather could bless an enterprise, mine was blessed beyond words. It seemed to me that Nature had taken an interest in my little project and was determined to do the thing handsomely. As I mounted higher, the light flung its dazzling presence on all things. The air stood still to take it; the green glittered within the green, the blue burned beyond it; the dew on the forests gathered to dry into massive crystals, and beyond the brilliant void of space the clear snowfields stood out like planes of marble inserted in a field of lapis lazuli. The Swiss side of the Simplon has the beauty of a boundless luxury of green; the view remains gentle even in its immensity. The ascent is gradual and slow, and only when you reach the summit do you get a sense of proper mountain grimness. On this favoring day of mine, the snowy horrors of the opposite Aletsch Glacier seemed fairly to twinkle with serenity. It seemed to me when I reached the hospice that I had been winding for hours along the inner hollow of some mighty cup of verdure toward a rim of chiseled silver crowned with topaz. At the hospice I made bold to ask leave to rest. It stands on the bare topmost plateau of the pass, bare itself as the spot it consecrates and stern as the courage of the pious brothers, who administer its charities. It broods upon the scene with the true, bold, convent look, with rugged yellow walls and grated windows, striving to close in human weakness from blast and avalanche, as in valleys and cities to close it in from temptation and pollution. A few St. Bernard dogs were dozing outside in the chilly sunshine. I climbed the great stone steps which lift the threshold above the snowland, and tinkled the bell of appeal. Here for a couple of hours I was made welcome to the cold, hard fare of the convent. There was to my mind a solemn and pleasant fitness in my thus entering church-burdened Italy through the portal of the church, for from the convent door to the plain of Lombardy, it was all to be downhill work. I seemed to feel on my head the hands of especial benediction and to hear in my ears the premonition of countless future hours to be passed in the light of altar candles. The inner face of the hospice is well-nigh as cold and bare as the face it turns defiant to the Alpine snows. Huge stone corridors and ungarnished rooms, in which poor unacclimatized friars must sit aching and itching with chilblains in high midsummer; everywhere that peculiar perfume of churchiness—the *odeur de sacristie* and essence of incense—which impart throughout the world an especial pungency to Catholicism. Having the good fortune, as it happened, to be invited to dine with the prior, I found myself in fine priestly company. A dozen of us sat about the board in the greasy, brick-paved refectory, lined with somber cupboards of ponderous crockery, all in stole and cassock but myself. Several of the brothers were *in transitu* from below. Among them I had the pleasure of greeting my companion in the coupé to Brieg, slightly sobered perhaps by his relapse into the clerical ranks, but still timidly gracious and joyous. The prior himself,

however, especially interested me, so every inch was he a
prior—a priest dominant and militant. He was still young,
and familiar, I should say, with the passions of youth; tall
and powerful in frame, stout-necked and small-headed,
with a brave beak of a nose and closely placed, fine, but
sinister eyes. The simple, childish cut of his black cassock,
with its little linen band across his great pectoral expanse
as he sat at meat, seemed to denote a fantastic, ironic
humility. Was it a mere fancy of a romantic Yankee tourist
that he was more evil than gentle? Heaven grant, I
mused as I glanced at him, that his fierce and massive manhood be guided by the Lord's example. What was such
a man as that doing up there on a lonely mountaintop,
watching the snow clouds from closed windows and dol-
ing out restorative cognac to frost-bitten wagoners? He
ought to be down in the hard, dense world, fighting and
sinning for his mother Church. But he was one who could
bide his time. Unless I'm scribbling nonsense, it will come.
In deference probably to the esoteric character of a portion of the company, our conversation at dinner was not
rigidly clerical. In fact, when my attention wandered back
to its theme, I found the good brothers were talking of
Alexandre Dumas with a delightful air of protest and hear-
say and a spice of priestly malice. The great romancer,
I believe, had among his many fictions somewhere pro-
mulgated an inordinate fiction touching the manners and
customs of the hospice. The game being started, each of
them said his say and cast his pebble, weighted always
with an *"on dit,"* and I was amazed to find they were so
well qualified to reprobate the author of *Monte Cristo.*
When we had dined, my young Frenchman came and
took me by the arm and led me in great triumph over
the whole convent, delighted to have something to show
me—me who had come from America and had lent him
my overcoat. When at last I had under his auspices made
my farewell obeisance to the prior and started on my
downward course, he bore me company along the
road. But before we lost sight of the hospice, he gave me
his fraternal blessing. *"Allons!"* he was pleased to say,
"the next time I shall know an American"; and he gathered up his gentle petticoat, and, as I looked behind, I

saw his black stockings frolicking back over the stones by a short cut to the monastery.

I should like to be able to tell the veracious tale of that divine afternoon. I should like to be able to trace the soft stages by which those rugged heights melt over into a southern difference. Now at last in good earnest I began to watch for the *symptoms* of Italy. Now that the long slope began to tend downward unbroken, it was not absurd to fancy a few adventurous tendrils of southern growth might have crept and clambered upward. At a short distance beyond the hospice stands the little village of Simplon, where I believe the coach stops for dinner; the uttermost outpost, I deemed it, of the lower world, perched there like an empty shell, with its murmur not yet quenched, tossed upward and stranded by some climbing southern wave. The little inn at the Italian end of the street, painted in a bright Italian medley of pink and blue, must have been decorated by a hand which had learned its cunning in the land of the fresco. The Italian slope of the Simplon road commands a range of scenery wholly different from the Swiss. The latter winds like a thread through the blue immensity; the former bores its way beneath crag and cliff, through gorge and mountain crevice. But though its channel narrows and darkens, Italy nears and nears none the less. You suspect it first in—what shall I say?—the growing warmth of the air, a fancied elegance of leaf and twig; a little while yet, and they will curl and wanton to your heart's content. The famous Gorge of Gando, at this stage of the road, renews the somber horrors of the Via Mala. The hills close together above your head, and the daylight filters down their corrugated sides from three inches of blue. The mad torrent of the Dauria, roaring through the straitened vale, fills it forever with a sounding din, as—to compare poetry to prose—a railway train a tunnel. Emerging from the Gorge of Gando, you fairly breathe Italian air. The gusts of a mild climate come wandering along the road to meet you. Lo! Suddenly, by the still wayside, I came upon a sensation: a little house painted a hot salmon color, with a withered pine twig over the door in token of entertainment, and above this inscribed in square chirography—literally in Italics—*Osteria!* I stopped devotedly to quaff a glass of sour wine to Italy gained. The place seemed wrapped in a desolation of stillness, save that as I stood and thumped the doorpost, the piping cry of a baby rose from the loft above and tickled the mountain echoes. Anon came clattering down the stairs a nursing mother of peasants; she gave me her only wine, out of her own bottle, out of her only glass. While she stood to wait on me, the terrible cry of her infant became so painful that I bade her go and fetch him before he strangled; and in a moment she reappeared, holding him in her arms, pacified and utterly naked. Standing there with the little unswaddled child on her breast, and smiling simply from her glowing brow, she made a picture which, in coming weeks, I saw imitated more or less vividly over many an altar and in many a palace. Onward still, through its long-drawn evolutions, the valley keeps darkly together, as if to hold its own to the last against the glittering breadth of level Lombardy. In truth, I had gained my desire. If Italy meant stifling heat, this was the essence of Italy. The afternoon was waning, and the early shadows of the valley deepening into a dead summer night. But the hotter the better, and the more Italian! At last, at a turn in the road, I glimpsed the first houses of a shallow village, pressed against the mountain wall. It was Italy—the Dogana Isella!—so I quickened my jaded steps. I met a young officer strolling along the road in sky-blue trousers, with a mustache *à la* Victor Emanuel, puffing a cigarette and yawning with the sensuous ennui of Isella—the first of that swarming company of warriors whose cerulean presence, in many a rich street scene, in later hours touched up so brightly the foreground of the picture. A few steps more brought me to the Dogana and to my first glimpse of those massive and shadowy arcades so delightfully native to the south. Here it was my privilege to hear for the first time the music of an Italian throat vibrate upon Italian air. "Nothing to declare—*niente?*" asked the dark-eyed functionary, emerging from the arcade. *"Niente"* seemed to me delicious; I would have told a fib for the sake of repeating the word. Just beyond stood the inn, which seemed to me somehow not as the inns of Switzerland. Perched something aloft against the hillside, a vague, light tendency to break out into balconies and terraces and trellises seemed to enhance its simple façade. Its open windows had an air of being familiar with southern nights; with balmy dialogues, possibly, passing between languid ladies leaning on the iron rails, and lounging gentlemen, star-gazing from the road beneath at their mistresses' eyes. Heaven grant it should not be fastidiously neat, scrubbed, and furbished and *frotte* like those prosy taverns on the Swiss lakes! Heaven was generous. I was ushered into a room whereof the ceiling was frescoed with flowers and gems and cherubs, but whose brick-tiled floor would have been vastly amended by the touch of a wet cloth and broom. After repairing my toilet within the limits of my resources, I proceeded to order supper. The host, I remember, I decreed to have been the *chef de cuisine* of some princely house of Lombardy. He wore a grizzled mustache and a red velvet cap, with little gold earrings. I could see him, under proper inspiration, whip a towel around his waist, turn back his sleeves, and elaborate a masterly pasticcio. "I shall take the liberty," he said, "of causing monsieur to be served at the same time with a lady."

"With a lady—an English lady?" I asked.

"An Italian lady. She arrived an hour ago." And mine host paused a moment and honored me with a genial smile. "She is alone—she is young—she is pretty."

Stolid child of the north that I was, surely my smile of response was no match for his! But, nevertheless, in my heart I felt that fortune was kind. I went forth to stroll down the road while my repast was being served, and while daylight still lingered, to reach forward as far as possible into the beckoning land beyond. Opposite the inn the mountain stream, still untamed, murmured and tumbled between the stout parapet which edged the road and the wall of rock which enclosed the gorge. I felt indefinably curious, expectant, impatient. Here was Italy at last; but what next? Was I to eat my supper and go contentedly to bed? Was there nothing I could see, or do, or feel? I had been deeply moved, but I was primed for a deeper emotion still. Would it come? Along the road toward Domo d'Ossola, the evening shadows deepened and settled and filled the future with mystery. The future would take care of itself; but ah, for an intenser present! I stopped and gazed wistfully along the broad dim highway. At this moment I perceived beyond me, leaning against the parapet, the figure of a woman, alone and in meditation. Her two elbows rested on the stone coping, her two hands were laid against her ears to deaden the din of the stream, and her face, between them, was bent over upon the waters. She seemed young and comely. She was bareheaded; a black organdy shawl was gathered around her shoulders; her dress, of a light black material, was covered with a multitude of little puffs and flounces, trimmed and adorned with crimson silk. There was an air of intense meditation in her attitude; I passed near her without her perceiving me. I observed her black-brown tresses, braided by a cunning hand, but slightly disarranged by travel, and the crumpled disorder of her half-fantastic dress. She was a lady and an Italian; she was alone, young, and pretty— was she possibly my destined companion? A few yards beyond the spot at which she stood, I retraced my steps; she had now turned around. As I approached her, she looked at me from a pair of dark, expressive eyes. Just a hint of suspicion and defiance I fancied that at this moment they expressed. "Who are you, what are you, roaming so close to me?" they seemed to murmur. We were alone in this narrow pass, I a newcomer, she a daughter of the land; moreover, her glance had almost audibly challenged me; instinctively, therefore, and with all the deference I was master of, I bowed. She continued to gaze for an instant; then suddenly she perceived, I think, that I was utterly a foreigner and presumably a gentleman, and hereupon, briefly but graciously, she returned my salute. I went my way and reached the hotel. As I passed in, I saw the fair stranger come slowly along the road as if also to enter the inn. In the little dining room I found mine host of the velvet cap bestowing the finishing touches upon a small table set *en tête-à-tête* for two. I had heard, I had read, of the gracious loquacity of the Italian race and their sweet familiarities of discourse. Here was a chance to test the quality of the matter. The landlord, having poised two fantastically folded napkins directly vis-à-vis, glanced at me with a twinkle in his eye which seemed to bespeak recognition of this cunning arrangement.

"*A propos*," I said, "this lady with whom I am to dine? Does she wear a black dress with red flounces?"

"Precisely, signore. You have already had a glimpse of her? A pretty woman, isn't it so?"

"Extremely pretty. Who is the lady?"

"Ah!" And the landlord turned back his head and thrust out his chin, with just the least play of his shoulders. "That's the question! A lady of that age, with that face and those red flounces, who travels alone—not even a maid—you may well ask who she is! She arrived here an hour ago in a carriage from Domo d'Ossola, where, her *vetturino* told me, she had arrived only just before by the common coach from Arona. But though she travels by the common vehicle, she is not a common person; one may see that with half an eye. She comes in great haste, but ignorant of the ways and means. She wishes to go by the diligence to Brieg. She ought to have waited at Domo, where she could have found a good seat. She didn't even take the precaution of engaging one at the office there. When the diligence stops here, she will have to fare as she can. She is pretty enough indeed to fare very well—or very ill; isn't it so, signore?" demanded the worthy Bonifazio, as I believe he was named. "Ah, but behold her strolling along the road, bareheaded, in those red flounces! What is one to say? After dusk, with the dozen officers in garrison here watching the frontier! Watching the ladies who come and go, *per Dio!* Many of them, saving your presence, signore, are your own compatriots. You'll not deny that some of them are a little free—a little bold. What will you have? Out of their own country! What else were the use of travel? But this one; eh! she's not out of her own country yet. Italians are Italians, signore, up to the frontier—eh! eh!" And the Signore Bonifazio indulged in a laugh the most *goguenard*. "Nevertheless, I have not kept an inn these twenty years without learning to know the sheep from the goats. This is an honorable lady, signore; it is for that reason that I have offered to you to sup with her. The other sort! One can always sup with them!"

It seemed to me that my host's fluent commentary was no meager foretaste of Italian frankness. I approached the window. The fair object of our conversation stood at the foot of the stone staircase which ascended to the

inn door, with the toe of her shoe resting upon the first
step. She was looking fixedly and pensively up the road
toward Switzerland. Her hand clasped the knob of the iron
balustrade, and her slight fingers played an impatient measure. She had begun to interest me. Her dark eyes, intent
upon the distant turn of the road, seemed to expand with
a vague expectancy. Whom was she looking for? Of what
romance of Italy was she the heroine? The *maître d'hôtel*
appeared at the head of the steps, and with a flourish of
his napkin, announced that the signora was served. She
started a little and then lightly shrugged her shoulders.
At the same moment, I caught her eye as I stood gazing
from the window. With a just visible deepening of her
color, she slowly ascended the steps. I was suddenly
seized with a sense of being dingy, travel-stained, un-
presentable to a woman so charming. I hastily retreated to
my room, and surveying myself in my dressing glass,
objurgated fortune that I lacked the wherewithal to amend
my attire. But I could at least change my cravat. I had
no sooner replaced my black necktie by a blue one than
it occurred to me that the signora would observe the difference; but what then? It would hardly offend her.
With a timid hope that it might faintly gratify her as
my only feasible tribute to the honor of her presence, I
returned to the dining room. She was seated and had
languidly addressed herself to the contents of her soup
plate. The worthy Bonifazio had adorned our little table
with four lighted candles and a centerpiece of Alpine
flowers. As I installed myself opposite my companion,
after having greeted her and received a murmured response,
it seemed to me that I was sitting down to one of those
factitious repasts which are served upon the French stage,
when the table has been moved close to the footlights and
the ravishing young widow and the romantic young artist
begin to manipulate the very *nodus* of the comedy.
Was the signora a widow? Our attendant, with his crimson
cap, his well-salted discourse, his light-handed gestures,
and his smile from behind the scenes, might have passed
for a classic *valet de théâtre*. I had the appetite of a man
who had been walking since sunrise, but I found ample
occasion, while I plied my knife and fork, to inspect the
signora. She merely pretended to eat; and to appeal, per-

haps, from the overflattering intentness of my vision, she opened an idle conversation with Bonifazio. I listened admiringly while the glancing shuttle of Italian speech passed rapidly from lip to lip. It was evident, frequently, that she remained quite heedless of what he said, losing herself forever in a kind of fretful intensity of thought. The repast was long and multifarious, and as he time and again removed her plate with its contents untouched, mine host would catch my eye and roll up his own with an air of mock commiseration, turning back his thumb at the same moment toward the region of his heart. *"Un coup de tête,"* he took occasion to murmur as he reached over me to put down a dish. But the more I looked at the fair unknown, the more I came to suspect that the source of her unrest lay deeper than in the petulance of wounded vanity. Her face wore to my eye the dignity of a deep resolution—a resolution taken in tears and ecstasy. She was some twenty-eight years of age, I imagined, though at moments a painful gravity resting upon her brow gave her the air of a woman who in youth has anticipated old age. How beautiful she was by natural gift I am unable to say, for at this especial hour of her destiny, her face was too serious to be fair and too interesting to be plain. She was pale, worn, and weary-looking, but in the midst of her weariness there flickered a fierce impatience of delay and forced repose. She was a gentle creature, turned brave and adventurous by the stress of fate. It burned bright in her soft, grave eyes, this longing for the larger freedom of the tarrying morrow. A dozen chance gestures indicated the torment of her spirit—the constant rapping of her knife against the table, her bread crumbed to pieces but uneaten, the frequent change from posture to posture of her full and flexible figure, shifting through that broad range of attitude—the very gamut of gracefulness—familiar to Italian women.

The repast advanced without my finding a voice to address her. Her secret puzzled me, whatever it was, but I confess that I was afraid of it. A *coup de tête!* Heaven only knew how direful a *coup!* My mind was flooded by the memory of the rich capacity of the historic womanhood of Italy. I thought of Lucrezia Borgia, of Bianca Capello, of the heroines of Stendahl. My fair friend seemed invested with an atmosphere of candid passion, which placed her quite apart from the ladies of my own land. The gallant soul of the Signor Bonifazio, however, had little sufferance for this pedantic view of things. Shocked by my apparent indifference to the privilege of my rare position, he thrust me by the shoulders into the conversation. The signora eyed me for a moment not ungraciously, and then, "Do you understand Italian?" she asked.

I had come to Italy with an ear quite unattuned, of course, to the spoken tongue, but the mellow cadence of the signora's voice rang in upon my senses like music. "I understand *you*," I said.

She looked at me gravely, with the air of a woman used to receive compliments without any great flutter of vanity. "Are you English?" she abruptly asked.

"English is my tongue."

"Have you come from Switzerland?"

"He has walked from Brieg!" proclaimed our host.

"Ah, you happy men, who can walk—who can run—who needn't wait for coaches and conductors!" The signora uttered these words with a smile of acute though transient irony. They were followed by a silence. Bonifazio, seeing the ice was broken, retired with a flourish of his napkin and a contraction of his eyelids as much in the nature of a wink as his respect for me, for the signora, and for himself allowed. What was the motive of the signora's impatience? I had a presentiment that I should learn. The Italians are confidential—of this I had already received sufficient assurance—and my companion, with her lucid eye and her fine, pliable lips, was a bright example of the eloquent genius of her race. She sat idly pressing with her fork the crimson substance out of a plateful of figs, without raising them to her lips.

"You are going over into Switzerland," I said, "and you are in haste."

She eyed me a minute suspiciously. "Yes, I'm in haste!"

"I, who have just begun to feel the charm of Italy," I rejoined, "can hardly understand being in haste to leave it."

"The charm of Italy!" cried the signora with a slightly

cynical laugh. "Foreigners have a great deal to say about it."

"But you, a good Italian, certainly know what we mean."

She shrugged her shoulders—an operation she performed more gracefully than any woman I ever saw, unless it be Mlle. Madeleine Brohan of the Théâtre Français. "For me it has no charm! I have been unhappy here. Happiness for me is *there!*" And with a superb nod of her head she indicated the transalpine world. Then, as if she had spoken a thought too freely, she rose suddenly from her chair and walked away to the window. She stepped out on the narrow balcony, looked intently for an instant up and down the road and at the band of sky above it, and then turned back, into the room. I sat in my place, divided between my sense of the supreme sweetness of figs and my wonder at my companion's mystery. "It's a fine night!" she said. And with a little jerk of impatience she flung herself into an armchair near the table. She leaned back, with her skirt making a great wave around her and her arms folded. I went on eating figs. There was a long silence. "You've eaten at least a dozen figs. You'll be ill!" said the signora at last.

This was friendly in its frankness. "Ah, if you only knew how I enjoy them!" I cried, laughing. "They are the first I ever tasted. And this the first Asti wine. We don't have either in the north. If figs and Asti wine are for anything in your happiness, signora," I added, "you had better not cross the Alps. See, the figs are all gone. Do you think it would hurt me to have any more?"

"Truly," cried the signora, "I don't know what you English are made of!"

"You think us very coarse and given up altogether to eating and drinking?" She gave another shrug tempered by a smile. "To begin with, I am not an Englishman. And in the second place, you'd not call me coarse if you knew— if you only knew what I feel this evening. Eh! Such thick-coming fancies!"

"What are your fancies?" she demanded with a certain curiosity gleaming in her dark eye.

"I *must* finish this Asti!" This I proceeded to do. I am very glad I did, moreover, as I borrowed from its mild

and luscious force something of the courage with which
I came to express myself. "I don't know how it is that
I'm talking Italian at such a rate. Somehow the words
come to me. I know it only from books. I have never
talked it."

"You speak as well," the signora graciously affirmed,
"as if you had lived six months in the country."

"Half an hour in your society," said I, "is as profitable
as six months elsewhere."

"Bravo!" she responded. "An Italian himself couldn't
say it better."

Sitting before me in the vague candlelight, beautiful,
pale, dark-browed, sad, the signora seemed to me an incorporate image of her native land. I had come to pay it
my devotions. Why not perform them at her feet? "I
have come on a pilgrimage," I said. "To understand what
I mean, you must have lived, as I have lived, in a land
beyond the seas, barren of romance and grace. This Italy
of yours, on whose threshold I stand, is the home of
history, of beauty, of the arts—of all that makes life
splendid and sweet. Italy, for us dull strangers, is a magic
word. We cross ourselves when we pronounce it. We are
brought up to think that when we have earned leisure
and rest—at some bright hour, when fortune smiles—
we may go forth and cross oceans and mountains and
see on Italian soil the primal substance—the Platonic
'idea'—of our consoling dreams and our richest fancies.
I have been brought up in these thoughts. The happy
hour has come to me—Heaven be praised!—while I am
still young and strong and sensitive. Here I sit for the
first time in the enchanted air in which love and faith
and art and knowledge are warranted to become deeper
passions than in my own chilly clime. I begin to behold
the promise of my dreams. It's Italy. How can I tell you
what that means to one of us? Only see already how
fluent and tender of speech I've become. The air has a perfume; everything that enters my soul, at every sense, is
a suggestion, a promise, a performance. But the best thing
of all is that I have met *you, bella donna!* If I were to tell
you how you seem to me, you would think me either in-
sincere or impertinent. *Ecco!*"

She listened to me without changing her attitude or

without removing her fathomless eyes from my own. Their blue-black depths, indeed, seemed to me the two wells of poetic unity, from which I drew my somewhat transcendental allocution. She was puzzled, I think, and a little amused, but not offended. Anything from an Inglese! But it was doubtless grateful to feel these rolling waves of sentiment break softly at her feet, chained as she was, like Andromeda, to the rock of a lonely passion. With an admirable absence of *minauderie,* "How is it that I seem to you, signore?" she asked.

I left my place and came round and stood in front of her. "Ever since I could use my wits," I said, "I have done little else than fancy dramas and romances and love tales, and lodge them in Italy. You seem to me as the heroine of all my stories."

There was perhaps a slight movement of coquetry in her reply: "Your stories must have been very dull, signore," and she gave a sad smile.

"Nay, in future," I said, "my heroines shall be more like you than ever. Where do you come from?" I seated myself in the chair she had quitted. "But it's none of my business," I added. "From anywhere. In Milan or Venice, in Bologna or Florence, Rome or Naples, every grave old palazzo I pass, I shall fancy your home. I'm going the whole length of Italy. My soul, what things I shall see!"

"You please me, signore. I say to you what I wouldn't say to another. I came from Florence. Shall you surely go there?"

"I have reasons," I said, "for going there more than elsewhere. In Florence"—and I hesitated, with a momentary horror at my perfect unreserve—"in Florence I am to meet my—my *promessa sposa.*"

The signora's face was instantly irradiated by a generous smile. "Ah!" she said, as if now for the first time she really understood me.

"As I say, she has been spending the summer at the Baths of Lucca. She comes to Florence with her mother in the middle of September."

"Do you love her?"

"Passionately."

"Is she pretty?"

"Extremely. But not like you. Very fair, with blue eyes."

"How long since you have seen her?"

"A year."

"And when are you to be married?"

"In November, probably, in Rome."

She covered me for a moment with a glance of the largest sympathy. "Ah, what happiness!" she cried abruptly.

"After our marriage," I said, "we shall go down to Naples. Do you know Naples?"

Instead of answering, she simply gazed at me, and her beautiful eyes seemed to grow larger and more liquid. Suddenly, while I sat in the benignant shadow of her vision, I saw the tears rise to her lids. Her face was convulsed and she burst into sobs. I remember that in my amazement and regret I suddenly lost my Italian. "Dearest lady," I cried in my mother tongue, "forgive me that I have troubled you. Share with me at least the sorrow that I have aroused." In an instant, however, she had brushed away her tears and her face had recovered its pale composure. She tried even to smile.

"What will you think of me?" she asked. "What do you think of me already?"

"I think you are an extremely interesting woman. You are in trouble. If there is anything I can do for you, pray say the word."

She gave me her hand. I was on the point of raising it to my lips. "No—*à l'Anglaise*," she said, and she lightly shook my own. "I like you—you're an honest man —you don't try to make love to me. I should like to write a note to your *promessa sposa* to tell her she may trust you. You can't help me. I have committed myself to God and the Holy Virgin. They will help me. Besides, it's only a little longer. Eh, it's a long story, signore! What is said in your country of a woman who travels alone at night without even a servant?"

"Nothing is said. It's very common."

"Ah! Women must be very happy there, or very unhappy! Is it never supposed of a woman that she has a lover? That is worst of all."

"Fewer things are 'supposed' of women there than

here. They live more in the broad daylight of life. They make their own law."

"They must be very good then—or very bad. So that a man of fancy like you, with a taste for romance, has to come to poor Italy, where he can suppose at leisure! But we are not all romance, I assure you. With me, I promise you, it's no light-minded *coup de tête*." And the signora enforced her candid assurance with an almost imperious nod. "I know what I'm doing. Eh! I'm an old woman. I've waited and waited. But now my hour has come! Ah, the heavenly freedom of it! Ah, the peace— the joy! Just God, I thank thee!" And sitting back in her chair, she folded her hands on her bosom and closed her eyes in a kind of ecstasy. Opening them suddenly, she perceived, I suppose, my somewhat intent and dilated countenance. Breaking then into a loud, excited laugh, "How you stare at me!" she cried. "You think I've at least poisoned my husband. No, he's safe and sound and strong! On the contrary, I've forgiven him. I forgive him with all my heart, with all my soul; there! I call upon you to witness it. I bear him no rancor. I wish never to think of him again; only let me never see him—never hear of him! Let him never come near me: I shall never trouble him! Hark!" She had interrupted herself and pressed her hand with a startled air upon my arm. I listened, and in a moment my ear caught the sound of rolling wheels on the hard high road. With a great effort at self-composure, apparently, she laid her finger on her lips. "If it should be he—if it should be he!" she murmured. "Heaven preserve me! Do go to the window and see."

I complied and perceived a two-horse vehicle advancing rapidly from the Italian quarter. "It's a carriage of some sort from Italy," I said. "But what—whom do you fear?"

She rose to her feet. "That my husband should overtake me," and she gave a half-frantic glance round the room, like a hunted stag at bay. "If it should be he, protect me! Do something, say something—anything! Say I'm not fit to go back to him. He wants me because he thinks me good. Say I'm not good—to your knowledge. Oh, signore—Holy Virgin!" Recovering herself, she sank into a chair and sat stiff and superb, listening to the deepening sound of the wheels. The vehicle approached, reached the inn, passed it, and went on to the Dogana.

"You're safe," I said. "It's not a posting-chaise, but a common wagon with merchandise."

With a hushed sign of relief, she passed her hand over her brow, and then looking at me: "I have lived these three days in constant terror. I believe in my soul he has come in pursuit of me; my hope is in my having gained time through his being absent when I started. My nerves are broken. I have neither slept nor eaten, nor till now have I spoken. But I *must* speak! I'm frank; it's good to take a friend when you find one."

I confess that to have been thus freely admitted by the fair fugitive into the whirling circle of her destiny was one of the keenest emotions of my life. "I know neither the motive of your flight nor the goal of your journey," I answered; "but if I may help you and speed you, I will joyfully turn back from the threshold of Italy and give you whatever furtherance my company may yield. To go with you," I added, smiling, "will be to remain in Italy, I assure you."

She acknowledged my offer with a glance more potent than words. "I'm going to a friend," she said after a silence. "To accept your offer would be to make friendship cheap. He is lying ill at Geneva; otherwise I shouldn't be *thus!* But my head is on fire. This room is close; it smells of supper. Do me the favor to accompany me into the air."

She gathered her shawl about her shoulders, I offered her my arm, and we passed into the entry toward the door. In the doorway stood mine host, with his napkin under his arm. He drew himself up as we approached, and as if to deprecate a possible imputation of scandal, honored us with a bow of the most ceremonious homage. We descended the steps and strolled along the road toward the Swiss frontier. A vague remnant of daylight seemed to linger imprisoned in the narrow gorge. We passed the Dogana and left the village behind us. My thoughts reverted as we went to the aching blank of my fancy as I entered Isella an hour before. It seemed to palpitate now with a month's experience. Beyond the village, a narrow bridge spans the stream and leads to a path which climbs the opposite hillside. We diverged from the road and lingered on the bridge while the sounding torrent gushed beneath us, flashing in the light of the few stars which sparkled in our narrow strip of sky, like diamonds tacked upon a band of velvet. I remained silent, thinking a passive silence the most graceful tribute to the signora's generous intentions. "I will tell you all!" she said at last. "Do you think me pretty? But you needn't answer. The less you think so, the more you'll say it. I *was* pretty! I don't pretend to be so now. I have suffered too much. I have a miserable fear that when *he* sees me, after these three years, he'll notice the loss of my beauty. But, *povrino!* He is perhaps too ill to notice anything. He is young—a year younger than I—twenty-seven. He is a painter; he has a most beautiful talent. He loved me four years ago, before my marriage. He was a friend of my poor brother, who was fatally wounded at the battle of Mentana, where he fought with Garibaldi. My brother, Giuseppino, was brought home with his wound; he died in a week. Ernesto came to make a drawing of his face before we lost it forever. It was not the first time I had seen him, but it was the first time we understood each other. I was sitting by poor Giuseppino's bedside, crying—crying! He, too, cried while he drew and made great blisters on the paper. I know where to look for them still. They loved each other devotedly. I, too, had loved my brother, for my mother was dead, and my father was not a mother—not even a father! Judge for yourself! We placed together the love which each of us had borne for Giuseppino, and it made a great love for each other. It was a misfortune; but how could we help it? He had nothing but his talent, which as yet was immature. I had nothing at all but the poor little glory of my father's being a Marchese, without a *soldo*, and my prettiness! But you see what has become of that! My father was furious to have given his only son to that scoundrel of a Garibaldi, for he is of that way of thinking. You should have heard the scene he made me when poor Ernesto in despair asked leave to marry me. My husband, whom I had never seen or at least never noticed, was at that time in treaty for my hand. By his origin he was little better than a peasant, but he had made a fortune in trade, and he was very well pleased to marry a *marchesina*. It's not every man who is willing to take a

penniless girl; it was the first chance and perhaps the best.
So I was given over blindfold, bound hand and foot, to
that brute. Eh! What I hadn't brought in cash I had to
pay down in patience. If I were to tell you what I've suffered these three years, it would bring tears to your eyes
—Inglese as you are. But they are things which can't be
told. He is a peasant, with the soul of a peasant—the
taste, the manners, the vices of a peasant. It was my great
crime that I was proud. I had much to be proud of. If
I had only been a woman of his own sort! To pay him
in his own coin! Ernesto, of course, had been altogether
suppressed. He proposed to me to escape with him before
my marriage, and I confess to you that I would have
done it if I could. I tried in vain; I was too well watched.
I implored him then to go away till better days, and he
at last consented to go to Paris and pursue his studies.
A week after my marriage he came to bid me farewell.
My husband had taken me to Naples to make me believe
I was not wretched. Ernesto followed me, and I contrived
to see him. It lasted three minutes by the clock; I have
not seen him since. In three years I have had five letters
from him; they are here in my dress. I am sure of his
love; I don't need to have him write, to tell me. I have
answered him twice. These letters—seven in all, in three
years!—are all my husband has to reproach me with. He
is furious at not having more. He knows, of course, that
I love another; he knows that to bear such things a woman
must borrow strength somewhere. I have had faith, but
it has not been all faith! My husband has none; nothing
is sacred to him, not the Blessed Virgin herself. If you
were to hear the things he says about the Holy Father!
I have waited and waited. I confess it, I have hoped at times
that my husband would die. But he has the health of a peasant. He used to strike me—to starve me—to lock me up
without light or fire. I appealed to my father, but, I'm sorry
to say it, my father is a coward! Heaven forgive me! I'm saying dreadful things here! But, ah, signore, let me breathe at
last! I've waited and waited, as I say, for this hour! Heaven
knows I have been good. Though I stand here now, I have
not trifled with my duties. It's not coquetry! I determined to
endure as long as I could, and then to break—to break
forever! A month ago strength and courage left me; or

rather, they came to me! I wrote to Ernesto that I would come to him. He answered that he would come down to meet me—if possible at Milan. Just afterward he wrote me in a little scrawl in pencil that he had been taken ill in Geneva, and that if I could, I must come alone, before he got worse. Here I am then, alone, pursued, frantic with ignorance and dread. Heaven only keep him till I come. I shall do the rest! Exactly how I left home, I can't tell you. It has been like a dream! My husband—God be praised!—was obliged to make a short absence on business, of which I took advantage. My great trouble was getting a little money. I never have any. I sold a few trinkets for a few francs—hardly enough! The people saw I was too frightened to make a stand, so that they cheated me. But if I can only come to the end! I'm certain that my husband has pursued me. Once I get to Switzerland, we can hide. Meanwhile I'm in a fever. I've lost my head. I began very well, but all this delay has so vexed and confused me. I hadn't even the wit to secure a place in the coach at Domo d'Ossola. But I shall go if I have to sit on the roof—to crouch upon the doorstep. If I had only a little more money, so that I needn't wait for coaches. To overtake me, my husband, for once in his life, won't count his *lire!*"

I listened with a kind of awe to this torrent of passionate confidence. I had got more even than I had bargained for. The current of her utterance seemed to gather volume as it came, and she poured out her tragic story with a sort of rapturous freedom. She had unburdened at last her heavy heart. As she spoke, the hot breath of her eloquence seemed to pass far beyond my single attentive sense and mingle joyously with the free air of the night. Her tale, in a measure, might be untrue or imperfect, but her passion, her haste, her sincerity, were imperiously real. I felt, as I had never felt it, the truth of the poet's claim for his touch of nature. I became conscious of a hurrying share in my companion's dread. I seemed to hear in the trembling torrent the sound of rapid wheels. I expected every moment to see the glare of lights along the road, before the inn, then a strong arm locked about her waist, and, in the ray of a lantern from the carriage window, to catch the mute agony of her solemn eyes. My heart beat fast; I was part and parcel of a romance! Come! The dénouement shouldn't fail by any prosy fault of mine.

"How I've talked!" cried the signora after a brief pause. "And how you stare at me! Eh! Don't be afraid. I've said all, and it has done me good. You'll laugh with your *promessa sposa* about that crazy creature who was flying from her husband. The idea of people not being happy in marriage, you'll say to her!"

"I thank you with all my heart," I said, "for having trusted me as you have. But I'm almost sorry you have taken the time. You oughtn't to be lingering here while your husband is making the dust fly."

"That's easy to say, signore, but I can't walk to Brieg, like you. A carriage costs a hundred and fifty francs. I have only just enough to pay my place in the coach."

I drew out my *portemonnaie* and emptied it in my hand; it contained a hundred and seventy francs. *"Ecco!"* I said, holding them out to her.

She glanced at them an instant and then, with a movement which effectually rounded and completed my impression of her simple and passionate sincerity, seized with both her hands my own hand as it held them. "Ah, the Blessed Virgin be praised!" she cried. "Ah, you're an angel from heaven! Quick, quick! A carriage, a carriage!"

She thrust the money into her pocket, and without waiting for an answer, hurried back to the road and moved swiftly toward the inn. I overtook her as she reached the doorstep, where our host was enjoying a pipe in the cool. "A carriage!" she cried. "I must be off. Quick, without delay! I have the money; you shall be well paid. Don't tell me you haven't one. There must be one here. Find one, prepare it, lose not a moment. Do you think I can lie tossing here all night? I shall put together my things and give you ten minutes! You, sir, see that they hurry!" And she rapidly entered the house.

Bonifazio stared, somewhat aghast at the suddenness and the energy of her requisition. Fearing that he might not be equal to the occasion, I determined to take him by his gallantry. "Come, my friend," I said, "don't stand scratching your head, but *act*. I know you admire the signora. You don't want to see so charming a woman in trouble. You don't wish to have a scandal in your inn. It is of the first importance that she should leave in ten minutes. Stir up your hostler."

A wise grin illumined his face. "Ah," said he, "it's as bad as that. I had my notions. I'll do what I can." He exerted himself to such good purpose that in the incredibly short period of twenty minutes, a small closed carriage was drawn by a couple of stout horses to the door. Going in to summon the fair fugitive, I found her in the dining room, where, fretting with impatience, and hooded and shawled, she had suffered a rather bungling chambermaid to attempt the insertion of a couple of necessary pins. She swept past me on her exit as if she had equally forgotten my face and her obligations, and entered the carriage with passionate adjurations of haste. I followed her and watched her take her place, but she seemed not even to see me. My hour was over. I had added an impulse to her straining purpose; its hurrying current had left me alone on the brink. I could not resist the influence of a poignant regret at having dropped from her consciousness. Learning from a peasant who was lounging near at hand that an easy footpath wound along the side of the mountain and struck the high road at the end of half an hour's walk, I immediately discovered and followed it. I saw beneath me in the dimness as I went the white high road, with the carriage slowly beginning its ascent. Descending at last from the slope, I met the vehicle well on its way up the mountain and motioned to the driver to stop. The poor signora, haunted with the fear of interruption, thrust her pale face from the window. Seeing me, she stared an instant almost vacantly, and then passing her hand over her face, broke into a glorious smile. Flinging open the carriage door from within, she held out her two hands in farewell.

"Give me your blessing," she cried, "and take mine! I had almost forgotten you. Love is selfish, signore. But I should have remembered you later and cried with gratitude. My Ernesto will write to you. Give me your card—write me your address, there in the carriage lamp. No? As you please, then. Think of me kindly. And the young girl you marry—use her well—love her if only a little—it will be enough. We ask but a little, but we need that. *Addio!*" and she raised her two hands to her lips, seemed for an instant to exhale her whole soul upon her finger-tips, and flung into the air a magnificent Italian kiss.

I returned along the winding footpath more slowly, a wiser, possibly a sadder man than a couple of hours before. I had entered Italy, I had tasted of sentiment, I had assisted at a drama. It was a good beginning. I found Bonifazio finishing his pipe before the inn. "Well, well, signore," he cried, "what does it all mean?"

"Aren't you enough of an Italian to guess?" I asked.

"Eh, eh, it's better to be an Inglese and to be told," cried Bonifazio with a twinkle.

"You must sleep tonight with an ear open," I said. "A personage will arrive posthaste from Domo. Stop him if you can."

Bonifazio scratched his head. "If a late supper or an early breakfast will stop him!" he murmured. I looked deep into his little, round eye, expecting to read there the recipe for the infusion of a sleeping potion into *café au lait*.

My room that night was close and hot, and my bed none of the best. I tossed about in a broken sleep. I dreamed that I was lying ill in a poor tavern at Naples, waiting, waiting with an aching heart, for the arrival from the Baths of Lucca of a certain young lady, who had been forced by her mother, Mrs. B. of Philadelphia, into a cruel marriage with a wealthy Tuscan *contadino*. At last, I seemed to hear a great noise without and a step on the stairs; through the opened door rushed in my *promessa sposa*. Her blue eyes were bright with tears, and she wore a flounced black dress trimmed with crimson silk. The next moment she was kneeling at my bedside crying, "Ernesto, Ernesto!" At this point I awoke into the early morning. The noise of horses and wheels and voices came up from outside. I sprang from my bed and stepped to my open window. The huge, high-piled, yellow diligence from Domo d'Ossola had halted before the inn. The door of the coupé was open; from the aperture half-emerged the personage. "A peasant," she had called him, but he was well *dicrotti*, though he *had* counted his lire and taken the diligence. He struck me as of an odd type for an Italian: dark, sandy hair; a little sandy mustache, waxed at the ends, and sandy wiskers *à l'Anglaise*. He had a broad face, a large nose, and a small, keen eye, without any visible brows. He wore a yellow silk handkerchief tied as a nightcap about his head, and in spite of the heat, he was very much muffled. On the steps stood Bonifazio, cap in hand, smiling and obsequious.

"Is there a lady here?" demanded the gentleman from the coupé. "A lady alone—good-looking—with little luggage?"

"No lady, signore," said Bonifazio. "Alas! I have an empty house. If *eccellenza* would like to descend——"

"Have you had a lady—yesterday, last night? Don't lie."

"We had three, *eccellenza*, a week ago—three Scotch ladies going to Baveno. Nay, three days since we had a *prima donna* on her way to Milan."

"Damn your Scotch *prima donna!*" said the other. "Have you had my wife?"

"The wife of *eccellenza*? Save the ladies I mention, we have had neither wife nor maid. Would *eccellenza* like a cup of coffee?"

"Sangue di Dio!" was *eccellenza's* sole response. The coupé door closed with a slam, the conductor mounted, the six horses started, and the great mountain coach rolled away.

The Madonna of the Future

WE had been talking about the masters who had achieved but a single masterpiece—the artists and poets who but once in their lives had known the divine afflatus and touched the high level of the best. Our host had been showing us a charming little cabinet picture by a painter whose name we had never heard, and who, after this one spasmodic bid for fame, had apparently relapsed into fatal mediocrity. There was some discussion as to the frequency of this phenomenon, during which, I observed, H—— sat silent, finishing his cigar with a meditative air and looking at the picture, which was being handed round the table. "I don't know how common a case it is," he said at last, "but I've seen it. I've known a poor fellow who painted his one masterpiece, and"— he added with a smile—"he didn't even paint that. He made his bid for fame and missed it." We all knew H—— for a clever man who had seen much of men and manners and had a great stock of reminiscences. Someone immediately questioned him further, and, while I was engrossed with the raptures of my neighbor over the little picture, he was induced to tell his tale. If I were to doubt whether it would bear repeating, I should only have to remember how that charming woman, our hostess, who had left the table, ventured back in rustling rose color to pronounce our lingering a want of gallantry, and, finding us a listening circle, had sunk into her chair in spite of our cigars and heard the story out so graciously that when the catastrophe was reached, she glanced across at me and showed me a tender tear in each of her beautiful eyes.

It relates to my youth, and to Italy: two fine things!

(H——— began.) I had arrived late in the evening at Florence, and while I finished my bottle of wine at supper, had fancied that, tircd traveler though I was, I might pay the city a finer compliment than by going vulgarly to bed. A narrow passage wandered darkly away out of the little square before my hotel, and looked as if it bored into the heart of Florence. I followed it and at the end of ten minutes emerged upon a great piazza, filled only with the mild autumn moonlight. Opposite rose the Palazzo Vecchio like some huge civic fortress, with the great bell tower springing from its embattled verge like a mountain pine from the edge of a cliff. At its base, in its projected shadow, gleamed certain dim sculptures which I wonderingly approached. One of the images, on the left of the palace door, was a magnificent colossus shining through the dusky air like some young god of defiance. In a moment I recognized him as Michelangelo's David. I turned with a certain relief from his sinister strength to a slender figure in bronze, stationed beneath the high, light loggia which opposes the free and elegant span of its arches to the dead masonry of the palace; a figure supremely shapely and graceful; gentle, almost, in spite of his holding out with his light, nervous arm the snaky head of the slaughtered Gorgon. His name is Perseus, and you may read his story, not in the Greek mythology, but in the memoirs of Benvenuto Cellini. Glancing from one of these fine fellows to the other, I probably uttered some irrepressible commonplace of praise, for, as if provoked by my voice, a man rose from the steps of the loggia, where he had been sitting in the shadow, and addressed me in good English—a small, slim personage, clad in a sort of black velvet tunic (as it seemed), and with a mass of auburn hair, which gleamed in the moonlight escaping from a little medieval biretta. In a tone of the most insinuating deference, he asked me for my "impressions." He seemed picturesque, fantastic, slightly unreal. Hovering there in this consecrated neighborhood, he might have passed for the genius of aesthetic hospitality—if the genius of aesthetic hospitality were not commonly some shabby little *custode,* flourishing a calico pocket handkerchief and openly resentful of the divided franc. This fantasy was made none the less plausible by the fine tirade with which he greeted my embarrassed silence.

"I've known Florence long, sir, but I've never known her so lovely as tonight. It's as if the ghosts of her past were abroad in the empty streets. The present is sleeping; the past hovers about us like a dream made visible. Fancy the old Florentines strolling up in couples to pass judgment on the last performance of Michel, of Benvenuto! We should come in for a precious lesson if we might overhear what they say. The plainest burgher of them, in his cap and gown, had a taste in the matter! That was the prime of art, sir. The sun stood high in heaven, and his broad and equal blaze made the darkest places bright and the dullest eyes clear. We live in the evening of time! We grope in the gray dusk, carrying each our poor little taper of selfish and painful wisdom, holding it up to the great models and to the dim ideal and seeing nothing but overwhelming greatness and dimness. The days of illumination are gone! But do you know I fancy—I fancy"— and he grew suddenly almost familiar in this visionary fervor—"I fancy the light of that time rests upon us here for an hour! I have never seen the David so grand, the Perseus so fair! Even the inferior productions of John of Bologna and of Baccio Bandinelli seem to realize the artist's dream. I feel as if the moonlit air were charged with the secrets of the masters, and as if, standing here in religious contemplation, we might—we might witness a revelation!" Perceiving at this moment, I suppose, my halting comprehension reflected in my puzzled face, this interesting rhapsodist paused and blushed. Then with a melancholy smile, "You think me a moonstruck charlatan, I suppose. It's not my habit to hang about the piazza and pounce upon innocent tourists. But tonight, I confess, I'm under the charm. And then, somehow, I fancied you, too, were an artist!"

"I'm not an artist, I'm sorry to say, as you must understand the term. But pray make no apologies. I am also under the charm; your eloquent reflections have only deepened it."

"If you're not an artist, you're worthy to be one!" he rejoined with a bow. "A young man who arrives at Florence late in the evening and, instead of going prosaically to bed or hanging over the travelers' book at his hotel, walks forth without loss of time to pay his *devoirs* to the beautiful, is a young man after my own heart!"

The mystery was suddenly solved; my friend was an American! He must have been, to take the picturesque so prodigiously to heart. "None the less so, I trust," I answered, "if the young man is a sordid New Yorker."

"New Yorkers," he solemnly proclaimed, "have been munificent patrons of art!"

For a moment I was alarmed. Was this midnight reverie mere Yankee enterprise, and was he simply a desperate brother of the brush who had posted himself here to extort an "order" from a sauntering tourist? But I was not called to defend myself. A great brazen note broke suddenly from the faroff summit of the bell tower above us and sounded the first stroke of midnight. My companion started, apologized for detaining me, and prepared to retire. But he seemed to offer so lively a promise of further entertainment that I was indisposed to part with him, and suggested that we should stroll homeward together. He cordially assented, so we turned out of the piazza, passed down before the statued arcade of the Uffizi, and came out upon the Arno. What course we took I hardly remember, but we roamed slowly about for an hour, my companion delivering by snatches a sort of moon-touched aesthetic lecture. I listened in puzzled fascination and wondered who the deuce he was. He confessed with a melancholy but all-respectful head shake to his American origin. "We are the disinherited of art!" he cried. "We are condemned to be superficial! We are excluded from the magic circle. The soil of American perception is a poor little, barren, artificial deposit. Yes! We are wedded to imperfection. An American, to excel, has just ten times as much to learn as a European. We lack the deeper sense. We have neither taste nor tact nor force. How should we have them? Our crude and garish climate, our silent past, our deafening present, the constant pressure about us of unlovely circumstance, are as void of all that nourishes and prompts and inspires the artist as my sad heart is void of bitterness in saying so! We poor aspirants must live in perpetual exile."

"You seem fairly at home in exile," I answered, "and

Florence seems to me a very pretty Siberia. But do you know my own thought? Nothing is so idle as to talk about our want of a nutritive soil, of opportunity, of inspiration, and all the rest of it. The worthy part is to do something fine! There's no law in our glorious Constitution against that. Invent, create, achieve! No matter if you've to study fifty times as much as one of these! What else are you an artist for? Be you our Moses," I added, laughing and laying my hand on his shoulder, "and lead us out of the house of bondage!"

"Golden words—golden words, young man!" he cried with a tender smile. " 'Invent, create, achieve!' Yes, that's our business: I know it well. Don't take me, in Heaven's name, for one of your barren complainers—querulous cynics who have neither talent nor faith. I'm at work!"—and he glanced about him and lowered his voice as if this were a quite peculiar secret,—"I'm at work night and day. I've undertaken a *creation!* I'm no Moses; I'm only a poor, patient artist; but it would be a fine thing if I were to cause some slender stream of beauty to flow in our thirsty land! Don't think me a monster of conceit," he went on as he saw me smile at the avidity with which he adopted my fantasy. "I confess that I'm in one of those moods when great things seem possible! This is one of my nervous nights—I dream waking! When the south wind blows over Florence at midnight, it seems to coax the soul from all the fair things locked away in her churches and galleries; it comes into my own little studio with the moonlight and sets my heart beating too deeply for rest. You see I am always adding a thought to my conception! This evening I felt that I couldn't sleep unless I had communed with the genius of Michel!"

He seemed deeply versed in local history and tradition, and he expatiated *con amore* on the charms of Florence. I gathered that he was an old resident and that he had taken the lovely city into his heart. "I owe her everything," he declared. "It's only since I came here that I have really lived, intellectually. One by one, all profane desires, all mere worldly aims, have dropped away from me and left me nothing but my pencil, my little notebook (and he tapped his breast pocket) and the worship of the pure masters—those who were pure because they were innocent, and those who were pure because they were strong!"

"And have you been very productive all this time?" I asked with amenity.

He was silent a while before replying. "Not in the vulgar sense!" he said at last. "I have chosen never to manifest myself by imperfection. The good in every performance I have reabsorbed into the generative force of new creations; the bad—there's always plenty of that—I have religiously destroyed. I may say, with some satisfaction, that I have not added a mite to the rubbish of the world. As a proof of my conscientiousness"—and he stopped short and eyed me with extraordinary candor, as if the proof were to be overwhelming—"I've never sold a picture! 'At least no merchant traffics in my heart!' Do you remember the line in Browning? My little studio has never been profaned by superficial, feverish, mercenary work. It's a temple of labor, but of leisure! Art is long. If we work for ourselves, of course we must hurry. If we work for her, we must often pause. She can wait!"

This had brought us to my hotel door, somewhat to my relief, I confess, for I had begun to feel unequal to the society of a genius of this heroic strain. I left him, however, not without expressing a friendly hope that we should meet again. The next morning my curiosity had not abated; I was anxious to see him by common daylight. I counted upon meeting him in one of the many aesthetic haunts of Florence, and I was gratified without delay. I found him in the course of the morning in the Tribune of the Uffizi—that little treasure chamber of perfect works. He had turned his back on the Venus di Medici, and with his two arms resting on the railing which protects the pictures and his head buried in his hands, he was lost in the contemplation of that superb triptych of Andrea Mantegna—a work which has neither the material splendor nor the commanding force of some of its neighbors, but which, glowing there with the loveliness of patient labor, suits possibly a more constant need of the soul. I looked at the picture for some time over his shoulder; at last, with a heavy sigh, he turned away and our eyes met. As he recognized me, a deep blush rose to his face; he fancied, perhaps, that he had made a fool of

himself overnight. But I offered him my hand with a
frankness which assured him I was not a scoffer. I knew
him by his ardent *chevelure;* otherwise, he was much
altered. His midnight mood was over, and he looked as
haggard as an actor by daylight. He was far older than I
had supposed, and he had less bravery of costume and
gesture. He seemed the quite poor, patient artist he had
proclaimed himself, and the fact that he had never sold
a picture was more obvious than glorious. His velvet
coat was threadbare, and his short, slouched hat, of an
antique pattern, revealed a rustiness which marked it an
"original," and not one of the picturesque reproductions
which brethren of his craft affect. His eye was mild and
heavy, and his expression singularly gentle and acquies-
cent; the more so for a certain pallid leanness of visage
which I hardly knew whether to refer to the consuming
fire of genius or to a meager diet. A very little talk, however, cleared his brow and brought back his eloquence.

"And this is your first visit to these enchanted halls?" he
cried. "Happy, thrice happy youth!" And taking me by
the arm, he prepared to lead me to each of the pre-
eminent works in turn and show me the cream of the
gallery. But before we left the Mantegna, he pressed my
arm and gave it a loving look. "*He* was not in a hurry," he
murmured. "He knew nothing of 'raw Haste, half-sister
to Delay'!" How sound a critic my friend was I am unable
to say, but he was an extremely amusing one; over-
flowing with opinions, theories, and sympathies, with dis-
quisition and gossip and anecdote. He was a shade too
sentimental for my own sympathies, and I fancied he was
rather too fond of superfine discriminations and of dis-
covering subtle intentions in the shallow felicities of chance.
At moments, too, he plunged into the sea of metaphysics
and floundered a while in waters too deep for intellectual
security. But his abounding knowledge and happy judgment
told a touching story of long attentive hours in this wor-
shipful company; there was a reproach to my wasteful
saunterings in so devoted a culture of opportunity. "There
are two moods," I remember his saying, "in which we may
walk through galleries, the critical and the ideal. They
seize us at their pleasure, and we can never tell which is
to take its turn. The critical mood, oddly, is the genial

one; the friendly, the condescending. It relishes the pretty
trivialities of art, its vulgar clevernesses, its conscious
graces. It has a kindly greeting for anything which looks
as if, according to his light, the painter had enjoyed doing
it—for the little Dutch cabbages and kettles, for the taper
fingers and breezy mantles of late-coming Madonnas, for the
little blue-hilled pastoral, skeptical Italian landscapes.
Then there are the days of fierce, fastidious longing—
solemn church-feasts of the intellect—when all vulgar
effort and all petty success is a weariness, and everything
but the best—the best of the best—disgusts. In these
hours, we are relentless aristocrats of taste. We'll not take
Michel for granted, we'll not swallow Raphael whole!"

The gallery of the Uffizi is not only rich in its possessions,
but peculiarly fortunate in that fine architectural accident,
as one may call it, which unites it—with the breadth of
river and city between them—to those princely chambers
of the Pitti Palace. The Louvre and the Vatican hardly
give you such a sense of sustained enclosure as those
long passages projected over street and stream to establish
a sort of inviolate transition between the two palaces of
art. We passed along the gallery in which those precious
drawings by eminent hands hang chaste and gray above the
swirl and murmur of the yellow Arno, and reached the
ducal saloons of the Pitti. Ducal as they are, it must be
confessed that they are imperfect as showrooms, and that,
with their deep-set windows and their massive moldings,
it is rather a broken light that reaches the pictured walls.
But here the masterpieces hang thick, and you seem to
see them in a luminous atmosphere of their own. And the
great saloons, with their superb dim ceilings, their outer
wall in splendid shadow, and the somber opposite glow
of mellow canvas and dusky gilding, make, themselves, almost as fine a picture as the Titians and Raphaels they
imperfectly reveal. We lingered briefly before many a
Raphael and Titian; but I saw my friend was impatient,
and I suffered him at last to lead me directly to the goal
of our journey—the most tenderly fair of Raphael's Vir-
gins, the Madonna in the Chair. Of all the fine pictures of
the world, it seemed to me this is the one with which
criticism has least to do. None betrays less effort, less of
the mechanism of effect and of the irrepressible discord

between conception and result, which shows dimly in so many consummate works. Graceful, human, near to our sympathies as it is, it has nothing of manner, of method; nothing, almost, of style; it blooms there in rounded softness, as instinct with harmony as if it were an immediate exhalation of genius. The figure melts away the spectator's mind into a sort of passionate tenderness which he knows not whether he has given to heavenly purity or to earthly charm. He is intoxicated with the fragrance of the tenderest blossom of maternity that ever bloomed on earth.

"That's what I call a fine picture," said my companion, after we had gazed awhile in silence. "I have a right to say so, for I've copied it so often and so carefully that I could repeat it now with my eyes shut. Other works are of Raphael: this *is* Raphael himself. Others you can praise, you can qualify, you can measure, explain, account for: this you can only love and admire. I don't know in what seeming he walked among men while this divine mood was upon him; but after it, surely, he could do nothing but die; this world had nothing more to teach him. Think of it a while, my friend, and you'll admit that I'm not raving. Think of his seeing that spotless image, not for a moment, for a day, in a happy dream, as a restless feverfit, not as a poet in a five minutes' frenzy, time to snatch his phrase and scribble his immortal stanza, but for days together, while the slow labor of the brush went on, while the foul vapors of life interposed, and the fancy ached with tension, fixed, radiant, distinct, as we see it now! What a master, certainly! But ah, what a seer!"

"Don't you imagine," I answered, "that he had a model, and that some pretty young woman?"

"As pretty a young woman as you please! It doesn't diminish the miracle! He took his hint, of course, and the young woman, possibly, sat smiling before his canvas. But, meanwhile, the painter's idea had taken wings. No lovely human outline could charm it to vulgar fact. He saw the fair form made perfect; he rose to the vision without tremor, without effort of wing; he communed with it face to face and resolved into finer and lovelier truth the purity which completes it as the perfume completes the rose. That's what they call idealism; the word's vastly abused, but the thing is good. It's my own creed, at any rate. Lovely Madonna, model at once and muse, I call you to witness that I too am an idealist!"

"An idealist, then," I said, half-jocosely, wishing to provoke him to further utterance, "is a gentleman who says to Nature in the person of a beautiful girl, 'Go to, you're all wrong! Your fine is coarse, your bright is dim, your grace is gaucherie. This is the way you should have done it!' Isn't the chance against him?"

He turned upon me almost angrily, but perceiving the genial flavor of my sarcasm, he smiled gravely. "Look at that picture," he said, "and cease your irreverent mockery! Idealism is *that!* There's no explaining it; one must feel the flame! It says nothing to Nature, or to any beautiful girl, that they'll not both forgive! It says to the fair woman, 'Accept me as your artist-friend, lend me your beautiful face, trust me, help me, and your eyes shall be half my masterpiece!' No one so loves and respects the rich realities of nature as the artist whose imagination caresses and flatters them. He knows what a fact may hold (whether Raphael knew, you may judge by his portrait behind us there, of Tommaso Inghirami); but his fancy hovers above it, as Ariel above the sleeping prince. There is only one Raphael, but an artist may still be an artist. As I said last night, the days of illumination are gone; visions are rare; we have to look long to see them. But in meditation we may still woo the ideal; round it, smooth it, perfect it. The result—the result"—here his voice faltered suddenly, and he fixed his eyes for a moment on the picture; when they met my own again they were full of tears—"the result may be less than this, but still it may be good; it may be *great!*" he cried with vehemence. "It may hang somewhere, in after years, in goodly company, and keep the artist's memory warm. Think of being known to mankind after some such fashion as this! Of hanging here through the slow centuries in the gaze of an altered world, living on and on in the cunning of an eye and hand that are part of the dust of ages, a delight and a law to remote generations; making beauty a force and purity an example!"

"Heaven forbid," I said, smiling, "that I should take the wind out of your sails; but doesn't it occur to you that beside being strong in his genius, Raphael was happy in a certain good faith of which we have lost the trick? There are people, I know, who deny that his spotless Madonnas are anything more than pretty blondes of that period, enhanced by the Raphaelesque touch, which they declare is a profane touch. Be that as it may, people's religious and aesthetic needs went hand in hand, and there was, as I may say, a demand for the Blessed Virgin, visible and adorable, which must have given firmness to the artist's hand. I'm afraid there is no demand now."

My companion seemed painfully puzzled; he shivered, as it were, in this chilling blast of skepticism. Then shaking his head with sublime confidence: "There is always a demand!" he cried. "That ineffable type is one of the eternal needs of man's heart; but pious souls long for it in silence, almost in shame; let it appear, and this faith grows brave. How *should* it appear in this corrupt generation? It can't be made to order. It could, indeed, when the order came, trumpet-toned, from the lips of the Church herself, and was addressed to genius panting with inspiration. But it can spring now only from the soil of passionate labor and culture. Do you really fancy that while, from time to time, a man of complete artistic vision is born into the world, that image can perish? The man who paints it has painted everything. The subject admits of every perfection, —form, color, expression, composition. It can be as simple as you please, and yet as rich, as broad and pure, and yet as full of delicate detail. Think of the chance for flesh in the little naked, nestling child, irradiating divinity; of the chance for drapery in the chaste and ample garment of the mother! Think of the great story you compress into that simple theme! Think, above all, of the mother's face and its ineffable suggestiveness, of the mingled burden of joy and trouble, and tenderness turned to worship, and the worship turned to far-seeing pity! Then look at it all in perfect line and lovely color, breathing truth and beauty and mastery!"

"*Anch' io son pittore!*" I cried. "Unless I'm mistaken, you've a masterpiece on the stocks. If you put all that in, you'll do more than Raphael himself did. Let me know when your picture is finished, and wherever in the wide world I may be, I'll post back to Florence and salute—the *Madonna of the future!*"

He blushed vividly and gave a heavy sigh, half of protest, half of resignation. "I don't often mention my picture, in so many words. I detest this modern custom of premature publicity. A great work needs silence, privacy, mystery even. And then, do you know, people are so cruel, so frivolous, so unable to imagine a man's wishing to paint a Madonna at this time of day, that I've been laughed at—laughed at, sir!" And his blush deepened to crimson. "I don't know what has prompted me to be so frank and trustful with you. You look as if you wouldn't laugh at me. My dear young man"—and he laid his hand on my arm—"I'm worthy of respect. Whatever my talents may be, I'm honest. There's nothing grotesque in a pure ambition, or in a life devoted to it!"

There was something so sternly sincere in his look and tone that further questions seemed impertinent. I had repeated opportunity to ask them, however, for after this we spent much time together. Daily, for a fortnight, we met by appointment to see the sights. He knew the city so well, he had strolled and lounged so often through its streets and churches and galleries, he was so deeply versed in its greater and lesser memories, so imbued with the local genius, that he was an altogether ideal *valet de place,* and I was glad enough to leave my Murray at home and gather facts and opinions alike from his gossiping commentary. He talked of Florence like a lover and admitted that it was a very old affair; he had lost his heart to her at first sight. "It's the fashion to talk of all cities as feminine," he said, "but, as a rule, it's a monstrous mistake. Is Florence of the same sex as New York, as Chicago? She's the sole true woman of them all; one feels towards her as a lad in his teens feels to some beautiful older woman with a 'history.' It's a sort of aspiring gallantry she creates." This disinterested passion seemed to stand my friend in stead of the common social ties; he led a lonely life, apparently, and cared for nothing but his work. I was duly flattered by his having taken my frivolous self into his favor, and by his generous sacrifice of precious hours, as they must have been, to my society. We spent many of these hours among those early paintings in

which Florence is so rich, returning ever and anon with
restless sympathies to wonder whether these tender blos-
soms of art had not a vital fragrance and savor more precious than the full-fruited knowledge of the later works. We
lingered often in the sepulchral chapel of San Lorenzo,
and watched Michelangelo's dim-visaged warrior sitting
there like some awful genius of doubt and brooding behind his eternal mask upon the mysteries of life. We stood
more than once in the little convent chambers where Fra
Angelico wrought, as if an angel indeed had held his
hand, and gathered that sense of scattered dews and early
bird notes which makes an hour among his relics seem
like a morning stroll in some monkish garden. We did all
this and much more, wandered into dark chapels, damp
courts, and dusty palace rooms in quest of lingering hints
of fresco and lurking treasures of carving. I was more and
more impressed with my companion's prodigious single-
ness of purpose. Everything was a pretext for some wild
aesthetic rhapsody or reverie. Nothing could be seen or
said that didn't end sooner or later in a glowing discourse
on the true, the beautiful, and the good. If my friend was
not a genius, he was certainly a monomaniac, and I
found as great a fascination in watching the odd lights
and shades of his character as if he had been a creature
from another planet. He seemed, indeed, to know very
little of this one, and lived and moved altogether in his
own little province of art. A creature more unsullied by
the world it is impossible to conceive, and I often thought
it a flaw in his artistic character that he hadn't a harmless
vice or two. It amused me vastly at times to think that he
was of our shrewd Yankee race; but, after all, there could
be no better token of his American origin than this same
fantastic fever. The very heat of his devotion was a sign
of conversion; those born to European opportunity
manage better to reconcile enthusiasm with comfort. He
had, moreover, all our native mistrust for intellectual discretion and our native relish for sonorous superlatives.
As a critic he was vastly more generous than just, and his
mildest terms of approbation were "glorious," "superb,"
and "magnificent." The small change of admiration seemed
to him no coin for a gentleman to handle; and yet, frank
as he was intellectually, he was personally altogether a

mystery. His professions, somehow, were all half-professions, and his allusions to his work and circumstances left something dimly ambiguous in the background. He was modest and proud and never spoke of his domestic matters. He was evidently poor, yet he must have had some slender independence, since he could afford to make so merry over the fact that his culture of ideal beauty had never brought him a penny. His poverty, I supposed, was his motive for never inviting me to his lodging nor mentioning its whereabouts. We met either in some public place or at my hotel, where I entertained him as freely as I might without appearing to be moved by charity. He seemed always hungry, which was his nearest approach to a "redeeming vice." I made a point of asking no impertinent questions, but each time we met I ventured to make some respectful allusion to the *magnum opus,* to inquire, as it were, as to its health and progress. "We're getting on, with the Lord's help," he would say with a grave smile. "We're doing well. You see I have the grand advantage that I lose no time. These hours I spend with you are pure profit. They're *suggestive!* Just as the truly religious soul is always at worship, the genuine artist is always in labor. He takes his property wherever he finds it, and learns some precious secret from every object that stands up in the light. If you but knew the rapture of observation! I gather with every glance some hint for light, for color or relief! When I get home, I pour out my treasures into the lap of my Madonna. Oh, I'm not idle! *Nulla dies sine linea.*"

I was introduced in Florence to an American lady whose drawing room had long formed an attractive place of reunion for the foreign residents. She lived on the fourth floor, and she was not rich; but she offered her visitors very good tea, little cakes at option, and conversation not quite to match. Her conversation had mainly an aesthetic flavor, for Mrs. Coventry was famously "artistic." Her apartment was a sort of Pitti Palace *au petit pied.* She possessed "early masters" by the dozen—a cluster of Peruginos in her dining room, a Giotto in her boudoir, an Andrea del Sarto over her parlor chimney piece. Backed by these treasures, and by innumerable bronzes, mosaics, majolica dishes, and little worm-eaten diptychs showing angular saints on gilded panels, our hostess enjoyed the dignity of a sort of high priestess of the arts. She always wore on her bosom a huge miniature copy of the Madonna della Seggiola. Gaining her ear quietly one evening, I asked her whether she knew that remarkable man, Mr. Theobald.

"Know him!" she exclaimed; "know poor Theobald! All Florence knows him, his flame-colored locks, his black velvet coat, his interminable harangues on the beautiful, and his wonderous Madonna that mortal eye has never seen and that mortal patience has quite given up expecting."

"Really," I cried, "you don't believe in his Madonna?"

"My dear ingenuous youth," rejoined my shrewd friend, "has he made a convert of you? Well, we all believed in him once; he came down upon Florence and took us by storm. Another Raphael, at the very least, had been born among men, and poor, dear America was to have the credit of him. Hadn't he the very hair of Raphael flowing down on his shoulders? The hair, alas, but not the head! We swallowed him whole, however; we hung upon his lips and proclaimed his genius on the housetops. The women were all dying to sit to him for their portraits and be made immortal, like Leonardo's Joconde. We decided that his manner was a good deal like Leonardo's—mysterious and inscrutable and fascinating. Mysterious it certainly was; mystery was the beginning and the end of it. The months passed by, and the miracle hung fire; our master never produced his masterpiece. He passed hours in the galleries and churches, posturing, musing, and gazing; he talked more than ever about the beautiful, but he never put brush to canvas. We had all subscribed, as it were, to the great performance, but as it never came off, people began to ask for their money again. I was one of the last of the faithful; I carried devotion so far as to sit to him for my head. If you could have seen the horrible creature he made of me, you would admit that even a woman with no more vanity than will tie her bonnet straight must have cooled off then. The man didn't know the very alphabet of drawing! His strong point, he intimated, was his sentiment; but is it a consolation, when one has been painted a fright, to

know it has been done with peculiar gusto? One by one,
I confess, we fell away from the faith, and Mr. Theobald didn't lift his little finger to preserve us. At the first
hint that we were tired of waiting and that we should like
the show to begin, he was off in a huff. 'Great work requires time, contemplation, privacy, mystery! O ye of
little faith!' We answered that we didn't insist on a great
work; that the fine-art tragedy might come at his convenience; that we merely asked for something to keep us
from yawning, some inexpensive little *lever de rideau.*
Hereupon the poor man took his stand as a genius mis-
conceived and persecuted, an *âme méconnue,* and
washed his hands of us from that hour! No, I believe he
does me the honor to consider me the head and front
of the conspiracy formed to nip his glory in the bud—a
bud that has taken twenty years to blossom. Ask him if he
knows me, and he'd tell you I'm a horribly ugly old woman
who has vowed his destruction because he wouldn't paint
her portrait as a *pendant* to Titian's Flora. I fancy
that since then he has had none but chance followers,
innocent strangers like yourself, who have taken him at
his word. The mountain's still in labor; I've not heard
that the mouse has been born. I pass him once in a
while in the galleries, and he fixes his great dark eyes on
me with a sublimity of indifference, as if I were a bad
copy of a Sassoferrato. It is a long time ago now that I
heard that he was making studies for a Madonna who was
to be a résumé of all the other Madonnas of the Italian
school, like that antique Venus who borrowed a nose from
one great image and an ankle from another. It's certainly
a masterly idea. The parts may be fine, but when I
think of my unhappy portrait I tremble for the whole.
He has communicated this fine idea under the pledge
of solemn secrecy to fifty chosen spirits, to every one
he has ever been able to buttonhole for five minutes.
I suppose he wants to get an order for it, and he's not
to blame, for heaven knows how he lives. I see by
your blush," my hostess frankly continued, "that you
have been honored with his confidence. You needn't
be ashamed, my dear young man; a man of your
age is none the worse for a certain generous credulity.
Only allow me to give you a word of advice: keep your

credulity out of your pockets. Don't pay for the picture till it's delivered. You've not been treated to a
peep at it, I imagine. No more have your fifty predeces-
sors in the faith. There are people who doubt whether there
is any picture to be seen. I fancy, myself, that if one were
to get into his studio, one would find something very like
the picture in that tale of Balzac's—a mere mass of in-
coherent scratches and daubs, a jumble of dead paint!"

I listened to this pungent recital in silent wonder. It had
a painfully plausible sound, and was not inconsistent with
certain shy suspicions of my own. My hostess was a clever
woman, and presumably a generous one. I determined
to let my judgment wait upon events. Possibly she was
right; but if she was wrong, she was cruelly wrong! Her
vision of my friend's eccentricities made me impatient
to see him again and examine him in the light of public
opinion. On our next meeting, I immediately asked him
if he knew Mrs. Coventry. He laid his hand on my arm
and gave me a sad smile. "Has she taxed *your* gallantry at
last?" he asked. "She's a foolish woman. She's frivolous
and heartless, and she pretends to be serious and kind.
She prattles about Giotto's second manner and Vittoria
Colonna's liaison with 'Michel'—one would think that
Michel lived across the way and was expected in to take
a hand at whist—but she knows as little about art, and
about the conditions of production, as I know about Bud-
dhism. She profanes sacred words," he added more vehemently, after a pause. "She cares for you only as someone to hand teacups in that horrible mendacious little
parlor of hers, with its trumpery Peruginos! If you
can't dash off a new picture every three days to show to
her guests, she tells them in plain English you're an im-
poster!"

This attempt of mine to test Mrs. Coventry's accuracy
was made in the course of a late-afternoon walk to the
quiet old church of San Miniato, on one of the hilltops
which directly overlook the city, from whose gate you are
guided to it by a stony and cypress-bordered walk, which
seems a most fitting avenue to a shrine. No spot is more
propitious to lingering repose than the broad terrace in
front of the church, where, lounging against the parapet,
you may glance in slow alternation from the black and yel-

low marbles of the church façade, seamed and cracked
with time and wind-sown with a tender flora of its own,
down to the full domes and slender towers of Florence and
over to the blue sweep of the wide-mouthed cup of
mountains into whose hollow the little treasure city has
been dropped. I had proposed, as a diversion from the
painful memories evoked by Mrs. Coventry's name,
that Theobald should go with me the next evening to the
opera, where some rarely played work was to be given.
He declined, as I had half-expected, for I had observed that
he regularly kept his evenings in reserve and never alluded to his manner of passing them. "You have reminded me before," I said, smiling, "of that charming
speech of the Florentine painter in Alfred de Mus-
set's Lorenzaccio: *'I do no harm to anyone. I pass my
days in my studio. On Sunday, I go to the Annunziata or
to Santa Maria; the monks think I have a voice; they dress
me in a white gown and a red cap, and I take a share in
the choruses, sometimes I do a little solo: these are the
only times I go into public. In the evening, I visit my
sweetheart; when the night is fine, we pass it on her balcony.'* I don't know whether you have a sweetheart, or
whether she has a balcony. But if you're so happy, it's
certainly better than trying to find a charm in a third-
rate prima donna."

He made no immediate response, but at last he turned
to me solemnly. "Can you look upon a beautiful woman
with reverent eyes?"

"Really," I said, "I don't pretend to be sheepish, but
I should be sorry to think I was impudent." And I asked
him what in the world he meant. When at last I had assured him that I could undertake to temper admiration
with respect, he informed me, with an air of religious
mystery, that it was in his power to introduce me to the
most beautiful woman in Italy. "A beauty with a soul!"

"Upon my word," I cried, "you're extremely fortunate.
And I shall rejoice to witness the conjunction."

"This woman's beauty," he answered, "is a lesson, a
morality, a poem! It's my daily study."

Of course, after this, I lost no time in reminding him of
what, before we parted, had taken the shape of a promise. "I feel somehow," he had said, "as if it were a sort

of violation of that privacy in which I have always contemplated her beauty. This is friendship, my friend. No hint of her existence has ever fallen from my lips. But with too great a familiarity, we are apt to lose a sense of the real value of things, and you perhaps will throw some new light upon it and offer a fresher interpretation."

We went accordingly by appointment to a certain ancient house in the heart of Florence—the precinct of the Mercato Vecchio—and climbed a dark, steep staircase to the very summit of the edifice. Theobald's beauty seemed as jealously exalted above the line of common vision as the Belle aux Cheveux d'Or in her tower top. He passed without knocking into the dark vestibule of a small apartment, and flinging open an inner door, ushered me into a small saloon. The room seemed mean and somber, though I caught a glimpse of white curtains swaying gently at an open window. At a table, near a lamp, sat a woman dressed in black, working at a piece of embroidery. As Theobald entered, she looked up calmly, with a smile; but seeing me, she made a movement of surprise and rose with a kind of stately grace. Theobald stepped forward, took her hand, and kissed it, with an indescribable air of immemorial usage. As he bent his head, she looked at me askance, and I thought she blushed.

"*Ecco la Serafina!*" said Theobald frankly, waving me forward. "This is a friend, and a lover of the arts," he added, introducing me. I received a smile, a courtesy, and a request to be seated.

The most beautiful woman in Italy was a person of a generous Italian type and of great simplicity of demeanor. Seated again at her lamp with her embroidery, she seemed to have nothing whatever to say. Theobald, bending toward her in a sort of Platonic ecstasy, asked her a dozen paternally tender questions as to her health, her state of mind, her occupations, and the progress of her embroidery, which he examined minutely and summoned me to admire. It was some portion of an ecclesiastical vestment —yellow satin wrought with an elaborate design of silver and gold. She made answer in a full, rich voice, but with a brevity which I hesitated whether to attribute to native reserve or to the profane constraint of my presence. She had been that morning to confession; she had also been to market, and had bought a chicken for dinner. She felt very happy; she had nothing to complain of, except that the people for whom she was making her vestment, and who furnished her materials, should be willing to put such rotten silver thread into the garment, as one might say, of the Lord. From time to time, as she took her slow stitches, she raised her eyes and covered me with a glance which seemed at first to denote a placid curiosity, but in which, as I saw it repeated, I thought I perceived the dim glimmer of an attempt to establish an understanding with me at the expense of our companion. Meanwhile, as mindful as possible of Theobald's injunction of reverence, I considered the lady's personal claims to the fine compliment he had paid her.

That she was indeed a beautiful woman I perceived, after recovering from the surprise of finding her without the freshness of youth. Her beauty was of a sort which, in losing youth, loses little of its essential charm, expressed for the most part as it was in form and structure and, as Theobald would have said, in "composition." She was broad and ample, low-browed and large-eyed, dark and pale. Her thick, brown hair hung low beside her cheek and ear and seemed to drape her head with a covering as chaste and formal as the veil of a nun. The poise and carriage of her head was admirably free and noble, and the more effective that their freedom was at moments discreetly corrected by a little sanctimonious droop, which harmonized admirably with the level gaze of her dark and quiet eye. A strong, serene physical nature and the placid temper which comes of no nerves and no troubles seemed this lady's comfortable portion. She was dressed in plain, dull black, save for a sort of dark blue kerchief which was folded across her bosom and exposed a glimpse of her massive throat. Over this kerchief was suspended a little silver cross. I admired her greatly, and yet with a large reserve. A certain mild intellectual apathy belonged properly to her type of beauty, and had always seemed to round and enrich it, but this bourgeois Egeria, if I viewed her right, betrayed a rather vulgar stagnation of mind. There might have been once a dim, spiritual light in her face, but it had long since begun to wane. And furthermore, in plain prose, she was growing stout. My disap-

pointment amounted very nearly to complete disenchantment when Theobald, as if to facilitate my covert inspection, declaring that the lamp was very dim and that she
would ruin her eyes without more light, rose and fetched
a couple of candles from the mantelpiece, which he placed,
lighted, on the table. In this brighter illumination I perceived that our hostess was decidedly an elderly woman.
She was niether haggard nor worn nor gray: she was
simply coarse. The "soul" which Theobald had promised
seemed scarcely worth making such a point of; it was no
deeper mystery than a sort of matronly mildness of lip
and brow. I would have been ready even to declare that
that sanctified bend of the head was nothing more than the
trick of a person constantly working at embroidery. It
occurred to me even that it was a trick of a less innocent
sort; for, in spite of the mellow quietude of her wits, this
stately needlewoman dropped a hint that she took the situation rather less *au sérieux* than her friend. When he
rose to light the candles, she looked across at me with
a quick, intelligent smile and tapped her forehead with
her forefinger; then, as, from a sudden feeling of compassionate loyalty to poor Theobald, I preserved a blank
face, she gave a little shrug and resumed her work.

What was the relation of this singular couple? Was
he the most ardent of friends or the most respectful of
lovers? Did she regard him as an eccentric youth whose
benevolent admiration of her beauty she was not ill-
pleased to humor at this small cost of having him climb
into her little parlor and gossip of summer nights? With
her decent and somber dress, her simple gravity, and that
fine piece of priestly needlework, she looked like some
pious lay member of a sisterhood, living by special permission outside her convent walls. Or was she maintained
here aloft by her friend in comfortable leisure, so that he
might have before him the perfect, eternal type, uncor-
rupted and untarnished by the struggle for existence? Her
shapely hands, I observed, were very fair and white; they
lacked the traces of what is called "honest toil."

"And the pictures, how do they come on?" she asked
of Theobald, after a long pause.

"Finely, finely! I have here a friend whose sympathy
and encouragement give me new faith and ardor."

Our hostess turned to me, gazed at me a moment rather inscrutably, and then tapping her forehead with the gesture she had used a minute before, "He has a magnificent genius!" she said with perfect gravity.

"I'm inclined to think so," I answered with a smile.

"Eh, why do you smile?" she cried. "If you doubt it, you must see the *bambino!*" And she took the lamp and conducted me to the other side of the room, where on the wall, in a plain, black frame, hung a large drawing in red chalk. Beneath it was festooned a little bowl for holy water. The drawing represented a very young child, entirely naked, half-nestling back against his mother's gown, but with his two little arms outstretched, as if in the act of benediction. It was executed with singular freedom and power, and yet seemed vivid with the sacred bloom of infancy. A sort of dimpled elegance and grace, in the midst of its boldness, recalled the touch of Correggio. "That's what he can do!" said my hostess. "It's the blessed little boy whom I lost. It's his very image, and the Signor Teobaldo gave it me as a gift. He has given me many things beside!"

I looked at the picture for some time and admired it vastly. Turning back to Theobald, I assured him that if it were hung among the drawings in the Uffizi and labeled with a glorious name, it would hold its own. My praise seemed to give him extreme pleasure; he pressed my hands, and his eyes filled with tears. It moved him apparently with the desire to expatiate on the history of the drawing, for he rose and made his adieux to our companion, kissing her hand with the same mild ardor as before. It occurred to me that the offer of a similar piece of gallantry on my own part might help me to know what manner of woman she was. When she perceived my intention, she withdrew her hand, dropped her eyes solemnly, and made me a severe courtesy. Theobald took my arm and led me rapidly into the street.

"And what do you think of the divine Serafina?" he cried with fervor.

"It's certainly good solid beauty!"

He eyed me an instant askance, and then seemed hurried along by the current of remembrance. "You should have seen the mother and the child together, seen them as I first saw them—the mother with her head draped in a shawl, a divine trouble in her face, and the *bambino* pressed to her bosom. You would have said, I think, that Raphael had found his match in common chance. I was coming in, one summer night, from a long walk in the country, when I met this apparition at the city gate. The woman held out her hand. I hardly knew whether to say, 'What do you want?' or to fall down and worship. She asked for a little money. I saw that she was beautiful and pale. She might have stepped out of the stable of Bethlehem! I gave her money and helped her on her way into the town. I had guessed her story. She, too, was a maiden mother, and she had been turned out into the world in her shame. I felt in all my pulses that here was my subject marvelously realized. I felt like one of the old convent artists who had had a vision. I rescued them, cherished them, watched them as I would have done some precious work of art, some lovely fragment of fresco discovered in a moldering cloister. In a month—as if to deepen and consecrate the pathos of it all—the poor little child died. When she felt that he was going, she held him up to me for ten minutes, and I made that sketch. You saw a feverish haste in it, I suppose; I wanted to spare the poor little mortal the pain of his position. After that, I doubly valued the mother. She is the simplest, sweetest, most natural creature that ever bloomed in this brave old land of Italy. She lives in the memory of her child, in her gratitude for the scanty kindness I have been able to show her, and in her simple religion! She's not even conscious of her beauty; my admiration has never made her vain. Heaven knows I've made no secret of it. You must have observed the singular transparency of her expression, the lovely modesty of her glance. And was there ever such a truly virginal brow, such a natural classic elegance in the wave of the hair and the arch of the forehead? I've studied her; I may say I know her. I've absorbed her little by little; my mind is stamped and imbued, and I have determined now to clinch the impression; I shall at last invite her to sit for me!"

" 'At last—at last'?" I repeated, in much amazement. "Do you mean that she has never done so yet?"

"I've not really had—a—a sitting," said Theobald,

speaking very slowly. "I've taken notes, you know; I've got my grand fundamental impression. That's the great thing! But I've not actually had her as a model, posed and draped and lighted, before my easel."

What had become for the moment of my perception and my tact I am at a loss to say; in their absence, I was unable to repress a piece of *brusquerie* which I was destined to regret. We had stopped at a turning, beneath a lamp. "My poor friend," I exclaimed, laying my hand on his shoulder, "you've *dawdled!* She's an old, old woman —for a Madonna!"

It was as if I had brutally struck him; I shall never forget the long, slow, almost ghastly look of pain with which he answered me. "Dawdled—old, old!" he stammered. "Are you joking?"

"Why my dear fellow, I suppose you don't take the woman for twenty?"

He drew a long breath and leaned against a house, looking at me with questioning, protesting, reproachful eyes. At last, starting forward, and grasping my arm: "Answer me solemnly: does she seem to you truly old? Is she wrinkled, is she faded, am I blind?"

Then at last I understood the immensity of his illusion; how, one by one, the noiseless years had ebbed away and left him brooding in charmed inaction, forever preparing for a work forever deferred. It seemed to me almost a kindness now to tell him the plain truth. "I should be sorry to say you're blind," I answered, "but I think you're deceived. You've lost time in effortless contemplation. Your friend was once young and fresh and virginal; but, I protest, that was some years ago. Still, she has *beaux restes*. By all means make her sit for you!" I broke down; his face was too horribly reproachful.

He took off his hat and stood passing his handkerchief mechanically over his forehead. *"De beaux restes?* I thank you for sparing me the plain English. I must make up my Madonna out of *beaux restes!* What a masterpiece she'll be! Old—old! Old—old!" he murmured.

"Never mind her age," I cried, revolted at what I had done, "never mind my impression of her! You have your memory, your notes, your genius. Finish your picture in a month. I proclaim it beforehand a masterpiece, and I hereby offer you for it any sum you may choose to ask."

He stared, but he seemed scarcely to understand me. "Old—old!" he kept stupidly repeating. "If she is old, what am I? If her beauty has faded, where—where is my strength? Has life been a dream? Have I worshiped too long—have I loved too well?" The charm, in truth, was broken. That the chord of illusion should have snapped at my light, accidental touch showed how it had been weakened by excessive tension. The poor fellow's sense of wasted time, of vanished opportunity, seemed to roll in upon his soul in waves of darkness. He suddenly dropped his head and burst into tears.

I led him homeward with all possible tenderness, but I attempted neither to check his grief, to restore his equanimity, nor to unsay the hard truth. When we reached my hotel, I tried to induce him to come in. "We'll drink a glass of wine," I said, smiling, "to the completion of the Madonna!"

With a violent effort he held up his head, mused for a moment with a formidably somber frown, and then giving me his hand, "I'll finish it," he cried, "in a month! No, in a fortnight! After all, I have it *here!*" and he tapped his forehead. "Of course she's old! She can afford to have it said of her—a woman who has made twenty years pass like a twelvemonth! Old—old! Why, sir, she shall be eternal!"

I wished to see him safely to his own door, but he waved me back and walked away with an air of resolution, whistling and swinging his cane. I waited a moment and then followed him at a distance and saw him proceed to cross the Santa Trinità Bridge. When he reached the middle, he suddenly paused, as if his strength had deserted him, and leaned upon the parapet, gazing over into the river. I was careful to keep him in sight; I confess that I passed ten very nervous minutes. He recovered himself at last, and went his way, slowly and with hanging head.

That I should really have startled poor Theobald into a bolder use of his long-garnered stores of knowledge and taste, into the vulgar effort and hazard of production, seemed at first reason enough for his continued silence and absence; but as day followed day without his either

calling or sending me a line, and without my meeting him
in his customary haunts, in the galleries, in the chapel at
San Lorenzo, or strolling between the Arno-side and the
great hedge-screen of verdure which, along the drive of
the Cascine, throws the fair occupants of barouche and
phaeton into such becoming relief—as for more than a
week I got neither tidings nor sight of him, I began to
fear that I had fatally offended him and that, instead of
giving a wholesome impetus to his talent, I had brutally
paralyzed it. I had a wretched suspicion that I had made
him ill. My stay at Florence was drawing to a close, and
it was important that, before resuming my journey, I
should assure myself of the truth. Theobald to the last had
kept his lodging a mystery, and I was altogether at a loss
where to look for him. The simplest course was to make
inquiry of the beauty of the Mercato Vecchio, and I confess that unsatisfied curiosity as to the lady herself coun-
seled it as well. Perhaps I had done her injustice, and she
was as immortally fresh and fair as he conceived her. I
was, at any rate, anxious to behold once more the ripe
enchantress who had made twenty years pass for a
twelvemonth. I repaired accordingly, one morning, to her
abode, climbed the interminable staircase, and reached
her door. It stood ajar, and as I hesitated whether to
enter, a little serving maid came clattering out with an
empty kettle, as if she had just performed some savory
errand. The inner door, too, was open, so I crossed the
little vestibule and entered the room in which I had formerly been received. It had not its evening aspect. The
table, or one end of it, was spread for a late breakfast,
and before it sat a gentleman—an individual, at least,
of the male sex—dealing justice upon a beefsteak and
onions and a bottle of wine. At his elbow, in friendly
proximity, was placed the lady of the house. Her attitude,
as I entered, was not that of an enchantress. With one
hand she held in her lap a plate of smoking macaroni;
with the other she had lifted high in air one of the pendu-
lous filaments of this succulent compound, and was in the
act of slipping it gently down her throat. On the uncovered
end of the table, facing her companion, were ranged half
a dozen small statuettes, of some snuff-colored substance

resembling terra cotta. He, brandishing his knife with ardor, was apparently descanting on their merits.

Evidently, I darkened the door. My hostess dropped her macaroni—into her mouth—and rose hastily with a harsh exclamation and a flushed face. I immediately perceived that the Signora Serafina's secret was even better worth knowing than I had supposed, and that the way to learn it was to take it for granted. I summoned my best Italian, I smiled and bowed and apologized for my intrusion; and in a moment, whether or no I had dispelled the lady's irritation, I had, at least, recalled her prudence. I was welcome, she said; I must take a seat; this was another friend of hers, also an artist, she declared with a smile which was almost amiable. Her companion wiped his mustache and bowed with great civility. I saw at a glance that he was equal to the situation. He was presumably the author of the statuettes on the table, and he knew a money-spending *forestiere* when he saw one. He was a small, wiry man, with a clever, impudent, *retroussé* nose, a sharp little black eye, and waxed ends to his mustache. On the side of his head he wore jauntily a little crimson velvet smoking cap, and I observed that his feet were encased in brilliant slippers. On Serafina's remarking with dignity that I was the friend of Mr. Theobald, he broke out into that fantastic French in which Italians so freely indulge and declared with fervor that Mr. Theobald was a magnificent genius.

"I'm sure I don't know," I answered with a shrug. "If you're in a position to affirm it, you have the advantage of me. I've seen nothing from his hand but the bambino yonder, which certainly is fine."

He declared that the bambino was a masterpiece, a pure Correggio. It was only a pity, he added with a knowing smile, that the sketch had not been made on some good bit of genuine old panel. The Signora Serafina hereupon protested that Mr. Theobald was the soul of honor and that he would never lend himself to a deceit. "I'm not a judge of genius," she said, "and I know nothing of pictures. I'm but a poor, simple widow, but I know that the Signor Teobaldo has the heart of an angel and the virtue of a saint. He's my benefactor," she added sententiously. The afterglow of the somewhat sinister flush with which she had greeted me still lingered in her cheek, and perhaps did not favor her beauty; I could not but fancy it a wise custom of Theobald's to visit her only by candle-light. She was coarse, and her poor adorer was a poet.

"I have the greatest esteem for him," I said; "it is for this reason that I have been uneasy at not seeing him for ten days. Have you seen him? Is he perhaps ill?"

"Ill! Heaven forbid!" cried Serafina, with genuine vehemence.

Her companion uttered a rapid expletive and reproached her with not having been to see him. She hesitated a moment; then she simpered the least bit and bridled. "He comes to see me—without reproach! But it would not be the same for me to go to him, though, indeed, you may almost call him a man of holy life."

"He has the greatest admiration for you," I said. "He would have been honored by your visit."

She looked at me a moment sharply. "More admiration than you. Admit that!" Of course, I protested with all the eloquence at my command, and the Signore Serafina then confessed that she had taken no fancy to me on my former visit, and that, Theobald not having returned, she believed I had poisoned his mind against her. "It would be no kindness to the poor gentleman, I can tell you that," she said. "He has come to see me every evening for years. It's a long friendship! No one knows him as well as I."

"I don't pretend to know him, or to understand him," I said. "He's a mystery! Nevertheless he seems to me a little—" And I touched my forehead and waved my hand in the air.

Serafina glanced at her companion a moment, as if for inspiration. He contented himself with shrugging his shoulders, as he filled his glass again. The signora hereupon gave me a more softly insinuating smile than would have seemed likely to bloom on so candid a brow. "It's for that that I love him!" she said. "The world has so little kindness for such persons. It laughs at them, and despises them, and cheats them. He is too good for this wicked life! It's his fancy that he finds a little paradise up here in my poor apartment. If he thinks so, how can I help it? He has a strange belief—really, I ought to be ashamed to tell you—that I resemble the Blessed Virgin: Heaven forgive me! I let him think what he pleases, so long as it makes him happy. He was very kind to me once, and I am not one that forgets a favor. So I receive him every evening civilly, and ask after his health, and let him look at me on this side and that! For that matter, I may say it without vanity, I was worth looking at once! And he's not always amusing, poor man! He sits sometimes for an hour without speaking a word, or else he talks away without stopping on art and nature, and beauty and duty, and fifty fine things that are all so much Latin to me. I beg you to understand that he has never said a word to me that I mightn't decently listen to. He may be a little cracked, but he's one of the saints."

"Eh!" cried the man, "the saints were all a little cracked!"

Serafina, I fancied, left part of her story untold, but she told enough of it to make poor Theobald's own statement seem intensely pathetic in its exalted simplicity. "It's a strange fortune, certainly," she went on, "to have such a friend as this dear man—a friend who's less than a lover and more than a friend." I glanced at her companion, who preserved an impenetrable smile, twisted the end of his mustache, and disposed of a copious mouthful. Was *he* less than a lover? "But what will you have?" Serafina pursued. "In this hard world, one mustn't ask too many questions; one must take what comes and keep what one gets. I've kept my good friend for twenty years, and I do hope that, at this time of day, signore, you've not come to turn him against me!"

I assured her that I had no such design and that I should vastly regret disturbing Mr. Theobald's habits or convictions. On the contrary, I was alarmed about him, and I should immediately go in search of him. She gave me his address and a florid account of her sufferings at his nonappearance. She had not been to him for various reasons, chiefly because she was afraid of displeasing him, as he had always made such a mystery of his home. "You might have sent this gentleman!" I ventured to suggest.

"Ah," cried the gentleman, "he admires the Signora

Serafina, but he wouldn't admire me." And then, confidentially, with his finger on his nose, "He's a purist!"

I was about to withdraw, on the promise that I would inform the Signora Serafina of my friend's condition, when her companion, who had risen from table and girded his loins apparently for the onset, grasped me gently by the arm and led me before the row of statuettes. "I perceive by your conversation, signore, that you are a patron of the arts. Allow me to request your honorable attention for these modest products of my own ingenuity. They are brand-new, fresh from my atelier, and have never been exhibited in public. I have brought them here to receive the verdict of the Signora Serafina, who is a good critic, for all she may pretend to the contrary. I am the inventor of this peculiar style of statuette—of subject, manner, material, everything. Touch them, I pray you; handle them; you needn't fear. Delicate as they look, it is impossible they should break! My various creations have met with great success. They are especially admired by Americans. I have sent them all over Europe—to London, Paris, Vienna! You may have observed some little specimens in Paris, on the Boulevard, in a shop of which they constitute the specialty. There is always a crowd about the window. They form a very pleasing ornament for the mantelshelf of a *jeune homme élégant,* for the boudoir of a *jolie femme.* You couldn't make a prettier present to a person with whom you wished to exchange a harmless joke. It is not classic art, signore, of course; but, between ourselves, isn't classic art sometimes rather a bore? Caricature, burlesque—*la charge,* as the French say—has hitherto been confined to paper, to the pen and pencil. Now, it has been my inspiration to introduce it into statuary. For this purpose I have invented a peculiar plastic compound which you will permit me not to divulge. That's my secret, signore! It's as light, you perceive, as cork, and yet as firm as alabaster! I frankly confess that I really pride myself as much on this little stroke of chemical ingenuity as upon the other element of novelty in my creations—my types. What do you say to my types, signore? The idea is bold; does it strike you as happy? Cats and monkeys—monkeys and cats—all human life is there! Human life, of course, I mean, viewed with the eye of the satirist! To combine sculpture and satire, signore, has been my unprecedented ambition. I flatter myself that I have not egregiously failed."

As this jaunty Juvenal of the chimney piece delivered himself of his seductive allocution, he took up his little groups successively from the table, held them aloft, turned them about, rapped them with his knuckles, and gazed at them lovingly with his head on one side. They consisted each of a cat and a monkey, fantastically draped, in some preposterously sentimental conjunction. They exhibited a certain sameness of motive and illustrated chiefly the different phases of what, in delicate terms, may be called gallantry and coquetry; but they were strikingly clever and expressive, and were at once very perfect cats and monkeys and very natural men and women. I confess, however, that they failed to amuse me. I was doubtless not in a mood to enjoy them, for they seemed to me peculiarly cynical and vulgar. Their imitative felicity was revolting. As I looked askance at the complacent little artist, brandishing them between finger and thumb and caressing them with an amorous eye, he seemed to me himself little more than an exceptionally intelligent ape. I mustered an admiring grin, however, and he blew another blast. "My figures are studied from life! I have a little menagerie of monkeys whose frolics I contemplate by the hour. As for the cats, one has only to look out of one's back window! Since I have begun to examine these expressive little brutes, I have made many profound observations. Speaking, signore, to a man of imagination, I may say that my little designs are not without a philosophy of their own. Truly, I don't know whether the cats and monkeys imitate us, or whether it's we who imitate them." I congratulated him on his philosophy, and he resumed: "You will do me the honor to admit that I have handled my subjects with delicacy. Eh, it was needed, signore! I have been free, but not licentious. Just a hint, you know! You may see as much or as little as you please. These little groups, however, are no measure of my invention. If you will favor me with a call at my studio, I think that you will admit that my combinations are really infinite. I likewise execute figures to command. You have perhaps some little motive—the fruit of your own

philosophy of life, signore—which you would like to have
interpreted. I can promise to work it up to your satisfaction; it shall be as malicious as you please. Allow me
to present you with my card, and to remind you that my
prices are moderate. Only sixty francs for a little group
like that. My statuettes are as durable as bronze—*ære
perennius,* signore—and, between ourselves, I think they
are more amusing."

As I pocketed his card, I glanced at the worthy Serafina, wondering whether she had an eye for contrasts. She
had picked up one of the little couples and was tenderly
dusting it with a feather broom.

What I had just seen and heard had so deepened my
compassionate interest in my deluded friend that I took
a summary leave and made my way directly to the house
designated by the Signora Serafina. It was in an obscure
corner of the opposite side of the town, and presented a
sombre and squalid appearance. An old woman in the
doorway, on my inquiring for Theobald, ushered me in
with a mumbled blessing and an expression of relief that
the poor gentleman had a friend. His lodging seemed to
consist of a single room at the top of the house. On getting no answer to my knock, I opened the door, sup-
posing that he was absent; so that it gave me a certain
shock to find him sitting there helpless and dumb. He
was seated near the single window, facing an easel which
supported a large canvas. On my entering, he looked up at
me blankly, without changing his position, which was
that of absolute lassitude and dejection, his arms loosely
folded, his legs stretched before him, his head hanging on
his breast. Advancing into the room, I perceived that
his face vividly corresponded with his attitude. He was
pale, haggard, and unshaven, and his dull and sunken eye
gazed at me without a spark of recognition. I had been
afraid that he would greet me with fierce reproaches, as
the cruelly officious friend who had turned his peace to
bitterness, and I was relieved to find that my appearance
awakened no visible resentment. "Don't you know me?"
I asked as I put out my hand. "Have you already forgotten me?"

He made no response, kept his position stupidly, and
left me staring about the room. It spoke most plaintively

for itself. Shabby, sordid, naked, it contained, beyond the wretched bed, but the scantiest provision for personal comfort. It was bedroom at once and studio—a grim ghost of a studio. A few dusty casts and prints on the walls, three or four old canvases turned face inward, and a rusty-looking color box formed, with the easel at the window, the sum of its appurtenances. The place savored horribly of poverty. Its only wealth was the picture on the easel, presumably the famous Madonna. Averted as this was from the door, I was unable to see its face; but at last, sickened by the vacant misery of the spot, I passed behind Theobald, eagerly and tenderly, and yet I can hardly say that I was surprised at what I found—a canvas that was a mere dead blank, cracked and discolored by time. This was his immortal work! But though not surprised, I confess I was powerfully moved, and I think that for five minutes I could not have trusted myself to speak. At last, my silent nearness affected him; he stirred and turned, and then rose and looked at me with a slowly kindling eye. I murmured some kind, ineffective nothings about his being ill and needing advice and care, but he seemed absorbed in the effort to recall distinctly what had last passed between us. "You were right," he said with a pitiful smile, "I'm a dawdler! I'm a failure! I shall do nothing more in this world. You opened my eyes; and, though the truth is bitter, I bear you no grudge. Amen! I've been sitting here for a week, face to face with the truth, with the past, with my weakness and poverty and nullity. I shall never touch a brush! I believe I've neither eaten nor slept. Look at that canvas!" he went on, as I relieved my emotion in the urgent request that he would come home with me and dine. "That was to have contained my masterpiece! Isn't it a promising foundation? The elements of it are all *here*." And he tapped his forehead with that mystic confidence which had marked the gesture before. "If I could only transpose them into some brain that had the hand, the will! Since I've been sitting here taking stock of my intellects, I've come to believe that I have the material for a hundred masterpieces. But my hand is paralyzed now, and they'll never be painted. I never began! I waited and waited to be worthier to begin, and wasted my life in preparation. While I fancied my creation was growing, it was dying. I've taken it all too hard! Michelangelo didn't, when he went at the Lorenzo! He did his best at a venture, and his venture is immortal. *That*'s mine!" And he pointed with a gesture I shall never forget at the empty canvas. "I suppose we're a genus by ourselves in the providential scheme—we talents that can't act, that can't do or dare! We take it out in talk, in plans and promises, in study, in visions! But our visions, let me tell you," he cried, with a toss of his head, "have a way of being brilliant, and a man hasn't lived in vain who has seen the things I have! Of course, you'll not believe in them when that bit of worm-eaten cloth is all I have to show for them, but to convince you, to enchant and astound the world, I need only the hand of Raphael. I have his brain. A pity, you'll say, I haven't his modesty. Ah, let me babble now; it's all I have left! I'm the half of a genius! Where in the wide world is my other half? Lodged perhaps in the vulgar soul, the cunning, ready fingers of some dull copyist or some trivial artisan who turns out by the dozen his easy prodigies of touch! But it's not for me to sneer at him; he at least does something. He's not a dawdler! Well for me if I had been vulgar and clever and reckless, if I could have shut my eyes and dealt my stroke!"

What to say to the poor fellow, what to do for him, seemed hard to determine; I chiefly felt that I must break the spell of his present inaction and remove him from the haunted atmosphere of the little room it seemed such cruel irony to call a studio. I cannot say I persuaded him to come out with me; he simply suffered himself to be led, and when we began to walk in the open air, I was able to measure his pitifully weakened condition. Nevertheless, he seemed in a certain way to revive, and murmured at last that he would like to go to the Pitti Gallery. I shall never forget our melancholy stroll through those gorgeous halls, every picture on whose walls seemed, even to my own sympathetic vision, to glow with a sort of insolent renewal of strength and luster. The eyes and lips of the great portraits seemed to smile in ineffable scorn of the dejected pretender who had dreamed of competing with their glorious authors; the celestial candor, even, of the Madonna in the Chair, as we paused in perfect silence before her, was tinged with the sinister irony of the women of Leonardo. Perfect silence, indeed, marked our whole progress—the silent of a deep farewell; for I felt in all my pulses, as Theobald, leaning on my arm, dragged one heavy foot after the other, that he was looking his last. When we came out, he was so exhausted that, instead of taking him to my hotel to dine, I called a carriage and drove him straight to his own poor lodging. He had sunk into an extraordinary lethargy; he lay back in the carriage, with his eyes closed, as pale as death, his faint breathing interrupted at intervals by a sudden gasp, like a smothered sob or a vain attempt to speak. With the help of the old woman who had admitted me before, and who emerged from a dark back court, I contrived to lead him up the long, steep staircase and lay him on his wretched bed. To her I gave him in charge, while I prepared in all haste to seek a physician. But she followed me out of the room with a pitiful clasping of her hands.

"Poor, dear, blessed gentleman," she murmured; "is he dying?"

"Possibly. How long has he been thus?"

"Since a night he passed ten days ago. I came up in the morning to make his poor bed and found him sitting up in his clothes before that great canvas he keeps there, and, poor, dear, strange man, says his prayers to! He had not been to bed, nor since then, properly! What has happened to him? Has he found out about the Serafina?" she whispered with a glittering eye and a toothless grin.

"Prove at least that one old woman can be faithful," I said, "and watch him well till I come back." My return was delayed, through the absence of the English physician on a round of visits and my vainly pursuing him from house to house before I overtook him. I brought him to Theobald's bedside none too soon. A violent fever had seized our patient, and the case was evidently grave. A couple of hours later I knew that he had brain fever. From this moment I was with him constantly, but I am far from wishing to describe his illness. Excessively painful to witness, it was happily brief. Life burned out in delirium. A certain night that I passed at his pillow, listening to his wild snatches of regret, of aspiration, of rapture and awe at the phantasmal pictures with which his brain seemed to swarm, recurs to my memory now like some stray page from a lost masterpiece of tragedy. Before a week was over we had buried him in the little Protestant cemetery on the way to Fiesole. The Signora Serafina, whom I had caused to be informed of his illness, had come in person, I was told, to inquire about its progress, but she was absent from his funeral, which was attended by but a scanty concourse of mourners. Half a dozen old Florentine sojourners, in spite of the prolonged estrangement which had preceded his death, had felt the kindly impulse to honor his grave. Among them was my friend Mrs. Coventry, whom I found, on my departure, waiting at her carriage door at the gate of the cemetery.

"Well," she said, relieving at last with a significant smile the solemnity of our immediate greeting, "and the great Madonna? Have you seen her, after all?"

"I've seen her," I said; "she's mine—by bequest. But I shall never show her to you."

"And why not, pray?"

"My dear Mrs. Coventry, you'd not understand her!"

"Upon my word, you're polite."

"Excuse me; I'm sad and vexed and bitter." And with reprehensible rudeness, I marched away. I was excessively impatient to leave Florence; my friend's dark spirit seemed diffused through all things. I had packed my trunk to start for Rome that night, and meanwhile, to beguile my unrest, I aimlessly paced the streets. Chance led me at last to the church of San Lorenzo. Remembering poor Theobald's phrase about Michelangelo—"He did his best at a venture"—I went in and turned my steps to the chapel of the tombs. Viewing in sadness the sadness of its immortal treasures, I fancied, while I stood there, that the scene demanded no ampler commentary. As I passed through the church again to depart, a woman, turning away from one of the side altars, met me face to face. The black shawl depending from her head draped picturesquely the handsome visage of the Signora Serafina. She stopped as she recognized me, and I saw that she wished to speak. Her eye was bright and her ample bosom heaved in a way that seemed to portend a certain sharpness of reproach. But the expression of my own face, apparently, drew the sting from her resentment, and she addressed me in a tone in which bitterness was tempered by a sort of dogged resignation. "I know it was you, now, that separated us," she said. "It was a pity he ever brought you to see me! Of course, you couldn't think of me as he did. Well, the Lord gave him, the Lord has taken him. I've just paid for a nine days' mass for his soul. And I can tell you this, signore, I never deceived him. Who put it into his head that I was made to live on holy thoughts and fine phrases? It was his own fancy, and it pleased him to think so. Did he suffer much?" she added more softly, after a pause.

"His sufferings were great, but they were short."

"And did he speak of me?" She had hesitated and dropped her eyes; she raised them with her question, and revealed in their somber stillness a gleam of feminine confidence which, for the moment, revived and illumined her beauty. Poor Theobald! Whatever name he had given his passion, it was still her fine eyes that had charmed him.

"Be contented, madam," I answered, gravely.

She dropped her eyes again, and was silent. Then exhaling a full, rich sigh, as she gathered her shawl together: "He was a magnificent genius!"

I bowed, and we separated.

Passing through a narrow side street on my way back to my hotel, I perceived above a doorway a sign which it seemed to me I had read before. I suddenly remembered that it was identical with the superscription of a card that I had carried for an hour in my waistcoat pocket. On the threshold stood the ingenious artist whose claims to public favor were thus distinctly signalized, smoking a pipe in the evening air and giving the finishing polish with a bit of rag to one of his inimitable "combinations." I caught the expressive curl of a couple of tails. He recognized me, removed his little red cap with a most obsequious bow, and motioned me to enter his studio. I returned his bow and passed on, vexed with the apparition. For a week afterward, whenever I was seized among the ruins of Roman greatness with some peculiarly poignant memory of Theobald's transcendent illusions and deplorable failure, I seemed to hear a fantastic, impertinent murmur, "Cats and monkeys, monkeys and cats; all human life is there!"

The Last of the Valerii

I HAD had occasion to declare more than once that if my goddaughter married a foreigner I should refuse to give her away. And yet when the young Conte Valerio was presented to me, in Rome, as her accepted and plighted lover, I found myself looking at the happy fellow, after a momentary stare of amazement, with a certain paternal benevolence; thinking, indeed, that from the picturesque point of view (she with her yellow locks and he with his dusky ones) they were a strikingly well-assorted pair. She brought him up to me half-proudly, half-timidly, pushing him before her and begging me with one of her dove-like glances to be very polite. I don't know that I am addicted to rudeness, but she was so deeply impressed with his grandeur that she thought it impossible to do him honor enough. The Conte Valerio's grandeur was perhaps nothing for a young American girl who had the air and almost the habits of a princess to sound her trumpet about, but she was desperately in love with him, and not only her heart, but her imagination, was touched. He was extremely handsome, and with a more significant sort of beauty than is common in the handsome Roman race. He had a sort of sunken depth of expression and a grave, slow smile, suggesting no great quickness of wit, but an unimpassioned intensity of feeling which promised well for Martha's happiness. He had little of the light, inexpensive urbanity of his countrymen, and more of a sort of heavy sincerity in his gaze which seemed to suspend response until he was sure he understood you. He was perhaps a little stupid, and I fancied that to a political or aesthetic question the reply would be particularly slow. "He is good and strong and brave," the young girl however assured me, and I easily believed her. Strong the Conte Valerio certainly was; he had a head and throat like some of the busts in the Vatican. To my eye, which has looked at things now so long with the painter's purpose, it was a real perplexity to see such a throat rising out of the white cravat of the period. It sustained a head as massively round as that of the familiar bust of the Emperor Caracalla and covered with the same dense sculptural crop of curls. The young man's hair grew superbly; it was such hair as the old Romans must have had when they walked bareheaded and bronzed about the world. It made a perfect arch over his low, clear forehead and prolonged itself on cheek and chin in a close, crisp beard, strong with its own strength and unstiffened by the razor. Neither his nose nor his mouth was delicate; but they were powerful, shapely, and manly. His complexion was of a deep glowing brown which no emotion would alter, and his large, lucid eyes seemed to stare at you like a pair of polished agates. He was of middle stature, and his chest was of so generous a girth that you half-expected to hear his linen crack with its even respirations. And yet, with his simple human smile, he looked neither like a young bullock nor a gladiator. His powerful voice was the least bit harsh, and his large, ceremonious reply to my compliment had the massive sonority with which civil speeches must have been uttered in the age of Augustus. I had always considered my goddaughter a very American little person, in all delightful meanings of the word, and I doubted if this sturdy young Latin would understand the transatlantic element in her nature; but, evidently, he would make her a loyal and ardent lover. She seemed to me, in her blonde prettiness, so tender, so appealing, so bewitching, that it was impossible to believe he had not more thoughts for all this than for the pretty fortune which it yet bothered me to believe that he must, like a good Italian, have taken the exact measure of. His own worldly goods consisted of the paternal estate, a villa within the walls of Rome, which his scanty funds had suffered to fall into somber disrepair. "It's the villa she's in love with, quite as much as the count," said her mother. "She dreams of converting the count; that's all very well. But she dreams of refurnishing the villa!"

The upholsterers were turned into it, I believe, before the wedding, and there was a great scrubbing and sweeping of saloons and raking and weeding of alleys and avenues. Martha made frequent visits of inspection while these ceremonies were taking place, but one day, on her return, she came into my little studio with an air of amusing horror. She had found them *scraping* the sarcophagus in the great ilex walk, divesting it of its mossy coat, divesting it of the sacred green mold of the ages! This was their idea of making the villa comfortable. She had made them transport it to the dampest place they could find; for next after that slow-coming, slow-going smile of her lover, it was the rusty complexion of his patrimonial marbles that she most prized. The young count's conversion proceeded less rapidly, and, indeed, I believe that his betrothed brought little zeal to the affair. She loved him so devoutly that she believed no change of faith could better him, and she would have been willing for his sake to say her prayers to the sacred Bambino at Epiphany. But he had the good taste to demand no such sacrifice, and I was struck with the happy promise of a scene of which I was an accidental observer. It was at St. Peter's, one Friday afternoon, during the vesper service which takes place in the Chapel of the Choir. I met my goddaughter wandering happily on her lover's arm, her mother being established on her camp stool near the chapel door. The crowd was collected thereabout, and the body of the church was empty. Now and then the high voices of the singers escaped into the outer vastness and melted slowly away into the incense-thickened air. Something in the young girl's step and the clasp of her arm in her lover's told me that her contentment was perfect. As she threw back her head and gazed into the magnificent immensity of vault and dome, I felt that she was in that enviable mood in which all consciousness revolves on a single center, and that her sense of the splendors around her was one with the ecstasy of her trust. They stopped before that somber group of confessionals which proclaims so portentously the world's sinfulness, and Martha seemed to make some almost passionate protestation. A few minutes later I overtook them.

"Don't you agree with me, dear friend," said the count,

who always addressed me with the most affectionate deference, "that before I marry so pure and sweet a creature as this, I ought to go into one of those places and confess every sin I ever was guilty of—every evil thought and impulse and desire of my grossly evil nature?"

Martha looked at him, half in deprecation, half in homage, with a look which seemed at once to insist that her lover could have no vices, and to plead that, if he had, there would be something magnificent in them. "Listen to him!" she said, smiling. "The list would be long, and if you waited to finish it, you would be late for the wedding! But if you confess your sins for me, it's only fair I should confess mine for you. Do you know what I have been saying to Camillo?" she added, turning to me with the half-filial confidence she had always shown me and with a rosy glow in her cheeks; "that I want to do something more for him than girls commonly do for their lovers—to take some step, to run some risk, to break some law, even! I'm willing to change my religion, if he bids me. There are moments when I'm terribly tired of simply staring at Catholicism; it will be a relief to come into a church to kneel. That's, after all, what they are meant for? Therefore, *Camillo mio,* if it casts a shade across your heart to think that I'm a heretic, I'll go and kneel down to that good old priest who has just entered the confessional yonder and say to him, 'My father, I repent, I abjure, I believe. Baptize me in the only faith.' "

"If it's as a compliment to the count," I said, "it seems to me he ought to anticipate it by turning Protestant."

She had spoken lightly and with a smile, and yet with an undertone of girlish ardor. The young man looked at her with a solemn, puzzled face and shook his head. "Keep your religion," he said. "Everyone his own. If you should attempt to embrace mine, I'm afraid you would close your arms about a shadow. I'm a poor Catholic! I don't understand all these chants and ceremonies and splendors. When I was a child, I never could learn my catechism. My poor old confessor long ago gave me up; he told me I was a good boy but a *pagan!* You must not be a better Catholic than your husband. I don't understand your religion any better, but I beg you not to change it for mine. If it has helped to make you what you are, it must be good." And taking the young girl's hand, he was about to raise it affectionately to his lips, but suddenly remembering that they were in a place unaccordant with profane passions, he lowered it with a comical smile. "Let us go!" he murmured, passing his hand over his forehead. "This heavy atmosphere of St. Peter's always stupefies me."

They were married in the month of May and we separated for the summer, the contessa's mama going to illuminate the domestic circle in New York with her reflected dignity. When I returned to Rome in the autumn, I found the young couple established at the Villa Valerio, which was being gradually reclaimed from its antique decay. I begged that the hand of improvement might be lightly laid on it, for as an unscrupulous old genre painter, with an eye to "subjects," I preferred that ruin should accumulate. My goddaughter was quite of my way of thinking, and she had a capital sense of the picturesque. Advising with me often as to projected changes, she was sometimes more conservative than myself; and I more than once smiled at her archeological zeal, and declared that I believed she had married the count because he was like a statue of the Decadence. I had a constant invitation to spend my days at the Villa, and my easel was always planted in one of the garden walks. I grew to have a painter's passion for the place and to be intimate with every tangled shrub and twisted tree, every moss-coated vase and moldy sarcophagus and sad, disfeatured bust of those grim old Romans who could so ill afford to become more meager-visaged. The place was of small extent; but though there were many other villas more pretentious and splendid, none seemed to me more deeply picturesque, more romantically idle and untrimmed, more encumbered with precious antique rubbish, and haunted with half-historic echoes. It contained an old ilex walk in which I used religiously to spend half an hour every day —half an hour being, I confess, just as long as I could stay without beginning to sneeze. The trees arched and intertwisted here along their dusky vista in the quaintest symmetry, and as it was exposed uninterruptedly to the west, the low evening sun used to tranfuse it with a sort of golden mist and play through it—over leaves and knotty boughs and mossy marbles—with a thousand crimson fingers. It was filled with disinterred fragments of sculpture—nameless statues and noseless heads and rough-hewn sarcophagi, which made it deliciously solemn. The statues used to stand there in the perpetual twilight like conscious things, brooding on their gathered memories. I used to linger about them, half-expecting they would speak and tell me their stony secrets—whisper heavily the whereabouts of their moldering fellows, still unrecovered from the soil.

My goddaughter was idyllically happy and absolutely in love. I was obliged to confess that even rigid rules have their exceptions, and that now and then an Italian count is an honest fellow. Camillo was one to the core, and seemed quite content to be adored. Their life was a kind of childlike interchange of caresses, as candid and unmeasured as those of a shepherd and shepherdess in a bucolic poem. To stroll in the ilex walk and feel her husband's arm about her waist and his shoulder against her cheek; to roll cigarettes for him while he puffed them in the great marble-paved rotunda in the center of the house; to fill his glass from an old rusty red amphora—these graceful occupations satisfied the young countess.

She rode with him sometimes in the tufty shadow of aqueducts and tombs and sometimes suffered him to show his beautiful wife at Roman dinners and balls. She played dominoes with him after dinner and carried out in a desultory way a daily scheme of reading him the newspapers. This observance was subject to fluctuations caused by the count's invincible tendency to go to sleep— a failing his wife never attempted to disguise or palliate. She would sit and brush the flies from him while he lay picturesquely snoozing, and if I ventured near him, would place her finger on her lips and whisper that she thought her husband was as handsome asleep as awake. I confess I often felt tempted to reply to her that he was at least as entertaining, for the young man's happiness had not multiplied the topics on which he readily conversed. He had plenty of good sense, and his opinions on practical matters were always worth having. He would often come and sit near me while I worked at my easel and offer a friendly criticism. His taste was a little crude, but his eye was excellent, and his measurement of the resemblance between some point of my copy and the original as trustworthy as that of a mathematical instrument. But he seemed to me to have either a strange reserve or a strange simplicity—to be fundamentally unfurnished with "ideas." He had no beliefs, or hopes, or fears—nothing but senses, appetites, and serenely luxurious tastes. As I watched him strolling about looking at his fingernails, I often wondered whether he had anything that could properly be termed a soul, and whether good health and good nature were not the sum of his attributes. "It's lucky he's good-natured," I used to say to myself; "for if he were not, there is nothing in his conscience to keep him in order. If he had irritable nerves instead of quiet ones, he would strangle us as the young Hercules strangled the poor little snakes. He's the natural man! Happily, his nature is gentle, and I can mix my colors at my ease." I wondered what he thought about and what passed through his mind in the sunny leisure which seemed to shut him in from that modern workaday world of which, in spite of my passion for bedaubing old panels with ineffective portraiture of moldy statues against screens of box, I still flattered myself I was a member. I went so far as to believe that he sometimes withdrew from the world altogether. He had moods in which his consciousness seemed so remote and his mind so irresponsive and dumb that nothing but a powerful caress or a sudden violence was likely to arouse him. Even his lavish tenderness for his wife had a quality which I but half-relished. Whether or no he had a soul himself, he seemed not to suspect that she had one. I took a godfatherly interest in what it had not always seemed to me crabbed and pedantic to talk of as her moral development. I fondly believed her to be a creature susceptible of the finer spiritual emotions. But what was becoming of her spiritual life in this interminable heathenish honeymoon? Some fine day she would find herself tired of the count's *beaux yeux* and make an appeal to his mind. She had, to my knowledge, plans of study, of charity, of worthily playing her part as a Contessa Valerio—a position as to which the family records furnished the most memorable examples. But if the count found the newspapers soporific, I doubted if he would turn Dante's pages very fast for his wife, or smile with much zest at the anecdotes of Vasari. How could he advise her, instruct her, sustain her? And if she became a mother, how could he share her responsibilities? He doubtless would assure his little son and heir a stout pair of arms and legs and a magnificent crop of curls, and sometimes remove his cigarette to kiss a dimpled spot, but I found it hard to picture him lending his voice to teach the lusty urchin his alphabet, or his prayers, or the rudiments of infant virtue. One accomplishment, indeed, the count possessed which would make him an agreeable playfellow; he carried in his pocket a collection of precious fragments of antique pavement—bits of porphyry and malachite and lapis and basalt—disinterred on his own soil and brilliantly polished by use. With these you might see him occupied by the half-hour, playing the simple game of catch-and-toss, ranging them in a circle, tossing them in rotation, and catching them on the back of his hand. His skill was remarkable; he would send a stone five feet into the air and pitch and catch and transpose the rest before he received it again. I watched with affectionate jealousy for the signs of a dawning sense, on Martha's part, that she was the least bit strangely mated. Once or twice, as the weeks went by, I fancied I read them, and that she looked at me with eyes which seemed to remember certain old talks of mine in which I had declared—with such verity as you please—that a Frenchman, an Italian, a Spaniard, might be a very good fellow, but that he never really respected the woman he pretended to love; but for the most part, I confess, these dusky broodings of mine spent themselves easily in the charmed atmosphere of our fine old villa. We were out of the modern world and had no business with modern scruples. The place was so bright, so still, so sacred to the silent, imperturbable past that drowsy contentment seemed a natural law; and sometimes when, as I sat at my work, I saw my companions passing arm-in-arm across the end of one of the long-drawn vistas and, turning back to my palette, found my colors dimmer for the radiant vision, I could easily believe that I was some loyal old chronicler of a perfectly poetical legend.

It was a help to ungrudging feelings that the count, yielding to his wife's urgency, had undertaken a series of systematic excavations. To excavate is an expensive luxury, and neither Camillo nor his latter forefathers had possessed the means for a disinterested pursuit of archeology. But his young wife had persuaded herself that the much-trodden soil of the villa was as full of buried treasures as a bride-cake of plums, and that it would be a pretty compliment to the ancient house which had accepted her as mistress to devote a portion of her dowry to bringing its moldy honors to the light. I think she was not without a fancy that this liberal process would help to disinfect her Yankee dollars of the impertinent odor of trade. She took learned advice on the subject and was soon ready to swear to you, proceeding from irrefutable premises, that a colossal gilt-bronze Minerva mentioned by Strabo was placidly awaiting resurrection at a point twenty rods from the northwest angle of the house. She had a couple of grotesque old antiquaries to lunch, whom having plied with unwonted potations, she walked off their legs in the grounds; and though they agreed on nothing else in the world, they individually assured her that properly conducted researches would probably yield an unequaled harvest of discoveries. The count had been not only indifferent, but even averse, to the scheme, and had more than once arrested his wife's complacent allusions to it by an unaccustomed acerbity of tone. "Let them lie, the poor disinherited gods, the Minerva, the Apollo, the Ceres, you are so sure of finding," he said, "and don't break their rest. What do you want of them? We can't worship them. Would you put them on pedestals to stare and mock at them? If you can't believe in them, don't disturb them. Peace be with them!" I remember being a good deal impressed by a vigorous confession drawn from him by his wife's playfully declaring in answer to some remonstrances in this strain that he was veritably superstitious. "Yes, by Bacchus, I am superstitious!" he cried. "Too much so, perhaps! But I'm an old Italian, and you must take me as you find me. There have been things seen and done here which leave strange influences behind! They don't touch you doubtless, who come of another race. But they touch me, often, in the whisper of the leaves and the odor of the moldy soil and the blank eyes of the old statues. I can't bear to look the statues in the face. I seem to see other strange eyes in the empty sockets, and I hardly know what they say to me. I call the poor old statues ghosts. In conscience, we've enough on the place already, lurking and peering in every shady nook. Don't dig up any more, or I won't answer for my wits!"

This account of Camillo's sensibilities was too fantastic not to seem to his wife almost a joke, and though I imagined there was more in it, he made a joke so seldom that I should have been sorry to cut short the poor girl's smile. With her smile she carried her point, and in a few days arrived a kind of explorer with a dozen workmen armed with pickaxes and spades. For myself, I was secretly vexed at these energetic measures, for, though fond of disinterred statues, I disliked the disinterment and deplored the profane sounds which were henceforth to break the leisurely stillness of the gardens. I especially objected to the personage who conducted the operations, an ugly, little, dwarfish man who seemed altogether a subterranean genius, a moldy gnome of the underworld, and went prying about the grounds with a malicious smile which suggested more delight in the money the Signor Conte was going to bury than in the expected marbles and bronzes. When the first sod had been turned, the count's mood seemed to alter, and his curiosity got the better of his scruples. He sniffed delightedly the odor of the humid earth, and stood watching the workmen as they struck constantly deeper with a kindling wonder in his eyes. Whenever a pickaxe rang against a stone, he would utter a sharp cry, and be deterred from jumping into the trench only by the little explorer's assurance that it was a false alarm. The near prospect of discoveries seemed to act upon his nerves, and I met him more than once strolling restlessly among his cedarn alleys, as if at last he had fallen athinking; he took me by the arm and made me walk with him, and discoursed ardently of the chance of a "find." I rather marveled at his sudden zeal, and wondered whether he had an eye to the past or to the future—to the beauty of possible Minervas and Apollos or to their market value. Whenever the count would come and denounce his little army of spadesmen a set of loitering vagabonds, the little explorer would glance at me with a sarcastic

twinkle which seemed to hint that excavations were a
snare. We were kept some time in suspense, for several
false beginnings were made. The earth was probed in the
wrong places. The count began to be discouraged and to
prolong his abbreviated siesta. But the little explorer,
who had his own ideas, shrewdly continued his labors,
and as I sat at my easel, I heard the spades ringing against
the dislodged stones. Now and then I would pause, with
an uncontrollable acceleration of my heartbeat. "It *may*
be," I would say, "that some marble masterpiece is stir-
ring there beneath its lightening weight of earth! There
are as good fish in the sea—*I may* be summoned to welcome another Antinoüs back to fame—a Venus, a Faun,
an Augustus!"

One morning it seemed to me that I had been hearing
for half an hour a livelier movement of voices than usual,
but as I was preoccupied with a puzzling bit of work, I
made no inquiries. Suddenly, a shadow fell across my
canvas, and I turned around. The little explorer stood
beside me, with a glittering eye, cap in hand, his forehead bathed in perspiration. Resting in the hollow of his
arm was an earthstained fragment of marble. In answer to
my questioning glance, he held it up to me, and I saw it
was a woman's shapely hand. "Come!" he simply said
and led the way to the excavation. The workmen were
so closely gathered around the open trench that I saw
nothing till he made them divide. Then, full in the sun and
flashing it back, almost, in spite of her moldy incrusta-
tions, I beheld, propped up with stones against a heap
of earth, a majestic marble image. She seemed to me
almost colossal, though I afterward perceived that she
was of perfect human proportions. My pulses began to
throb, for I felt she was something great and that it was
great to be among the first to know her. Her marvelous
beauty gave her an almost-human look, and her absent
eyes seemed to wonder back at us. She was amply draped,
so that I saw that she was not a Venus. "She's a Juno,"
said the explorer decisively; and she seemed, indeed,
an embodiment of celestial supremacy and repose. Her
beautiful head, bound with a single band, could have
bent only to give the nod of command; her eyes looked
straight before her; her mouth was implacably grave; one

hand, outstretched, appeared to have held a kind of imperial wand; the arm from which the other had been broken hung at her side with the most classical majesty. The workmanship was of the rarest finish, and though perhaps there was a sort of vaguely modern attempt at character in her expression, she was wrought, as a whole, in the large and simple manner of the great Greek period. She was a masterpiece of skill and a marvel of preservation. "Does the count know?" I soon asked, for I had a guilty sense that our eyes were taking something from her.

"The Signor Conte is at his siesta," said the explorer, with his skeptical grin. "We don't like to disturb him."

"Here he comes!" cried one of the workmen, and we made way for him. His siesta had evidently been suddenly broken, for his face was flushed and his hair disordered.

"Ah, my dream—my dream was right then!" he cried and stood staring at the image.

"What was your dream?" I asked as his face seemed to betray more dismay than delight.

"That they'd found a Juno, and that she rose and came and laid her marble hand on mine—eh?" said the count excitedly.

A kind of awestruck, guttural *a-ah!* burst from the listening workmen.

"This is the hand!" said the little explorer, holding up his perfect fragment. "I've had it this half-hour, so it can't have touched you."

"But you're apparently right as to her being a Juno," I said. "Admire her at your leisure." And I turned away, for if the count was superstitious, I wished to leave him free to relieve himself. I repaired to the house to carry the news to my goddaughter, whom I found slumbering— dreamlessly, it appeared—over a great archeological octavo. "They've touched bottom," I said. "They've found a Juno of Praxiteles at the very least!" She dropped her octavo and rang for a parasol. I described the statue, but not graphically, I presume, for Martha gave a little sarcastic grimace.

"A long, fluted *peplum*," she said. "How very odd! I don't believe she's beautiful."

"She's beautiful enough, *figliocciamia*," I answered, "to make you jealous."

We found the count standing before the resurgent goddess in fixed contemplation, with folded arms. He seemed to have recovered from the irritation of his dream, but I thought his face betrayed a still deeper emotion. He was pale, and gave no response as his wife caressingly clasped his arm. I'm not sure, however, that his wife's attitude was not a livelier tribute to the perfection of the image. She had been laughing at my rhapsody as we walked from the house, and I had bethought myself of a statement I had somewhere seen that women lack the perception of the purest beauty. Martha, however, seemed slowly to measure our Juno's infinite stateliness. She gazed a long time silently, leaning against her husband, and then stepped half-timidly down on the stones which formed a rough base for the figure. She laid her two rosy, ungloved hands upon the stony fingers of the goddess and remained for some moments pressing them in her warm grasp and fixing her living eyes upon the inexpressive brow. When she turned around, her eyes were bright with an admiring tear—a tear which her husband was too deeply absorbed to notice. He had apparently given orders that the workmen should be treated to a cask of wine in honor of their discovery. It was now brought and opened on the spot, and the little explorer, having drawn the first glass, stepped forward, hat in hand, and obsequiously presented it to the countess. She only moistened her lips with it and passed it to her husband. He raised it mechanically to his own; then, suddenly, he stopped, held it a moment aloft, and poured it out slowly and solemnly at the feet of the Juno.

"Why, it's a libation!" I cried. He made no answer and walked slowly away.

There was no more work done that day. The laborers lay on the grass, gazing with the native Roman relish of a fine piece of sculpture, but wasting no wine in pagan ceremonies. In the evening, the count paid the Juno another visit and gave orders that on the morrow she should be transferred to the casino. The casino was a deserted gardenhouse built in not ungraceful imitation of an Ionic temple, in which Camillo's ancestors must often have

assembled to drink cool syrups from Venetian glasses
and listen to learned madrigals. It contained several dusty
fragments of antique sculpture, and it was spacious
enough to enclose that richer collection of which I began
fondly to regard the Juno as but the nucleus. Here,
with short delay, this fine creature was placed, serenely
upright, a reversed funereal *cippus* forming a sufficiently
solid pedestal. The little explorer, who seemed an expert
in all the offices of restoration, rubbed her and scraped
her with mysterious art, removed her earthy stains, and
doubled the luster of her beauty. Her mellow substance
seemed to glow with a kind of renascent purity and bloom,
and, but for her broken hand, you might have fancied she
had just received the last stroke of the chisel. Her fame
remained no secret. Within two or three days, half a
dozen inquisitive *cognoscenti* posted out to obtain sight
of her. I happened to be present when the first of these
gentlemen (a German in blue spectacles, with a portfolio
under his arm) presented himself at the villa. The
count, hearing his voice at the door, came forward and
eyed him coldly from head to foot.

"Your new Juno, Signor Conte," began the German,
"is, in my opinion, much more likely to be a certain
Proserpine—"

"I've neither a Juno nor a Proserpine to discuss with
you," said the count curtly. "You're misinformed."

"You've dug up no statue?" cried the German. "What
a scandalous hoax!"

"None worthy of your learned attention. I'm sorry you
should have the trouble of carrying your little notebook
so far." The count had suddenly become witty!

"But you've something, surely. The rumor is running
through Rome."

"The rumor be damned!" cried the Count savagely.
"I've *nothing,* do you understand? Be so good as to say
so to your friends."

The answer was explicit, and the poor archeologist departed, tossing his flaxen mane. But I pitied him and
ventured to remonstrate with the count. "She might as
well be still in the earth, if no one is to see her," I said.

"*I'm* to see her: that's enough!" he answered with the
same unnatural harshness. Then, in a moment, as he

caught me eying him askance in troubled surprise, "I hated his great portfolio. He was going to make some hideous drawing of her."

"Ah, that touches me," I said. "I have been planning to make a little sketch."

He was silent for some moments, after which he turned and grasped my arm, with less irritation, but with extraordinary gravity. "Go in there toward twilight," he said, "and sit for an hour and look at her. I think you'll give up your sketch. If you don't, my good old friend —you're welcome!"

I followed his advice, and as a friend, I gave up my sketch. But an artist is an artist, and I secretly longed to attempt it. Orders strictly in accordance with the count's reply to our German friend were given to the servants, who, with an easy Italian conscience and a gracious Italian persuasiveness, assured all subsequent inquirers that they had been regrettably misinformed. I have no doubt, indeed, that, in default of larger opportunity, they made condolence remunerative. Further excavation was, for the present, suspended, as implying an affront to the incomparable Juno. The workmen departed, but the little explorer still haunted the premises and sounded the soil for his own entertainment. One day he came to me with his usual ambiguous grimace. "The beautiful hand of the Juno," he murmured; "what has become of it?"

"I've not seen it since you called me to look at her. I remember when I went away I saw it lying on the grass near the excavation."

"Where I placed it myself! After that it disappeared. *Ecco!*"

"Do you suspect one of your workmen? Such a fragment as that would bring more *scudi* than most of them ever looked at."

"Some, perhaps, are greater thieves than the others. But if I were to call up the worst of them and accuse him, the count would interfere."

"He must value that beautiful hand, nevertheless."

The little expert in disinterment looked about him and winked. "He values it so much that he himself purloined it. That's my belief, and I think that the less we say about it the better."

"Purloined it, my dear sir? After all, it's his own property."

"Not so much as that comes to. So beautiful a creature is more or less the property of everyone; we've all a right to look at her. But the count treats her as if she were a sacrosanct image of the Madonna. He keeps her under lock and key and pays her solitary visits. What does he do, after all? When a beautiful woman is in stone, all you can do is to look at her. And what does he do with that precious hand? He keeps it in a silver box; he has made a relic of it!" And the little explorer began to titter grotesquely and walked away.

He left me musing uncomfortably and wondering what the deuce he meant. The count certainly chose to make a mystery of the Juno, but this seemed a natural incident of the first rapture of possession. I was willing to wait for a free access to her, and in the meantime I was glad to find that there was a limit to his constitutional apathy. But as the days elapsed, I began to be conscious that his enjoyment was not communicative, but strangely cold and shy and somber. That he should admire a marble goddess was no reason for his despising mankind, but he really seemed to be making invidious comparisons between us. From this untender proscription his charming wife was not excepted. At moments, when I tried to persuade myself that he was neither worse nor better company than usual, her face condemned my optimism. She said nothing, but she wore a constant look of pathetic perplexity. She sat at times with her eyes fixed on him with a kind of appealing remonstrance and tender curiosity, as if pitying surprise held resentment yet awhile in check. What passed between them in private, I had, of course, no warrant to inquire. Nothing, I imagined, and that was the misery. It was part of the misery, too, that he seemed impenetrable to these mute glances and looked over her head with an air of superb abstraction. Occasionally, he noticed me looking at him in urgent deprecation, and then for a moment his heavy eye would sparkle, half, as it seemed, in defiant irony, and half with a strangely stifled impulse to justify him-

self. But from his wife he kept his face inexorably, cruelly
averted, and when she approached him with some per-
suasive caress, he received it with an ill-concealed shudder. I inwardly protested and raged. I grew to hate the
count and everything that belonged to him. "I was a
thousand times right," I cried; "an Italian count may
be mighty fine, but he won't *wear!* Give us some wholesome young fellow of our own blood, who'll play us
none of these dusky Old-World tricks. Painter as I am,
I'll never recommend a picturesque husband!" I lost my
pleasure in the villa, in the purple shadows and glowing
lights, the mossy marbles and the long-trailing profile of the
Alban Hills. My painting stood still; everything looked
ugly. I sat and fumbled with my palette, and seemed to
be mixing mud with my colors. My head was stuffed
with dismal thoughts; an intolerable weight seemed to
lie upon my heart. The Count became, to my imagination, a dark efflorescence of the evil germs which history
had implanted in his line. No wonder he was fore-
doomed to be cruel. Was not cruelty a tradition in his
race, and crime an example? The unholy passions of his
forefathers stirred blindly in his untaught nature and
clamored dumbly for an issue. What a heavy heritage it
seemed to me, as I reckoned it up in my melancholy
musings, the count's interminable ancestry! Back to the
profligate revival of arts and vices—back to the bloody
medley of medieval wars—back through the long, fitfully
glaring dusk of the early ages to its ponderous origin in
the solid Roman state, back through all the darkness
of history, it seemed to stretch, losing every feeblest
claim on my sympathies as it went. Such a record was in
itself a curse, and my poor girl had expected it to sit
as lightly and gratefully on her consciousness as her
feather on her hat! I have little idea how long this painful situation lasted. It seemed the longer from my goddaughter's continued reserve and my inability to offer
her a word of consolation. A sensitive woman, disappointed
in marriage, exhausts her own ingenuity before she
takes counsel. The count's preoccupations, whatever they
were, made him increasingly restless; he came and went
at random, with nervous abruptness; he took long rides
alone and, as I inferred, rarely went through the form of

excusing himself to his wife; and still, as time went on, he came no nearer explaining his mystery. With the lapse of time, however, I confess that my apprehensions began to be tempered with pity. If I had expected to see him propitiate his urgent ancestry by a crime, now that his native rectitude seemed resolute to deny them this satisfaction, I felt a sort of comparative gratitude. A man couldn't be so gratuitously somber without being unhappy. He had always treated me with that antique deference to a grizzled beard for which elderly men reserve the flames of their general tenderness for waning fashions, and I thought it possible he might suffer me to lay a healing hand upon his trouble. One evening, when I had taken leave of my goddaughter and given her my useless blessing in a silent kiss, I came out and found the count sitting in the garden in the mild starlight and staring at a moldy Hermes nestling in a clump of oleander. I sat down by him and informed him roundly that his conduct needed an explanation. He half-turned his head, and his dark pupil gleamed an instant.

"I understand," he said, "you think me crazy!" And he tapped his forehead.

"No, not crazy, but unhappy. And if unhappiness runs its course too freely, of course our poor wits are sorely tried."

He was silent awhile, and then, "I'm not unhappy!" he cried abruptly. "I'm prodigiously happy. You wouldn't believe the satisfaction I take in sitting here and staring at that old weather-worn Hermes. Formerly I used to be afraid of him; his frown used to remind me of a little, bushy-browed old priest who taught me Latin and looked at me terribly over the book when I stumbled in my Virgil. But now it seems to me the friendliest, jolliest thing in the world, and suggests the most delightful images. He stood pouting his great lips in some old Roman's garden two thousand years ago. He saw the sandaled feet treading the alleys and the rose-crowned heads bending over the wine; he knew the old feasts and the old worship, the old Romans and the old gods. As I sit here, he speaks to me, in his own dumb way, and describes it all! No, no, my friend, I'm the happiest of men!"

I had denied that I thought he was crazy, but I suddenly began to suspect it, for I found nothing reassuring in this singular rhapsody. The Hermes, for a wonder, had kept his nose; and when I reflected that my dear countess was being neglected for this senseless pagan block, I secretly promised myself to come the next day with a hammer and deal him such a lusty blow as would make him too ridiculous for a sentimental tête-à-tête. Meanwhile, however, the count's infatuation was no laughing matter, and I expressed my sincerest conviction when I said, after a pause, that I should recommend him to see either a priest or a physician.

He burst into uproarious laughter. "A priest! What should I do with a priest, or he with me? I never loved them, and I feel less like beginning than ever. A priest, my dear friend," he repeated, laying his hand on my arm, "don't set a priest at me, if you value *his* sanity! My confession would frighten the poor man out of his wits. As for a doctor, I never was better in my life, and unless," he added abruptly, rising and eying me askance, "you want to poison me, in Christian charity I advise you to leave me alone."

Decidedly, the count *was* unsound, and I had no heart, for some days, to go back to the villa. How should I treat him, what stand should I take, what course did Martha's happiness and dignity demand? I wandered about Rome, revolving these questions, and one afternoon found myself in the Pantheon. A light spring shower had begun to fall, and I hurried for refuge into the great temple which its Christian altars have but half-converted into a church. No Roman monument retains a deeper impress of ancient life, or verifies more forcibly the memory of these old beliefs which we are apt to regard as dim fables. The huge, dusky dome seems to the spiritual ear to hold a vague reverberation of pagan worship, as a gathered shell holds the rumor of the sea. Three or four persons were scattered before the various altars; another stood near the center, beneath the aperture in the dome. As I drew near, I perceived he was the count. He was planted with his hands behind him, looking up first at the heavy rain clouds, as they crossed the great bull's-eye, and then down at the besprinkled circle on the pavement. In those days the pavement was rugged and cracked and magnificently old, and this ample space, in free communion with the weather, had become as moldy and mossy and verdant as a strip of garden soil. A tender herbage had sprung up in the crevices of the slabs, and the little microscopic shoots were twinkling in the rain. This great weather current, through the unclosed apex of the temple, deadens most effectively the customary odors of incense and tallow and transports one to a faith that was on friendly terms with nature. It seemed to have performed this office for the count; his face wore an indefinable expression of ecstasy, and he was so rapt in contemplation that it was some time before he noticed me. The sun was struggling through the clouds without, and yet a thin rain continued to fall and came drifting down into our gloomy enclosure in a sort of illuminated drizzle. The count watched it with the fascinated stare of a child watching a fountain, and then turned away, pressing his hand to his brow, and walked over to one of the ornamental altars. Here he again stood staring, but in a moment wheeled about and returned to his former place. Just then he recognized me and perceived, I suppose, the puzzled gaze I must have fixed on him. He saluted me frankly with his hand, and at last came toward me. I fancied that he was in a kind of nervous tremor and was trying to appear calm.

"This is the best place in Rome," he murmured. "It's worth fifty St. Peters'. But do you know I never came here till the other day? I left it to the *forestieri*. They go about with their red books, and read about this and that, and think they know it. Ah! You must *feel* it— feel the beauty and fitness of that great open skylight. Now, only the wind and the rain, the sun and the cold come down; but of old—of old"—and he touched my arm and gave me a strange smile—"the pagan gods and goddesses used to come sailing through it and take their places at their altars. What a procession, when the eyes of faith could see it! Those are the things they have given us instead!" And he gave a pitiful shrug. "I should like to pull down their pictures, overturn their candlesticks, and poison their holy water!"

"My dear Count," I said gently, "you should tolerate

people's honest beliefs. Would you renew the Inquisition, and in the interest of Jupiter and Mercury?"

"People wouldn't tolerate my belief, if they guessed it!" he cried. "There's been a great talk about the pagan persecutions, but the Christians persecuted as well, and the old gods were worshiped in caves and woods as well as the new. And none the worse for that! It was in caves and woods and streams, in earth and air and water, they dwelt. And there—and here, too, in spite of all your Christian lustrations—a son of old Italy may find them still!"

He had said more than he meant, and his mask had fallen. I looked at him hard and felt a sudden outgush of the compassion we always feel for a creature irresponsibly excited. I seemed to touch the source of his trouble, and my relief was great, for my discovery made me feel like bursting into laughter. But I contented myself with smiling benignantly. He looked back at me suspiciously, as if to judge how far he had betrayed himself and in his glance I read, somehow, that he had a conscience we could take hold of. In my gratitude, I was ready to thank any gods he pleased. "Take care, take care," I said, "you're saying things which if the sacristan there were to hear and report—!" And I passed my hand through his arm and led him away. I was startled and shocked, but I was also amused and comforted. The count had suddenly become for me a delightfully curious phenomenon, and I passed the rest of the day in meditating on the strange ineffaceability of race characteristics. A sturdy young Latin I had called Camillo; sturdier, indeed, than I had dreamed him. Discretion was now misplaced, and on the morrow I spoke to my goddaughter. She had lately been hoping, I think, that I would help her to unburden her heart, for she immediately gave way to tears and confessed that she was miserable. "At first," she said, "I thought it was fancy, and not his tenderness that was growing less, but my exactions that were growing greater. But suddenly it settled upon me like a mortal chill—the conviction that he had ceased to care for me, that something had come between us. And the horrible thing has been the want of possible cause in my own conduct, or of other visible claim on his interest. I have racked my brain

to discover what I had said or done or thought to dis-
please him! And yet he goes about like a man too deeply
injured to complain. He has never uttered a harsh word
or given me a reproachful look. He has simply renounced
me. I have dropped out of his life."

She spoke with such an appealing tremor in her voice
that I was on the point of telling her that I had guessed
the riddle, and that this was half the battle. But I was
afraid of her incredulity. My solution was so fantastic,
so apparently farfetched, so absurd, that I resolved to
wait for convincing evidence. To obtain it, I continued
to watch the count, covertly and cautiously, but with a
vigilance which disinterested curiosity now made doubly
keen. I returned to my painting and neglected no pretext for hovering about the gardens and the neighborhood
of the casino. The count, I think, suspected my designs,
or at least my suspicions, and would have been glad to
remember just what he had suffered himself to say to me
in the Pantheon. But it deepened my interest in his extraordinary situation that, insofar as I could read his deeply
brooding face, he seemed to have grudgingly pardoned
me. He gave me a glance occasionally, as he passed me,
in which a sort of dumb desire for help appeared to
struggle with the instinct of mistrust. I was willing enough
to help him, but the case was prodigiously delicate and
I wished to master the symptoms. Meanwhile, I worked
and waited and wondered. Ah! I wondered, you may be
sure, with an interminable wonder; and, turn it over as I
would, I couldn't get used to my idea. Sometimes it offered itself to me with a perverse fascination which deprived me of all wish to interfere. The count took the
form of a precious psychological study, and refined feeling seemed to dictate a tender respect for his delusion. I
envied him the force of his imagination, and I used sometimes to close my eyes with a vague desire that when I
opened them, I might find Apollo under the opposite tree,
lazily kissing his flute, or see Diana hurrying with long
steps down the ilex walk. But for the most part, my host
seemed to me simply an unhappy young man, with an un-
wholesome mental twist which should be smoothed away
as speedily as possible. If the remedy was to match the

disease, however, it would have to be an ingenious compound!

One evening, having bidden my goddaughter good night, I had started on my usual walk to my lodgings in Rome. Five minutes after leaving the villa gate, I discovered that I had left my eyeglass—an object in constant use—behind me. I immediately remembered that, while painting, I had broken the string which fastened it around my neck and had hooked it provisionally upon the twig of a flowering almond tree within arm's reach. Shortly afterward I had gathered up my things and retired, unmindful of the glass; and now, as I needed it to read the evening paper at the Café Greco, there was no alternative but to retrace my steps and detach it from its twig. I easily found it and lingered awhile to note the curious night aspect of the spot I had been studying by daylight. The night was magnificent, and full-charged with the breath of the early Roman spring. The moon was rising fast and flinging her silver checkers into the heavy masses of shadow. Watching her at work, I strolled farther and suddenly came in sight of the casino. Just then the moon, which for a moment had been concealed, touched with a white ray a small marble figure which adorned the pediment of this rather factitious little structure. Its sudden illumination suggested that a rarer spectacle was at hand, and that the same influence must be vastly becoming to the imprisoned Juno. The door of the casino was, as usual, locked, but the moonlight was flooding the high-placed windows so generously that my curiosity became obstinate —and inventive. I dragged a garden seat around from the portico, placed it on end, and succeeded in climbing to the top of it and bringing myself abreast of one of the windows. The casement yielded to my pressure, turned on its hinges, and showed me the fancied scene—Juno visited by Diana. The beautiful image stood bathed in the radiant flood and shining with a purity which made her most persuasively divine. If by day her mellow complexion suggested faded gold, her substance now might have passed for polished silver. The effect was almost terrible; beauty so eloquent could hardly be inanimate. This was my foremost observation. I leave you to fancy whether my next was less interesting. At some distance from the foot of the statue, just out of the light, I perceived a figure lying flat on the pavement, prostrate apparently with devotion. I can hardly tell you how it completed the impressiveness of the scene. It marked the shining image as a goddess, indeed, and seemed to throw a sort of conscious pride into her stony mask. I of course immediately recognized this recumbent worshiper as the count, and while I stood gazing, as if to help me to read the full meaning of his attitude, the moonlight traveled forward and covered his breast and face. Then I saw that his eyes were closed and that he was either asleep or swooning. Watching him attentively, I detected his even respirations and judged there was no reason for alarm. The moonlight blanched his face, which seemed already pale with weariness. He had come into the presence of the Juno in obedience to that extraordinary need of which the symptoms had so woefully perplexed us, and exhausted either by compliance or resistance, he had sunk down at her feet in a stupid sleep. The bright moonshine soon aroused him, however; he muttered something and raised himself, vaguely staring. Then, recognizing his situation, he rose and stood for some time gazing fixedly at the shining statue with an expression which I fancied was not that of wholly unprotesting devotion. He uttered a string of broken words of which I was unable to catch the meaning, and then, after another pause and a long, melancholy moan, he turned slowly to the door. As rapidly and noiselessly as possible, I descended from my post of vigilance and passed behind the casino, and in a moment I heard the sound of the closing lock and of his departing footsteps.

The next day, meeting the little explorer in the grounds, I shook my finger at him with what I meant he should consider portentous gravity. But he only grinned like the malicious earth gnome to which I had always likened him and twisted his mustache, as if my menace was a capital joke. "If you dig any more holes here," I said, "you shall be thrust into the deepest of them and have the earth packed down on top of you. We have made enough discoveries, and we want no more statues. Your Juno has almost ruined us."

He burst out laughing. "I expected as much," he cried, "I had my notions!"

"What did you expect?"

"That the Signor Conte would begin and say his prayers to her."

"Good heavens! Is the case so common? Why did you expect it?"

"On the contrary, the case is rare. But I've fumbled so long in the monstrous heritage of antiquity that I have learned a multitude of secrets—learned that ancient relics may work modern miracles. There's a pagan element in all of us—I don't speak for you, *illustrissimi forestieri* —and the old gods have still their worshipers. The old spirit still throbs here and there, and the Signor Conte has his share of it. He's a good fellow, but between ourselves, he's an impossible Christian!" And this singular personage resumed his impertinent hilarity.

"If your previsions were so distinct," I said, "you ought to have given me a hint of them. I should have sent your spadesmen walking!"

"Ah, but the Juno is so beautiful!"

"Her beauty be blasted! Can you tell me what has become of the contessa's? To rival the Juno, she's turning to marble herself."

He shrugged his shoulders. "Ah, but the Juno is worth fifty thousand *scudi!*"

"I'd give a hundred thousand," I said, "to have her annihilated. Perhaps, after all, I shall want you to dig another hole."

"At your service!" he answered with a flourish, and we separated.

A couple of days later I dined, as I often did, with my host and hostess, and met the count face to face for the first time since his prostration in the casino. He bore the traces of it and sat plunged in somber distraction. I fancied that the path of the old faith was not strewn with flowers and that the Juno was becoming daily a harder mistress to serve. Dinner was scarcely over before he rose from table and took up his hat. As he did so, passing near his wife, he faltered a moment, stopped, and gave her—for the first time, I imagine—that vaguely imploring look which I had often caught. She moved her lips in inarticulate sympathy and put out her hands. He drew her toward him, kissed her with a kind of angry ardor, and strode away. The occasion was propitious, and further delay unnecessary.

"What I have to tell you is very strange," I said to the countess, "very fantastic, very incredible. But perhaps you'll not find it so bad as you feared. Your enemy is the Juno. The count—how shall I say it?—the count takes her *au sérieux*." She was silent, but after a moment she touched my arm with her hand, and I knew she meant that I had spoken her own belief. "You admired his antique simplicity: you see how far it goes. He has reverted to the faith of his fathers. Dormant through the ages, that imperious statue has silently aroused it. He believes in the pedigrees you used to dog-ear your school mythology with, trying to get by heart. In a word, dear child, Camillo is a pagan."

"I suppose you'll be terribly shocked," she answered, "if I say that he's welcome to any faith, if he will only share it with me. I'll believe in Jupiter, if he'll bid me! My sorrow's not for that: let my husband be himself! My sorrow is for the gulf of silence and indifference that has burst open between us. His Juno's the reality: I'm the fiction!"

"I've lately become reconciled to this gulf of silence and to your wearing for awhile a fabulous character. After the fable the moral! The poor fellow has but half-succumbed: the other half protests. The modern man is shut out in the darkness with his incomparable wife. How can he have failed to feel—vaguely and grossly, if it must have been, but in every throb of his heart—that you are a more perfect experiment of nature, a riper fruit of time, than those primitive persons for whom Juno was a terror and Venus an example? He pays you the compliment of believing you an inconvertible modern. He has crossed the Acheron, but he has left you behind, as a pledge to the present. We'll bring him back to redeem it. The old ancestral ghosts ought to be propitiated when a pretty creature like you has sacrificed the roses of her life. He has proved himself one of the Valerii; we shall see to it that he is the last, and yet that his decease shall leave the Conte Camillo in excellent health."

I spoke with a confidence which I had partly felt, for it seemed to me that if the count was to be touched it must be by the sense that his strange, spiritual excursion had not made his wife detest him. We talked long and to a hopeful end, for before I went away, my goddaughter expressed the desire to go out and look at the Juno. "I was afraid of her almost from the first," she said, "and have hardly seen her since she was set up in the casino. Perhaps I can learn a lesson from her and guess the secret of her influence."

For a moment I hesitated, with the fear that we might intrude upon the count's devotions. Then, as something in the young girl's face suggested that she had thought of this and felt a sudden impulse to pluck victory from the heart of danger, I bravely offered her my arm. The night was cloudy, and on this occasion, apparently, the triumphant goddess was to depend upon her own luster. But as we approached the casino, I saw that the door was ajar and that there was lamplight within. The lamp was suspended in front of the image, and it showed us that the place was empty. But the count had lately been there. Before the statue stood a roughly extemporized altar, composed of a nameless fragment of antique marble engraved with an illegible Greek inscription. We seemed really to stand in a pagan temple, and we gazed at the serene divinity with an impulse of spiritual reverence. It ought to have been deepened, I suppose, but it was rudely checked by our observing a curious glitter on the face of the low altar. A second glance showed us it was blood!

My companion looked at me in pale horror and turned away with a cry. A swarm of hideous conjectures pressed into my mind, and for a moment I was sickened. But at last I remembered that there is blood and blood, and the later Latins were not the anthropophagi.

"Be sure it's very innocent," I said, "a lamb, a kid, or a sucking calf!" But it was enough for her nerves and her conscience that it was a crimson trickle, and she returned to the house in great agitation. The rest of the night was not passed in a way to restore her to calmness. The count had not come in, and she sat up for him from hour to hour. I remained with her and smoked my cigar as composedly as I might, but internally I wondered what in horror's name had become of him. Gradually, as the hours wore away, I shaped a vague interpretation of those dusky portents—an interpretation none the less valid and devoutly desired for its being tolerably cheerful. The blood drops on the altar, I mused, were the last installment of his debt and the end of his delusion. They had been a happy necessity, for he was, after all, too gentle a creature not to hate himself for having shed them, not to abhor so cruelly insistent an idol. He had wandered away to recover himself in solitude, and he would come back to us with a repentant heart and an inquiring mind! I should certainly have believed all this more easily, however, if I could have heard his footstep in the hall. Toward dawn, as skepticism threatened to creep in with the gray light, I restlessly betook myself to the portico. Here in a few moments I saw him cross the grass, heavy-footed, splashed with mud, and evidently excessively tired. He must have been walking all night, and his face denoted that his spirit had been as restless as his body. He paused near me, and before he entered the house he stopped, looked at me a moment, and then held out his hand. I grasped it warmly, and it seemed to me to throb with all that he could not speak.

"Will you see your wife?" I asked.

He passed his hand over his eyes and shook his head. "Not now—not yet—some time!" he answered.

I was disappointed, but I convinced her, I think, that he had cast out the devil. She felt, poor girl, a pardonable desire to celebrate the event. I returned to my lodging, spent the day in Rome, and came back to the villa toward dusk. I was told that the countess was in the grounds. I looked for her cautiously at first, for I thought it just possible I might interrupt the natural consequences of a reconciliation; but failing to meet her, I turned toward the casino and found myself face to face with the little explorer.

"Does your Excellency happen to have twenty yards of stout rope about him?" he asked gravely.

"Do you want to hang yourself for the trouble you've stood sponsor to?" I answered.

"It's a hanging matter, I promise you. The countess

has given orders. You'll find her in the casino. Sweet-voiced as she is, she knows how to make her orders understood."

At the door of the casino stood half a dozen of the laborers on the place, looking vaguely solemn, like outlying dependants at a superior funeral. The countess was within, in a position which was an answer to the surveyor's riddle. She stood with her eyes fixed on the Juno, who had been removed from her pedestal and lay stretched in her magnificent length upon a rude litter.

"Do you understand?" she said. "She's beautiful, she's noble, she's precious, but she must go back!" And, with a passionate gesture, she seemed to indicate an open grave.

I was hugely delighted, but I thought it discreet to stroke my chin and look sober. "She's worth fifty thousand *scudi*."

She shook her head sadly. "If we were to sell her to the Pope and give the money to the poor, it wouldn't profit us. She must go back—she must go back! We must smother her beauty in the dreadful earth. It makes me feel almost as if she were alive; but it came to me last night with overwhelming force, when my husband came in and refused to see me, that he'll not be himself as long as she is above ground. To cut the knot we must bury her! If I had only thought of it before!"

"Not before!" I said, shaking my head in turn. "Heaven reward our sacrifice now!"

The little surveyor, when he reappeared, seemed hardly like an agent of the celestial influences, but he was deft and active, which was more to the point. Every now and then he uttered some half-articulate lament, by way of protest against the countess's cruelty, but I saw him privately scanning the recumbent image with an eye which seemed to foresee a malicious glee in standing on a certain unmarked spot on the turf and grinning till people stared. He had brought back an abundance of rope, and having summoned his assistants, who vigorously lifted the litter, he led the way to the original excavation, which had been left unclosed with the project of further researches. By the time we reached the edge of the grave, the evening had fallen and the beauty of our marble vic-

tim was shrouded in a dusky veil. No one spoke—if
not exactly for shame, at least for regret. Whatever our
plea, our performance looked, at least, monstrously profane. The ropes were adjusted and the Juno was slowly
lowered into her earthy bed. The countess took a handful
of earth and dropped it solemnly on her breast. "May it
lie lightly, but forever!" she said.

"Amen!" cried the little surveyor with a strange, mock-
ing inflection; and he gave us a bow, as he departed,
which betrayed an agreeable consciousness of knowing
where fifty thousand *scudi* were buried. His underlings
had another cask of wine, the result of which, for them,
was a suspension of all consciousness and a subsequent
irreparable confusion of memory as to where they had
plied their spades.

The countess had not yet seen her husband, who had
again apparently betaken himself to communion with the
great god Pan. I was, of course, unwilling to leave her to
encounter alone the results of her momentous deed. She
wandered into the drawing room and pretended to occupy herself with a bit of embroidery, but in reality she
was bravely composing herself for an "explanation." I
took up a book, but it held my attention as feebly. As
the evening wore away, I heard a movement on the
threshold and saw the count lifting the tapestried curtain
which masked the door and looking silently at his wife.
His eyes were brilliant, but not angry. He had missed the
Juno—and rejoiced! The countess kept her eyes fixed
on her work, and drew her silken stitches like an image of
wifely contentment. The image seemed to fascinate him.
He came in slowly, almost on tiptoe, walked to the chimney piece, and stood there in a sort of rapt contemplation. What had passed, what was passing, in his mind, I
leave to your own apprehension. My goddaughter's hand
trembled as it rose and fell, and the color came into her
cheek. At last, she raised her eyes and sustained the gaze
in which all his returning faith seemed concentrated. He
hesitated a moment, as if her very forgiveness kept the
gulf open between them, and then he strode forward,
fell on his two knees, and buried his head in her lap. I
departed as the count had come in, on tiptoe.

He never became, if you will, a thoroughly modern man; but one day, years after, when a visitor to whom he was showing his cabinet became inquisitive as to a marble hand suspended in one of its inner recesses, he looked grave and turned the lock on it. "It is the hand of a beautiful creature," he said, "whom I once greatly admired."

"Ah—a Roman?" said the gentleman with a smirk.

"A Greek," said the count with a frown.

Four Meetings

I SAW her but four times, but I remember them vividly; she made an impression upon me. I thought her very pretty and very interesting—a charming specimen of a type. I am very sorry to hear of her death, and yet, when I think of it, why should I be sorry? The last time I saw her she was certainly not—but I will describe all our meetings in order.

1

THE first one took place in the country, at a little tea party, one snowy night. It must have been some seventeen years ago. My friend Latouche, going to spend Christmas with his mother, had persuaded me to go with him, and the good lady had given in our honor the entertainment of which I speak. To me it was really entertaining. I had never been in the depths of New England at that season. It had been snowing all day and the drifts were knee-high. I wondered how the ladies had made their way to the house, but I perceived that at Grimwinter a *conversazione* offering the attraction of two gentlemen from New York was felt to be worth an effort.

Mrs. Latouche in the course of the evening asked me if I "didn't want to" show the photographs to some of the young ladies. The photographs were in a couple of great portfolios, and had been brought home by her son, who, like myself, was lately returned from Europe. I looked around and was struck with the fact that most of the young ladies were provided with an object of interest more absorbing than the most vivid sun picture. But there was a person standing alone near the mantelshelf, and looking round the room with a small, gentle smile which seemed at odds, somehow, with her isolation. I looked at her a moment and then said, "I should like to show them to that young lady."

"Oh yes," said Mrs. Latouche, "she is just the person. She doesn't care for flirting; I will speak to her."

I rejoined that if she did not care for flirting, she was, perhaps, not just the person, but Mrs. Latouche had already gone to propose the photographs to her.

"She's delighted," she said, coming back. "She is just the person, so quiet and so bright." And then she told me the young lady was, by name, Miss Caroline Spencer, and with this she introduced me.

Miss Caroline Spencer was not exactly a beauty, but she was a charming little figure. She must have been close upon thirty, but she was made almost like a little girl, and she had the complexion of a child. She had a very pretty head, and her hair was arranged as nearly as possible like the hair of a Greek bust, though it was presumable that she had never seen a Greek bust save in plaster. She was "artistic," I suspected, so far as Grimwinter allowed such tendencies. She had a soft, surprised eye, and thin lips, with very pretty teeth. Round her neck she wore what ladies call, I believe, a "ruche," fastened with a very small pin in pink coral, and in her hand she carried a fan made of plaited straw and adorned with pink ribbon. She wore a scanty, black silk dress. She spoke with a kind of soft precision, showing her white teeth between her narrow but tender-looking lips, and she seemed extremely pleased, even a little fluttered, at the prospect of my demonstrations. These went forward very smoothly, after I had moved the portfolios out of their corner and placed a couple of chairs near a lamp. The photographs were usually things I knew— large views of Switzerland, Italy and Spain, landscapes, copies of famous buildings, pictures, and statues. I said what I could about them, and my companion, looking at them as I held them up, sat perfectly still, with her straw fan raised to her underlip. Occasionally, as I laid one of the pictures down, she said very softly, "Have you seen that place?" I usually answered that I had seen it several

times (I had been a great traveler), and then I felt that
she looked at me askance for a moment with her pretty
eyes. I had asked her at the outset whether she had been
to Europe; to this she answered, "No, no, no," in a little,
quick, confidential whisper. But after that, though she
never took her eyes off the pictures, she said so little that
I was afraid she was bored. Accordingly, after we had
finished one portfolio, I offered, if she desired it, to
desist. I felt that she was not bored, but her reticence
puzzled me and I wished to make her speak. I turned
around to look at her and saw that there was a faint
flush in each of her cheeks. She was waving her little fan
to and fro. Instead of looking at me, she fixed her eyes
upon the other portfolio, which was leaning against the
table.

"Won't you show me that?" she asked with a little
tremor in her voice. I could almost have believed she was
agitated.

"With pleasure," I answered, "if you are not tired."

"No, I am not tired," she affirmed. "I like it—I love it."

And as I took up the other portfolio, she laid her hand
upon it, rubbing it softly.

"And have you been here, too?" she asked.

On my opening the portfolio, it appeared that I had
been there. One of the first photographs was a large view
of the Castle of Chillon, on the Lake of Geneva.

"Here," I said, "I have been many a time. Is it not
beautiful?" And I pointed to the perfect reflection of the
rugged rocks and pointed towers in the clear, still water.
She did not say, "Oh, enchanting!" and push it away to
see the next picture. She looked awhile, and then she
asked if it was not where Bonivard, about whom Byron
wrote, was confined. I assented and tried to quote some
of Byron's verses, but in this attempt I floundered, helpless.

She fanned herself a moment and then repeated the
lines correctly, in a soft, flat, and yet agreeable voice. By
the time she had finished, she was blushing. I compli-
mented her and told her she was perfectly equipped for
visiting Switzerland and Italy. She looked at me askance
again to see whether I was serious, and I added that if
she wished to recognize Byron's descriptions, she must go

abroad speedily; Europe was getting sadly dis-Byronized.

"How soon must I go?" she asked.

"Oh, I will give you ten years."

"I think I can do it within ten years," she answered very soberly.

"Well," I said, "you will enjoy it immensely; you will find it very charming." And just then I came upon a photograph of some nook in a foreign city which I had been very fond of and which recalled tender memories. I discoursed (as I suppose) with a certain eloquence; my companion sat listening, breathless.

"Have you been *very* long in foreign lands?" she asked, some time after I had ceased.

"Many years," I said.

"And have you traveled everywhere?"

"I have traveled a great deal. I am very fond of it, and, happily, I have been able."

Again she gave me her sidelong gaze.

"And do you know the foreign languages?"

"After a fashion."

"Is it hard to speak them?"

"I don't believe you would find it hard," I gallantly responded.

"Oh, I shouldn't want to speak—I should only want to listen," she said. Then, after a pause, she added: "They say the French theater is so beautiful."

"It is the best in the world."

"Did you go very often?"

"When I was first in Paris I went every night."

"Every night!" And she opened her clear eyes very wide. "That to me is"—and she hesitated a moment—"is very wonderful." A few minutes later she asked, "Which country do you prefer?"

"There is one country I prefer to all others. I think you would do the same."

She looked at me a moment, and then she said softly, "Italy?"

"Italy," I answered softly, too, and for a moment we looked at each other. She looked as pretty as if, instead of showing her photographs, I had been making love to her. To increase the analogy, she glanced away, blushing. There was a silence, which she broke at last by saying:

"That is the place which—in particular—I have thought of going to."

"Oh! That's the place—that's the place!" I said.

She looked at two or three photographs in silence.

"They say it is not so dear."

"As some other countries? Yes, that is not the least of its charms."

"But it is all pretty dear, is it not?"

"Europe, you mean?"

"Going there and traveling. That has been the trouble. I have very little money. I teach," said Miss Spencer.

"Of course, one must have money," I said, "but one can manage with a moderate amount."

"I think I should manage. I have laid something by, and I am always adding a little to it. It's all for that." She paused a moment, and then went on with a kind of suppressed eagerness, as if telling me the story were a rare, but a possibly impure satisfaction. "But it has not been only the money; it has been everything. Everything has been against it. I have waited and waited. It has been a mere castle in the air. I am almost afraid to talk about it. Two or three times it has been a little nearer, and then I have talked about it and it has melted away. I have talked about it too much," she said hypocritically, for I saw that such talking was now a small, tremulous ecstasy. "There is a lady who is a great friend of mine; she doesn't want to go; I always talk to her about it. I tire her dreadfully. She told me once she didn't know what would become of me. I should go crazy if I did not go to Europe, and I should certainly go crazy if I did."

"Well," I said, "you have not gone yet, and nevertheless you are not crazy."

She looked at me a moment and said:

"I am not so sure. I don't think of anything else. I am always thinking of it. It prevents me from thinking of things that are nearer home—things that I ought to attend to. That is a kind of craziness."

"The cure for it is to go," I said.

"I have a faith that I shall go. I have a cousin there."

We turned over some more photographs, and I asked her if she had always lived at Grimwinter.

"Oh, no, sir," said Miss Spencer. "I have spent twenty-three months in Boston."

I answered, jocosely, that in that case foreign lands would probably prove a disappointment to her, but I quite failed to alarm her.

"I know more about them than you might think," she said with her shy, neat, little smile. "I mean by reading; I have read a great deal. I have not only read Byron; I have read histories and guidebooks. I know I shall like it!"

"I understand your case," I rejoined. "You have the native American passion—the passion for the picturesque. With us, I think, it is primordial—antecedent to experience. Experience comes and only shows us something we have dreamed of."

"I think that is very true," said Caroline Spencer. "I have dreamed of everything; I shall know it all."

"I am afraid you have wasted a great deal of time."

"Oh yes, that has been my great wickedness."

The people about us had begun to scatter; they were taking their leave. She got up and put out her hand to me, timidly, but with a peculiar brightness in her eyes.

"I am going back there," I said as I shook hands with her. "I shall look out for you."

"I will tell you," she answered, "if I am disappointed."

And she went away, looking delicately agitated and moving her little straw fan.

2

A few months after this I returned to Europe, and some three years elapsed. I had been living in Paris, and, toward the end of October, I went from that city to Havre, to meet my sister and her husband, who had written me that they were about to arrive there. On reaching Havre I found that the steamer was already in; I was nearly two hours late. I repaired directly to the hotel, where my relatives were already established. My sister had gone to bed, exhausted and disgusted by her voyage; she was a wretchedly poor sailor, and her suf-

ferings on this occasion had been extreme. She wished,
for the moment, for undisturbed rest, and was unable to
see me for more than five minutes. It was agreed that
we should remain at Havre until the next day. My
brother-in-law, who was anxious about his wife, was unwilling to leave her room, but she insisted upon his going
out with me to take a walk and recover his land legs. The
early autumn day was warm and charming, and our
stroll through the bright-colored, busy streets of the
old French seaport was sufficiently entertaining. We
walked along the sunny, noisy quays and then turned into
a wide, pleasant street which lay half in sun and half in
shade—a French provincial street, that looked like an
old watercolor drawing: tall, gray, steep-roofed, red-
gabled, many-storied houses; green shutters on windows
and old scrollwork above them; flowerpots in balconies
and white caps in doorways. We walked in the shade;
all this stretched away on the sunny side of the street
and made a picture. We looked at it as we passed along;
then, suddenly, my brother-in-law stopped, pressing my
arm and staring. I followed his gaze and saw that we had
paused just before coming to a café, where, under an
awning, several tables and chairs were disposed upon
the pavement. The windows were open behind; half a
dozen plants in tubs were ranged beside the door; the
pavement was besprinkled with clean bran. It was a nice
little, quiet, old-fashioned café; inside, in the comparative dusk, I saw a stout, handsome woman with pink
ribbons in her cap perched up with a mirror behind her
back, smiling at some one who was out of sight. All
this, however, I perceived afterward; what I first observed was a lady sitting alone outside at one of the little
marble-topped tables. My brother-in-law had stopped to
look at her. There was something on the little table, but
she was leaning back quietly, with her hands folded, looking down the street, away from us. I saw her only in
something less than profile; nevertheless, I instantly felt
that I had seen her before.

"The little lady of the steamer!" exclaimed my brother-
in-law.

"Was she on your steamer?" I asked.

"From morning till night. She was never sick. She

used to sit perpetually at the side of the vessel with her hands crossed that way, looking at the eastward horizon."

"Are you going to speak to her?"

"I don't know her. I never made acquaintance with her. I was too seedy. But I used to watch her and—I don't know why—to be interested in her. She's a dear little Yankee woman. I have an idea she is a school-mistress taking a holiday—for which her scholars have made up a purse."

She turned her face a little more into profile, looking at the steep, gray house-fronts opposite to her. Then I said:

"I shall speak to her myself."

"I wouldn't; she is very shy," said my brother-in-law.

"My dear fellow, I know her. I once showed her photographs a whole winter's evening, at a tea party."

And I went up to her. She turned and looked at me, and I saw she was in fact Miss Caroline Spencer. But she was not so quick to recognize me; she looked startled. I pushed a chair to the table and sat down.

"Well," I said, "I hope you are not disappointed!"

She stared, blushing a little; then she gave a small jump which betrayed recognition.

"It was you who showed me the photographs—at Grimwinter!"

"Yes, it was I. This happens very charmingly, for I feel as if it were for me to give you a formal reception here—an official welcome. I talked to you so much about Europe."

"You didn't say too much. I'm so happy!" she softly exclaimed.

Very happy she looked. There was no sign of her being older; she was as gravely, decently, demurely pretty as before. If she had seemed before a thin-stemmed, mild-hued flower of Puritanism, it may be imagined whether in her present situation this delicate bloom was less apparent. Beside her an old gentleman was drinking absinthe; behind her the *dame de comptoir* in the pink ribbons was calling *"Alcibiade! Alcibiade!"* to the long-aproned waiter. I explained to Miss Spencer that my companion had lately been her shipmate, and my brother-in-law came up and was introduced to her. But she looked at him as if she had never seen him before, and I remembered that he had told me that her eyes were always fixed upon the eastward horizon. She had evidently not noticed him, and, still timidly smiling, she made no attempt whatever to pretend that she had. I stayed with her at the café door, and he went back to the hotel and to his wife. I said to Miss Spencer that this meeting of ours in the first hour of her landing was really very strange, but that I was delighted to be there and receive her first impressions.

"Oh, I can't tell you," she said: "I feel as if I were in a dream. I have been sitting here for an hour, and I don't want to move. Everything is so picturesque. I don't know whether the coffee has intoxicated me; it's so delicious."

"Really," said I, "if you are so pleased with this poor old, prosaic, shabby Havre, you will have no admiration left for better things. Don't spend your admiration all the first day; remember it's your intellectual letter of credit. Remember all the beautiful places and things that are waiting for you; remember that lovely Italy!"

"I'm not afraid of running short," she said gaily, still looking at the opposite houses. "I could sit here all day, saying to myself that here I am at last. It's so dark, and old, and different."

"By the way," I inquired, "how come you to be sitting here? Have you not gone to one of the inns?" For I was half-amused, half-alarmed at the good conscience with which this delicately pretty woman had stationed herself in conspicuous isolation at a café door.

"My cousin brought me here," she answered. "You know I told you I had a cousin in Europe. He met me at the steamer this morning."

"It was hardly worth his while to meet you if he was to desert you so soon."

"Oh, he has only left me for half an hour," said Miss Spencer. "He has gone to get my money."

"Where is your money?"

She gave a little laugh.

"It makes me feel very fine to tell you! It is in some circular notes."

"And where are your circular notes?"

"My cousin has them."

This statement was very serenely uttered, but—I can hardly say why—it gave me a certain chill. At the moment, I should have been utterly unable to say why. I knew nothing of Miss Spencer's cousin, and the presumption was in his favor, since he *was* her cousin. But I felt suddenly uncomfortable at the thought that half an hour after her landing her scanty funds should have passed into his hands.

"Is he to travel with you?" I asked.

"Only as far as Paris. He is an art student there. I wrote to him that I was coming, but I never expected him to come off to the ship. I supposed he would only just meet me at the train in Paris. It is very kind of him. But he *is* very kind—and very bright."

I instantly became conscious of an extreme curiosity to see this bright cousin who was an art student.

"He is gone to the banker's?" I asked.

"Yes, to the banker's. He took me to a hotel—such a queer, quaint, delicious little place, with a court in the middle, and a gallery all round, and a lovely landlady, in such a beautifully fluted cap, and such a perfectly fitting dress! After a while we came out to walk to the banker's, for I haven't got any French money. But I was very dizzy from the motion of the vessel, and I thought I had better sit down. He found this place for me here, and he went off to the banker's himself. I am to wait here till he comes back."

It may seem very fantastic, but it passed through my mind that he would never come back. I settled myself in my chair beside Miss Spencer and determined to await the event. She was extremely observant; there was something touching in it. She noticed everything that the movement of the street brought before us—the peculiarities of costumes, the shapes of vehicles, the big Norman horses, the fat priests, the shaven poodles. We talked of these things. There was something charming in her freshness of perception and the way her book-nourished fancy recognized and welcomed everything.

"And when your cousin comes back, what are you going to do?" I asked.

She hesitated a moment.

"We don't quite know."

"When do you go to Paris? If you go by the four o'clock train I may have the pleasure of making the journey with you."

"I don't think we shall do that. My cousin thinks I had better stay here a few days."

"Oh!" said I, and for five minutes said nothing more. I was wondering what her cousin was, in vulgar parlance, "up to." I looked up and down the street, but saw nothing that looked like a bright American art student. At last I took the liberty of observing that Havre was hardly a place to choose as one of the aesthetic stations of a European tour. It was a place of convenience, nothing more; a place of transit, through which transit should be rapid. I recommended her to go to Paris by the afternoon train, and meanwhile to amuse herself by driving to the ancient fortress at the mouth of the harbor—that picturesque, circular structure which bore the name of Francis the First and looked like a small castle of St. Angelo. (It has lately been demolished.)

She listened with much interest; then for a moment she looked grave.

"My cousin told me that when he returned he should have something particular to say to me, and that we could do nothing or decide nothing until I should have heard it. But I will make him tell me quickly, and then we will go to the ancient fortress. There is no hurry to get to Paris; there is plenty of time."

She smiled with her softly severe little lips as she spoke those last words. But I, looking at her with a purpose, saw just a tiny gleam of apprehension in her eye.

"Don't tell me now," I said, "that this wretched man is going to give you some bad news!"

"I suspect it is a little bad, but I don't believe it is very bad. At any rate, I must listen to it."

I looked at her again an instant. "You didn't come to Europe to listen," I said, "You came to see!" But now I was sure her cousin would come back; since he had something disagreeable to say to her, he certainly would come back. We sat a while longer, and I asked her about her plans of travel. She had them on her fingers' ends, and she told over the names with a kind of solemn distinctness: From Paris to Dijon and to Avignon, from Avignon to Marseilles and the Cornice road; thence to Genoa, to Spezia, to Pisa, to Florence, to Rome. It apparently had never occurred to her that there could be the least incommodity in her traveling alone, and since she was unprovided with a companion, I, of course, religiously abstained from kindling her suspicions.

At last, her cousin came back. I saw him turn toward us out of a side street, and from the moment my eyes rested upon him I felt that this was the bright American art student. He wore a slouch hat and a rusty black velvet jacket, such as I had often encountered in the Rue Bonaparte. His shirt collar revealed a large portion of a throat which, at a distance, was not strikingly statuesque. He was tall and lean; he had red hair and freckles. So much I had time to observe while he approached the café, staring at me with natural surprise from under his umbrageous coiffure. When he came up to us, I immediately introduced myself to him as an old acquaintance of Miss Spencer. He looked at me hard with a pair of little red eyes, then he made me a solemn bow in the French fashion, with his sombrero.

"You were not on the ship?" he said.

"No, I was not on the ship. I have been in Europe these three years."

He bowed once more, solemnly, and motioned me to be seated again. I sat down, but it was only for the purpose of observing him an instant. I saw it was time I should return to my sister. Miss Spencer's cousin was a queer fellow. Nature had not shaped him for a Raphaelesque or Byronic attire, and his velvet doublet and naked throat were not in harmony with his facial attributes. His hair was cropped close to his head; his ears were large and ill adjusted to the same. He had a lackadaisical carriage and a sentimental droop, which was peculiarly at variance with his small, strange-colored eyes. Perhaps I was prejudiced, but I thought his eyes treacherous. He said nothing for some time; he leaned his hands on his cane and looked up and down the street. Then at last, slowly lifting his cane and pointing with it, "That's a very nice bit," he remarked, softly. He had his head on one side, and his little eyes were half-closed. I followed the direction of his stick; the object it indicated was a red cloth hung out of an old window. "Nice bit of color," he continued, and without moving his head he transferred his half-closed gaze to me. "Composes well," he pursued. "Make a nice thing." He spoke in a strange, weak drawl.

"I see you have a great deal of eye," I replied. "Your cousin tells me you are studying art?" He looked at me in the same way without answering, and I went on with deliberate urbanity: "I suppose you are at the studio of one of those great men."

Still he looked at me, and then he said softly, "Gérôme."

"Do you like it?" I asked.

"Do you understand French?" he said.

"Some kinds," I answered.

He kept his little eyes on me; then he said, *"Je l'adore!"*

"Oh, I understand that kind!" I rejoined. Miss Spencer laid her hand upon her cousin's arm with a little pleased and flattered movement; it was delightful to be among people who were so easily familiar with foreign tongues. I got up to take leave and asked Miss Spencer where, in Paris, I might have the honor of waiting upon her. To what hotel should she go?

She turned to her cousin inquiringly, and he honored me again with his little languid leer. "Do you know the Hotel des Princes?"

"I know where it is."

"I shall take her there."

"I congratulate you," I said to Caroline Spencer. "I believe it is the best inn in the world; and in case I should still have a moment to call upon you here, where are you lodged?"

"Oh, it's such a pretty name," said Miss Spencer gleefully. "À la Belle Cuisinière,—the Beautiful Cook."

As I left them her cousin gave me a great flourish with his picturesque hat. My sister, as it proved, was not sufficiently restored to leave Havre by the afternoon train; so that, as the autumn dusk began to fall, I found myself at liberty to call at the sign of the "Beautiful Cook." I must confess that I had spent much of the interval in wondering what the disagreeable thing was that my charming friend's disagreeable cousin had been telling her. The Belle Cuisinière was a modest inn in a shady bystreet, where it gave me satisfaction to think Miss Spencer must have encountered local color in abundance. There was a crooked little court where much of the hospitality of the house was carried on; there was a staircase climbing to bedrooms on the outer side of the wall; there was a small, trickling fountain with a stucco statuette in the midst of it; there was a little boy in a white cap and apron cleaning copper vessels at a conspicuous kitchen door; there was a chattering landlady, neatly laced, arranging apricots and grapes into an artistic pyramid upon a pink plate. I looked about, and on a green bench outside of an open door labeled *Salle à Manger*, I perceived Caroline Spencer. No sooner had I looked at her than I saw that something had happened since the morning. She was leaning back on her bench, her hands were clasped in her lap, and her eyes were fixed upon the landlady, at the other side of the court, manipulating her apricots.

But I saw she was not thinking of apricots. She was staring absently, thoughtfully; as I came near her I perceived that she had been crying. I sat down on the bench beside her before she saw me; then, when she had done so, she simply turned around, without surprise, and rested her sad eyes upon me. Something very bad indeed had happened; she was completely changed.

I immediately charged her with it.

"Your cousin has been giving you bad news; you are in great distress."

For a moment she said nothing, and I supposed that she was afraid to speak, lest her tears should come back. But presently I perceived that in the short time that had elapsed since my leaving her in the morning, she had shed them all, and that she was now softly stoical and composed.

"My poor cousin is in distress," she said at last. "His news was bad." Then, after a brief hesitation: "He was in terrible want of money."

"In want of yours, you mean?"

"Of any that he could get—honestly. Mine was the only money."

"And he has taken yours?"

She hesitated again a moment, but her glance, meanwhile, was pleading.

"I gave him what I had."

I have always remembered the accent of those words as the most angelic piece of human intonation I have ever listened to.

Almost with a sense of personal outrage I jumped up.

"Good heavens!" I said, "do you call that getting it honestly?"

But I had gone too far; she blushed deeply. "We will not speak of it," she said.

"We *must* speak of it," I answered, sitting down again. "I am your friend; it seems to me you need one. What is the matter with your cousin?"

"He is in debt."

"No doubt! But what is the special fitness of your paying his debts?"

"He has told me all his story; I am very sorry for him."

"So am I! But I hope he will give you back your money."

"Certainly he will; as soon as he can."

"When will that be?"

"When he has finished his great picture."

"My dear young lady, confound his great picture! Where is this unhappy cousin?"

She certainly hesitated now. Then, "At his dinner," she answered.

I turned about and looked through the open door into the *salle à manger*. There, alone, at the end of a long table, I perceived the object of Miss Spencer's compassion—the bright young art student. He was dining too attentively to notice me at first, but in the act of setting down a well-emptied wineglass he caught sight of my observant attitude. He paused in his repast, and with his head on one side and his lank jaws slowly moving, fixedly returned my gaze. Then the landlady came lightly brushing by with her pyramid of apricots.

"And that nice little plate of fruit is for him?" I exclaimed.

Miss Spencer glanced at it tenderly.

"They do that so prettily!" she murmured.

I felt helpless and irritated. "Come now, really," I said; "do you approve of that great long fellow accepting your funds?" She looked away from me; I was evidently giving her pain. The case was hopeless; the great long fellow had "interested" her.

"Excuse me if I speak of him so unceremoniously," I said. "But you are really too generous, and he is not quite delicate enough. He made his debts himself—he ought to pay them himself."

"He has been foolish," she answered; "I know that. He has told me everything. We had a long talk this morning; the poor fellow threw himself upon my charity. He has signed notes to a large amount."

"The more fool he!"

"He is in extreme distress; and it is not only himself. It is his poor wife."

"Ah, he has a poor wife?"

"I didn't know it, but he confessed everything. He married two years since, secretly."

"Why secretly?"

Caroline Spencer glanced about her, as if she feared listeners. Then softly, in a little impressive tone—"She was a countess!"

"Are you very sure of that?"

"She has written me a most beautiful letter."

"Asking you for money, eh?" I pursued, brutally, cynically perhaps, but irresistibly.

"Asking me for confidence and sympathy," said Miss Spencer. "She has been disinherited by her father. My cousin told me the story, and she tells it in her own way in the letter. It is like an old romance. Her father opposed the marriage, and when he discovered that she had secretly disobeyed him, he cruelly cast her off. It is really most romantic. They are the oldest family in Provence."

I looked and listened, marveling. It really seemed that the poor woman was enjoying the "romance" of having a discarded countess-cousin, out of Provence, so deeply as almost to lose the sense of what the forfeiture of her money meant for her.

"My dear young lady," I said, "you don't want to be ruined for picturesqueness' sake?"

"I shall not be ruined. I shall come back before long to stay with them. The countess insists upon that."

"Come back! You are going home, then?"

She sat for a moment with her eyes lowered, then with a heroic suppression of a faint tremor of the voice:

"I have no money for traveling!" she answered.

"You gave it *all* up?"

"I have kept enough to take me home."

I gave an angry groan, and at this juncture Miss Spencer's cousin, the fortunate possessor of her precious purse and of the hand of the Provençal countess, emerged from the little dining room. He stood on the threshold for an instant, removing the stone from a plump apricot which he had brought away from the table; then he put the apricot into his mouth, and while he let it sojourn there, gratefully, stood looking at us, with his long legs apart and his hands dropped into the pockets of his velvet jacket. My companion got up, giving him a thin glance which I caught in its passage, and which seemed to designate a strange commixture of resignation and fascination—a sort of perverted enthusiasm. Ugly, vulgar, pretentious, dishonest as I thought the creature, he had appealed successfully to her eager but most innocent imagination. I was profoundly disgusted, but I had no warrant absolutely to interfere. Besides, I felt that it would be vain.

The young man waved his hand with a pictorial gesture. "Nice old court," he observed. "Nice mellow old place. Good tone in that brick. Nice crooked old staircase."

Decidedly, I was too much displeased. Without responding, I gave my hand to Caroline Spencer. She looked at me an instant with her little white face and expanded eyes, and as she showed her pretty teeth, I suppose she meant to smile.

"Don't be sorry for me," she said, "I am very sure I shall see something of Europe yet."

I told her that I should not bid her good-by, I should find a moment to come back the next morning. Her cousin, who had put on his sombrero again, flourished it off at me by way of a bow, with which I took my departure.

The next morning I came back to the inn, where I met in the court the landlady, more loosely laced than in the evening. On my asking for Miss Spencer, *"Partie,"* Monsieur," said the landlady. "She went away last night

at ten o'clock, with her—her—not her husband, eh?—
in fine, her *Monsieur*. They went down to the American
ship." I turned away; the poor girl had been about thirteen
hours in Europe.

3

I MYSELF, more fortunate, was there some five years
longer. During this period I lost my friend Latouche, who
died of a malarious fever during a tour in the Levant. One
of the first things I did on my return was to go up to
Grimwinter to pay a consolatory visit to his poor mother.
I found her in deep affliction, and I sat with her the whole
of the morning that followed my arrival (I had come in
late at night), listening to her tearful descant and singing
the praise of my friend. We talked of nothing else, and
our conversation terminated only with the arrival of a
quick little woman who drove herself up to the door in a
carryall, and whom I saw toss the reins upon the horse's
back with the briskness of a startled sleeper throwing
back the bedclothes. She jumped out of the carryall, and
she jumped into the room. She proved to be the minister's
wife and the great town gossip, and she had evidently, in
the latter capacity, a choice morsel to communicate.
I was as sure of this as I was that poor Mrs. Latouche
was not absolutely too bereaved to listen to her. It seemed
to me discreet to retire. I said I believed I would go
and take a walk before dinner.

"And, by the way," I added, "if you will tell me where
my old friend Miss Spencer lives, I will walk to her
house."

The minister's wife immediately responded. Miss
Spencer lived in the fourth house beyond the Baptist
church; the Baptist church was the one on the right, with
that queer, green thing over the door; they called it a
portico, but it looked more like an old-fashioned bed-
stead.

"Yes, do go and see poor Caroline," said Mrs. Latouche. "It will refresh her to see a strange face."

"I should think she had had enough of strange faces!" cried the minister's wife.

"I mean, to see a visitor," said Mrs. Latouche, amending her phrase.

"I should think she had had enough of visitors!" her companion enjoined. "But you don't mean to stay ten years," she added, glancing at me.

"Has she a visitor of that sort?" I inquired, perplexed.

"You will see the sort!" said the minister's wife. "She's easily seen; she generally sits in the front yard. Only take care what you say to her, and be very sure you are polite."

"Ah, she is so sensitive?"

The minister's wife jumped up and dropped me a courtesy—a most ironical courtesy.

"That's what she is, if you please. She's a countess!"

And pronouncing this word with the most scathing accent, the little woman seemed fairly to laugh in the countess's face. I stood a moment, staring, wondering, remembering.

"Oh, I shall be very polite!" I cried, and grasping my hat and stick, I went on my way.

I found Miss Spencer's residence without difficulty. The Baptist church was easily identified, and the small dwelling near it, of a rusty white, with a large central chimney stack and a Virginia creeper, seemed naturally and properly the abode of a frugal old maid with a taste for the picturesque. As I approached, I slackened my pace, for I had heard that someone was always sitting in the front yard, and I wished to reconnoiter. I looked cautiously over the low, white fence which separated the small garden space from the unpaved street, but I descried nothing in the way of a countess. A small, straight path led up to the crooked doorstep, and on either side of it was a little grass plot, fringed with currant bushes. In the middle of the grass, on either side, was a large quince tree, full of antiquity and contortions, and beneath one of the quince trees were placed a small table and a couple of chairs. On the table lay a piece of unfinished embroidery and two or three books in bright-colored paper covers. I went in at the gate and paused halfway along the path, scanning the place for some further token of its occupant, before whom—I could hardly have said why—I hesitated abruptly to present myself. Then I saw that the poor little house was very shabby. I felt a sudden doubt of my right to intrude, for curiosity had been my motive, and curiosity here seemed singularly indelicate. While I hesitated, a figure appeared in the open doorway and stood there looking at me. I immediately recognized Caroline Spencer, but she looked at me as if she had never seen me before. Gently, but gravely and timidly, I advanced to the doorstep, and then I said, with an attempt at friendly badinage:

"I waited for you over there to come back, but you never came."

"Waited where, sir?" she asked softly, and her light-colored eyes expanded more than before.

She was much older; she looked tired and wasted.

"Well," I said, "waited at Havre."

She stared; then she recognized me. She smiled and blushed and clasped her two hands together.

"I remember you now," she said. "I remember that day."

But she stood there, neither coming out nor asking me to come in. She was embarrassed.

I, too, felt a little awkward. I poked my stick into the path.

"I kept looking out for you, year after year," I said.

"You mean in Europe?" murmured Miss Spencer.

"In Europe, of course! Here, apparently, you are easy enough to find."

She leaned her hand against the unpainted doorpost, and her head fell a little to one side. She looked at me for a moment without speaking, and I thought I recognized the expression that one sees in women's eyes when tears are rising. Suddenly she stepped out upon the cracked slab of stone before the threshold and closed the door behind her. Then she began to smile intently, and I saw that her teeth were as pretty as ever. But there had been tears too.

"Have you been there ever since?" she asked almost in a whisper.

"Until three weeks ago. And you—you never came back?"

Still looking at me with her fixed smile, she put her hand behind her and opened the door again.

"I am not very polite," she said. "Won't you come in?"

"I am afraid I incommode you."

"Oh no!" she answered, smiling more than ever.

And she pushed back the door, with a sign that I should enter.

I went in, following her. She led the way to a small room on the left of the narrow hall, which I supposed to be her parlor, though it was at the back of the house, and we passed the closed door of another apartment, which apparently enjoyed a view of the quince trees. This one looked out upon a small woodshed and two clucking hens. But I thought it very pretty, until I saw that its elegance was of the most frugal kind; after which, presently, I thought it prettier still, for I had never seen faded chintz and old mezzotint engravings, framed in varnished autumn leaves, disposed in so graceful a fashion. Miss Spencer sat down on a very small portion of the sofa, with her hands tightly clasped in her lap. She looked ten years older, and it would have sounded very perverse now to speak of her as pretty. But I thought her so; or at least I thought her touching. She was evidently agitated. I tried to appear not to notice it, but suddenly, in the most inconsequent fashion —it was an irresistible memory of our little friendship at Havre—I said to her:

"I do incommode you. You are distressed."

She raised her two hands to her face, and for a moment kept it buried in them. Then, taking them away:

"It's because you remind me——" she said.

"I remind you, you mean, of that miserable day at Havre?"

She shook her head.

"It was not miserable. It was delightful."

"I never was so shocked," I rejoined, "as when, on going back to your inn the next morning, I found you had set sail again."

She was silent a moment; and then she said:

"Please let us not speak of that."

"Did you come straight back here?" I asked.

"I was back here just thirty days after I had gone away."

"And here you have remained ever since?"

"Oh, yes!" she said gently.

"When are you going to Europe again?"

This question seemed brutal, but there was something that irritated me in the softness of her resignation, and I wished to extort from her some expression of impatience.

She fixed her eyes for a moment upon a small sunspot on the carpet; then she got up and lowered the window blind a little to obliterate it. Presently, in the same mild voice, answering my question, she said:

"Never!"

"I hope your cousin repaid you your money."

"I don't care for it now," she said, looking away from me.

"You don't care for your money?"

"For going to Europe."

"Do you mean that you would not go if you could?"

"I can't—I can't," said Caroline Spencer. "It is all over; I never think of it."

"He never repaid you, then!" I exclaimed.

"Please—please," she began.

But she stopped; she was looking toward the door. There had been a rustling and a sound of steps in the hall.

I also looked toward the door, which was open, and now admitted another person—a lady who paused just within the threshold. Behind her came a young man. The lady looked at me with a good deal of fixedness—long enough for my glance to receive a vivid impression of herself. Then she turned to Caroline Spencer, and with a smile and a strong foreign accent:

"Excuse my interruption!" she said. "I knew not you had company—the gentleman came in so quietly."

With this, she directed her eyes toward me again.

She was very strange; yet my first feeling was that I had seen her before. Then I perceived that I had only seen ladies who were very much like her. But I had seen them very far away from Grimwinter, and it was an odd sensation to be seeing her here. Whither was it the sight of her seemed to transport me? To some dusky landing before a shabby Parisian *quatrième*——to an open door revealing a mussy antechamber, and to madame leaning over the banisters, while she holds a faded dressing gown together and bawls down to the portress to bring up her coffee. Miss Spencer's visitor was a very large woman, of middle age, with a plump, dead-white face, and hair drawn back *à la chinoise*. She had a small, penetrating eye and what is called in French an agreeable smile. She wore an all pink cashmere dressing gown, covered with white embroideries, and like "madame," in my momentary vision, she was holding it together in front with a bare and rounded arm, and a plump and deeply dimpled hand.

"It is only to spick about my *café*," she said to Miss Spencer with her agreeable smile. "I should like it served in the garden under the leetle tree."

The young man behind her had now stepped into the room, and he also stood looking at me. He was a pretty-faced little fellow, with an air of provincial foppishness —a tiny Adonis of Grimwinter. He had a small, pointed nose, a small, pointed chin, and, as I observed, the most diminutive feet. He looked at me foolishly, with his mouth open.

"You shall have your coffee," said Miss Spencer, who had a faint red spot in each of her cheeks.

"It is well!" said the lady in the dressing gown. "Find your bouk," she added, turning to the young man.

He looked vaguely round the room.

"My grammar, d'ye mean?" he asked with a helpless intonation.

But the large lady was looking at me curiously and gathering in her dressing gown with her white arm.

"Find your bouk, my friend," she repeated.

"My poetry, d'ye mean?" said the young man, also gazing at me again.

"Never mind your bouk," said his companion. "Today we will talk. We will make some conversation. But we must not interrupt. Come," and she turned away. "Under the leetle tree," she added for the benefit of Miss Spencer. Then she gave me a sort of salutation and a "Monsieur!" with which she swept away again, followed by the young man.

Caroline Spencer stood there with her eyes fixed upon the ground.

"Who is that?" I asked.

"The countess, my cousin."

"And who is the young man?"

"Her pupil, Mr. Mixter."

This description of the relation between the two persons who had just left the room made me break into a little laugh. Miss Spencer looked at me gravely.

"She gives French lessons; she has lost her fortune."

"I see," I said. "She is determined to be a burden to no one. That is very proper."

Miss Spencer looked down on the ground again.

"I must go and get the coffee," she said.

"Has the lady many pupils?" I asked.

"She has only Mr. Mixter. She gives all her time to him."

At this I could not laugh, though I smelled provocation. Miss Spencer was too grave.

"He pays very well," she presently added with simplicity. "He is very rich. He is very kind. He takes the countess to drive." And she was turning away.

"You are going for the countess's coffee?" I said.

"If you will excuse me a few moments?"

"Is there no one else to do it?"

She looked at me with the softest serenity.

"I keep no servants."

"Can she not wait upon herself?"

"She is not used to that."

"I see," said I as gently as possible. "But before you go, tell me this: who is this lady?"

"I told you about her before—that day. She is the wife of my cousin, whom you saw."

"The lady who was disowned by her family in consequence of her marriage?"

"Yes; they have never seen her again. They have cast her off."

"And where is her husband?"

"He is dead."

"And where is your money?"

The poor girl flinched; there was something too method-
ical in my questions.

"I don't know," she said wearily.

But I continued a moment.

"On her husband's death this lady came over here?"

"Yes, she arrived one day."

"How long ago?"

"Two years."

"She has been here ever since?"

"Every moment."

"How does she like it?"

"Not at all."

"And how do *you* like it?"

Miss Spencer laid her face in her two hands an instant,
as she had done ten minutes before. Then, quickly, she
went to get the countess's coffee.

I remained alone in the little parlor; I wanted to see
more—to learn more. At the end of five minutes the
young man whom Miss Spencer had described as the
countess's pupil came in. He stood looking at me for a
moment with parted lips. I saw he was a very weak-eyed
young man.

"She wants to know if you won't come out there?" he
observed at last.

"Who wants to know?"

"The countess. That French lady."

"She has asked you to bring me?"

"Yes, sir," said the young man feebly, looking at
my six feet of stature.

I went out with him, and we found the countess sitting
under one of the little quince trees in front of the house.
She was drawing a needle through the piece of embroidery
which she had taken from the small table. She pointed
graciously to the chair beside her. I seated myself.
Mr. Mixter glanced about him and then sat down in the
grass at her feet. He gazed upward, looking with parted
lips from the countess to me.

"I am sure you speak French," said the countess, fixing
her brilliant little eyes upon me.

"I do, madam, after a fashion," I answered, in the
lady's own tongue.

"*Voilà!*" she cried most expressively. "I knew it so

soon as I looked at you. You have been in my poor dear country."

"A long time."

"You know Paris?"

"Thoroughly, madame." And with a certain conscious purpose I let my eyes meet her own.

She presently, hereupon, moved her own and glanced down at Mr. Mixter.

"What are we talking about?" she demanded of her attentive pupil.

He pulled his knees up, plucked at the grass with his hand, stared, blushed a little.

"You are talking French," said Mr. Mixter.

"La belle découverte!" said the countess. "Here are ten months," she explained to me, "that I am giving him lessons. Don't put yourself out not to say he's a fool; he won't understand you."

"I hope your other pupils are more gratifying," I remarked.

"I have no others. They don't know what French is in this place; they don't want to know. You may therefore imagine the pleasure it is to me to meet a person who speaks it like yourself." I replied that my own pleasure was not less, and she went on drawing her stitches through her embroidery, with her little finger curled out. Every few moments she put her eyes close to her work, near-sightedly. I thought her a very disagreeable person; she was coarse, affected, dishonest, and no more a countess than I was a caliph. "Talk to me of Paris," she went on. "The very name of it gives me an emotion! How long since you were there?"

"Two months ago."

"Happy man! Tell me something about it. What were they doing? Oh, for an hour of the boulevards!"

"They were doing about what they are always doing—amusing themselves a good deal."

"At the theaters, eh?" sighed the countess. "At the *cafés-concerts*—at the little tables in front of the doors? *Quelle existence!* You know I am a Parisienne, monsieur," she added, "to my fingertips."

"Miss Spencer was mistaken, then," I ventured to rejoin, "in telling me that you are a Provençale."

She stared a moment, then she put her nose to her embroidery, which had a dingy, desultory aspect. "Ah, I am a Provençale by birth; but I am a Parisienne by—inclination."

"And by experience, I suppose?" I said.

She questioned me a moment with her hard little eyes.

"Oh, experience! I could talk of that if I wished. I never expected, for example, that experience had *this* in store for me." And she pointed with her bare elbow, and with a jerk of her head, at everything that surrounded her—at the little white house, the quince tree, the rickety paling, even at Mr. Mixter.

"You are in exile!" I said, smiling.

"You may imagine what it is! These two years that I have been here I have passed hours—hours! One gets used to things, and sometimes I think I have got used to this. But there are some things that are always beginning over again. For example, my coffee."

"Do you always have coffee at this hour?" I inquired.

She tossed back her head and measured me.

"At what hour would you prefer me to have it? I must have my *demi-tasse* after breakfast."

"Ah, you breakfast at this hour?"

"At midday—*comme cela se fait*. Here they breakfast at a quarter past seven! That 'quarter past' is charming!"

"But you were telling me about your coffee," I observed, sympathetically.

"My *cousine* can't believe in it; she can't understand it. She's an excellent girl; but that little cup of black coffee, with a drop of cognac, served at this hour—they exceed her comprehension. So I have to break the ice every day, and it takes the coffee the time you see to arrive. And when it arrives, monsieur! If I don't offer you any of it, you must not take it ill. It will be because I know you have drunk it on the boulevards."

I resented extremely this scornful treatment of poor Caroline Spencer's humble hospitality, but I said nothing, in order to say nothing uncivil. I only looked on Mr. Mixter, who had clasped his arms round his knees and was watching my companion's demonstrative graces in solemn fascination. She presently saw that I was observing him; she glanced at me with a little, bold, explanatory smile. "You know, he adores me," she murmured, putting her nose into her tapestry again. I expressed the promptest credence and she went on. "He dreams of becoming my lover! Yes, it's his dream. He has read a French novel; it took him six months. But ever since that he has thought himself the hero and me the heroine!"

Mr. Mixter had evidently not an idea that he was being talked about; he was too preoccupied with the ecstasy of contemplation. At this moment Caroline Spencer came out of the house, bearing a coffee-pot on a little tray. I noticed that on her way from the door to the table she gave me a single, quick, vaguely appealing glance. I wondered what it signified; I felt that it signified a sort of half-frightened longing to know what, as a man of the world who had been in France, I thought of the countess. It made me extremely uncomfortable. I could not tell her that the countess was very possibly the runaway wife of a little *coiffeur*. I tried suddenly, on the contrary, to show a high consideration for her. But I got up; I couldn't stay longer. It vexed me to see Caroline Spencer standing there like a waiting maid.

"You expect to remain some time at Grimwinter?" I said to the countess.

She gave a terrible shrug.

"Who knows? Perhaps for years. When one is in misery! *Chère belle*," she added, turning to Miss Spencer, "you have forgotten the cognac!"

I detained Caroline Spencer as, after looking a moment in silence at the little table, she was turning away to get this missing delicacy. I silently gave her my hand in farewell. She looked very tired, but there was a strange hint of prospective patience in her severely mild little face. I thought she was rather glad I was going. Mr. Mixter had risen to his feet and was pouring out the countess's coffee. As I went back past the Baptist church, I reflected that poor Miss Spencer had been right in her presentiment that she should still see something of Europe.

Selected Bibliography

OTHER WORKS BY HENRY JAMES

A Passionate Pilgrim, 1871   Story
Transatlantic Sketches, 1875   Travel
Roderick Hudson, 1876   Novel
The American, 1877   Novel
French Poets and Novelists, 1878   Criticism
The Europeans, 1878   Novel
Daisy Miller, 1878   Novella
An International Episode, 1878   Novella
Hawthorne, 1879   Criticism
Washington Square, 1880   Novel
The Portrait of a Lady, 1881   Novel
The Bostonians, 1886   Novel
The Princess Casamassima, 1886   Novel
Partial Portraits, 1888   Criticism
The Reverberator, 1888   Novella
The Aspern Papers, 1888   Story
The Tragic Muse, 1890   Novel
The Figure in the Carpet, 1896   Story
The Spoils of Poynton, 1897   Novel
What Maisie Knew, 1897   Novel
In the Cage, 1898   Novella
The Turn of the Screw, 1898   Story
The Awkward Age, 1899   Novel
The Sacred Fount, 1901   Novel
The Wings of the Dove, 1902   Novel
The Beast in the Jungle, 1903   Story
The Ambassadors, 1903   Novel
The Golden Bowl, 1904   Novel
The American Scene, 1907   Travel
The Jolly Corner, 1908   Story
The Bench of Desolation, 1910   Story
A Small Boy and Others, 1913   Autobiography

Notes of a Son and Brother, 1914   Autobiography
Notes on Novelists, 1914   Criticism
The Middle Years, 1917   Autobiography

SELECTED BIOGRAPHY AND CRITICISM

Beach, Joseph Warren. *The Method of Henry James.* New Haven: Yale University Press, 1918.

Dupee, F. W. *Henry James: His Life and Writings.* New York: Doubleday & Company, Inc., 1956.

———(ed.) *The Question of Henry James.* New York: Henry Holt & Company, 1945.

Edel, Leon. *Henry James—The Untried Years.* Philadelphia: J. B. Lippincott Company; London: Hart-Davis, 1953.

Leavis, F. R. *The Great Tradition.* New York: George W. Stewart, Publisher; London: Chatto & Windus, Ltd., 1948.

Lubbock, Percy (ed.). *The Letters of Henry James.* 2 vols. London: The Macmillan Company, Ltd., 1920.

Matthiessen, F. O. *Henry James: The Major Phase.* New York: Oxford University Press, 1944; London: Oxford University Press, 1946.

———*The James Family: A Group Biography.* New York: Alfred A. Knopf, Inc., 1947.

———and Murdock, Kenneth B. (eds.) *The Notebooks of Henry James.* New York and London: Oxford University Press, 1947.

McCarthy, Harold T. *Henry James: The Creative Process.* New York: Thomas Yoseloff, Publisher, 1958.

Poirier, William R. *The Comic Sense of Henry James.* New York: Oxford University Press; London: Chatto & Windus, Ltd., 1960.

West, Rebecca. *Henry James.* New York: Henry Holt & Company, 1916.

A NOTE ON THE TEXT

The text of each of these eight stories is that of the first publication in one of the magazines. James made extensive revisions of two of these stories, "The Madonna of the Future" and "Four Meetings," for the New York Edition of his Novels and Tales (1907–1909). These revised texts are not suitable for this volume, which presents all the stories as the early readers of James's fiction first saw them.

The magazine publication of the eight stories was as follows:

"The Story of a Year," *Atlantic Monthly*, March, 1865

"My Friend Bingham," *Atlantic Monthly*, March, 1867

"The Story of a Masterpiece," *Galaxy*, January–February, 1868

"A Light Man," *Galaxy*, July, 1869

"At Isella," *Galaxy*, August, 1871

"The Madonna of the Future," *Atlantic Monthly*, March, 1873

"The Last of the Valerii," *Atlantic Monthly*, January, 1874

"Four Meetings," *Scribner's Monthly*, November, 1877

American SIGNET Classics

50¢ except where noted

THE ADVENTURES OF HUCKLEBERRY FINN *by Mark Twain*
Afterword by George P. Elliott   (#CD5)

THE ADVENTURES OF TOM SAWYER *by Mark Twain*
Afterword by George P. Elliott   (#CD2)

THE AMBASSADORS *by Henry James*
Afterword by R. W. Stallman   (#CD12)

THE AUTOCRAT OF THE BREAKFAST TABLE
   by Oliver Wendell Holmes
Afterword by Eleanor Tilton   (#CD53)

THE CALL OF THE WILD and Selected Stories *by Jack London*
Foreword by Franklin Walker   (#CD20)

DEMOCRACY *by Henry Adams*
Foreword by Henry D. Aiken   (#CD48)

THE FALL OF THE HOUSE OF USHER and Other Tales
   by Edgar Allan Poe
Afterword by R. B. Blackmur   (#CD29)

THE FARM *by Louis Bromfield*
Afterword by Russell Lord   (#CD49)

GEORGIA BOY *by Erskine Caldwell*
Afterword by Robert Cantwell   (#CD57)

THE GREAT MEADOW *by Elizabeth Madox Roberts*
Afterword by Willard Thorp   (#CD52)

THE HOUSE OF THE SEVEN GABLES *by Nathaniel Hawthorne*
Afterword by Edward C. Sampson   (#CD58)

THE JUNGLE *by Upton Sinclair*
Foreword by Robert B. Downs   (#CD36)

English SIGNET Classics

50¢ except where noted

TO OUR READERS

We welcome your request for our free catalog of SIGNET and MENTOR books. If your dealer does not have the books you want, you may order them by mail, enclosing the list price plus 5¢ a copy to cover mailing. The New American Library of World Literature, Inc., P.O. Box 2310, Grand Central Station, New York 17, N. Y.